"I haven't seen *you* since I was eighteen, but I've been home quite a few times between then and now. I'm a bit hurt you hadn't noticed. I hear you've been busy since you became *the sheriff*."

The boy wilder than the horses her father used to tame had become the man put in charge of policing the entire county.

"Don't worry, you're not the only one surprised by the news," he said. "Though I am impressed at your reaction. Last time we saw each other, you were more on the reserved side."

Remi couldn't help but laugh at that.

"I was a mouse," she exclaimed. "It took college for me to open up."

It was Declan's turn to laugh.

"Being the sheriff has shown me the value of holding your cards close to your chest."

Remi leaned back to mirror his stance.

"Well, it looks like we might have switched personalities since we last saw each other."

Even though she said it, Remi didn't believe it.

SHOWDOWN WITH THE SHERIFF

TYLER ANNE SNELL

Previously published as *Last Stand Sheriff*
and *Small-Town Face-Off*

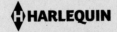

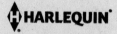

Recycling programs
for this product may
not exist in your area.

ISBN-13: 978-1-335-42721-2

Showdown with the Sheriff

Copyright © 2022 by Harlequin Books S.A.

Last Stand Sheriff
First published in 2020. This edition published in 2022.
Copyright © 2020 by Tyler Anne Snell

Small-Town Face-Off
First published in 2017. This edition published in 2022.
Copyright © 2017 by Tyler Anne Snell

This edition published by arrangement with Harlequin Books S.A.

For questions and comments about the quality of this book,
please contact us at CustomerService@Harlequin.com.

Harlequin Enterprises ULC
22 Adelaide St. West, 41st Floor
Toronto, Ontario M5H 4E3, Canada
www.Harlequin.com

Printed in U.S.A.

CONTENTS

WINDING ROAD REDEMPTION

Tyler Anne Snell genuinely loves all genres of the written word. However, she's realized that she loves books filled with sexual tension and mysteries a little more than the rest. Her stories have a good dose of both. Tyler lives in Alabama with her same-named husband and their mini "lions." When she isn't reading or writing, she's playing video games and working on her blog, *Almost There*. To follow her shenanigans, visit tylerannesnell.com.

Books by Tyler Anne Snell

Harlequin Intrigue

Visit the Author Profile page
at Harlequin.com for more titles.

LAST STAND SHERIFF

This book is for Tyler, my husband.
Thank you for always being my smart, hilarious
and cat-loving rock. If you're reading this,
then let's go make some brownies.

Chapter One

Declan Nash wasn't having the greatest of days.

Not only was it raining cats and dogs and elephants, his trusty old pickup had decided not to be so trusty.

"Come on, Fiona." He rubbed the dash trying to coo the truck into stopping her lurching and ominous rattling sound. Fiona the Ford wasn't impressed. Declan admitted defeat by taking the upcoming exit. There was a gas station at the corner of the short road. He pulled in, sighing. "After everything we've been through, you decide to pitch a fit now and here of all places?"

The city of Kilwin, Tennessee, was an hour out from where he had been on the highway. Which meant his hometown of Overlook was an hour and twenty minutes out of reach.

Not that he was reaching for it.

He might have been the sheriff of Wildman County but, as of that morning, he was just a man on vacation.

Or, at least, he was trying to be.

Declan sighed into the empty cab again. His dark blue Stetson, one he only wore on his off days—which meant he hardly ever wore it—sat on the passenger seat mocking him.

"You're about to become an umbrella," he told it.

The rain was having a great old time drenching Declan to the bone after he got out and propped up his hood. He hadn't parked under the gas station awning, worried about his truck catching fire and making a bad situation way worse. That decision got him wet but was reassuring as steam billowed up, angry, at him from next to the engine. There was also an overpowering oil smell.

Declan jogged back to the cab and grabbed his phone.

Just in time for the interior lights to blink out.

His battery had died.

So, Fiona was finally going to pitch a fit. After fifteen years of not making a peep, she was doing it during the first vacation he'd taken in at least five.

Declan hung his head and swore. The motion dumped water from his hat into his seat.

Declan swore some more, spied the diner next to the gas station and decided that he was at least going to get some coffee out of all of this. He could deal with the truck once the rain let up.

Still, he grabbed his duffel bag knowing there wasn't an inch in this world to give when it came to the accordion file he had tucked in with his boxers and toothbrush.

"We'll get you figured out, Fiona," he told his truck with a pat after locking her up. He dashed across the gas station parking lot and right into the diner. When he pushed through the front door, heralded in by a chime, an older woman with a nice smile met him.

"When it rains it pours, huh?" she greeted, motioning to one of the large-pane windows that ran along the front of the building. He could see his truck through the one next to the last booth. "We have some fresh hand towels in the kitchen. I can get you some to dry off a little if you'd like."

Declan took his hat off and pressed it against his chest. He gave the woman—Agnes, according to her name tag—a smile that he meant.

"That would be much appreciated, thank you."

Agnes went off to the kitchen while Declan took the booth in the corner so he could keep an eye on his truck. He set his duffel on the floor next to the seat.

Then he had a moment of internal crisis.

His hands itched to open his bag and pull the folder out, to riffle through the pages he'd already read and reread countless times. To look at every piece of evidence that had been collected for over twenty-five years. To see his own notes and compare them to the ones his father had made when he had been a detective.

Then Declan heard an inner voice warning of doing just that.

It wasn't his conscience; it was a collective featuring Madi, Caleb and Desmond. They'd all made it clear that they were concerned Declan was blurring the line between dedication and obsession. That finding justice, finding the truth, wasn't worth the toll of the quality of his life.

Not after the same obsession had taken their father's life.

Since Declan was their big brother, a part of him prickled at being directed at what to do or, more aptly, what not to do. Just as quickly, though, as his gruffness reared its head, he'd remind himself that in the small town of Overlook, they weren't just bystanders.

Madi, Caleb and Desmond had told him that from experience they knew what it was like to be slowly consumed by a mystery. He had to learn to let go and live a little.

Considering the case was about their abduction, Declan figured they might have a point.

Now, though, with his truck broken down and the rain trapping him inside a diner that had only two other patrons, Declan couldn't help deciding his vacation hadn't *really* started yet. This was more of a pit stop. Which meant if he looked at the files now, it didn't count against him.

Agnes returned with a few hand towels, cutting off the physical action of taking the folder out. He ordered a coffee and some bacon and eggs and returned the towels. Then he retrieved the folder and put it down on the tabletop with minimal guilt and maximum focus.

He hadn't been there at the park that day.

He hadn't been attacked and taken and held in a basement.

He hadn't had to trick a man and fight to get out as the three scared and hurt eight-year-olds had done.

He hadn't had to make the terrifying trek through the woods to find help.

No, Declan hadn't been there at all.

He'd been too consumed with his own little world to notice the triplets had disappeared until an hour after the fact.

And then he'd had to wait with the rest of Overlook for three days, hoping and praying they would find nothing but good news.

Declan could still feel the helplessness that had nearly crushed him during the wait.

And now?

Now Declan was older, smarter.

Now Declan had focus and patience and a lot more experience.

Now Declan was the sheriff.

He couldn't save the triplets from what had happened, but he could damn sure finally give them the peace they deserved.

The rain continued to fall. Music from the kitchen floated to the front. Declan didn't wrestle with his choice anymore. The diner would actually be the perfect place to look over the newer evidence. No one from his family at his shoulder. No one from the sheriff's department by his side.

He opened the folder.

No one was going to distract him here.

The time for questions was over. Now it was time for answers.

Remi was, as her cousin Claudette said, a "Hot Mess Susan."

Not the worst thing she'd been called in her thirty-three years of life but definitely not the most flattering, either.

What was worse than being called a Hot Mess Susan?

When the nickname actually applied to her.

And now, pulling into the diner off Exit 41B, it definitely applied.

Remi cut the engine in a parking spot and let out a sigh that had apparently been trapped in her chest for the last hundred miles. It dragged down her shoulders, slouched her back and put pressure on the stress headache that had been brewing all morning.

"'Go see your father,'" she muttered to no one, adopting her mother's pushy voice. "'It'll be fun. Stop stalling, Remi. It'll be *fine*.'"

Her mother wasn't right about much…and she was wrong about that, too. It hadn't been fine. In fact, it had been awful and exactly what she had expected.

Josh and Jonah had met her with hugs and sibling love, and then all of that mush had soured when their father had sat them down at the dinner table. The questions had started and they'd all daggered her. Remi had felt like she was interviewing for her job at Towne & Associates all over again. However, instead of sitting across from a group of public accountants she was looking at three cowboys who didn't understand a lick of why she'd left the ranch all those years ago in the first place.

Which was why she hadn't told them of her current problem. One that she'd been wrestling with before she ever decided to heed her mother's advice and go see the Hudson men in Overlook.

How she ever thought they'd take a second to think outside of the ranch and help her, she didn't know.

But now with the rain hitting the roof of her car, reminding her that she didn't have a rain jacket or an umbrella, Remi felt her troubles being pulled back to her. That, and the weather, had been one of the reasons she'd taken the exit and parked herself outside of a diner. It's neon open sign was a distraction she was ready to fully embrace.

She grabbed her purse, tucked her phone in the waist of her exercise leggings and tried to think about how see-through her shirt was going to become just from her short jaunt between the car and the front doors.

Then she ran.

And immediately became drenched.

A chime sounded over the door as Remi danced inside. She was met with cool air that made her now-wet clothes cold. A song was playing somewhere in the small space, and through the cook's window behind the counter a man gave her a look. An older woman in uniform also looked through the window and called out.

"Be with you in a sec, hon!"

Remi gave a polite smile and decided not to check her shirt to see if her bra was showing through the beige. Instead, she ran a hand through her dirty-blond hair that was probably dark now and took a quick look at the few patrons already seated.

To her right was a couple immersed in their own conversation, and a gray-haired man in a booth two down from her spot in the middle of the space. Straight ahead was a woman and her small son at the counter, making quick work of what looked like apple pie. To her left sat one man in the last booth.

He was facing her but looking down at the table. Remi noted first that he had wide, muscled shoulders; second, that he had dark brown hair as messy as hers must be; and, third, that he was, even with his face angled down, attractive. Then, with a little start, Remi realized the fourth and most intriguing detail.

She dripped water across the linoleum and walked right up to a face she hadn't seen in ages.

"Declan Nash?"

The cowboy hat resting on the table was all the confirmation she needed, but the man still raised his eyes to hers and nodded. Remi couldn't help feeling a bit of heat as he looked at her directly.

She saw both the boy her father had warned her about

when they were kids and the man who had grown up quite nicely.

When he cut a grin and recognition flared behind his green eyes, Remi felt more heat rising in her.

"Well, if it isn't Remi Hudson."

Declan surprised her by standing and extending his hand. She felt her eyebrow quirk up as she shook his hand.

The young Declan hadn't been so formal, especially when it came to her. Why shake the hand of the person you're competing with or fighting against?

He didn't make a thing about her questioning look as he motioned to the seat opposite him. Before he officially asked her to sit, he looked behind her.

"Are you here alone?"

She didn't miss his glance down at her left hand.

So she held that hand up and thumped her ring finger.

"Alone in the diner and single outside of it."

Declan chuckled as Remi slid across the plastic seat. Her wet leggings made it squeak.

"I don't think I've seen you this close to Overlook since we were, what, nineteen?" He closed the folder on the tabletop and leaned back against his seat. The new position highlighted how the years had been more than kind to the man. His face was all angles and strong. The bump in his nose from the time he broke it after getting into a fight with Cody Callers at a house party when they were sixteen was still visible but, instead of looking awkward as it had then, now it added to the intrigue that was him.

Because, while Remi had known the wild child that was Declan Nash, she hadn't seen him since graduation day.

"I haven't seen *you* since I was eighteen, but I've been home quite a few times between then and now. I'm a bit hurt you haven't noticed. It's not like Hudson Heartland isn't the Nash Family Ranch's next-door neighbor or anything."

"There's a good hundred acres or so between the ranches, so forgive me for not having superhero-grade vision," he teased.

"You're forgiven, I suppose. Besides, I hear you've been busy since you became *the sheriff*."

Saying it out loud created the same shock she'd felt the first time her father had told her about the eldest Nash sibling running for sheriff. When he'd won, well, that had been a much stronger shock.

The boy wilder than the horses her father used to tame had become the man put in charge of policing the entire county.

"Don't worry, you're not the only one surprised by the news," he said. "Though I am impressed at your reaction. Last time we saw each other you were more on the reserved side."

Remi couldn't help but laugh at that.

"I was a mouse," she exclaimed. "It took college for me to open up and see the virtue of speaking my mind. Something I assume you can relate to."

It was Declan's turn to laugh.

"Being the sheriff has shown me the value of holding your cards close to your chest."

Remi leaned back to mirror his stance.

"Well, it looks like we might have switched personalities since we last saw each other."

Even though she said it, Remi didn't believe it. People couldn't change their stripes. Not when it came to someone as wild and bold as Declan.

The waitress appeared at their table, took Remi's order and was kind enough to give her a hand towel to dab off the excess water. Declan was polite enough to keep his eyes north of her potentially see-through shirt. Sure, he'd been wild when they were younger, but his mama had still raised him right when it came to respecting women.

"So what brings you to this diner?" Remi got around to asking. She looked at the folder beneath his hand. "Is it work related?"

Declan took the folder and slid it beneath his cowboy hat.

"I was actually on my way to one of my deputy's rental cabins for a long weekend." He pointed out the window. The rain had, of course, lessened a minute or two after she'd entered the diner. "You see that—"

"You mean Fiona?" she finished. Like the cowboy hat, Declan had had that truck for years and years. She'd recognize it anywhere and probably would have earlier had it not been raining so hard when she'd pulled up.

Declan smirked.

"Yeah. Fiona." He sighed. "She finally decided to have a fit. I was going to call my roadside assistance when the rain died down since, well, I don't know much about cars."

"Except stealing them from Rodney Becker's garage to prove you were smarter than him," she added.

Declan lowered his voice but there was humor in it.

"Listen here, Huds, you promised you'd take that one to the grave."

The way Declan said the nickname he'd used for her

when they were in high school, all rumbling baritone, made some of the heat at seeing him swirl around again. She held up her hands in surrender.

"I keep my promises. But, may I point out, you're not in Overlook right now. In fact, you're not even in Wildman County."

He shrugged.

"You can't be too careful about these things. You know how powerful talk in town can be. One slipup and that's all we'll hear about for years."

He said it in a joking way, but she heard the resentment deep in his words.

Remi was an Overlook native. Her parents had been born and raised in town, and she and her brothers had been born and raised there, too. It was impossible to keep people from talking in a small town, but when it came to the Nashes it was an entirely different ball game.

After what had happened to the triplets, the family had been become famous. A horrible fame that, as far as she knew, hadn't gone away despite the years that had passed.

Remi's coffee showed up at just the right time, and the two of them spent the next half hour talking about the people they'd gone to school with, old friends and annoyances, and what had been going on with their respective families. They hit all the social cues that were expected of a conversation between old acquaintances.

He was sorry to hear about her parents' divorce, and she was happy to hear about his siblings' marriages and kids.

He could barely talk around his laughter about Clay Reynolds being arrested for public intoxication after his girlfriend bought him a fake lottery ticket, and she admitted, with much shame, that she'd dated Matthew Shaker for a year after running into him on campus.

He seemed interested in what her stepfather, Dave, did for a living, and she genuinely was excited that Claire's Café was expanding into the shop next door due to its popularity.

It wasn't until he excused himself to call about Fiona that Remi realized she didn't want the conversation to end just yet.

So when he said that a local mechanic couldn't look at his truck for a few days and would tow it back to Overlook instead, she decided she could take an hour detour back to town.

As long as he'd be with her.

"I don't want to inconvenience you," he said at her offer of driving him back. She waved off his concern.

"You're the one who's going to listen to me talk about my work dilemma all the way there," she said. "May I remind you that I'm an accountant so, honestly, you might just want to ride with the tow truck driver."

Declan smirked.

Hot dog, what a sight.

"I'm always being asked about my job, I'd love to listen to someone else's for a change."

They paid their bill, made arrangements for the tow truck and then headed back to the town they'd both had a mind to leave that morning.

Then the rain went from crummy to bad to worse. It was only when they were between Kilwin and Overlook that they admitted defeat and pulled into another parking lot.

This time it was for a surprisingly nice motel.

"Fun fact," Declan said, pointing in the direction of the vacancy sign. "My sister-in-law is good friends with the woman who owns this place."

"Then I bet you could get us a good deal on a room, huh?"

Remi had meant it as a joke.

Yet, when she looked at Declan, his cowboy hat on his head and a smirk on his lips, she wasn't quite sure of her own intentions.

She'd always wondered how a kiss between them would feel.

When Declan's eyes moved down to her lips, she had a suspicion he was just as curious.

Chapter Two

A month later and Declan's patience was spread so thin it was damn near transparent.

"Cooper, you called *me* out here, not the other way around," he reminded the always-a-little-left-of-the-law young man. "I have a press conference in a few hours that I need to prep for. I don't have time to just be shooting the breeze."

They were outside the local hardware store, standing in the parking lot between Declan's truck and Cooper's little sports car. Declan was wearing his uniform and had his sheriff's badge hanging on his belt. The black Stetson on his head had just been cleaned. Cooper had on a well-worn Nirvana graphic tee, hole-ridden jeans and an expression that said he needed some prodding to get to talking.

"Come on, Coop," he added. "I'm not a mind reader over here."

The man, twenty-two, cut his eyes to the lot around them and sucked on his teeth a second. Then he got to the point.

"Okay, well, don't get your panties all in a twist, but I've heard a rumor that I don't think you've heard yet." He shrugged. "Since you helped me out of that dumb warrant last year I figured telling you about it would be a good way to say we're even."

Declan cocked his head to the side, instantly curious. There weren't many rumors that didn't make it to every pair of ears in Overlook. Considering Cooper lived in town, Declan couldn't imagine he hadn't already heard it, too.

A day without talk about the Nash family, especially over everything that had happened in the last few years, was rare.

"I'm listening."

Cooper stood up straight, no longer leaning against his car, and dropped his voice a little. Declan couldn't help but angle forward.

"You know the Waypoint, right?"

Declan nodded. It was a bar in the city of Kilwin, twenty minutes from Overlook. The clientele had been mostly law enforcement back in the day. Now it catered to the crowd in the newly erected business plaza across the block from it. A family friend who was a detective with the Kilwin Police Department had said the new vibe was too modern and trendy for him. Declan hadn't been there in months.

"Well, for the last month or so there's been a lot of talk about what happened to your family. You know, with the, well you know." Declan nodded again. There was always some kind of talk, even in Kilwin, about the triplets' abduction, despite it having taken place decades ago. That wasn't anything new.

What Cooper said next was.

"Some guy keeps talking about a note in the wall at the cabin and everyone who knows the story keeps telling him he doesn't know what he's talking about. But he just keeps talking about that darn note in the wall, preaching it like it's gospel. It's probably nothing but I thought I'd let you know."

"A note in the wall," Declan repeated, still not sold.

Cooper shrugged.

"He said it's in the hallway and hidden real good. Said it took the law a while to find it, but I didn't remember hearing that."

There had never been a note found in a wall or otherwise at the cabin where the triplets had been held in the basement apartment. Considering it had been swarmed with law enforcement for months, and revisited by his father for years, Declan was sure he would have known about any note that had been found.

"It sounds like you were listening to a drunk guy wanting attention," Declan said.

Cooper shrugged again.

"Listen, if it had been Piper or that Grant guy who are always trying to rope you into their pyramid schemes, I wouldn't have said anything," he said in defense. "But this guy only ever had one beer in front of him, and it was mostly full. And his suit was so high-end he just kind of seemed to have his crap more together, you know?"

Declan had spent his career in law enforcement learning how to perfect his facial expressions and body language. How to control it so it didn't betray how he was really feeling. In that moment it took all his training to keep his face impassive and his body from visibly tensing.

"That bar has a lot of men in suits, though," Declan said, playing the devil's advocate, careful not to get ahead of himself. "I'm sure more than one of them has their crap together."

"Not like this guy. This dude looked like he belonged on a magazine cover. He looked way out of place there."

Declan's phone started to vibrate. He pulled it out to see a text from his chief deputy, Mayne Cussler. They needed to prep for the press conference.

He sighed.

"I have to get going," he said. Then, with a little more politeness he addressed the young man directly. "Thanks for the info. I do appreciate the effort."

Cooper nodded with a smile.

"Just trying to stay in the sheriff's good graces!"

"I thought you were trying to repay a debt?"

"Can't I do both?"

He laughed and got into his car. Declan, despite the text, hung back as Cooper disappeared down the road.

A note in the wall.

A man in a bar.

A man in a fancy suit.

The last two Declan had run into over the past few years. In fact, a man in a bar had been a detail in the chaos that all three of his siblings had gone through in their personal lives recently.

There had always been a man in a bar who had given bad ideas to bad people.

A man in a fancy suit? They'd run into a few of them, too. Most recently, a man in a high-end suit had gotten tangled up in a dangerous situation with Desmond and his then girlfriend, now wife, Riley. One who actually bore the same scar that the triplets' abductor had had.

Though he wasn't the man who had done it, that had been the last new lead they'd had in years.

But a note in the wall of the cabin where they were held?

That was a new one.

And coupled with a man in a suit at a bar?

That was too enticing not to investigate.

Declan put his truck into Drive and moved out onto the road, pointing in the direction that would lead him to that cabin. His phone started to vibrate and he was ready to stall, when he saw the caller ID wasn't one he recognized.

"Nash, here," he answered.

"Hey, Declan, it's me."

That voice gave him a split reaction.

Confusion and primal excitement.

Remi Hudson.

He hadn't seen her since she'd dropped him off at the ranch.

The day *after* they'd stopped at the motel.

"Well, hey there, Huds. How's it going?"

Hesitation, silent and as loud as could be, was his answer. Declan moved the phone away from his face to make sure the call hadn't dropped.

It hadn't.

Remi finally responded.

"I'm, uh, actually in town and was wondering if we could get together?"

She sounded different. Distracted.

It made his gut go on high alert.

"Yeah, sure. I have a press conference in two hours. Can it wait until after then?"

"Oh, yeah, that's fine. Can you just call me back

when you're ready? I'll be at my dad's but would prefer to meet up somewhere else."

That didn't surprise Declan. During their last meeting he'd gotten the impression that she was having some issues with her father, Gale, and her brothers. He hadn't pried and he still wouldn't when they met up.

"How about I call you when I'm done and we can meet at my house?"

"Okay, great. Yeah, okay. Well, I guess I'll talk to you later."

Remi ended the call before Declan could say another word.

For the next few minutes he wondered why she sounded so off, but when he turned onto *the* road that eventually led to *the* cabin, all thoughts flew back to the past.

Declan tightened his grip on the steering wheel.

Being haunted by the past was never a good feeling.

REMI FELT LIKE she was about to vibrate out of her skin with nerves. Which wasn't like her at all. Not anymore. Not since she'd grown up.

Yet, there she was, driving up Winding Road toward the Nash Family Ranch that sat at its end while the butterflies in her stomach hitched a ride for free.

It was only December 10, but it felt like a lifetime had passed since she'd last been here dropping Declan off at his house. She'd been lucky then to avoid his family all while she and the sheriff had been able to avoid talking about what they'd done, *several* times, at the motel. That had been fine by Remi.

She'd always wondered what it was like to kiss Dec-

Ian outside of a teenage dare and she had found out. Along with a few other exciting things.

Declan hadn't seemed put out in the slightest at their time together, or that it had to end.

They had separate, nonintersecting lives. The only reason they'd run into each other in the first place at the diner had been a fluke. Nothing more, nothing less.

Sure, the entire ride back to her home in Nashville had been filled with thoughts of the man. She'd compared the quiet, reflective Declan to the wild child she'd grown up with. She had tried to recall every piece of gossip about his life since she'd moved away after graduation, and she'd kept thinking about the *move* that had made her see fireworks. Remi would also be lying if she didn't admit thinking about Declan had become a routine thing. Maybe not every second of every day, but occasionally she'd found that her mind had wandered right to a cowboy with a gruff exterior and the softest lips she ever did kiss.

Then *it* had happened.

The heat. And not the good kind of heat. The kind that made her feel sick and worried that she was somehow dying from some rare disease. One second she was *fine* with a capital *F.* The next she was opening her windows and sticking her head out into the cold night air.

When it happened two more times over a few days, Remi had done the only sensible thing.

She'd googled.

Her anxiety had gone through the roof as sicknesses she was *sure* she suffered from filled her computer screen. It just about soared when one answer in particular kept recurring.

That's when she became a mathematician. One who

tore through the house looking for her phone and its calendar app. When the numbers didn't match up, she ran them again.

Then she'd given herself a pep talk about the stress of the huge life-changing decision she'd just made.

It was *stress*.

That was it.

That was all.

"Stress my butt," Remi told the inside of her car now as she passed under the ranch's entrance sign with a snort. Remi might have become a woman ready to say what was on her mind, but that didn't mean she was always eloquent about it.

The Nash Family Ranch had several things in common with the Hudson Heartland, and Remi never got tired of admiring both.

The Nashes owned several hundred acres of the most beautiful fields, stretches of forest, natural bodies of water, as well as picturesque farmhouses, barns and a stable. In the distance the rise and fall of mountains could be admired. From Hudson Heartland those mountains were closer. Remi and her brothers had spent many a hiking trip out on them.

The main difference between the ranches was the number of homes on the properties. On their property there were only two. The biggest, a four-thousand-square-foot house was where she'd grown up and where her father and brothers lived now. On the other side of the ranch stood the second home, which belonged to Jerri and Margot Heath. In a role reversal that had been quite the talk of Overlook when it had first happened, Margot was the stable master while her husband kept the main house clean and the useless-with-cooking Hudson brood fed. Their son, around Remi's age, hadn't felt comfortable with the arrangement as he'd gotten older. The moment he'd turned eighteen he'd moved out west.

Not that Remi could fault him for doing almost the same thing she had done.

The Nash family, on the other hand, had several homes across their acreage. According to Declan, not only did he have his own house on the property, but so did Caleb and his wife, Nina, Desmond and his wife, Riley, and his mother, Dorothy, who still lived in the main house. There was even a new set of structures she'd never seen. The Wild Iris Retreat was a nice walk from the stable and run by Dorothy, Nina and Molly, a family friend who also happened to be one of the only friends Remi had kept in touch with once she'd left Overlook.

Remi had been particularly curious about the retreat, considering Madi and her husband, Julian, ran a bed-and-breakfast on the other side of town but she hadn't pried too much for any more details. Being around Declan had been bad for her focus, especially after they'd done what they had.

It was like eating a slice of the best cake you'd ever tasted and then having to sit next to the rest of it and pretend your mouth wasn't still watering.

A different kind of heat engulfed Remi at the memory. Even hearing Declan's voice over the phone had had an effect on her. She wondered if the feeling was mutual. He'd seemed so surprised by her call that Remi couldn't help but feel a little sting.

As she pulled up to his house, Remi couldn't begin to guess how the news she was about to deliver to the cowboy would be received.

Not only had she taken his advice on her career troubles and decided to accept the job she'd been offered in Colorado, she'd found out two weeks later while packing up her house that she was pregnant.

With Declan's child.

Remi cut her engine in his driveway and jumped out into the cold air. The sound of tires against gravel forced her attention to the truck pulling up behind her from the main road.

Declan gave her a polite smile through the windshield as he parked.

Boy, was she about to blow his mind.

Chapter Three

"Do you mind if we ride out somewhere? I could really use a second set of eyes."

The moment Declan saw Remi outside of her car, he'd had the idea that she could be exactly what he needed. The cabin in the woods was empty, just as it had been for years and years. Declan had swept the hallway before looking through every other part of the space, trying to find a clue he'd somehow missed.

Then he'd left for the press conference.

But his mind was still in that cabin, suspicious of the man in the suit.

When he saw Remi, he realized what he needed was peace of mind. He needed a second pair of eyes, ones that weren't as close to the case as he was.

He needed her to confirm there was nothing there.

Then he could let it go.

For now.

Remi's eyebrow rose in question. She tilted her head to the side a fraction. Her hair shifted at the movement in a sheet across her shoulders. She'd cut it since he'd seen her last.

It looked good.

Then again, Remi always looked good.

"Do I need to wear my good dress?"

Declan didn't understand until she pointed to his suit blazer, pressed button-up, and slacks. He chuckled.

"No. I have to get spiffy for the press conferences," he said. "Something about jeans and flannel not being appropriate."

Remi looked him up and down openly. Declan tried not to do the same.

While he'd in no way expected to do what they had done the day *and night* his truck had broken down outside of town, the truth was they had. And they'd been good at it, too. Just as they'd both been clear about it being a one-time thing.

Two ships passing in the night.

Catching up, and dressing down, with a friend.

Remi had a promotion in wait, he had a county to protect.

She'd left town for one reason; he had stayed for many.

They'd been adults about parting ways. Coolheaded and relaxed.

That didn't mean Declan hadn't occasionally thought he smelled her perfume or snorted at a joke she'd told during their time together.

Remi had been fun to hang out with when they were kids, even when she was quiet. Adult Remi had been a change that he had still enjoyed, as the woman said exactly what was on her mind.

But now, standing opposite her, there was a hesitation that seemed to be moving across her expression. Declan realized he might have done it again. He'd focused on the case more than he had the present. Remi was in front of him, in Overlook, and there he was ready trying to rope her into playing junior detective. Why was she here?

Still, it was hard to forget about the note in the wall. It clawed at his mind, despite the company.

"We don't have to go if this can't wait or can't ride along with us?" he ventured.

"Location won't change the conversation," she said with a shrug. "But I am worried you don't remember that I'm an accountant and *not* a detective."

"I need a second opinion, is all."

"And you picked me because you know I have a lot of those?"

She started to walk around him toward the truck. Declan opened the door for her before answering.

"I know you're about the details," he said. Then, moving to the driver's side and sliding in, he gave her an even look. "And I'd like a civilian and non-Nash to help look for those details."

Remi's eyebrow rose again. Declan noted the freckles he'd remembered from her teenage years were still peppered around her eyes and across her cheeks.

"Where exactly are we going?"

Declan put the truck in Reverse. He didn't answer until they were back on the main road that ran through the ranch, heading toward Winding Road.

"The Well Water Cabin."

He could detect her confusion without her voicing t right away. She shifted, her hair moving across the at's fabric as she must have turned to look at him. He hed and explained.

heard about a man in a bar who keeps talking a note in the wall that law enforcement missed. like a weird riddle or bad nursery rhyme, I

know, but I went there earlier and looked around anyways. Like I thought, it was empty. But there are so
many coincidences that have popped up lately that I'm
inclined to think it might be worth looking into." He
gave her a quick look and half shrug. "I also know how
close I am to this case and how many times I've been
over every single detail. I could be missing something I
haven't seen *because* I've seen it too much. You know?"

"Like having someone else proofread an email before you send it off because you've read it too many
times already."

Declan snorted.

"Exactly. There could be nothing there and I just
can't let go, which I know is a concern. Or, there could
be something." He gave her a sidelong glance as they
slowed going through the main gate. "I need another
set of eyes to proofread."

Remi nodded and stared out the windshield. Her
brows were knotted together in thought.

"And asking Caleb, the actual detective, would be
worse than going by yourself," she surmised. "Not to
mention, he probably doesn't want to go back there in
the first place."

"None of them do. Ma won't even drive on the road
that leads up to the place. Not that I blame any of them.
They've had their fill for more than a lifetime."

Out of his periphery he saw Remi nod again.

One thing he had valued in his friendship with her
when they were younger was her ability to not enjoy
the drama surrounding the triplets' abduction. Some
people thrived on it, still bringing the case up in casual
conversation with throwaway theories about the man
behind it. Ones they thought up on their lunch break

and brought up like it was some party game. Declan's father had entertained any and all of them, but Declan had had the benefit of seeing his father run himself into the ground and had changed tactics. He and Caleb had heard many theories and kept their expectations at zero.

Still, Declan knew his family wished people would stay quiet about it. He did, too. He and his siblings had spent middle and high school dealing with children and teens with no tact. He'd hoped that as they aged their need to reach into the past and stir up gossip would ebb away.

It hadn't for a majority of Overlook residents.

Yet, Remi had never been one of those people. Whether they were kids or teens, she only spoke on the subject when he brought it up. Even then she stayed thoughtful, not at all interested in fanning the fire.

Now, sitting next to her, Declan was reminded of that thoughtful girl who had been his friend even though she'd adopted a new outgoing personality since college. A part of him wished he'd kept in touch when she left. The other part reminded him that she'd left to get away from Overlook and start a new, different life.

It was for the better.

"What do you mean coincidences?" Remi asked. "People *talking* about the case? Surely that can't be out of the ordinary for around here."

It was Declan's turn to hesitate. The man in the suit. The man in the bar. The man with the scar on his hand. All of that information had been kept within the family and only between the detectives at the sheriff's department and his chief deputy, Cussler. Everyone knew what it meant for any potential new information on the case to get out. What was already a long shot of an investigation would become impossible.

Declan had dropped his guard for one night with Remi, it was true, but they weren't in that room anymore. They weren't in her car, heading home before heading in opposite directions.

What he knew held a weight that he didn't want to put on her even though Declan was taking her back to the scene.

She didn't have to know everything to be helpful, and he decided then and there that he could keep some things from her without being a grade A jackass.

"A few cases have had a similarity that could be connected," he went with. "Again, it might just be someone doing it on purpose to throw us off or pull our legs, but I can't let it go just yet unless I know for sure."

"So, we need to find a note in the wall or nothing at all."

"That's the goal."

Remi smiled. Declan knew because he heard it clearly in her voice. He was surprised at how much he was reminded again of the girl he'd known. Even when she had been quiet, he'd always been able to tell when she was smiling without looking at her.

"Well, I'm sure not about to say no to the sheriff, now am I?"

THE ROAD THAT led to the Well Water Cabin looked like many roads to older houses in Overlook. Dirt mixed with gravel, tree-lined, worn by weather, age and use. Narrow, too. If you met another vehicle you just had to pray you had the good luck that at least one of the two wasn't a truck and that there was enough room to crunch onto the nearly nonexistent shoulder so the other could pass by.

Isolated but not without purpose.

Yet, the road that led to Well Water was different.

It felt almost forgotten. Or maybe lost. Not because of its location and beautiful scenery, nestled within one of the thickest parts of the forest that stretched across Overlook, but because people had tried to lose it.

There was an eeriness that crept into every visitor's bones when driving up to the cabin. Whether they admitted it out loud or not. Remi was sure of that just as the odd feeling moved across her like she'd walked into a cold spot during the summer heat.

While she'd had every intention of telling the man about her pregnancy as soon as she could, he'd said just about the only thing that had made her wait. Or, really, if she was being honest it was the way he'd looked when he talked about going to the cabin. His eyes had somehow softened and remained hard at the same time. Like someone trying their damnedest to appear the picture of strength while trying to hide the vulnerability tearing at them.

It was such an intriguing and surprising juxtaposition that Remi had decided to tell Declan after they had examined the cabin. Maybe the news would cheer him up.

Maybe it wouldn't.

Either way Remi didn't believe there was a note in the cabin, hidden in the wall or not.

Someone would have found it by now.

At least she thought so.

"How did you get in?" she asked as he followed the last curve before the cabin. "Did the Fairhopes give the department a copy of the key?"

The Fairhopes had owned Well Water for years before the abduction. They had lived in Chicago and used the cabin as a vacation home when it struck their fancy. Remi had heard through the grapevine that, after being interviewed and investigated extensively, the family hadn't been back to Overlook. Remi realized she didn't know if anyone else had rented the place from them.

Declan's voice went hard.

"I own it."

Remi's hair slapped her cheeks, she turned her head so fast.

"You own it?"

Declan's jaw was set. He nodded.

"Dad bought it from the Fairhopes. When he passed, it passed on to me."

"That gives me some mixed feelings, I'll be honest."

"You're not the only one."

You'd never guess such a cute, quaint cabin could breed such heartache, confusion and fear.

Well Water came into view like the beautiful terror it was.

Remi had never been inside but, like most of Overlook, had found her way to the outside to look.

A true log cabin exterior with a storybook chimney and wraparound porch. The green on the window trim and front door had aged well over the years, but the front gardens had not. They were equally overgrown and barren.

Declan parked next to the mailbox. Remi watched as he pulled a key out of the middle console. The hardness in his voice had transferred to his body.

She had no doubt he was becoming the sheriff.

There was no banter-heavy lead-up to going inside.

No flourish or outpouring of emotion. Declan got out, Remi followed. He unlocked the front door, she moved past him. He hung back by the door, she started to explore. It was a silent dance between them. One that completely consumed her.

As long as they were in *the* cabin, all thoughts of being pregnant with Declan's child, moving to Colorado and how insanely different her life was about to become quieted.

Then it was just the two of them in an empty cabin.

Chapter Four

Well Water wasn't a spacious place by any means. The layout was simple. The front door opened into a narrow hallway that went back to the kitchen but opened up to the living space on the right and two small bedrooms and one bathroom on the left. The stairs to the basement were pushed against the only stretch of wall between the living room and the doorway to the kitchen. Down there, however, things took a turn for the creepy. That was where the Nash triplets had been locked up. A basement apartment was how it had been described in the news. A bedroom, kitchenette and bathroom.

A door that had once had four sets of locks on the outside.

Remi didn't want to go down there yet. Instead, she walked through every room upstairs with fresh attention.

First of all, she was surprised that the cabin was fully furnished. She'd expected to walk into an empty, stale space. Instead, it looked very much like a vacation home, albeit from the eighties. Some furniture was covered with drop cloths, other pieces had a thin layer of dust. Again, she never would have picked this place to be the site of a town-wide legend whose story continued to terrorize.

Remi was careful as she picked her way through each room until eventually she made it back to the hallway.

Declan looked like a statue leaning against the wall opposite the bedroom and bathroom doors. Cast in stone, the man was rigid. Jaw set sharp and intimidating, shoulders broad and unrivaled, muscles a testament to his discipline and focus, and bright green eyes narrowed and seeing only the past. Remi felt a tug at her heartstrings for him. The greatest upset in her family life throughout her existence was her parents' divorce and, honestly, it had been a blessing for everyone. She hadn't had to deal with fear and then death like he had.

And she certainly hadn't taken those experiences and been elected into a job that dealt in both on more than one occasion.

"If there's something here, I'm not seeing it," she said with sympathy. He nodded and tried to smile. It fell short, but Remi wasn't going to fault him for it.

"It's okay. I guess I didn't expect there to be something."

Remi glanced at the stairs across from him.

"So do we go down there next?"

Declan sighed. He took off his Stetson and thumped it against his thigh.

"This place has gotten a lot of attention but downstairs is another story altogether. I'm confident that not even a speck of dirt has gone undocumented from that apartment." His attempt at a smile dissolved completely. It looked so odd in comparison to the faded but still bright blue paint that covered the hallway's walls. The rest of the rooms were painted in similar, bright shades.

Remi had somewhat expected wallpaper given the date of the cabin, but all the other rooms had a texture to them like they'd been sponged instead.

She guessed the Fairhopes hadn't liked the effort since the hall didn't have the same effect. It looked like they'd simply painted over wallpaper. Remi could see the seam right above the wooden chair rail that ran around the hall.

"We can go," Declan continued. "You've already done enough by just coming out here."

He pushed away from the wall, but Remi didn't move. She felt her eyebrows furrow in together as she continued to stare at the wall.

"What is it?" Declan asked. He turned around after Remi pointed.

"That seam that's been painted over."

"You mean the wallpaper? Yeah, they painted over it."

Remi shook her head, finger still poised in midair, and looked around the small hallway.

"Where are the other seams?" she asked. "If you paint over wallpaper you're going to see more than one, or bubbles from the paint over the paper. Something over the chair rail or at the corners. Not just *one* seam. No one is that good at painting over wallpaper, especially not in the eighties or nineties."

Declan touched the seam beneath the paint.

"Unless it's not a seam from wallpaper."

Green eyes met hers. Remi saw the excitement. The potential. The possibility that they were close to something new. She felt it, too.

What she didn't expect was what happened next.

Declan touched the wall next to the seam and then

reared his arm back and punched that same spot. Remi gasped as his fist went right through the drywall.

"Declan!"

"I'm okay," he said. Then he did it again, beneath the hole he'd just made. It expanded the open space. Remi was prepared to grab his arm to keep him from doing it again when he slowly put his hand into the hole and pulled more of the drywall out. It came off with ease. He tossed the blue-painted chunks to the left of her. There was no trace of wallpaper on any of the pieces.

Then he kicked the wall, opening a new hole.

Remi took a step back.

It was oddly intriguing to watch the man pull, punch and kick away an entire panel of drywall with such ease. And in a blazer and slacks, no less.

Soon there was a Declan-sized hole in the wall. Remi moved closer again as the sheriff stepped just enough inside of the hole to peer straight at the spot where the seam was. Without looking anywhere else, he pulled two things from two separate pockets of his blazer.

One was a pair of plastic gloves, which he put on with lightning speed and precision. The other was a pocketknife.

He opened it, wordlessly.

Then he slid the blade beneath the seam like an expert surgeon.

Remi held her breath.

The chill from outside had found its way into the cabin. Goose bumps moved across her skin.

A long, agonizing minute crept by.

When it was over Declan had cut out what had made the seam.

"My God," he breathed out after holding it up. He

met Remi's gaze with a look of total bewilderment. "Huds, it's a piece of paper."

THE PAPER WAS small but thick. One side was covered in paint, but the blue hadn't bled all the way through. The ink that was scrawled across the other side, the one that had been against the original cream-colored wall, was still legible.

In fact, it was nearly pristine.

"What does it say?"

Remi followed him into the kitchen, careful to keep her distance as he gently laid the paper down on one of the counters. The power was off, but the natural light kept the first floor bright. Still, Declan set the paper beneath the window that ran across the kitchen wall, not wanting to miss a thing.

"It's a name." The handwriting was tight, neat. Declan didn't recognize it, though he did the name. "Justin Redman."

"Who? Is that all it says?" Remi went from a careful distance to right up against his side. She smelled like the beach. Sunscreen and sunshine. It might have knocked him off his game had they been in a different setting.

But not now.

Not here with the note from the wall.

"That's all it says," he confirmed, tilting the paper up so she could see it better. "Justin Redman."

"Does that name mean something to you?"

Declan nodded.

"He was a part of one of the cases my dad was working when the triplets were taken. Aggravated assault. Redman was attacked outside of the old gas station at the turnoff to County Road 11. The one that shut down when we were around fifteen, sixteen. He couldn't give a good description and there were no witnesses. Then Redman died in a car accident. The department never found out who attacked him but suspected it was drug related." Declan pulled out his phone to take pictures. "I don't know why his name would be here. Or, for the matter, why it was painted against the wall."

"Or how that man in the bar knew about it," Remi added.

A shot of adrenaline went through Declan.

"Or how he knew about it," he repeated, chewing the words over.

Remi shifted and walked away. Declan took several pictures before laying the paper gently back down on the cabinet.

"What are you doing?" he called.

"What do you think I'm doing? I'm looking at the walls again! Check for any seams or bubbles or discoloration. If there's one hidden piece of paper, who knows how many more there might be!"

Declan followed his rising excitement and Remi's instructions. Together they inspected the first-floor walls in silence. Sometimes Remi would be the one running her hands over different spots, other times Declan would rub certain stretches of faded paint.

When they ended their search at the top of the stairs again, Declan took pictures of the wall he'd partially demolished.

It had been easy to punch through the drywall but had left his hand stinging. A glance down showed blood. He tried to keep that hand out of Remi's view.

"What now? Do we go downstairs and look?" Declan was surprised at how eager Remi was to help. Surprised and pleased. It helped remind him how easy it had been to hang out with her as kids and teens. Being in her company was nice now, even if they were looking for hidden clues in walls.

It also reminded him how bizarre their current situation was compared to them hanging out in the loft space of his family's barn or out behind the high school complaining about Mrs. Darlene's too-hard geometry homework and Coach Kelly's ridiculous rules about dressing for PE.

Declan was surprised at himself for what he said next.

"We got way more than I bargained for already. I need to take that paper back to the department and do some digging. I can come back out here later and look downstairs, though I stand by there being not a speck of dirt or dust down there that hasn't been cataloged already." He motioned to the walls around him. "This, though... This was a surprise."

"Are you sure you don't want to keep looking? I don't mind."

Declan shook his head.

"You've done more than enough already, Huds. Thank you, I mean it."

Remi's cheeks darkened slightly. From rosy to rosier. She was blushing. It was an endearing sight.

"It was no problem."

Declan went out to his truck, grabbed one of the plastic sandwich bags he always carried in the cab, and bagged the note. Remi waited outside, leaning against the truck and looking off into the woods. It was a nice sight when he came back out, ready to leave.

It wasn't until they were both back in the cab of the

truck that Declan realized the weight of what they'd just done.

What they'd found.

A new clue to the abduction case.

The case that had torn his family apart.

The case that changed all of their lives.

Justin Redman. Declan had already reviewed the cases his father had worked on through his career. Michael Nash had been a great detective. Which had been the leading point of fact that had contributed to his obsession with the case and then led to his downfall. He was the great detective who couldn't for the life of him solve an inch of what had happened to his own family, in his own hometown.

It wore him down until there was nothing left.

And now Declan had a piece of something his father had never seen.

Could this be the missing part of the puzzle that finally led to some answers?

Could he finally help his family find the peace they'd been searching for?

A hand touched his arm. Declan was startled by it. Remi's eyebrow was arched, her expression soft.

"Did you say something?"

She smiled. It was soft, too.

"I asked if you were okay."

Declan took off his hat and set it down on the center console. A restlessness was starting to settle on him. An itch he needed to scratch. But that was how it had started with his dad—focusing to the point of isolating himself.

Declan didn't want to do that.

Not to the woman who had seen what he couldn't.

"Sorry," he said, starting the truck. "I get caught in my own head sometimes. Yeah, I'm good."

"And that blood on your hands?"

Declan smirked.

"Hazard of the job."

That earned a snort from Remi, and soon they were back on the dirt road.

The farther away they got away from Well Water, the more he tried to relax and be in the moment.

It wasn't until they were on the main road pointed back to Winding Road that Declan realized how much of a grade A jackass he'd still managed to be.

"What are you doing?" Remi asked the moment he slowed and started to pull onto the grassy shoulder.

Declan switched on his flashers, put the truck in Park, and turned in his seat to face her.

"You called me because you said you wanted to talk, and I pulled you out to a crime scene without even asking what it was that you wanted to talk about. I swear my mama taught me manners. Now what's on your mind?"

A peculiar look changed Remi's expression from confusion to somewhere between amusement and hesitation. He thought she might not tell him for a moment, but then she angled in her seat to face him better and began.

"Well, you know how stressed I was trying to decide if I should take the job in Colorado and you said you thought I should?"

He nodded.

"Yeah! You said it would be a huge step in your career, right?"

It was Remi's turn to nod.

"It would be and, the Monday after I left here last, I accepted the position."

Declan smiled.

"That's great, Huds! You busted your tail to get it!"

Remi's cheeks tinted a darker shade of rosy again.

"It *is* great. I've actually already started packing up the house. What's *not* great is how slow that's been going since the morning sickness kicked in last week."

For a second, Declan thought he heard her wrong. Then Remi raised her eyebrows as if to say, *Yeah, you heard me right, big man.* When she didn't speak for another moment, Declan realized he must have heard her right.

Then he finally added up some things he should have probably already been questioning.

Declan might not have been as good a detective as his father or his brother but, by God, he'd be a damn near a fool to not understand the real reason Remi Hudson had come back to town again.

Chapter Five

"You're pregnant."

It was more a statement than a question, one that didn't seem to match Declan's increasingly inquisitive expression. Remi didn't know what she had hoped to see from the man at the news but was glad, at least, he hadn't tried to rebuff her immediately.

And that she hadn't had to spell it out for him, either.

"According to the lab tech who took my blood and the nurse who called me with the results," she said with a nod. "Not to mention more than a few tests." Remi pulled her phone out and went to the Gallery app. When she got to the cluster of pregnancy test photos she'd taken originally in disbelief, she passed him the phone.

Declan was quiet as he swiped through them. There was another odd contrast between the muscled sheriff and her pink-and-blue-floral phone case. He stopped on the last picture and zoomed in with his fingers, expanding the part of the digital test that clearly read "pregnant."

"You're pregnant," he repeated when he was done. Remi took her phone back. Their fingers touched. Declan was warm. Just as he had been the night that had led them to this moment.

"I didn't notice at first that my period didn't come, and then when I did I assumed it was because of stress, but then I was *just so hot* and Googled my symptoms. I started to do the math. I grabbed a test and made an appointment the next day for the blood draw. Though they took a urine test, too, and it was also positive."

Declan's expression was passing from curious to shocked. His green eyes, tall grass in a breeze, were the size of quarters. A man trying to process as much information as he could while seeking out more.

"But we used protection," he pointed out.

"And yet, here we are at almost six weeks. I guess the Nash swimmers are Olympians."

"Six weeks?" Declan's voice jumped at that.

"Five weeks, five days. Based on conception since, well, that was easy to pin down." Remi held her phone up again. "I have an app that I can show you. It explains *a lot*, which is good because I grew up with three men and—" Before she could finish the thought Declan's cell phone shifted their focus. A rhythmic set of beeps filled the space of the cab around them. Remi could see the caller ID read Detective Santiago. Declan didn't reach for it.

"My news isn't going anywhere," she said with a light laugh. "You can answer the phone. I won't be offended."

Declan still wavered, but by the fourth ring he hit Answer.

"What's up, Jazz?"

A woman's voice floated from the receiver, though Remi couldn't hear what she was saying. A slight panic took over as Remi realized she didn't know if Declan had started seeing someone in the time after they'd been together. She *had* told him several times he needed to lighten up and live a little as they'd been trapped between the sheets together. Had he taken her advice as she'd taken his about her promotion?

And, if so, did it really matter?

Remi did want children. Eventually. Now was unexpected, but she was taking the surprise with a cautious, slightly terrified smile of acceptance. Telling Declan had never been a question in her mind.

However, her expectations of a future together had never been set.

Declan Nash might have been wild when they were younger, but his love for his family had never been in question. He adored his mother, looked up to his father, and he'd die to protect each and every one of his siblings. The man he was now? Remi was seeing the sheriff, a respected man filled with responsibility and the need to protect. Even now, years and years later, he was still trying to protect that same family he'd fiercely loved when they were younger.

No, there was no doubt in Remi's mind that Declan would absolutely step up to his role as father.

What she *didn't* know was what that meant for the two of them in the future.

And where that future might take place.

Because, as much as she liked and respected the man next to her, Remi hadn't for a moment wavered in her desire to move to Colorado. As she'd told Declan when they last spoke, her new job wasn't just a career maker. It paid extremely well.

Financial stability hadn't always been something the Hudson family could claim, and Remi would be damned if she didn't change that for her kid.

She didn't have to hear the conversation going on next to her to read the changes in Declan's demeanor. The shift to sheriff was quick. His brow furrowed, his forehead crinkled, and a frown ate away whatever emotions he was feeling about the news she'd given him.

He nodded even though Detective Santiago couldn't see it.

"Yeah, you were right," he said, gruff. "Thanks for the heads-up. I appreciate it." A sigh pulled his chest down. "Yeah. I'll head that way after I change. Give me twenty."

He ended the call. Then he was staring again.

"I have a *situation* I need to take care of at work."

"Everything okay?"

That sigh came back. She didn't like how it brought the man down.

"Everything is up in the air," he answered. "I'll know more when I get there. Is that okay?"

Remi held her hands up to show no offense was being taken again.

"Listen, I promise you that me being pregnant hopefully isn't going anywhere. We can talk about it more later on. If you want."

Declan's expression was hard.

"I want to."

He put them back on the main road and soon they were on Winding Road, leading up to the ranch. In the time between their stop and the arch that read Nash Family Ranch, Declan had called two people and hurriedly given them information she didn't understand. Remi wasn't trying to snoop, though. Instead, she watched out the window as trees whipped by. Winter had stripped some of them bare. Others were shades of dark green and dark brown. Remi wondered if it would snow for Christmas.

How would the holidays look now?

She started her new job two days into the New Year. This was the last time she'd be in Tennessee for the foreseeable future.

How would her family take the news that she was moving so far away? Not well, she imagined. The last time she'd come to town she'd almost told them about the decision she had to make. To accept the new position or not. Yet, she'd found herself back in their old fights of leaving the ranch for school and after. Moving to Colorado? She doubted that conversation would end in anything but a fight. Especially once she added in the news of a baby on the way.

"Sorry," Declan grumbled as he ended his last call. He cut the engine in the driveway at his house. "If it's not one thing, it's another."

"Well, I'm sure that note and, well, *this*—" Remi motioned to her stomach, which was bloated if she was being honest "—isn't helping your sheriff to-do list."

She meant the comment in humor; Declan didn't smile.

"How long are you in town for?"

"Until Christmas, though I might head back if I need a break from the boys at the ranch."

"Have you told them yet? About, you know?"

Remi let out a sigh that mimicked Declan's earlier stress-infused ones.

"No. Other than the nurse and lab tech, you're the only one I've told so far." She gave him a look she hoped was severe. "And I'd like to keep it on the down low for now. Not only is it too early to tell anyone, I also feel like *we* need to talk it out first."

"Agreed. What about tonight?" He nodded out the windshield. "I can make us dinner. If you don't mind subpar cooking."

Remi couldn't help laughing.

"Considering the microwave was my most-used appliance at my rental in Nashville, anything you make I bet would be ten times better than what I would cobble together at Heartland."

After they got out of the truck, Declan paused next to her car door. He looked like he wanted to say something and couldn't seem to find the right words. Remi felt a wave of sympathy wash over her. In its wake was a surprising and vicious pull of the fear of the unknown.

She could have misjudged the man opposite her. Children and teens *did* grow up, and there was no denying he had. He could still love his family. That didn't mean he would want to be a part of their child's life.

Either way, Remi wasn't about to find the answer right now. She put her hand out and patted Declan on the shoulder.

"Let me know when you want me to come over and I'll be here," she said, trying to sound happier than her thoughts had just become. "And try not to stress too much about everything. I can already see some wrinkles trying to break through."

He smiled. It was tight.

"I guess you're too short to see some of the gray hairs I've been sprouting already."

"Just remember, that's when cowboy hats serve a dual purpose. Slap that puppy on and aim that stress somewhere else. Okay?"

He nodded, but she knew her words were just words. They didn't have the power to wring the stress from his life. Just as his didn't have the power to smooth over hers.

He opened her car door and shut it gently when Remi was inside. By the time she was pulling out of the driveway, she couldn't help but look in her rearview.

Declan was already gone.

COOPER MANN LOOKED two shades of panicked when Declan walked into the viewing room at the sheriff's department. The young rebel was handcuffed to the metal table in the room opposite, visibly freaking out even though there was a thick, soundproofed two-way mirror between them.

Detective Jazz Santiago, Caleb's partner and best friend, shook her head in greeting.

"I couldn't believe the call when it came in," she started. "I almost asked if there was another Cooper Mann who drove a white Corvette with a piece of duct tape along the bumper."

"But there's not," he finished.

She shook her head.

"Still hard to believe, though."

Declan had to agree with her there.

"Where's the woman he tried to grab? You said her name was Lydia?"

Jazz pulled a slip of paper out of her pants pocket. She handed it over. "Lydia Cartwright" was written in sloppy handwriting. It was a far cry from the neatness of the note he'd found less than two hours ago.

If the current situation hadn't been what it was, Declan would have considered telling Jazz what he had found. Even though she and her husband had lived in Overlook for years, they weren't locals. Her fascination with the triplet abduction stopped and started only when it was relevant to the conversation and only if that conversation was started by a Nash. Her loyalty, friendship and top-notch detective skills would be an asset to figuring out whatever it was that Declan and Remi had found.

Yet, he held his tongue and forced himself to focus on the present and the woman who had almost been kidnapped herself.

"She's at the hospital getting seen about still," Jazz answered. Her shoulders tensed. "He cut up her face pretty good with the keys on his key ring. You can still see some of her blood on his hands."

Declan cursed beneath his breath. Sure enough he could make out smears across parts of Cooper's hands and fingers.

"Is Caleb out there with her already?"

Caleb had been one of his calls as Declan tried to assess the situation before knowing all of the facts. He'd needed to deploy one of his best to figure out those facts. Pronto. But then he'd spent the majority of the ride over talking to his chief deputy. Mayne Cussler was, and had been, Declan's right-hand man for a while now. When Declan had nearly died a few years ago, Cussler had stepped up in a big way while making it known he liked where he was.

"Being sheriff one day could be nice," he'd said once Declan had been cleared for work again. "But I like where I am right now."

Cussler was a reserved man, quiet. He hadn't been as much when Declan had told him that Cooper Mann had tried to abduct a woman. In fact, Declan had heard the man cuss more during their conversation on the drive over than Declan had heard in the ten years of knowing him.

"Yeah. He and Nina were downtown with Parker when you called so he was able to get there pretty quick," Jazz answered. "He said he'd update us the second he finds something out."

Declan nodded. He tried to untangle the knots of facts threaded together in his head. One line of thought was begging to be pulled out, but Jazz angled her body toward him and dropped her voice before he could inspect it.

"Cooper isn't asking for a lawyer. He's asking for you. He said you two met up today?"

The question of "why" was clear in her expression, yet he was glad there was no suspicion there. She might not have been Declan's partner but she trusted him.

Which made his omission of the entire truth even harder to tell her.

"He heard a rumor about the triplets' abduction case and wanted to pass it on to me, to pay me back for helping clear his warrant."

Jazz's eyes widened considerably.

"What was the rumor?"

That one thread of thought, begging to be pulled out, became the only one left in his head.

"It doesn't matter," he said, anger rising. "I have a feeling it was all just a distraction."

The paper in the plastic bag in Declan's pocket felt heavier. The hope Declan had been harboring since Remi had pointed out the seam in the hallway was now souring into him feeling like an idiot.

Cooper Mann had, for whatever reason, set him up.

He should have known better.

And that just made Declan angrier.

"It's time for me to have a little talk with our friend."

Chapter Six

Cooper was sweating bullets. His face had paled considerably from earlier that morning. There was a slight shake to him. He wasn't exactly the picture of a man who had brazenly attacked and then tried to kidnap a woman. But Declan was no stranger to the adage that looks could be deceiving.

He settled into the metal chair opposite Cooper in the interrogation room and laced his fingers over the top of the table, leaning in. Declan was outraged and trying his best not to let it show.

Cooper, again, wasn't faring well when it came to keeping his own emotions in check. Declan didn't get a word in before the young man was nearly talking over himself to get his side of the story out.

"I didn't do this, man, you gotta know that, right? She came after *me*!"

"Don't call me 'man,'" Declan responded, voice even. "It's Sheriff Nash."

Cooper's eyes widened, a deer caught in headlights. He shook his head.

"*She* came at *me*, Sheriff Nash," he tried again. "Honest to God, I was just stopping to get something to eat, and she got my attention and then *bam*!" He tried

to bring his hands up to his face. The handcuffs kept the
movement from extending past his chest, so he jerked
his head down to meet his hands. He didn't touch his
face but made stabbing motions. "She grabbed my keys
out of my hand and started shredding her own face!"

If Caleb had been sitting next to him, Declan imagined he would have snorted and said something along
the lines of *Well, that's a new one.*

However, Declan wasn't in the mood in the slightest.
He wasn't about to encourage Cooper's story.

"The man who called 911 said he came out of the
shop because he heard her screaming and saw *you* trying to push *her* into your car."

Cooper made a strangled sound between frustration
and fear. He hit his hands against the top of the table.

"I was trying to get her *out* of my car! After she did
that crazy thing to her face, she opened my door and
tried to get in! I thought she was trying to carjack me!
Then someone was grabbing me and you guys showed
up acting like I was the bad guy!"

Declan didn't roll his eyes.

He wanted to, though.

"Why would she want to do all of that?" he asked.

"The hell if I know! She's crazy!"

Cooper was nearly panting. Declan believed something traumatic had happened. What he was having
a hard time believing was that Cooper had been the
victim.

"You have to understand how this looks from my
point of view, Cooper," Declan said, easy on the tone.
"First you come to me today about new information on
the abduction case and then you're seen with an injured
woman who swears you tried to abduct *her.* Were you

trying to use the triplets' abduction to distract me from you trying the same? Or were you just trying to double your chances at making headline news?"

Cooper opened and closed his mouth a few times. Objectively, Declan thought the boy looked terrified and surprised at the accusation. Then again, trying to abduct someone on his watch wasn't just an affront to Declan's job, it was a hard prod into his family's past.

He wasn't going to give Cooper an inch.

Not until he had proof otherwise.

"After we finish talking to Ms. Cartwright, I'll be back in here," Declan said, standing to his full height and drawing in his chest with authority and sincerity. He adjusted his Stetson and made sure his sheriff's badge was showing. "Then we're going to get to the bottom of this. And, Cooper? If you lie to me, you're going pay for that lie. It's as simple as that. Got it?"

This time Cooper found his words. They jumbled together as he again tried to tell Declan he was innocent, that Lydia had been the one lying, and he'd just been in the wrong place at the wrong time.

Declan shut the door behind him with Cooper still talking.

Jazz met him in the hallway.

"This is going to be a nightmare in the press," she said. "Cussler can only sweet-talk Delores and the media away for so long."

"I know." Declan sighed. "Which is why we have to move fast and get this thing settled before it takes over the town."

Declan didn't call.

Remi shrugged deeper into her jacket and kept her

leisurely pace along the dirt path across Hudson Heartland. It went from the front door of the house all the way to the front gate, and she was on her way back for the second pass. The distance wasn't anything she couldn't handle, yet she felt a soreness already creeping into her legs. She was also somewhat out of breath.

Was that a pregnancy thing?

Or was she just looking for pregnancy symptoms and finding her own when there were none?

Remi shook her head. She needed to calm down. Her next appointment was at eight weeks, a little too far away if she was being honest, and she'd given herself that deadline to figure out what the heck was going to happen next for her, her child and Declan.

She knew the sheriff was out there being the sheriff, yet, when seven o'clock turned into eight and then nine, Remi had felt a sting of rejection at his absence. Rescheduling their talk was okay—she'd understand that—but Declan hadn't even texted her.

The reasons he hadn't gotten in touch with her all stemmed from issues Remi had been afraid of when she found out about the pregnancy.

Declan being so busy with work that he'd forgotten about their chat was the leading suspect in her mind. Which opened up a Pandora's box of potential issues for her. One, Declan's job was chaotic and dangerous. Not a point against him but definitely not a point of stability for Remi's comfort or liking. Two, he was a sheriff who didn't just do his job, he *was* his job.

She took in a deep, cooling breath. She'd recognized the look in Declan's eyes after finding the note. It was one of purpose. It was one of excitement. It was a solid stubbornness.

Stubbornness to do whatever it took to see through what he meant to see through.

She'd encountered it before in her father. A dogged approach to life: the job came first because it had to, the rest of them be damned.

Remi knew the balance between family and obligation to protect that family was a difficult dance. One her father had lost when she was younger, resulting in her parents' divorce. And that had revolved around taming horses for clients and then boarding horses, not solving kidnapping cases and trying to protect an entire county of people.

She also knew that she and Declan were friends who had *momentarily* become more.

Could she really expect him to keep her within his orbit? Especially with his job?

And if Declan *hadn't* forgotten about her?

Well, then, that was another set of issues she'd have to deal with.

Remi saw movement ahead of her. The outline of a man was illuminated by the exterior lights set up around the house. For a moment her stomach turned into an excited mess of static, then she realized the proportions of the man didn't fit the wide stature of the sheriff.

He came close enough that the light shifted. Jonah had his eyebrow raised in question.

"You know it's cold out here, right?" he greeted, zipping up the plaid monstrosity their mother had given him a few Christmases ago. Of all the Hudson clan, Jonah and Remi resembled each other the most. Lean, on the shorter side, dark blond hair, and freckles that had faded since they were children. Along with their mother, they both had almond-brown eyes. Remi had liked to think hers resembled more of a burning ember in the right light, but she seriously doubted Jonah would ever want such a frilly descriptor of his features.

Jonah Hudson might have looked like her, but he was all their father in personality. No-nonsense, no-frills, just hard work and a stifling need to guilt others about family obligation while rising to equally intense and set-way-too-high family expectations. Jonah might have been a year younger than her but Remi had always felt he was light-years older.

Even now his gaze felt belittling.

It did nothing for her current mood.

"You know that's what jackets are made for, right?" She motioned to hers and returned his eyebrow raise.

Jonah rolled his eyes but turned so he was at her shoulder. He matched her steps as she followed the curve of the path that went around the house and to the back porch.

"I don't know why you're out here right now anyways," Jonah kept on. "Last I heard you weren't a fan of the ranch. Now you show up two weeks early for the holidays and you're out walking it?"

Remi groaned.

"Just because I don't want to run the ranch doesn't mean I can't love it, you know," she shot back, neck getting hot as her anger spiked.

Jonah raised his hands in surrender.

"I didn't come out here to fight," he backtracked. "I saw you and thought I'd join you. Dad and Josh are in a mood together."

Remi heard the annoyance she often felt for the three Hudson men coming out of one of those men now. Her anger took a turn for the curious.

"Really? I didn't pick up on that at supper."

Jonah's breath misted out in front of him for the smallest of seconds. It wasn't cold enough to sustain a more noticeable cloud. It *did* show Remi a frustrated side of her brother that wasn't, for once, aimed at her.

"You haven't exactly been around the last few years so that doesn't surprise me. Dad and Josh butt heads more and more every day, but ever since Josh started dating this new woman he's been more *vocal* than normal. One moment he's talking about turning the ranch back into *the* place to tame and train horses, the next he's talking about running off into the sunset with this new fling."

Remi was absolutely stunned at that news. A common theme she'd encountered since leaving for college had been how living a life outside of the ranch was akin to familial treason. Josh hadn't pulled any punches as Remi had decided to commit that treason with every new choice that wasn't coming back to Overlook and taking an interest in Hudson Heartland.

"A fling is making him rethink his gospel?" Remi mocked, unable to keep the bad feelings of her brother's disappointment from slinking into her words. "Does that mean I finally get a pass if he decides to run off into the sunset?"

"This is serious, Remi," Jonah tried. "He barely knows this woman and yet he's ready to throw everything he's worked for away? For what? A few rounds in the sack?"

Remi made a disgusted noise.

"I don't need to hear that," she said. "Please and thank you."

They made it to the back porch. The light in their

father's bedroom room was off. Josh's room was at the other corner of the house along the back. His light was on. Jonah looked up at it with concern clear on his face.

Despite their differences and the chasm that had opened up between them since becoming adults, Remi softened and took pity on her little brother.

"Josh will be fine. He's been the dutiful son, brother and horse trainer since he could walk and talk. Let him have his moment. If you don't, you'll only be pushing him to do the exact thing you don't want him to in the first place." Remi placed her hand on Jonah's shoulder. He gave her a look that also clearly said he wasn't used to the sibling closeness. Still, he didn't pull away. "It wouldn't hurt for you to relax a little, too. Maybe spend less time worrying about those two—" she motioned to her father's room and then Josh's "—and a little more about yourself. When's the last time *you* had a fling?"

Jonah snorted. Remi was glad he hadn't taken offense to what she'd said.

"I'll have you know that I actually went out on a blind date last week, thank you very much."

Remi couldn't stop the wide grin that moved across her face.

"Oh, yeah? And how did that go?"

Jonah shrugged. It was a cocky movement.

"Must have been okay since we're supposed to meet up tomorrow."

Remi laughed and bumped her shoulder against his.

"Way to go there, Jonah boy! What's her name? Do I know her?"

He was already walking to the back door, shaking his head.

"She's new in town but, even if she wasn't, I'm not

going to give you any ammo to dog me...or stalk her online."

"Oh, come on! That's not fair!" Remi followed him inside, mood lifting. It was nice to laugh with her brother. It made her forget for a moment about the insecurities swarming in her head. "How old is she? What does she do? When did she move to Overlook?"

Jonah kept shaking his head. He hurried to the stairs but paused when she threw out a last teasing insult.

"Did you know that you're a wet blanket? Has anyone ever told you that?" Remi said.

Jonah rolled his eyes.

"Her name is Lydia," he said. "And that's all you're getting."

He dashed up the stairs. Remi didn't follow. Her eyes caught on an old picture framed on the wall next to the stairs. It was of her and her father. She was sitting on a horse, her father standing next to them.

He was beaming, no doubt sure about the future.

One with his wife, his ranch, and his eldest child on a path that would certainly lead to taking over that same ranch.

But the thing about certainty was that it didn't exist.

At least, not for Remi.

She ran a hand over her stomach. Then she pulled out her cell phone.

There were no missed calls or texts.

Remi looked back at the picture for a few more moments. Then she went to bed.

Chapter Seven

Remi fell asleep next to an empty fruit-snack wrapper and woke up to Jonah looking a far cry from the humor-filled man he had been when they parted ways at the stairs the night before.

"What's wrong?" she asked, sitting bolt upright. She couldn't remember the last time Jonah had even been in her childhood room.

"You have a visitor out on the front porch," he said, his voice weirdly low. "I thought I'd give you a warning since Dad doesn't seem to much care for the Nashes and he's the one who's out there talking to him."

Remi tossed the blanket off her, threw her legs over the side of the bed and rushed to the window. Unlike her brothers' and father's rooms, hers was the only front-facing bedroom. Which meant from her window she couldn't see the covered front porch, but she *could* see the truck parked in the drive.

Declan.

It wasn't ladylike but Remi cussed under her breath. Jonah snorted and headed back for the door.

"Probably way friendlier than Dad is being to the sheriff," he said over his shoulder.

Remi didn't doubt that one bit.

She hurried to the bathroom and got presentable like it was the big triathlon she'd been practicing all year to win. Teeth brushed, face washed, mascara applied, hair detangled, and a blue flannel button-up with jeans and boots put on. She knew she could stand to be slower if she wanted. On his own Declan was already a grumpy spot for Gale Hudson. Him coming to the ranch to ask to see his daughter?

Remi bet every paycheck she'd ever made at Towne & Associates that the only way the sheriff was coming inside was if he had a warrant. And even then he might have to bust out the handcuffs to keep her father from making a scene.

December stuck to its guns on mimicking a real winter. Remi ripped her jacket off the hook by the front door and walked into the cold without properly bracing herself for it. She sucked in a breath as she tried to zip up the jacket, all while trying to gauge the situation on the porch.

Declan was standing on the bottom step, her father on the top. The latter was leaning against the railing, all casual. Declan, however, was tense. His badge had been pinned to the outside of his jacket. He greeted Remi with a smile.

It was also tense.

"Hey," Remi said, sliding into whatever conversation they'd been having. She caught Declan's gaze. "I saw your truck and thought you might be here for me?"

"And why would you think that?" her father asked so fast she got whiplash looking back at him. A heat pulsed up her neck and into her cheeks. It was born from embarrassment and quick anger.

It could have been pregnancy hormones; it could

have been the fact that her father had barely said two words to her since she'd come back for the holidays.

"Because why would anyone want to visit a bunch of grumpy men holed up in one house?" she shot back, deciding it didn't matter what was fueling her sudden fire.

Her father turned, surprised but obviously ready for rebuttal. Remi was, too.

Declan went to the next step. When he spoke, his tone was so harsh that both Hudsons redirected their attention.

"I'm actually here for Jonah."

Neither Hudson said a word for a moment. Remi was too busy nursing the stab of disappointment that had pierced her. Declan hadn't called the night before and now he wasn't even there for her.

His expression softened.

"But I would like to talk to you after."

"Why do you need Jonah?" Her father had lost all illusions of being casual.

Declan's jaw was hard. He seemed to choose his words carefully.

"An incident happened yesterday involving an acquaintance of his and I'd like to ask him a few questions."

Remi shared a confused look with her father. Well, *her* expression expressed *confusion*. Her father's read *defiance*.

Declan must have recognized it.

He took one more step up the stairs. When he spoke he kept her father's eye contact.

"This isn't a request, Gale."

Whether it was intentional or not, Declan shifted in his jacket, which made his sheriff's badge catch the sun's glare. It was enough to get her father moving, though he grumbled as he did so.

When Gale was back in the house, Remi descended to the step Declan was on.

"What's going on? Is Jonah in trouble? I mean he's a pain in the backside, but you know he's harmless, right?"

Declan didn't give away anything with his expression.

"He's not in trouble, but I still need to talk to him."

"You? Why not one of your detectives?" Remi lowered her voice. "Is this about the note from Well Water?"

Declan was quick to shake his head.

"It's about that call I got yesterday. I'll explain after I talk with him."

Remi's emotions fluctuated again. She couldn't help what she said next. "Will you call me like you did last night? Or should I just wait around again and hope you'll show up tomorrow instead?"

Declan's entire demeanor shifted, but she didn't have a chance to see what emotion it was shifting into.

"Remi, I—" he said but the front door opened again. Jonah came out, followed by their dad. "I want to talk to you after this," Declan finished instead. Then he met Jonah's stare with another impassive expression.

"Jonah can we talk in private for a minute?" Unlike their father, Jonah agreed without fuss. They walked out to Declan's truck and stopped by its hood.

Remi couldn't hear what they were saying as, alongside her father, she watched their body language. It changed quickly. Jonah clearly was surprised and then angry.

But not at Declan. In fact, Declan put his hand on Jonah's shoulder for a moment.

Then Jonah turned on his heel, yanked his keys from his pocket and was rushing to his car. That put Remi and her father into action. While he went to Jonah, Remi went to Declan.

"What's going on? What's wrong?"

Declan didn't seem offended or angry that Jonah was obviously leaving the conversation. He watched as Jonah quickly spoke to her dad.

"A woman was attacked in an attempted kidnapping yesterday," he explained, not mincing words. "She said she knew Jonah so I thought I'd ask him a few questions to help clarify some things for me."

Remi gasped.

"Lydia?"

"Wait. You know her?"

"I heard about her last night. Jonah went on a blind date with her. Is she okay?"

"Yeah. Shaken up and has some superficial wounds, but she's okay. Considering."

Stressed wasn't the word that described Declan in that moment. It wasn't strong enough. The crinkles at the edge of his eyes that showed a life that had had many a laugh were woefully absent when he met her stare.

"Have you had breakfast yet? I need to eat if I have any hope of continuing to think straight."

Remi didn't have to think about it long. She hurried back to the house for her purse and phone and was sliding into the cab of his truck soon after. It wasn't until they were off Heartland that she realized they were headed toward town and not the Nash Family Ranch.

Which meant they weren't going to be alone after all.

Remi wondered if Declan had made that decision on purpose.

DOWNTOWN OVERLOOK WAS SIMPLE. A main strip with shops, eateries and slow but even foot traffic no matter the day. From the aptly named Main Street there were a few branching streets that led to a park, businesses and one that even went all the way to Second Wind, Desmond's foundation.

When Declan suggested getting something to eat, though, his mind only went to Claire's Café. It was a local favorite and run by a friend. One who, unlike most of the town, knew not to pester Declan for information when it came to a current case. Claire smiled from behind the counter after they walked in and motioned quickly to a table in the corner of the room. Partially hidden behind the pastry cabinet, it gave its patrons a slight privacy advantage while still keeping the front door in sight. Considering it was a seat-yourself establishment, that meant Claire was trying to help him out.

Which meant the town had picked up on the story of Lydia and Cooper way faster than he'd hoped.

Which *also* meant that the press conference he would be attending in two hours might not be soon enough.

"Ahh. I haven't been here in way too long," Remi said with obvious fondness. "Please tell me her homemade pecan squares are still a thing."

Declan pulled out her chair and eyed the glass cabinet near them.

"They are and it looks like she just made a new batch. You got lucky."

Remi grinned and only stood again when Claire

bustled over. They hugged, said all the pleasant, polite things exchanged between old friends and then Claire dropped any guise that that was the real reason she'd come over.

"Declan, I thought you should know that all anyone was talking about this morning was Cooper and what he did to that poor woman," she said, lowering her voice so the handful of patrons already in the restaurant couldn't hear. "And, if it were me, I'd avoid talking to the new news editor of the paper. Delores doesn't say it out loud but I can tell she's having a hard time keeping Kellyn from doing the whole tabloid thing instead of using the facts."

Declan took off his hat and decided if he sighed every time he felt like it, then he might never get the chance to talk. Or breathe.

"Thanks, Claire," he said. "I'll make sure to keep a wide berth until the press conference today."

She tapped the tabletop in confirmation and went to get them two pecan squares and two coffees. Remi changed her order to decaf before Claire could get too far away.

"I've been away a lot longer than I realized," she said. "Who are Delores and Kellyn?"

"Delores Dearborn is the editor in chief of the *Overlook Explorer* and Kellyn is the latest news editor. While we—that being me and the department—are personal fans of Delores, we're definitely on the fence about Kellyn. She likes to…*sensationalize* every story she gets her hands on. Sometimes at the expense of the facts. Delores has had her hands full keeping her on track since there aren't a lot of people at the moment who could or would want to take her place. Overlook might be a magnet for some pretty dramatic stories on occasion but it's not the most exciting place in between them."

Remi glanced at the people settled in at a few of the tables across the room.

"Like a kidnapping attempt. The same day we found a note in the wall at Well Water," she whispered.

"I'm not so sure the note even is legit anymore," he admitted. "The man who told me where the note was just so happens to be the same one who tried to take Lydia."

Remi's eyes widened in surprise.

"You think he put it there recently to—what—distract you? That seems pretty darn elaborate for something he surely could have done easier."

Declan shrugged.

"That's the only thing that makes sense right now for me. It wasn't a secret that Dad had been working on Justin Redman's case back in the day. Picking his name to write down would definitely link back to the right time frame."

"That's all so wild." Her expression softened. "Considering I'm stressed out about this, I have to believe you're just swamped with it. How do you cope?"

Declan wanted to say he didn't. His version of coping with the stresses of the job was throwing himself deeper into that job to try to put whatever case was going on to bed. Instead, he smiled at Claire's reappearance with pecan squares and coffee. He pointed to both when she walked away.

"Sweets and coffee help."

Remi laughed. It was a light sound and it helped his mood.

It also made him feel another wave of guilt.

"Listen, Huds, I'm sorry about last night. This case just got really involved and by the time I realized what time it was I didn't want to wake you." He held up one hand in a Stop motion. "I know that's no excuse, but not calling you had nothing to do *with* you. I'm sorry."

A small smile passed over Remi's lips. It was fleeting.

"It's okay. I get it. Really, I do." She took a steady breath. Her lips, glossy and pink, parted. Declan read her body language before she spoke a word. She was about to tell him something.

Something important.

Declan didn't have a chance to find out what that something was.

Suddenly all hell broke loose outside the café. Without thought he threw himself between the rest of the café and Remi and their unborn child.

DECLAN HAD HIS gun up and out. Every patron in the room backed away from the front door. Claire, who was behind the counter with wide, searching eyes, moved behind the baked goods case. She shared a worried look with Remi.

The screeching tires and screaming had happened in an instant. Just as quickly as the appearance of Declan in front of her as a human shield. She'd barely had time to register that anything was wrong before the wall of a man was between her and the door.

Remi reached out to touch that same man, drawn to his protection like her other hand had been drawn to her stomach, linking the three of them in one fight if needed. It was a bizarre reaction Remi didn't have the time to address. When the screaming outside didn't result in an attack inside, Declan finally moved.

"Stay here," he barked over his shoulder, gun still raised.

Remi watched the door bang shut behind him but couldn't see what the commotion was through the front windows. Whatever had happened must have been just out of view.

Remi's heart hammered in her chest.

She still had her hand raised from touching Declan.

The screaming outside stopped.

But the fear rooting her feet to the ground and snaking up to her heart did not.

Chapter Eight

Declan almost mistook the bystander helping the woman as the person who had hurt her.

"Hands where I can see them," Declan ordered on reflex.

Then the details filtered in.

There were three people outside. One was an older man, gray hair haloed around a bald spot that shone in the patch of sunlight not covered by Claire's awning. He stood in the street, his full attention on the other two people outside. Which brought Declan to the younger man kneeling on the sidewalk.

He had dreads pulled back against a plaid button-up and a nice tie. They matched his pants and dress shoes. They did *not* match the blood that was on the arm of his shirt or the woman leaning against him.

Declan realized it was her scream he'd heard.

Blood, bright and angry, was smeared across her cheek. She held it with one hand and the man held her with both of his. He didn't let go as he addressed Declan.

"That man just jumped out of a car and hit her, then took off!" He motioned his head to the side.

Declan lowered his gun and followed the man's sight

line, already mentally calling in backup to search the area for the man in question.

Yet, Declan couldn't believe his eyes.

A few yards away there was a man with red hair standing in the middle of the street. When he saw Declan, he smiled.

"Stop right—" Declan started to yell.

The man turned on his heel and ran like a bat out of hell.

"Call 911," he said to the man on the sidewalk.

Then he lowered his gun and dug his heels into the concrete.

Boots and dress shoes slapping the ground echoed across Main Street as the man of the hour hauled over the span of two blocks. Unlike Caleb, Declan was more muscle than speed. Unlike the man he was chasing, however, Declan was the sheriff and damned determined.

His legs burned as he pushed every muscle to eat up the distance between them. Shouts behind him filled the street as shop owners and patrons came outside to see what all the fuss was about. Declan sidestepped two bystanders with shouts to get back inside. That effort, plus yelling out for the man in question to stop, cost him a bit of endurance. But when the man hung a right around the hardware store at the intersection of Main and Juniper streets, Declan could have laughed.

Whoever the man was, he wasn't a local. Or, at least, hadn't been downtown in a while.

Tilting forward into the run, Declan curved around the corner of the building and immediately had to swerve around an orange caution cone. And then another. The intersection, sidewalk and part of the hardware store were in a construction zone thanks to a nasty spring storm that had used the trees across the street as battering rams. This week they'd started repaving the sidewalk. The road was still sectioned off.

The man didn't know that.

He cursed something awful, already halfway through a stretch of wet cement. Two cones with tape between them were knocked over. A string of workers were littered around the street and watched as Declan let out his booming voice once more.

"Sheriff's department, *stop now!*"

One man, a long-haired younger worker, sprang into action and tried to grab the culprit. Instead, he became a human shield. One that was erected so fast all Declan could do was stop and huff. The man he had been chasing grabbed the younger one and put a gun Declan hadn't yet seen against his temple, stopping them both in the wet cement.

"You stop or he dies," he panted out. He pressed the gun against the man's head again. It made him wince.

Declan didn't move his aim, but he did freeze.

"Whoa there, buddy," he tried, dropping some of the command in his voice and picking up some, as Caleb's wife said, goodwill honey. Some people responded the way Declan wanted to the commanding voice. He had a gut feeling the man with the gun across from him wasn't one of those people. "Take it easy."

He glanced between Declan and the men in neon vests along the road.

"No one do anything stupid," Declan called to them. When the man's gaze was back to him, he addressed him directly. "Drop the gun, let him go, and let's just talk. There's no need for this to go any further."

The man in question did something Declan wasn't expecting. And certainly didn't like.

He laughed.

"And what would we talk about, Sheriff?" he called. "The weather? Christmas plans? How you may be a good shot, but there's no way this would end in a good light if *you* don't put down *your* gun?"

He laughed again and then settled into a smirk.

"I'll make you a deal, though," he continued before Declan could say a word. "Throw your gun into the wet cement and I'll throw you this." He shook the young man he was holding enough to put emphasis on his control of his well-being.

A worker near Declan cussed loudly. He was older and, even with just a glance, undeniably favored the man caught between Declan and his target. It was probably his son.

Which made Declan even more uneasy at the balance of power between him and the smirking man.

"Who are you?" Declan stalled. "What do you want?"

"I'm someone who wants you to *throw your gun* into the cement."

The man didn't lose his smirk but Declan could see his patience was going as he pressed the gun harder against his hostage's head. The man winced.

Declan relented.

There were too many variables, and he didn't have the upper hand with any of them.

"Fine," he said, lowering his gun. "Just let's stay calm."

Declan's service weapon could be replaced, yet he

couldn't deny he didn't like seeing it hit the light gray muck and sink in an inch or so.

He also didn't like how it felt to be that vulnerable.

There wasn't anything stopping the man from using them all as target practice.

They were at a severe disadvantage.

That is, until the younger man he held against him decided to even the playing field. He brought his elbow back so fast that Declan almost missed it.

What he didn't miss was the other man groaning out in pain as that elbow bit into his stomach. It was enough to make him lose his stance. Which also made him lose his target.

"Son of a—" The man cried out, trying to regain his composure. His captive wasn't having it. The younger man ducked and spun as much as the wet cement would allow and grabbed for the wrist of the hand holding the gun.

Declan wasn't about to wait around to see the outcome. He jumped into the cement and slogged over. He wasn't alone. Every man wearing a construction vest converged, even though the gun was still in hand.

Pride swelled in Declan's chest despite the fact that he'd much prefer there be no civilians in danger. Yet, the man who had grown up in Overlook couldn't help but be proud.

It was a feeling he carried with him as he closed the space between them with speed. Declan heard the gun hit the muck beneath them just before his shoulder connected with the attacker's chest. They sank into the cement, and Declan knew he'd won.

The man didn't fight back as Declan got to his knees and kept his hand pressed down on the man's chest.

"Don't you dare move unless I tell you," Declan

ordered. The construction workers flanked him. He looked back at the discarded gun and scooped it up.

The man's head was just above the cement while his body had sunk in a bit. He smiled.

Declan didn't like when a losing man smiled.

It usually meant he didn't care enough to notice he'd lost or he hadn't actually lost at all.

A twisting thought pushed those worries aside. Declan got to his feet and the man merely pushed up on his elbows as best he could. He met Declan's gaze. In the chase and struggle, part of his shirt had drooped down around the collar.

That was when Declan saw the tattoo.

A scorpion.

The brand of the Fixers, the men and women in suits who had a reputation for being the organization other criminals called when a job was too hard to do. Or too messy to carry out.

Declan swore.

The man kept on smiling.

That twisting thought turned into a question. Declan heard the low thrum of ascending rage in his own voice as he asked it.

"Why didn't you just get back into your car after you hit that woman? Why run away if you could have driven away?"

The man was absolutely enjoying himself when he answered. It made Declan's blood run cold.

"Because, *Sheriff*, I knew the only way to get you to leave that café was if I ran."

THE WOMAN CLUTCHING at her face said her name was Rose Ledbetter. She, like Remi, the pedestrian named

Sam who was holding her, and the patrons of Claire's Café, had no idea why the man had jumped out of the car to attack her and then run off. One second she had been on her way down the sidewalk and the next she'd been pistol-whipped by a stranger.

"Pistol-whipped?" Remi asked, fear flowing out of her words before her body could feel it. "He had a gun?"

Rose nodded, whimpering along with the movement. She sat at the table Remi and Declan had been sharing while the rest of the patrons crowded around. Claire was behind the counter, on the phone with the sheriff's department.

"I only saw it after he'd already hit me with it," Rose said. "I—I thought he would shoot me, but he ran instead."

"And Declan chased him."

Chased the man with the gun, she wanted to add but didn't.

Declan was the sheriff. Dealing with bad guys who had guns wasn't new to him. However, the fear uncoiling in Remi's chest was.

Declan wasn't just a boy she'd had a crush on as a girl or kissed once as a teenager. He wasn't just a man she'd shared a bed with after getting reacquainted. He also wasn't just a man who made her question if she wanted to be more than the friends they used to be.

No.

Now, and forever, he'd be the father of her kid.

No matter if they became enemies, lovers or any variation in between.

Declan Nash had cemented his place in her life the moment she'd seen the first positive pregnancy test.

And now?

Now he'd chased a man with a gun.

Normal or not, that made Remi afraid.

A feeling that must have translated into an expression she didn't have time to hide.

Sam, standing between them, looked her in the eye and was fierce with his words.

"The sheriff will be all right."

Remi gave him a small smile.

That smile died right after.

The door to the café opened with a bang. Remi already knew it wouldn't be Declan standing in the doorway, if only for the almost-violent movement, but she hoped all the same.

When she saw a man in a suit wearing a grin, a gun at his side, Remi couldn't help but suck in a breath. She wasn't alone. Everyone around her tensed.

No one spoke until the man walked farther inside. A woman in a matching pantsuit came in behind him and stopped just inside the doorway. She held her gun, aiming it at Claire.

"End the call, show me the screen, and then put it down on the counter," she ordered. Her accent was weirdly devoid of anything Remi could place. Not that it mattered. Claire was staring at a gun. She did as she was told and soon was standing with the rest of them.

The man stopped a few feet from their makeshift line next to the table. There were seven of them in total. Remi stood between Sam and Claire, Rose stayed sitting behind them.

"Don't worry, everyone," the man started. "We're not going to kill anyone as long as no one here does anything stupid."

Remi's adrenaline spiked. He didn't say anything about not *hurting* them.

"Now, let us get down to business and then we'll leave." He scanned their faces quickly, moving his head to the side to see Rose behind them. She whimpered at the eye contact.

Then he was staring at Remi.

He looked her up and down.

"Looks like you might be perfect for the job," he said conversationally.

Remi's heart was hammering in her chest.

The job? she wanted to ask. Instead, all she could do was remember to breathe as he moved directly in front of her and started to pull his gun from its holster.

"Wait a second," Sam jumped in. The man in the suit held the gun but didn't aim it. He addressed Sam but raised his voice for the crowd.

"Anyone moves and you'll make me a liar," he interrupted. "I'll end up killing you all. We good?"

Sam was tense but didn't say a word. No one did. Not even Rose's whimpers could be heard. That went double for moving.

Remi didn't want to break the only rule they'd been given, but the moment he took a step away from them and moved the gun so it was aimed at her, she had no choice.

"I'm pregnant."

The words left her mouth on a trembling plea.

Surprisingly, it seemed to have an impact. The man in the suit glanced back at his partner then to Remi.

"You're not the first person to try and lie about that."

"I have pictures on my phone," she hurried. "Of the tests. It's on the table."

There was a moment where Remi was sure trying to save herself had done the opposite. That she'd been pregnant for such a short amount of time and had already made a wrong choice as a parent. That Declan was about to suffer from another senseless act.

Yet the man sighed.

"Well, that's more trouble than it's worth," he said. He started to lower the gun. Remi felt a part of her unclench. Then the man in the suit turned to Sam. "Which I suppose means bad luck for you."

When he raised his gun and shot, Remi didn't even have time to scream.

THE SOUND OF the gunshot carried down Main Street, around the corner and right into Declan's bones. He was running before the construction workers could utter a word after him. Declan didn't care that he was leaving the man in the suit with civilians.

He had the man's gun.

What he didn't have was eyes on Remi.

Declan cursed into the wind he was creating as he ran full tilt back to the café. The gun in his hand was partially covered in cement, but he could wield it like a club if he had to. Or he'd use his bare hands.

Anything to protect the patrons he'd left behind.

Anything to protect Remi.

The ferocity of that desire should have surprised him, but he didn't have the time to dwell. Sirens started to go off in the distance, and right outside the café a car screeched to a stop. A woman ran out of the café, a man behind her.

"Stop," Declan yelled, still too far away. Pedestrians and bystanders were dotting the openings of stores and buildings along the thoroughfare, or else Declan would have tried out his new gun.

As it was, he watched as the woman ducked into the passenger side of the car and a man in a suit jumped into the back. Neither one paid attention to him; neither did the driver. Declan couldn't make out who it was as they sped off and hung a left up toward the street that ran in front of the community parking lot.

Declan looked at their license plate.

Then his focus shifted to the café.

For the first time in his career, he hesitated. With his hand on the handle of the door, he imagined the worst.

In that moment Remi was both safe and not safe. All at the same time. Just as their unborn child was unharmed and *not*. Going inside would confirm one truth. Staying outside gave him the option of keeping hope even if there was none inside.

So, for the briefest of moments, Declan hesitated.

Just as quickly he remembered that a person couldn't live in a moment. They could treasure it. They could fear it, hate it, wish to never remember it, but *staying* in a moment wasn't realistic.

It wasn't fair.

It wasn't possible.

Declan pushed open the door and saw the blood first.

Then he saw her.

Chapter Nine

The last time Remi had been in the hospital she was six-teen and, oddly enough, Declan Nash had been within earshot. At the time he'd been with his brothers, Caleb and Desmond, while she had been with their friend Molly.

They'd been placed in a room outside of the ER unit because, as Remi's father said, Declan was a wild, dangerous boy. That same wild, dangerous boy had saved the day from the stupid yet fun game of Keep Away with a bag of chocolate-covered peanuts during their hike along the mountain. A hike they had gone on after skipping school.

Remi remembered it fondly, at least the part before they'd taken the game too seriously. Caleb had thrown the package of candy to Molly, and Molly and Remi had taken it too close to a sloped edge that had more tilt than either of them realized. Remi had lost her footing first, but Molly had let out a scream before either girl started their slide down the leaf-covered incline.

In hindsight Remi realized that scream was probably why Caleb had run the way he did after them, spurred on by memories of what had happened to him, Desmond and Madi when they were younger. At the time

Remi had barely hit the even ground with a groan before Caleb had lost his footing, too, and was tumbling down to meet them.

Remi remembered being terrified that she'd hurt herself enough to go to the hospital. That her father would add another notch to the post of reasons he disliked the Nash children. Yet, she'd been fine. A little bruised but no visibly broken bones or radiating pain. Though when Declan had made his way to her, he'd made her question herself. The concern in his eyes, the searching touch as his hands had seemingly been trying to find and fix whatever was hurt, and the warmth in his voice as he'd kept calm, had caused sixteen-year-old Remi to hope there was something that would keep Declan's careful attention on her.

That want had disappeared, however, when Molly and Caleb hadn't stopped their cries and grunts of pain after they were back on even ground. The walk to their vehicles had been spent trying to lay out all of their options, though they'd ultimately chosen to go with the only one that made sense.

Molly had broken her arm, Caleb had twisted his ankle, and Remi had caught lava-hot heat from her father for skipping school with her friend and a bunch of boys, Declan the Wild King among them.

Now Remi was in another room, Sam's, just off the ER in Overlook, this time older. Maybe not wiser, but with enough years between then and now to feel the full terror of a situation that could have been much worse.

When the door opened behind her, Remi didn't have time to hide the swirl of emotions starting to make her feel sick.

It was another moment of déjà vu. Declan came in,

sheriff's badge on his belt and cowboy hat firmly on his head, and stopped at her side. He looked at the hospital bed and spoke to her with a lowered voice.

"I'm going to cut to the chase and tell you it's not your fault," he said. "You watching him sleep off his pain meds isn't going to do anything other than feed that guilt fire I know you've been stoking for the last two hours."

"And me pretending he didn't take a bullet that was probably meant for me isn't going to make me walk around this hospital with any pep in my step." Her words were more harsh than she'd meant them. Still, she didn't take them back.

Declan's face went a bit stony.

"All you did was tell that man you were pregnant. *He's* the one who shot Sam. Not you. I'd like to see anyone else in your shoes do anything differently." Declan motioned to Sam on the bed. He was asleep, his biceps bandaged. The damage hadn't been that bad, but Sam was a local and his friend had been the attending nurse. Remi imagined that had played into the swiftness of the pain meds he'd been given, despite his injury not being severe. It was more of a graze than anything, they'd been told. "Sam didn't blame you for what happened. No reason to blame yourself. Okay?"

Remi sighed and nodded. She followed him back out into the hallway.

Since Declan had come through the café's doors they hadn't been alone. Now, though, Remi didn't know what to say or how to act.

Seeing Declan, after he'd chased Rose's attacker, come back into the café unhurt had been a relief unlike any other. That relief seemed to be reflected in him, though Remi couldn't know how much. Chaos had erupted around them. Only now was it calming down.

Remi didn't know how to handle it so she stuck with the questions that had been piling up since the man and woman in the suits had left.

"I heard the man you chased got away?" she started in, following along with Declan as he led them down the hallway.

His body tensed. He nodded.

"After the two at the café left they hightailed it around the block and made the men holding him let go." He swore and made no looks of apology for it. "My guess was he was only meant to get me away from Claire's so the other two could go in without meeting me and my gun."

"But why? What was the point of all of that? It seems a lot of trouble to go through for not trying to steal from us or kidnap anyone."

If it was possible, Declan tensed more.

"They were making a statement."

Remi felt her eyebrow rise in question. Declan seemed to catch himself. He shook his head slightly and stopped.

"I'll tell you more later when I know more. For now I need to talk to Rose and then go back to the scene. I can get a deputy to take you home, but I thought you might like some company." He rapped his knuckles against the closed door next to them. "Since this town talks so much I figured you might want to get on top of the news." Now he looked apologetic. "And if not, I'm sorry."

Remi had a sudden fear of whoever was on the other side of the door, but it vanished as soon as it opened.

Jonah gave a nod to Declan and then surprised her with a tight embrace.

"I ran into Declan in the lobby when I was at the vending machine," he said into her hair. "He told me to wait here since it was so hectic with everyone trying to get what happened straight."

Jonah pulled back and looked her up and down.

"Rusty called me and said he saw you coming out of the café with a woman who was all bloody. Are you okay?"

Remi nodded.

This was why Declan had already apologized. He must have known she wouldn't have told her family about what had happened if she could avoid it. Instead, apparently, the news was already traveling. It was best she get on top of it, starting with the closest relation to her.

She met Declan's eye. His expression was pinched. He was already getting lost in his own thoughts.

"I'll stay here, if that's okay," she said to him. Then she said to her brother, "If that's okay with you."

"I wasn't going to let you leave without telling me what's going on."

"Then this is where I'll leave you," Declan decided. He seemed to want to say more but stopped himself.

"Call me later?"

He nodded. It was a rigid movement.

Then he was gone.

Remi sighed and faced her brother. Then she realized why Jonah was there in the first place. Peeking around his shoulder she saw the covered legs of someone lying down in the bed in the center of the room.

"Is that Lydia?" she whispered.

"Yeah, she's asleep now, though. They just gave her something for the pain. She asked me not to leave her since she doesn't have anyone else in town." He smiled a little. Lydia must have left quite the impression on him.

Jonah motioned her farther inside the room and over to a couch next to the bed. Remi cringed as she saw the bandages over most of Lydia's face.

"It looks a lot worse than it is, I think," he said at her side. "But we can talk in here. I've been watching TV and it didn't bother her."

Remi settled into the seat next to him. Like being alone with Declan for the first time since everything had happened at Claire's, Remi was at a loss of what exactly to say to her brother. She loved him, she knew that, but there was more of a disconnect between them than there ever was one of understanding.

The Hudsons weren't the Nashes.

Tragedy hadn't tightly fused an already tightly fused family.

There was no triplet connection that created a unique bond between them.

There wasn't a sense of protectiveness that was forged from being in the public eye and at the center of rumors for years.

There was just a family of people who didn't understand the others' choices in life.

Which was why she became a coward when recounting what had happened at the café. Remi hesitated without an ounce of grace when she got to the reason the man in the suit had shot Sam instead of her.

She could have lied.

She could have omitted that part altogether.

She'd been caught between loving her brother and

worrying at his reaction to the news that he'd be an uncle.

He wasn't an idiot. He knew something was off.

"What aren't you saying, Remi? Tell me."

She felt like sighing and then realized how much she'd been doing that lately. Acting defeated or frustrated when, given everything that had happened, she had made it out unscathed. Lucky.

Plus, she figured she'd have to tell her family at some point. Why not now?

"The reason the man in the suit shot Sam and not me was because I told him something that changed his mind." Jonah gave her a questioning look. Remi put her hand on her stomach as she finished. "I told him I was pregnant."

Jonah's eyes widened. They trailed to her stomach and then back up to her gaze.

"And was that true or were you lying?"

"It's true."

Suspicion was quick to line his expression.

"Why didn't you tell us then?"

This time Remi did sigh.

"I wanted the father to be the first to know. I told him yesterday. We were supposed to talk about it today at the café when everything happened."

Jonah had never been considered book smart—he'd rather be outside than studying—but he was well versed in common sense. Remi watched as he connected the dots from the little information he had.

When he spoke his voice rose an octave.

"Declan Nash is the father." It wasn't a question. "When you gave him a ride back to Overlook…" He shook his head. "*That's* why he came to the house personally today instead of sending his brother or a deputy. He wanted to talk to you."

Remi nodded.

"No one else knows. Well, no one else *knew*. I was going to tell you and Josh and Dad after Christmas."

"After?" A look akin to hurt passed over his face. It pushed guilt and anger to the surface for Remi.

"I figured if I told you all right before I left I wouldn't have to hear everyone complaining that long." Jonah opened his mouth to, she guessed, protest. She cut him off. "Dad hasn't liked the Nashes for a long time. He's disliked Declan, specifically, for longer. Throw in the fact that the three of you love to tell me with every other breath that I'm dishonoring my family by 'abandoning' Heartland, I thought that hiding an unexpected, out-of-matrimony pregnancy until I had an escape was a smart, sane move to make. Don't you think?"

Jonah again looked like he wanted to object but then stopped himself. He let out a long breath and nodded.

"We're not the easiest people to talk with, huh?" He gave her a small smile. Remi snorted.

"Not unless we're talking horses."

Jonah gave an identical snort. Then his expression softened.

"And how do *you* feel about being pregnant with Declan's kid?"

Remi was honest.

"Nervous, terrified and weirdly excited."

"So… I'm allowed to be excited, too, right?" he asked.

"Right."

Jonah smiled.

"You know, I've always wanted to be an uncle."

Remi couldn't deny hearing him say that was a relief. It was a feeling that relaxed the part of her that had been tense since finding out she was pregnant.

However, with one glance at Lydia, bandaged and still in the nearby bed, Remi slid fully back into her worries.

Why had the man and woman in the suits attacked Sam?

Why had the other man attacked Rose?

And when was the next attack going to happen?

THE ONLY REASON Declan went back to the hospital that night was because he knew Remi was there.

He'd spent the last several hours putting out fires their suited attackers had created. There was no keeping their brazen attacks against Rose and Sam under wraps as they'd somewhat been able to do with Cooper Mann's attack on Lydia.

And even that news hadn't been out of the spotlight for long. Declan had gone to the press conference set up for what had happened with Lydia as planned and then had to add a vague recount of that morning's chase and attacks. The news editor Claire had warned him about, Kellyn, stood on the front lines with a recorder in her hand and hungry excitement in her eyes.

For once, Declan couldn't blame her or any of the others in attendance.

If Declan hadn't been used to chaos, he would have been overwhelmed.

The note in the wall.

An attempted kidnapping.

The reappearance of a man in a suit.

Three culprits getting away.

Remi Hudson pregnant with his child.

Declan didn't count the last point as a bad one, though he couldn't deny it was heavier than the rest.

Almost as heavy as the exhaustion weighing him down as he made his way to the hospital from the department. He'd called Remi when there was nothing more he could do for the night. When she said she'd brought dinner for her brother and Lydia, Declan had changed course without a second thought.

And when she came out to the lobby to meet him, Declan did something else without a second thought.

He relaxed. If only a little.

"You okay?" he said in greeting. She didn't look tired, but she did look annoyed.

"Well, I thought I was hungry, and then I smelled the chicken I brought Jonah and it made me gag," she said in one hurried breath. "And *now* all I can think about is Pop-Tarts." Her eyes swept over him. Her pink lips turned into a line of concern. "But I shouldn't complain. How are you?"

Declan opened his mouth, fully intending to lie, and then found that the idea didn't sit well with him. Not to Remi.

So he didn't.

"I'm dog-tired." It was a simple answer and a simple truth. "I haven't gotten much sleep lately."

The corner of Remi's lips turned up into a grin. She reached her hand out, palm facing upward. Declan felt his eyebrow rise in question.

"Then you're in luck. It sounds like you need a trusted friend and confidante to take the lead for a little bit. Give me your keys and I'll drive Fiona and you back to the ranch. All the while I can regale you with some of my most harrowing accounting stories, guaranteed to help you fall into a deep, relaxing sleep." When Declan didn't immediately agree, Remi pressed on. There was an edge to her voice. "You might not be the same boy I remember on some fronts, but your stubbornness seems to be intact. Then again, so is mine. You *look* exhausted and need some sleep. I'm fine and know how to get you home. Let me."

"What about your car?" he tried.

She rolled her eyes.

"I trust it'll be just fine in the parking lot, but I'll let Jonah know so he can check on it when he leaves. Okay?"

Declan relented. He dug out his keys and dropped them onto her palm.

"Good sheriff," she said with a smile. "Now, let's go home."

She took his elbow and turned him toward the door. Through the weight of exhaustion, the best Declan could tell, Remi didn't realize what she'd said.

Her gaze remained ahead, and there was no blush in her cheeks, no hesitation in her steps.

An off-the-cuff comment that didn't mean anything past a friend taking another home.

Yet those three words had packed quite the blow.

Let's go home.

It was right then that Declan realized something.

Something big. Something life changing.

But something he wasn't going to think about just yet.

Not when the men in the suits were out there.

Chapter Ten

Declan Nash lived in a simple house furnished with simple things. Remi walked into the entry and slowly turned in a circle to take in the open floor plan. The living room was to the left, the kitchen was straight ahead, and an open archway to the right showed a small office. The door off the living room must have led to the bedroom. Declan moved to it while waving her toward the kitchen.

She'd spent most of the car ride to the Nash Family Ranch complaining about being hungry, complaining about not being able to drink more than a cup of coffee and then complaining about how cold it was getting.

Remi didn't know if it was pregnancy hormones making her grumpy or if she was looking for safe topics to talk about. Nothing that brought their future with a child into account. Nothing about the uptick in Overlook's bad-guy population. Nothing about any notes in the wall.

Just the two of them going down a dark road, her complaining about nothing in particular and him nodding along.

It was nice in a way.

Comfortable.

But now they weren't on the road.

Remi accepted his hospitality by raiding his pantry with a squeal.

"You okay?" Declan called out from the open bedroom door.

"You have Pop-Tarts," she yelled back, mouth already watering.

Declan didn't respond, and Remi settled at the small four-chair dining table set up between the kitchen and the living room couch. She was already through half of her pastry when Declan reemerged.

It was a struggle to keep her jaw from hitting the tabletop.

Remi had seen Declan naked. That was how she came to be sitting at his table, scarfing down Pop-Tarts and knowing in less than ten minutes she'd have to go pee. Again. She knew that the boy she'd grown up around had developed a firm chest and stomach and all the lines that muscles had carved in between. He even had the V that some actors and models sported in the movies and magazines. The one that led the eyes from the stomach and right down into the imagination.

She'd run her fingers along one of those very same lines, marveling that she had found herself in the situation where that touch was wanted.

After that Remi hadn't had to imagine where those lines led.

So when her lust for the sheriff went from a passive five out of ten to a red-hot, volcanic two thousand in the span of him walking through the doorway to dropping down onto the couch cushion, Remi had to double-check the scene.

Declan wasn't naked, first of all.

In fact, he'd merely swapped out his button-down and pants for a plain tee and sleep pants.

But, boy oh boy, was he wearing them.

The shirt hugged his muscled frame while the pants hung lower and a bit baggier than his jeans. It was such a casual outfit, and yet somehow sexier.

It was a glimpse into Declan behind the scenes.

A place where he could just be.

It spoke of vulnerability and it spoke right to Remi's hormones, apparently.

"I couldn't remember if I had them or not," Declan said from his spot on the couch. He leaned back, put his feet up on the coffee table and met her eyes with a smile. If she looked like an idiot, he didn't say it. Even when she scrambled to look normal while finishing her bite of Pop-Tart. "I babysat Riley's nephew the other week and that boy was all about some frosted strawberry. I didn't really think about it until we were in the car."

Remi held up the uneaten portion in a salute.

"Well, I thank you for it."

Declan seemed satisfied that she was satisfied and leaned his head back, put his arms over his chest and closed his eyes.

"I'm sorry I'm so tired," he said after a yawn. "Sometimes I forget that I need to recharge, even though I tell Caleb and my deputies to do it all the time." His eyes opened again, but there was a lag to the movement. He didn't move his head as two grass-green eyes found hers.

Remi put her food down. She felt a tug at her heartstrings. Declan Nash might not be a great talker, but when he did speak he managed to put a whole lot into what he said. Simple statements, yet with so much depth they were nearly overwhelming for Remi to hear, especially when she thought of the always-smiling and mischievous boy she'd once kissed on a dare beneath the moon and stars when she was nothing more than a quiet girl.

The time after they'd parted ways had been kind to him in some respects, but Remi believed it had also run him down in others.

And then he said as much to her utter surprise.

"My dad always used to say that even though there's never enough time to do everything you want to do, there's always time to do at least one thing. Just make that one thing count." He let out a small breath and domed his fingers over his lap. Remi realized she was hanging on his every word. "I didn't think I had a *one thing* for years until I met Bobby Teague."

The name rang a bell.

"The mayor when we were teens?"

Declan shook his head.

"His son," he replied. "Not the nicest man, not the most patient, either. I didn't like him, just like his dad hadn't liked mine back in the day. They were men who wanted attention and became annoyed when they actually got it. A son who became an even grumpier version of his father. And then a pain in my backside. Then one day Bobby Teague came into the department with nothing but fear in him. His sister had gone on a date and hadn't returned to her house." Declan sat up a little. The frown of remembering settled into his lips as he took a moment. "It hadn't been twenty-four hours yet so we couldn't count it as a missing person but, well, after what happened to the triplets, the rules for missing persons in Wildman County are a bit different. I wasn't waiting around hoping that his sister was fine and was just lost in a new love bubble. And Bobby refused to be sidelined. So, he rode with me as we went all over town looking for her."

Remi saw the subtle shift in the man, though she couldn't place the emotion behind it.

"It took us a bit to track down where her date lived, but when we did everything changed between me and Bobby. His digs at me and my family, his sarcasm and ego getting into every word he said, it just all went away the moment we got to the end of that driveway. One second we were two people who didn't much like each other. Nothing in common. No love lost at all between us. And in the next, we were two people who wanted nothing more than for Lori Teague to be okay and would do anything to see that happen."

His words were tired and the rest of what he wanted to say seemed to stall out. Remi hated to prod the man, but she wanted to know what had happened.

"Was she there? At the date's house?"

"She was and she was fine, too," he said with a small smile. "Her phone had died so she hadn't gotten any of the calls and then she lost track of time…doing what happens with some dates, if you catch my drift."

"I do."

"It was a good call. One that could have turned out much worse. Weirdly enough, *that* was when I realized what it was that I wanted to be my *one* thing." Remi leaned in as Declan's expression hardened, resolute. "Making sure people like Bobby Teague didn't have to spend their lives worrying. Instead, they could sigh in relief or, ideally, never have the need." Declan shrugged. "So I threw everything I had into my career, to Overlook, to the county. I woke up worrying about everyone and went to bed wondering how I could make their lives better."

A vulnerability that Remi hadn't been prepared for took over the sheriff. Not only did it pull at her heart-strings, it made something else within her stir.

"When you told me you were pregnant, I didn't act the way I should have. Running off to work, losing track of time and not calling, and then pulling you back into trouble… I should have said, and done, more. It's just… Well, I think I've been so focused on what everyone else wants and needs for so long that, along the way, I forgot to wonder what it is I want."

Every part of Remi went on alert. She could have sworn if a pin had dropped in between his earlier words, she could have heard it as easily as if a bowling ball had been dropped onto the hardwood.

"And what do you want?" she chanced.

The father of her unborn child smiled.

"I know I want to be a part of my kid's life, from now until I'm old, gray, and then in the grave. Everything else? Well, I'm just too tired to think about any of that right now." His mood darkened. He didn't need to say it but Remi knew his thoughts had found their way back to Cooper Mann and then the attack and chase at Claire's.

It was the only reason she didn't push him for more.

And the only reason she didn't give any of what she wanted to say back.

Instead, Remi tried to be reassuring.

"No one has their entire life planned out. You'll have plenty of time to figure out what's next for you. Until then, why don't you go get some sleep."

Declan snorted. He kicked his feet up and swung his

legs over onto the couch. Then he slid down against the cushions with a sigh. It reminded Remi of when she slid into a much-needed warm bubble bath.

"I'm good right here," he said, his eyes closing. "Feel free to eat whatever else you want. There's a spare toothbrush in the cabinet over the sink and some more pj's in the dresser."

That surprised Remi.

"You want me to stay?"

He nodded, eyes still closed. Then he yawned.

"I can't make you but I'd feel better if you were close. Last time I—" He yawned again. This one was deeper, longer, too. The man was dancing near the edge of sleep, there was no denying it. "Last time I left you all hell broke loose. Not gonna happen again. Bed's yours."

Remi smiled into her Pop-Tart. Then she remembered something she needed to tell the man before sleep claimed him.

"Hey, Declan. I told Jonah about the baby in the hospital today."

Declan opened his eyes.

"Did you tell him I'm the father?"

"I did."

Declan surprised her with a nod and a simple response.

"Good."

Remi smiled. Declan returned it. Then his eyes closed and, just like that, Declan quieted. By the time Remi had finished her Pop-Tarts the man was sound asleep.

THE HOUSE WAS different in winter.

The heater made it smell like something was burning sometimes. Not like an all-out fire or anything but more of a lingering firepit smell that always reminded Declan of the day after a bonfire had burned out. That smell, rare since Declan hardly ever turned the heater on in the house, combined with the lack of noise he was used to surrounding the ranch, sometimes disoriented him when he first woke up. It didn't matter that he'd had just as many years knowing winter in Overlook as he'd known summer. There was just something about the cold outside that threw off his internal navigation and understandings.

Like when he opened his eyes to the darkness, smelled something burning and heard something he wasn't used to hearing.

Declan sat up so quickly he nearly pulled a muscle.

It was dark in his immediate area, but on the other side of the room there was a soft glow. That light was enough to show him a space he knew. It clicked in place with the smell of the heater and the feel of the couch beneath him.

And the old wool blanket he was particularly fond of that he'd thrown to the ground in half-asleep earnestness.

He rubbed at his eyes and then worked at blinking away the haze of sleep. Wondering what had wakened him, he turned toward a window. Through the open slats of the blinds he could just make out another glow, though this one wasn't as focused.

It was dawn, and Declan bet that routine had been the thing that had wakened him. He'd never quite shaken waking up early on the ranch as a kid, especially when school was out. As the oldest child he'd had the most to do. Now he normally used the time to go on a run or drink coffee and worry.

He snorted in the dark.

I sure am exciting, he thought ruefully.

His gaze returned to the soft glow nearest him. The one that he knew came from his bedside lamp in the bedroom. Moving slowly, careful to be quiet, Declan got up, went to the open doorway and looked inside.

Dark blond hair was splayed across a navy pillow-case while the covers he hadn't gotten beneath in days housed a woman wearing his clothes.

Remi.

She'd stayed.

Her face, slack with sleep, was turned toward Declan, as beautiful as when she was awake.

And what do you want?

Declan hadn't meant to come clean with what he was feeling the night before. He hadn't meant to admit he'd had tunnel vision with his job the last several years. Just as he hadn't meant to say that her news had finally made him confront the fact that he'd forgotten about himself in the grand scheme of things.

He'd honestly just been tired as hell and ready to fall asleep so he could start fresh in the morning. Yet, when he'd seen Remi sitting at the dining table eating a pack of Pop-Tarts of all things, Declan hadn't been able to stop himself. He'd seen the woman just as he'd seen the girl who had once been his friend.

He'd felt comfortable. So, he'd opened up.

What he *had* meant to say was his realization that, no matter what his future held, he knew without a doubt he wanted it to include their child. It was just a declaration he'd hoped to make in better circumstances, not in his sleep pants after a majorly crappy day.

Also, not immediately before he'd fallen asleep.

But there she'd been and there he'd told her.

And now there she was, asleep in his bed.

It wasn't a new sight for Declan to see her asleep. One time he'd seen her drift off at a school assembly, bored out of her mind. Lon McKinnley had tried to pull her hair to wake her then, so Declan had thumped the boy on the head and dared him in silence to do it again.

What *was* new was how it felt to watch her do so.

The urge to join her was almost as strong as the urge to run a hand across her cheek and tuck behind her ear the strands of hair that had escaped. To feel the warmth of her skin. To feel the smoothness. To—

Adrenaline shot through Declan's bloodstream. It zipped his spine straight and had him retreating into the living room to look for his phone.

Shame, deep and biting, mingled with the new sense of urgency.

How had he not put together the pieces before?

How had he been so blind to not understand what was going on?

Declan cussed, low and with vehemence.

How had he not seen the pattern until now?

Rose hadn't been targeted, per se, but her face had.

Sam wasn't the plan, getting shot in the arm was.

Just like Madi and Caleb.

The day they had been abducted.

Chapter Eleven

"He's not going to figure it out," the woman whined. Her name was Candy and, unlike it, she was not at all sweet. She'd spent the entire car ride back complaining that she hadn't been the one to shoot the man or hit the woman or even put a gun to the other man's head.

Candy was what some professionals might call a sociopath. For him, he thought of her as nothing more than a nuisance.

"He'll put it together," he assured her. "He's smart."

She snorted.

"He sure didn't seem like a man who had put it together at the hospital. He just stood there and made puppy dog eyes at the pregnant chick from the café."

"Remi Hudson," he interjected.

Candy cocked her head to the side at that.

"Hudson? As in—"

He nodded, not needing her to finish the thought.

"The very same."

Candy, for once, looked slightly satiated. It never lasted. Her need to always be doing *something* was a big part of why she'd been chosen to join him.

She rarely shied away from what they needed to do.

"Well, while this has some potential to finally be interesting, it won't matter at all if our dear sheriff doesn't put any of the pieces together. Why leave bread crumbs if the idiot won't ever follow them?"

He sighed.

"He's dealing with a lot. Give the man a few beats. He'll get to where we need him."

Candy's eyebrow rose in thinly disguised disgust.

"You sound like you're fond of the eldest Nash. Then again, I've heard you have a soft spot for all of the Nash kids. Had several chances to take them out over the last few years and now look where we are. Here, waiting for a man to find breadcrumbs."

Unlike some of the men and women he surrounded himself with, *he* kept his cool, even if he would have liked nothing more than to tell the woman off. Point out her brazen attitude would only ever get her, and maybe him, killed. That she might have joined them two years ago, but she was nowhere near his level.

"It wasn't my job to kill them, just like it's not my job to kill Declan now," he said, keeping his voice as crisp as the chill outside of the building above them. "I come up with plans and I follow plans. *That's* how I serve this organization and *that's* how I stay off the radar and alive."

"Whisperer."

He snorted at the moniker he'd been given by the men and women within their group. One that hadn't yet made it to any law enforcement ears.

"There's something to be said about the power of suggestion." He lost all humor. "Just like there's something to be said about the Nash family." He leaned across the table enough to focus her attention. Candy lost her humor, too. She might have been insolent nine times out of ten, but for that one time she knew when to bite her tongue and listen. "In the last few years people, for whatever reasons, have taken their cracks at them. Threatened them, attacked them, tried to hurt them and the people they loved. Now, answer me this…" He ran a thumb across the raised skin on his hand, a scar he'd had for years. "Who's still standing? The people who went after the Nashes or the Nashes themselves?"

Candy didn't answer.

She didn't have to because they knew exactly who had come out on top in those encounters.

"Respecting the enemy means you don't underestimate them," he added. "A lesson you might want to learn."

Candy opened her mouth, but approaching footsteps kept the words back. The man who filled the doorway next demanded quick respect with his silence.

Even more with the pointed stare. He addressed Candy, who tried her best to look as if she wasn't afraid of him.

"Go tell Hawthorne to shut up about today. You two keep bragging like you've done something a child couldn't easily do. Go."

Candy didn't sneer or back talk him or try to be clever. She fled the room like her life depended on it.

And maybe it did.

Depending on his mood, their boss could be a very *difficult* person to be around.

Still, when it came to the boss he wasn't like Candy. His fear of the boss was surrounded by a thin protective layer that had been built over time.

They had something in common.

Something none of the others had.

That didn't stop him from being worried that the boss was standing in front of him.

"I heard about yesterday. You did a good job." He came closer but didn't sit down. "I also heard that you didn't use Miss Hudson because she said she was pregnant."

"It was a complication I wanted to avoid. Once she said it out loud, it didn't matter if she was pregnant or not, that kind of news might have inspired someone else in the café to be a hero. I didn't have the time for it."

The boss nodded.

"I would have made the same call. No sense in muddling the message with unnecessary drama. But, as it turns out, she *is* pregnant." His expression transformed into something he hadn't seen in a long, long time. Glee. "With Declan Nash's child."

"You've got to be kidding me."

He shook his head with a little laugh.

"She told her brother in the hospital after yesterday's events."

For a moment the two marveled at the news. Then the boss slowly hardened back into the determination that had been driving him for over two decades.

"Using Declan was always a risk. Miss Hudson has taken that risk out entirely. We get her, we get him. The other Nashes will follow, trying to save the day." He moved back to the doorway, his mind no doubt already spinning a revision to his plan. Even though they'd gone over every variation there had been to it, every possible outcome, every contingency they could think of, the hair on the back of his neck stood on end when the boss got to the bottom line. The endgame. The only reason they were all there.

"Then we'll kill them all."

Chapter Twelve

Madi Nash had a thin scar across her cheekbone.

Caleb Nash had a scar across his upper arm from a bullet graze.

Desmond had a limp that would never fully heal.

Cooper Mann had none of the above. The only affliction he seemed to have was that he tended to be more nerves than anything else. Like right now, through the bars of a Wildman County cell. His eyes were wide and tired. He'd seen better days and it showed.

Instead of pleading his case, repeating over and over that he hadn't tried to take Lydia Cartwright, he simply watched Declan stop just outside of the bars. Even as Declan studied him, the young man remained quiet.

"Cooper, do you know what I did this morning before I got here?" Declan started. He didn't wait for Cooper to try to guess. "I went out to the impound lot and took a look at your car because something just isn't sitting right with me. You know what I found? An oddly clean car, leather seats that were well taken care of, and a CD player. I can appreciate you having one because I know that isn't the standard with newer cars, but I just have to question the CD that I found *in* it." Declan recalled the name from memory with a slight head tilt in question. "*How to Learn Spanish in Three Easy Steps.* It was on the third track of five and in the middle of a lesson. Were you listening to it before you got out of the car and saw Lydia?"

Cooper's eyes flitted from one side of the room to the other. He didn't move off the cot he'd been sitting on as he answered.

"Yeah, I was."

"Can I ask why?"

"Because I'm trying to learn Spanish," Cooper deadpanned. Declan almost laughed. He'd sure walked into that one.

"No. I mean, *why* are you trying to learn Spanish? Is it something you've been wanting to do for a while now or something you tried on a whim?" Cooper straightened. He crossed his arms over his chest, defensive. Declan sighed. "Cooper, I left a beautiful woman at my house and in my bed to go to the lot before hours to check your car and now I'm here. The case against you is already as damning as damning can be. Lydia Cartwright swears up and down that you are the man who attacked her. Answering me now, about a CD in your car, isn't going to do any more harm. Not answering will only make me grouchier than I already am."

Cooper seemed to weigh his options.

"A beautiful woman," he said. Declan thought he was repeating him and then realized it was an answer.

"A beautiful woman is why you're trying to learn Spanish?"

Cooper nodded.

"Her name is Inez. She works at Waypoint as one of the bartenders." He sighed deeply. It deflated him. "It was love at first sight for me. Dark hair, dark eyes, and this laugh thing she does when she's brushing drunk guys off. Most beautiful woman I ever saw."

"Have you asked her out?" Declan prodded when the man trailed off.

"Yeah," Cooper exclaimed with sudden vigor. "I sure did! And do you know what she said? 'Ask me in Spanish and then we'll talk.' Can you believe that?" Even though his voice was raised in frustration, it was clear he wasn't angry at the bartender. In fact, when he spoke again it was akin to being impressed. "Nothing worth having is ever easy, though, is it? I ordered the CD since I like driving around a lot. Was hoping to go back this coming weekend and show off but..." Cooper's face fell. Any and all feeling he'd had went with it. He didn't bother finishing his thought.

Sympathy started to sprout in Declan's chest. A seed that had always been there, watered by Cooper's story.

One that was growing now.

"Cooper Mann, come over here and look me in the eye," he barked, a little more forcefully than he meant.

But it did the trick.

Cooper hopped up and came to the bars. Through them he met Declan's stare.

"Why would you try to kidnap Lydia Cartwright if you were so worried about learning Spanish to ask out the most beautiful woman in the world this weekend?"

Cooper might have been nervous and he might have been scared, but he answered with a steady voice.

"I wouldn't."

And, by God, if Declan didn't believe him.

THERE WAS A package of Pop-Tarts on the kitchen counter with a sticky note stuck to it. Declan said he was sorry for leaving, but he'd gotten her car to his house and he'd call her later.

Remi was both let down and touched.

She changed back into her clothes, pocketed the pastries and decided it was time to go to Heartland.

While Jonah had promised to keep the pregnancy under wraps until she told Josh and their father, she remembered how bad Jonah had been at keeping secrets when they were younger. He had too much honor when it came to their father. He snitched quicker than Josh could gallop between the stables and Heartland's outer fence.

Which was pretty damn quick.

Remi still hadn't completely forgiven him for blabbing about the belly button piercing she'd gotten with her friend Molly in high school.

That fallout had lasted a good while.

At least now she couldn't be grounded.

There were clouds in the sky and the air was cold. Remi pulled up beside Josh's truck and could see her father's and Jonah's off to the side of the house. She decided dawdling wasn't going to make anything easier.

She took a deep breath, pushed out into the cold, and didn't make it two steps into the house before Jonah appeared.

"I told him you stayed at Molly's," he hurried in greeting. "I didn't know how you wanted to handle everything with the, you know, so I kind of panicked."

Despite her earlier annoyance, Remi laughed.

"Afraid he'll find out I was bunking with Declan?" she asked, lowering her voice. "Do you think he'd be worried I'd, I don't know, gotten pregnant?"

She gave him a look that showed she was teasing.

Jonah rolled his eyes but smiled.

"Listen, I'm just trying to keep the peace before you break it. Can't blame a guy for trying."

Remi started up the stairs.

"I blame whoever I want for whatever I want," she said, grinning. "Don't you forget that, Jonah Bruce."

Remi bounded up the stairs to the sound of Jonah being annoyed and locked herself in her room. One thing that had been a surprise for her about pregnancy so far was how energetic she was during some parts of the day. Like now she felt as if she'd already had an entire cup of coffee on top of eight hours of sound sleep. She knew these moments didn't always stick. Exhaustion and fatigue were always waiting around the corner, ready to strike. That had been her mother's only major symptom when she'd been pregnant. Remi hoped it would be the same for her going forward.

Then again, she wasn't holding her breath for that.

Remi took her prenatal vitamins, ate the Pop-Tarts on her bed and then went to take a nice, long shower. Her mind wandered to days when she was younger and her biggest concern was trying to keep her grades up and then right over to seeing the man in the suit shoot Sam.

She left the shower in a less good mood than when she'd gotten in.

Jonah and Josh were in the living room. One was reading, the other on his laptop.

"It's a rare sight to see you two inside," she noted. Jonah snorted. Josh was more direct. He always was, despite being the youngest. He had more of their mother in him than the rest of them.

"Until we get the ranch back to how it was, there will be a lot more downtime than what you remembered from when you last called this place home," he said, close to sneering. It made Remi's adrenaline spike in a flash of anger.

"This is my home as much as it is yours. Just because I left doesn't mean I didn't grow up here, same as you."

Josh pushed his laptop onto the couch cushion next to him.

"And just because you're visiting for the holidays doesn't mean we've forgotten how happy you were to leave in the first place. And how often you *don't* visit when it's not the holidays."

Guilt stabbed Remi quickly in the chest. Her anger overcompensated. She dropped her voice low, seething.

"And how often will you visit after you've skipped town with your one true love?"

Josh looked like a deer in the headlights. When he recovered, his expression matched her mood. He turned it on Jonah.

"You told *her*?"

Jonah abandoned his book.

"That *her* is our sister," Jonah defended. "Wouldn't you rather me tell *her* than Dad?"

Josh didn't have to chew on that question long. But that didn't mean he was ready to roll over. He whipped his head around to her so fast Remi was surprised it didn't pop right off.

"If you tell Dad so help me—"

"So help you what?" Remi interrupted. "Are you threatening me, baby brother? What you and the other two Hudson men keep seeming to forget is that before *'my betrayal of house and home'* I got to see you grow up, too." She laughed. It was unkind. "I saw you try to fight Marlin Crosby. Operative word, *try*."

Josh's face changed to the color of her cherry bomb lipstick.

"Marlin Crosby cheated," he said, frustration at the humiliating fight ringing clear through every word. "He rushed me when I was talking to *you two*!"

Remi took several steps forward, putting her into the same orbit as her brothers. Men might have been sitting a few feet from her, but all she saw were the little boys who used to annoy her to no end. Little boys playing at being adults while she had already graduated.

"He hit you from behind because you were too busy telling us, and everyone else watching, how you were going to beat him up. He didn't win because he cheated. He won because your mouth is bigger than your brain!"

That did it. That activated her younger brother like flipping a switch. He jumped up, face as red as ever, and she reacted by squaring her shoulders, ready to wrestle like they had done when they were kids.

"Whoa there!" Jonah was faster than either one of them. He put his body between them and hands out on Josh's chest.

Remi was ready to knock both of them silly, absolutely done with their talk of her abandoning her family because she had had the *audacity* to live her own life, but the sound of boots against hardwood silenced them all.

Gale Hudson filled the doorway between the living room and the kitchen. He must have come in through the back door and they hadn't heard him because, in hindsight, Remi realized they'd been yelling awfully loud.

"I can't ground you like I used to," their father started, voice always booming. "But I can sure enough make life harder for the lot of you if you don't stop your bellyaching. You hear me?"

All three Hudson children took a breath and relaxed their tensed muscles.

"Yes sir," they sang in a chorus.

Their father nodded, satisfied.

"Good. No one should be fighting this close to Christmas, if nothing else. What is it that your mom used to say about it?"

"Fighting on Christmas will only get you the present of shame," Jonah recalled. However, there was still some kick in Josh.

"She meant that about Christmas Day, not the rest of them."

"Well, then, I'm making an amendment," their father said. "No fighting during December."

This time it was Remi who decided to try her luck.

"Can I add 'no guilting your children for their life choices' to the list?"

"Remi," Jonah whispered in warning.

Their father, however, surprised them. He chuckled.

"Your mom used to say you reminded her of herself, but there's a lot of times I hear my stubbornness come out of your mouth." His expression softened. "Instead of you all yelling, why don't we make an early lunch and eat together? It's been a while."

And just like that all the tension left the room.

"Brunch," Remi said, following him into the kitchen.

"What?"

"It's called brunch. A meal between breakfast and lunch."

"Sounds like nonsense to me."

Remi laughed and soon the four of them were moving around the kitchen, preparing whatever food was in the fridge. It was nice. Their father started to complain about a horse they were boarding whose owner wouldn't stop calling him, while Josh pointed out that that was probably because she had a crush on him. Remi and Jonah were paired up to the side of the refrigerator and cringed at the news that someone had a crush on *their* dad when Josh slid a plated sandwich to her. It was and had been her favorite since she was a kid. A peace offering in the form of turkey, jalapeños, cheese and wheat bread.

Remi hesitated. Not because of the surprising offer but because she couldn't accept it. She didn't know a lot about pregnancy yet, but she did know she couldn't eat sandwich meat.

Jonah bumped her shoulder, a questioning look on his face.

She pointed to her stomach and shook her head.

He pointed to his plate. Leftover chicken potpie. *His* favorite.

Remi nodded.

If Jonah had accepted her pregnancy this fast, what was stopping her from giving the other two Hudson men the same chance to do the same?

Because old wounds don't heal just like that.

Remi might have gotten lucky with Jonah but that didn't guarantee it would be as easy with the others. So, she decided to keep stalling a little while longer. At least she could wait until she had a full stomach.

Her and Johan were in the middle of switching meals when an odd sound filled the house.

The doorbell.

For a moment they all looked at one another as if to

say, *We're all here so who is using the bell?* Everyone who frequented the ranch knew to knock because their dad hated the bell.

Except for Declan. He had no idea.

"I'll get it," Remi said, hurrying past the boys before they could answer it. Remi's phone was in her back pocket. She brought it out to check to see if she had a missed call or text from the man.

She hadn't.

And it wasn't him at the door, either.

Remi opened the door wide as soon as she saw the angry tears and stitches across the woman's face.

"Lydia?"

The last time Remi had seen the woman was right before she and Declan had left the hospital. The doctors had said she was being discharged but probably not until that afternoon. Jonah had told her he'd pick her up from the hospital himself when that happened.

Now there she was on their doorstep, wearing a blouse with blood on it and jeans that had a tear. It must have been the same outfit she'd been wearing when she was attacked by Cooper Mann.

It was a jarring sight. Made even more so by the fact that the woman didn't seem bothered by any of it.

"Hi there, Remi," she greeted in return. "Do you think I could come inside?"

"Oh, yeah, of course." Remi might have been thrown off her game, but she hadn't lost her manners. She stepped aside, waving Lydia into their home.

"Jonah is in the kitchen," she said, already moving that way. Lydia shook her head.

"I'm not here for Jonah," she said.

"Oh?"

Lydia smiled.

It should have been a red flag.

It should have been a lot of things.

What it wasn't was enough to make Remi use the phone in her hand to call for help.

Instead she listened, intently, for the reason.

"I'm here for you."

Chapter Thirteen

Lydia struck out before Remi could move a muscle.

The hit landed against her chest, just below the collarbone. It hurt. Remi staggered backward from the force and surprise. She didn't have a chance to catch herself. Her backside hit the hardwood just as her periphery was filled with the bulk of her father and Jonah.

They hadn't seen the hit.

Remi heard her father say her name just as Jonah called out to Lydia. Neither had a chance to finish their thoughts or get answers in return.

Lydia pulled out a gun and aimed it at the men.

Remi reacted on reflex.

From her angle on the floor she couldn't do much, but she was close enough to do something. She brought her fist up and paid the woman in kind for the hit she'd been given. But Remi could only get as high as her stomach from where she was on the ground.

It did the job well enough.

A gunshot exploded inside the house, pushing pain through Remi's ears at the sound just as fear rang through her heart, but Lydia gasped for different reasons.

She hadn't counted on the hit to the stomach, just as Remi hadn't counted on the hit to the chest.

Lydia stumbled but didn't fall. She kept the gun but lost her aim.

Remi took advantage of the distraction. She pushed up off the ground and right into the woman. Lydia completely lost her footing this time. Like a rag doll, the woman fell back and out onto the front porch.

Then Remi did the only thing her adrenaline and slightly good sense would let her do.

She slammed the door shut and threw the dead bolt.

The sound of Lydia cursing became the soundtrack behind the next important, life-altering thing in Remi's world. She turned, heart in her throat, and hoped to every god there ever was that none of her family had been shot.

Her father was rushing over to her. Josh and Jonah watched wide-eyed from the doorway.

No one was bleeding, no one was on the ground.

It was a relief that didn't last long.

"Get away from there," her father grunted out, grabbing her wrist. Another explosion went off as Lydia shot through the door. It barely missed them as her father slung Remi around and pushed her to the stairs. Remi didn't hesitate in running up them, out of line of the door.

"Stay low, boys," he yelled over his shoulder.

Remi hit the landing as another gunshot went off. It was followed by two more. She spun on her heel, but her father pushed her farther onto the second floor.

"There's a gun in my room," he said. Remi would have marveled at how calm he was being if not for the directive he gave her as he pulled her along with him to the bedroom at the end of the hall. "Call for help, Remi. Do it now."

Remi went for her phone only to have her stomach drop. Just as she had done with her phone after being hit by Lydia.

"I—I don't have it." She heard it then. In her voice. A waver of terror, strengthened by adrenaline and confusion.

They ran into the master bedroom and made a U-turn to the closet.

"That's okay." He was using his soothing voice. The one she'd once heard when she'd accidentally cut her hand with a knife and needed stitches. He'd brought her nerves down simply by the cadence of his voice.

Whether or not he agreed with her leaving town, there was a comfort in knowing that, with just the sound of his voice, her father could make her feel better.

"What about the landline?" she asked, hopeful. It didn't last long.

"I took the cordless to the kitchen yesterday. Haven't put it back."

Remi doubled back to the bedroom door as her father opened his safe in the closet. He'd always been diligent about keeping all weapons locked up, even when his children had grown, but what he had in there Remi had no idea.

She watched the hallway and the top of the stairs with a twist in her gut. Her brothers hadn't attempted to go for the second floor. She hoped they had fled through the back door as soon as the shots kept coming and that one of them had called for help.

"The front door open yet?" her father asked, rushing back to her side.

They both paused.

The house around them was eerily silent.

Remi opened her mouth, ready to call for her brothers, but her father grabbed her wrist.

"Shh, keep quiet," he whispered. "We don't know if she's alone or not, and we don't want to let her know exactly where we are."

He had shut the bedroom door and locked it when two things happened at once.

First, she heard glass shatter downstairs. The living room windows maybe.

Then she felt a peculiar wetness against her arm.

"I need you to listen to me," her father said, but Remi stopped him when she realized what that wetness was.

"You're bleeding."

The last few shots hadn't missed them.

At least, not her father.

"I'm okay," he tried, pulling her again. The wetness grew against her arm. He stopped when they were in the en suite, and turned to shut and lock the door.

Remi turned her attention to his bullet wound.

"Dad."

There was no denying he'd been hit. His button-up was turning dark at the side of his stomach. He was trying—and failing—to keep his left forearm pressed against it.

"I'm okay," he repeated.

Remi was devastated to hear the waver in his voice this time.

Instead of fear, she heard pain.

He swung around and showed her something else she hadn't had the mind to notice yet. It was a revolver. He held it out to her. Remi took it with a sob stuck in her throat.

"Do you remember how to use that? No safety and no cocking it between shots. Just shoot. Understood?"

"I don't want to use it. I want *you* to use it."

He shook his head and moved to the window.

"If there's more than one of them and they come up here, I want you to use the lattice next to Josh's room to get down to the ground. Then, only if it's clear, make it to the stable. That's where you're all supposed to go if bad stuff happens in the house. Josh and Jonah will be there."

Remi watched, her heart nearly crushed with help-lessness as the strongest man she knew fell against the wall and slid to the floor.

"Dad." It was all Remi could do not to yell. She knelt down in front of him, the hand not holding the revolver, trying helplessly to grab onto a part of him as if her touch alone could help heal him.

It did no such thing.

Dark eyes searched her face. His expression soft-ened, but his words were stern. Harsh.

"That was a good move you made with that woman downstairs, but bullets count for more than courage. You can take on one person—don't try to take more if there are more. Promise me, Remi. You run if there's more than one person out there and use that thing to protect your brothers. Don't be afraid to shoot."

Then he gave her that look.

That look of unconditional love. The same one her mother gave them. The same one her grandmother had given her mother before she'd passed away.

The love of a parent for a child.

The same love Remi already felt for hers.

She nodded.

And then, in the simplest of terms, she told her father the news she should have already told him.

"I'm pregnant."

Gale Hudson took all of two seconds to respond.

"Shoot to kill, baby girl."

Remi wanted to say more, to *do* more, but an awful sound cut off any conversation.

Wood splintered. A thud sounded.

Then a man spoke. Followed by another.

"We know you're in there," he yelled.

It wasn't her brothers.

Which meant Lydia wasn't alone.

Which meant Remi was supposed to abandon her father.

The doorknob shook.

Her father touched her stomach. Blood transferred to her shirt, but he got his point across with it.

He was trying to protect her.

And it was her turn to do the same for her child.

Remi looked at her father one last time and then slid the window up. She was up and out of it within a breath. Her shoes hit the roof that hung over the wraparound porch. The backyard was, at a glance, empty. No one shot at her. No one yelled.

She ran.

Josh's room was at the corner of the house. Attached to the overhang outside of his window was a thick lattice their mother had built herself. She'd wanted it for decoration. Her children had used it to sneak out of the house.

Now her daughter was using it to escape.

Why was Lydia there for her?

Who were the men?

Were there more?

Remi didn't have any answers. She knew only that she didn't want to find them by letting Lydia get ahold of her or her brothers. Sibling protectiveness combined with maternal protectiveness drove Remi's hands and feet as she got to the edge of the roof outside of Josh's room and onto the top of the lattice.

She slipped twice as she tried to find footholds not completely covered in vines, then dropped the last two feet to the ground. Pain radiated up her shins but she didn't stop.

Hudson Heartland had several stables. Some were at the front of the acreage, others were tucked toward the back. The stable they had been taught to go to if there was ever a fire, break-in or other disaster in the main house was a faded red barn a hundred yards or so from the back porch. It had housed Heartland's personal horses and had never been used by clients.

It also had a landline.

Remi ran full tilt toward it, knowing if anyone was on the roof or in the bathroom looking out, they'd see her. If anyone came after them they could just keep running until they made it to the woods.

The Hudson children knew the ranch.

She doubted Lydia and whoever was with her could claim the same.

At least, that was her hope as she struggled to breathe while running away from the house.

From her father.

Remi ignored the ache in her heart.

She had to protect her brothers.

She had to protect her baby.

"Lydia Cartwright didn't exist until five years ago."

Declan should have felt something at hearing the words out loud, but a part of him was going on autopilot. A routine created out of necessity for being sheriff. A detached acceptance of what he was learning. A bridge between throwing his hands in the air with anger and confusion and complete silence. An in-between where he could stay for a while until he figured out how he needed to, as sheriff, react to whatever news he received.

Caleb ran a hand through his dark hair and then hung his hand on the detective's badge on a chain around his neck. Jazz was sitting in the chair he was hovering over while both looked at the computer screen.

"Why do you say that?"

Caleb touched the computer screen, but Declan couldn't see what they were looking at.

"First of all, that's when all of her social media accounts popped up," he answered. "Secondly, that's also when her car was registered and she moved into an apartment in Kilwin…" He slid his finger across the screen. Jazz pulled it off the glass as if she'd done it countless times in their partnership. It didn't stop Declan's brother from continuing his explanation. "All within the span of a week. Before that there seems to be no trace of her. At least not on the internet or through the databases we have access to."

"But just because she isn't showing up on either doesn't mean Lydia didn't exist before then." Declan had to be the devil's advocate. Caleb looked up. His eyes were just as blue as Madi's and Des's.

"And yet you still think something's off with her," Caleb guessed.

Declan eyed the desks around them. A few deputies were in, their heads bent over paperwork. There wasn't any use in lying to his brother. Or Jazz, for that matter. They both were sharp as tacks when it came to reading someone. Even sharper when it came to their family and friends.

"I think Cooper Mann is telling the truth," he admitted. "I think Lydia either initiated the attack or carried it out against herself."

Caleb cringed. Jazz's sour expression wasn't too far off.

"Victim blaming is an absolute nonstarter, you know that, right?" Caleb pointed out. Declan didn't need the no-brainer statement. But, in this instance, his gut was starting to kick up a fuss.

Declan lowered his voice, leaning in so only they could hear him for sure.

"Which is why I want to be certain we check her out. If I'm wrong, then we've helped her case by shutting down any opposing argument Cooper's lawyer could put up in court. And if I'm right?" He shook his head. "Then we might start getting some answers around here. Some answers we desperately need."

Caleb kept his stare for a moment before sharing a look with Jazz. Declan remembered the first case they'd worked together as partners. Oil and water. Now? They could communicate in looks alone if they had to.

The look they shared must have been an agreement. Both nodded.

"So what do you want to do?" Caleb asked. "Want us to go talk to her?"

"What's her last known address? She said she lived in Overlook when we spoke in the hospital."

Jazz went back into the computer. It wasn't long before she had an answer. All three recognized the location. They'd passed that house countless times in the last year or so since Desmond's wife, Riley, used to live in the neighborhood with her twin and her son. Jenna and Hartley still resided in the house but Lydia's address, if memory served, was more toward the front of Willows Way.

Declan had to remind himself that just because he'd grown up in Overlook didn't mean he knew everyone who lived there, especially those who weren't long-time locals.

"Okay, let's divide and conquer on this." Declan looked at Jazz. "Keep digging here and see if you can find her employer. If you do, give them a call and feel them out about her. Caleb, I want you to go to Cooper's house." Declan pulled a key out of his pocket. That earned a questioning look from both detectives. "Cooper gave me permission. He lives alone and in an apartment over where Delores stays. The number is on the key." He tossed him the key. Caleb caught it with ease. "See if you can't find something that helps us see if he's innocent or if he's playing us."

"And you?"

"I'll head over to Lydia's house to see if anything jumps out at me."

"I'm assuming you don't have a key to that one?"

"I don't."

Caleb and Jazz shared another look with each other and didn't comment out loud on whatever conclusion they'd reached. Instead, they all went about their tasks immediately.

Declan looked at his phone before jumping into Fiona.

No missed calls or texts from his chief deputy, Cussler. Which meant no news or leads on the two men and woman who had been a scourge against Main Street.

That should have concerned him more than the other nagging thought prickling at the back of his mind.

There were also no missed calls or texts from Remi.

He'd gone years without any contact whatsoever.

Yet, there he was. Thinking about her. Wondering what she was doing now. Craving more contact.

He knew her car was gone from his house and she was probably back at Heartland. Usually knowing that much would have been enough. Now he found his thoughts circling the woman.

Declan pulled her number up on his phone. He nearly called it right then and there. Then he tossed the cell onto the seat next to him and started toward the neighborhood of Willows Way.

The best thing he could do was rein in the chaos and sift through it until he could make his home, his county and the people within it safe.

If he couldn't do that?

Then what good could he ever be for his child?

Chapter Fourteen

The house was nice. One story. Brick. A ranch-style. There was a small front porch and a welcome mat on the concrete. The gardens on either side of it were well-kept, as were the yard and exterior of the house.

The neighbors were more than a stone's throw away, and no one appeared to be home in at least three of the houses.

It looked like a normal scene. A single woman who lived alone in a nice house in a nice neighborhood in a nice town.

Yet, after Declan knocked on the front door several times, he couldn't stop his gut from being loud again.

He'd met liars. He'd met scum.

He'd dealt with con artists, thieves, killers and men and women who wanted to watch the world burn.

He knew clever people who had lit the metaphorical or—on occasion—real match and the hapless idiots who believed they needed to be the ones to put that flame right where it needed to go.

Declan had met a lot of people, and only after a career of meeting those people did he think he was a good enough judge of character. Still, he knew he could be wrong. No man, woman or child could escape that human flaw.

Being wrong was what made being right feel so good.

It gave you a goal.

It gave you a purpose.

It made Declan know, logically, that he might be wrong about Cooper Mann.

The only thing that stopped that thought from really taking root was another fact he knew to be true.

Cooper Mann wasn't that smart.

As his mother would say, bless his heart, but Cooper wasn't burdened with an abundance of common sense.

There was no way that that boy could try to fool someone into believing he hadn't done what he had.

No, what had Declan believing him had to do with something he'd seen. Or, really, hadn't.

Cooper wasn't trying to hide a single thing.

He was just trying to get someone to believe him.

He wasn't clever enough to do anything else.

Declan didn't get back into his truck when no one answered the door. He moved to the living room windows and peered inside. The wooden slats of the blinds were open and through them he could see a standard living room setup. Couches, a TV, art on the wall, and a pair of tennis shoes next to the coffee table.

Declan kept moving. He left the front porch and rounded the side of the house next to the driveway. The house was flush with the ground and gave him easy access to look into each of the rooms along the exterior wall.

Easy access to *try* to look into each of the rooms.

Blinds were closed tightly over each window. The

other side of the house was the same. Declan doubled back to the back porch. There were no blinds over the only window. He looked through it to a small, tidy kitchen.

Then he did something he shouldn't have.

He tried the back door.

When the knob turned without resistance, he expanded on what he shouldn't have been doing.

There were no beeps of an alarm or gasps of surprised houseguests. There was also no heat or air-conditioning. The smell of disuse was as prevalent as the chill. Although Declan didn't believe anyone was in the house, still his hand went to the butt of the service weapon at his hip. He moved past the kitchen and took the first right he could, gut as quiet as the silence around him. He opened the first door he came to.

Then he moved to the next closed door and opened it. He went across the house to the last bedroom. And, just to be thorough, he checked the bathroom and moved to the kitchen and peeked at cupboards and drawers.

Declan cussed. Loud and true.

Empty.

The bedrooms, the bathroom, the kitchen.

He didn't know what was going on, but Declan would bet his badge that no one lived in the house.

Which meant Lydia had lied.

THE BARN WASN'T COLD. Remi assumed they'd had the heaters running early that morning and the closed doors had kept in the warmth for the horses. There were two of them in the stables. Diamond Duke, a bay-and-white tobiano-patterned Tennessee walker who belonged to

Josh, and Raphael, a chestnut Tennessee walker who belonged to Jonah.

Remi didn't know them like she had her horse, Jackson, growing up, but seeing the beautiful horses in their stalls made her feel better. For a moment it was just like any other normal day on Heartland.

Just as the thought took root, it was torn away from her.

A hand slapped around Remi's mouth as someone grabbed her arm.

Her grip had tightened around the revolver, ready to listen to her father's directive, when Jonah's voice floated next to her ear.

"One of them is around here somewhere," he whispered. "Keep quiet."

He moved his hand and, once again, Remi was led from out in the open to somewhere more hidden. This time instead of a bedroom, Jonah led her into Diamond Duke's stall. The horse watched with little interest as they came inside and closed the door behind them. Then again, his favorite human was leaning against him, hand running over his pristine coat.

Relief at seeing that Josh and Jonah were unhurt was, once again, short-lived.

"Are you okay?" Jonah asked, turning her enough to look her up and down. His eyes widened at the blood. Their father's blood.

She nodded. Josh met her eye.

Jonah touched the blood on her shirt, looking for a wound. When he didn't find it he came to the same conclusion their brother already had. She could see it in both of their faces. Still, Josh voiced the question.

"Where's Dad?"

Remi knew this was the moment that could change everything. This was the moment she could do one of two things. She could let the unknown and the sorrow and the blood soaking through her father's shirt consume her. She could break down right then and there and let her brothers take over. Give them the gun, let them show her how they were both capable adults now and could handle themselves.

Or, she could woman up. Keep her father's promise and, instead of leaving Jonah and Josh to figure out how to get them all to safety, she could help. Show them that leaving the ranch didn't mean she'd retired the cowgirl.

"He made me leave him," she answered, no waver in her voice. It hardened like water being thrown into the freezing wind.

"He made you—" Josh started to repeat.

Remi didn't have time for it.

"He made me promise that we'd stay safe and that's what we're going to do," she steamrollered ahead. Remi looked to Jonah. Pain pinched his expression, though she knew it had nothing to do with anything physical. "Did you use the landline and call for help?"

He nodded, but then a different emotion momentarily took over his face.

"It didn't work. Not even a dial tone."

"And I'm assuming neither one of you have your cell phones."

It wasn't a question. Whereas most people around their ages were glued to their smartphones, Josh and Jonah were much like their father. There was no reason to have a phone out with the horses or while doing chores. Their father had preached that until it became second nature to *not* take their phones out of the house unless they were going to town. Even then Remi knew the chance of leaving the phones at the house was still great. The only reason she had bucked the anti-phone sentiment was because she'd stopped living on the ranch. Worrying about dropping her phone in horse droppings or having it crushed by a tractor hadn't been an issue in college or Nashville. Definitely not at her job as an accountant.

Which made the fact that the one time she actually *needed* it and didn't have it that much more frustrating.

"They're in the living room," Jonah answered. "Once the shooting started we had to bolt back into the kitchen and then out the back door."

"You said there's someone around here?" she asked, her mind building up a new plan.

"Right after we got in here we saw two men walking the backyard." Josh eyed the revolver in her hand. "They had guns."

"Two men were upstairs. Dad told me not to shoot if there was more than one. So five against three, including Lydia."

Jonah flinched at the name.

"Why is this even happening? Why is *she* here? Did I do this somehow? Is she here because of me? I don't understand!"

"Me." Her brothers' eyebrows rose in tandem. "Before Lydia attacked she said she was here for me."

"But why?" The question was barely out of Josh's mouth before Jonah's eyes widened even more. He looked at Remi, and she knew he'd stumbled onto the same theory she'd already been working on in the back of her mind.

One that made her stomach drop and blood boil at the same time.

"Is it because you're pregnant with the sheriff's baby?" Jonah asked. "She could have heard you tell me in the hospital."

"It's a long-shot guess but that's all I can figure. He's the only one of us who does anything that might catch this kind of heat."

"Wait, you're pregnant?"

Remi turned to Josh and nodded. She felt bad he was finding out like this but, as was the current story of her life, she just didn't have the time to address the topic with loving care.

The best she could do was give him a brief, apologetic smile.

Then it was down to business.

"Which is another reason we're about to get the hell out of here." Remi motioned to the gun, careful to keep its aim away from the three of them and Diamond Duke. "From what I remember this has eight rounds. I'm going to go ahead and assume our five bad guys all have guns, all have more bullets, and all know how to use them better than us." She waited a beat for her brothers to interject. They didn't. "So, since we haven't been able to call for help, standing our ground in here with eight bullets that aren't even guaranteed to hit their target sounds like an awful plan."

Remi looked to the stall across the aisle from them.

Raphael, ever content, let out a little neigh.

"Which is why we're going to focus on being the best cowboys we can be."

"You want us to ride out," Jonah said.

Remi nodded.

"Our best option is to put distance between us and them. Ride to the Nash Ranch and hope somebody's home."

"That's a long ride out in the open," Jonah pointed out. "Once we clear the last barn on Heartland that's easy pickings in the fields between us and them. What... maybe ten minutes or so."

Josh motioned around them.

"I'd rather be the fish in the pool than fish in the barrel." He put his hand on Remi's shoulder and nodded. His support rallied her even more.

"I'll unlatch the back doors. Y'all tack up your horses like our lives depend on it." Which they did.

"There's no doubles saddle in here. Going to be a bumpy ride for you," Josh said.

"Better than being those fish."

They got to work quickly. Remi went back to the door she'd come through and barred it, checked the main double doors to make sure they were still locked, and then hurried to the back two. They were usually only opened to take advantage of cool air and breezes for the horses. Now they were all that stood between her relative calm and all-out fear.

Remi checked that the doors were still locked. She undid the latch slowly, careful not to make a sound, but didn't open them.

Not yet.

She didn't know where any of the men or Lydia were. They could be in the house still or the area around the barn, or they could simply have left. The fact that she had no idea was terrifying.

How long ago had she run from her father's side? Five minutes ago? Ten? Maybe more?

If they were still on the ranch, Remi had to believe they'd check the closest building to the house. Sooner rather than later.

It put her nerves closer to the edge and sent pricks of adrenaline across her body. Her muscles tightened in anticipation. Her palms grew sweaty. Remi strained to listen past her brothers tacking up their horses in record time.

Then she heard something she'd prayed she wouldn't.

A feeling of dread rolled over in her stomach. The hairs on the back of her neck stood on end.

The door they'd all come in through might have been locked but someone jiggling the handle was like a gunshot in the silence. Remi hurried to the space between the horse stalls her brothers were in. Both had paused what they were doing.

"Keep going," she whispered.

Someone coming to the barn didn't change their plan. There was nowhere to hide, and their odds of five against one gun was still not something she wanted to test.

She stood there and listened.

The door was at the head of the barn, off to the left. Stalls blocked her view of it. If someone broke through she'd have a few seconds to react. Whether that was jumping on a horse or shooting.

"Done."

Remi could have sung in relief as her brothers whispered in unison. Josh opened his stall's door. Remi went to Jonah's.

Whoever was on the other side of the barn door decided they were done trying things the normal way. The *bang* of someone ramming the door made Diamond Duke do a little jump as Josh led him into the aisle. He waved Raphael through but didn't follow as he and Jonah went to the door. Remi held back, too, and together they heard another loud bang followed by the splintering of wood.

They'd run out of time.

There was no way all three of them could mount up and ride out now. Not without being targets.

What would Declan do?

The question popped into Remi's head so quickly she answered it before she thought of why she'd asked it in the first place.

She took a small step forward so that she was in front of her little brother and raised the revolver.

She wasn't going to let anyone hurt any more of her family.

Not today.

Not ever.

Chapter Fifteen

The moment he saw her, Declan thought he was dreaming.

Honest to God, he thought he'd somehow fallen asleep somewhere between Lydia's house, Winding Road and his mother's house.

He wasn't even supposed to *be* on his way to the main house on the Nash Family Ranch. After he'd discovered Lydia's place was empty, he'd called Caleb to tell him the news. Caleb thought that was wildly peculiar but hadn't been able to make it to Cooper's place yet to see if there were any more wildly peculiar finds. Instead, he'd said he was almost to their ranch.

"Cooper Mann's family must have some crazy Spidey senses," he'd said. "Ma just called and said his grandma June is sitting at her dining table, wanting to talk to us."

"Why didn't she go to the department or call us?"

Caleb had snorted.

"Southern women are most powerful when they have a glass of sweet tea in front of them and some kind of wicker chair beneath them. But seriously, if you had to talk to the law, wouldn't you rather do it while basking in Mom's hospitality?"

Declan had seen the logic in that. Plus, there was probably some way their mother knew June Mann through everything she did in the community. Which meant telling the older woman to go to the department was a no-no. Not unless they wanted to catch their mother's wrath.

So Declan had decided to meet his brother and Grandma June at the ranch. On the drive there he'd percolated the information he did and didn't have and had almost tuned so wholly into his own thoughts that he didn't clock the movement streaking across the field he was driving alongside.

If seeing Remi galloping through an open field, hair blowing in the wind behind her wasn't a dream then maybe it was fate.

Because Declan didn't have to know the circumstances around why she was booking it for him to know exactly where she was going.

The same place he was.

Declan might have spent a bit more time speculating dreams and fate and Lydia's empty home and Grandma June's unannounced arrival if the other shocking details hadn't filtered through.

Remi wasn't alone.

Her brother, Jonah judging by his height, was trailing behind her on another horse. While someone was pressed against Remi's chest. The man was slumped, head bent.

Something was wrong.

Something was horribly wrong.

Declan honked the horn, unlocked his phone and dialed the last number on his recent calls list. The second it rang he put it on speaker and then cut his wheel.

The Nash Family Ranch and Hudson Heartland both had fenced in most of their acreage. However, after a dispute that came before any of the children of either family were born, there was a stretch of land between them that neither believed the other should claim. A no-man's-land, his father had called it. Owned and not owned by two families. Their only agreement concerning the expanse was that neither could erect a fence or let livestock or horses roam there.

Declan had never cared about the space.

Until now.

Caleb answered the phone just as Declan navigated the slight dip of the road's shoulder and began driving out into the field. He honked the horn again. This time Remi turned her head to look.

She must have yelled something to Jonah. Both slowed.

"What's going on?" Caleb asked.

"Remi and Jonah are booking it on horses to the ranch through no-man's-land. Remi's carrying someone who looks hurt."

Rustling carried through the airwaves. Caleb was moving.

"How hurt we talking?"

Declan was eating up the distance between them and came to a stop a few yards off, not wanting to spook the horses.

He swore as Remi and Jonah trotted over.

"She's holding Josh and there's blood all over both of them."

Declan threw open the door, adrenaline shooting through him so fast that he thought it might make him explode. Josh was pressed against Remi's front, and he could see blood across her arm and the hand holding the reins.

And the gun she had clutched in the hand pressing Josh against her.

"Lydia Cartwright and at least four men are on the ranch," Remi dived in, panting. "Dad's upstairs in the house with a bullet in the stomach. Josh just got hit in the chest. They need a hospital. *Now*."

Declan put his phone between his shoulder and his ear.

"You get that?"

"Yeah," Caleb answered. "Calling for EMS and backup."

Jonah swung off his horse and Declan motioned to Josh. He was unconscious. Remi's expression was blank.

"Let's get Josh in the truck," he said. "Hold on, Caleb."

He dropped his phone into his front breast pocket and, together with Jonah, pulled Josh down from the horse. Remi stayed astride while the two of them slid Josh into the passenger seat.

Then Declan only had eyes for Remi.

If the blood on her arm and hand had been alarming, the blood on front of her shirt was downright heart-stopping. She caught his eye.

"It's my dad's, not mine."

Declan knew that shouldn't have made him feel better.

It did.

He pulled his phone back out.

"Caleb, call ahead to the ER and say we have Josh

Hudson with a gunshot wound to the chest coming in hot with Jonah and Remi in my truck."

Jonah didn't need any prodding. He looped around the truck to the open driver's side door. Declan held his hand up to Remi to help her down.

She wasn't having it. Her grip on the reins tightened.

Declan was reminded of the girl whose father used to tame wild horses. The one who could outride him and his siblings even if they'd never admit it. The girl who had grown up more cowgirl than he had cowboy, if he was being honest.

"You're going back to the house. So am I."

Remi straightened her shoulders.

Declan, Jonah and even Caleb spoke at once.

She didn't listen.

"I left Dad for my kid's sake. I'm going back for him for the same reason." She pulled the reins to the side, turning her horse around and effectively ending the discussion. She turned to Jonah. "Go. Now." Then she gave Declan a long, low look. "I can outride you and you know it. Telling me I can't go only wastes time we don't have."

What Declan felt at her statements of fact was jarring. On the one hand he wanted to cuff her and throw her into the truck, sending her off to safety, kicking and screaming if need be. On the other hand, he'd never been more proud.

Remi Hudson was a fighter.

So was he.

And they'd both be damned if their kid didn't get the chance to be, too.

Declan nodded to Jonah and then went to his horse.

"Caleb," he said, "Remi and I will be approaching from no-man's-land."

"Des is here so I'm bringing him with me. Be safe, keep your phone on and in your pocket."

"Roger that."

Remi and her family might have been near-professionals when it came to horseback riding, but that didn't mean Declan was an amateur. The second he was upright in the saddle and fingers laced around the reins, he felt something like what he thought a professional swimmer might feel when first diving into the lap pool. Adrenaline, natural and exciting, flooded his veins, tensing his muscles and making his heart gallop. Being on a horse was being at home.

He knew Remi felt the same.

In tandem they struck out back toward Heartland. Thundering across the field like a battle cry. Hooves against the earth. Cold air biting at their faces. Furious justice at their heels.

Two horses and their riders in sync.

It felt right, even if the reason they were riding was so wrong.

Declan glanced over at the woman next to him and knew without a doubt that he'd never find another person like her ever again.

Remi Hudson was one of a kind.

And he loved her for it.

Declan slowed as the barn nearest the house came into view. Thankfully, so did Remi. Although her bravado was still displayed fiercely across her face, he saw caution there, too. She'd come back for her father but wasn't about to put their child at unnecessary risk. At least, no more than coming back had.

"For us to get out on the horses I had to shoot one of them," she said with effort. Her cheeks were red with windburn and exertion. Being pregnant probably wasn't helping. He remembered how tired Madi and Nina had been during the beginnings of their pregnancies.

"Did you kill him?" he had to ask.

The question didn't even make her flinch.

"I thought I did but he shot Josh before I could make sure. We barely got him on the horse before another one of them ran into the barn. We took off, but no one shot at us again."

Declan nodded, hoping that one man was out of commission by now.

"Stay behind me," he said. "If anyone shoots at us, use me and the horses as cover if you have to."

Declan took the lead, trotting ahead with eyes peeled and gun in one hand.

No one moved.

He led them to the side of the barn facing away from the house and jumped off his horse. Remi followed suit. She hung back as he moved around the corner to look inside the barn.

Blood was in the aisle between the stalls. Two spots of them on opposite ends. There was no one inside to match them.

"The barn nearest the house is empty," he said down to his pocket so Caleb could hear through the speakerphone that was still on. Caleb said he understood.

"Des and I are coming up the drive now."

Declan could feel Remi's anxiety mounting as he peered around what used to be a door, splintered off the hinges and facing the house.

"No movement."

Caleb repeated the sentiment when they made it to the end of the driveway opposite them.

"Let's clear the house," Declan ordered. "Be careful."

Remi stuck to Declan's back as they moved to the house in a hurry. For the next few minutes the four of them went from room to room, only to clarify it was empty.

The men and Lydia were gone.

And the only things they'd left behind were blood and Gale Hudson.

Sirens blared up the driveway when they finally made it to the upstairs bathroom the Hudson patriarch was in.

It wasn't a pretty sight.

Remi cried out, pure anguish breaking down every part of the woman. She reached out for her father before she'd even cleared the doorway. Declan grabbed her, trying to shield her from a terrifying reality if only for a few seconds longer.

Even if he didn't know what had happened in the bathroom, it was clear that Gale had fought. Blood was smeared everywhere, the man himself in the middle of it all and as still as still could be.

Remi fought against Declan's chest.

Desmond ran past them and knelt beside Gale. He checked his pulse.

He didn't shake his head, but he didn't look relieved, either.

UNLIKE THE LAST time chaos had reigned within their orbit, Declan didn't leave Remi's side once.

From Heartland to the hospital to roaming the halls of the hospital to even standing outside of the bathroom door, the sheriff kept his cowboy hat on but metaphorically seemed to take his badge off.

"Go do what you need to," Remi had said after Josh had first gone into surgery. Declan had shaken his head. She'd noticed for the first time that day that dark stubble was lining his chin.

"I'm with you now," was all he'd said in response.

These were words that were comforting in an increasingly uncertain world, and words he stayed true to.

He made and answered phone calls, spoke to his brothers, deputies and chief deputy in person, and when it was time for her to relay everything that had happened at Heartland, he was the one who took her statement personally.

Remi had been ready to ride solo back to the ranch to try to save her dad but now she was grateful for the close proximity. Especially when, hours later, Jonah met them next to a vending machine in the lobby.

He ran a hand through his hair. He was exhausted.

"I just talked to the doctor about Dad."

Remi perked up at that. She'd been hovering around the hallways in the hopes of talking to a doctor sometime soon. Her father was still alive, a miracle by all accounts, and had gone through a series of touch-and-go surgeries. He'd only been sent to a room an hour ago. Josh, who had undergone his own surgery, had been out for four. He'd regained consciousness only to ask about them and then the "new fling" Jonah had told Remi about.

After a deputy had found and brought their phones to the hospital, Remi had made sure to call the woman after she realized how important she was to her brother. They had all been surprised when a brightly dressed, extremely expressive woman named Lilianna had rushed into the hospital and immediately to his bedside. Talking to the woman, seeing how worried she was, had eased Remi's guilt at leaving Josh's side.

It had given her more time to worry about their father.

"How is he?" Remi asked, heart jumping back into her throat. "Does he have to have another surgery?"

Jonah shook his head. Then he did something she'd truly not seen coming. He smiled.

"His rehab is going to be extensive and he'll have to take it easy for a long while to come, *but* the doc said he should be out of the woods now. He's stable and both surgeries did exactly what they wanted them to do." Remi threw her arms around her brother in an embrace. He spoke into her hair. "If you hadn't gotten him help as fast as you did, it would have been a different story."

Remi squeezed and then pulled away. She looked him in the eye with certainty.

"And if you hadn't gotten Josh here as fast as you did, *he* would have been in worse trouble, too."

Jonah took the truth with a smile that waned.

"But if I'd never gone out with Lydia—" he started.

"They would have still probably come," Declan finished.

They'd already had this conversation while waiting for Josh and their dad's surgeries to finish. Jonah told Declan and Caleb everything he knew about Lydia, which hadn't been much. She'd been nice and funny and had done a good job at pulling Jonah in with limited interaction.

The truth was, no one blamed him one bit, yet Remi

could see he'd be blaming himself for a long while despite that fact.

Jonah shook himself a little.

"Did you talk to Mom?"

"Yeah. Her flight got grounded because of the weather and it took all I had to convince her and Dave not to drive through it instead. She only relented after hearing that Josh and Dad would be okay. She'll call one of us tomorrow with an update but said *you* better call her soon."

Jonah glanced at Declan. He lowered his voice.

"Does she know? About the...you know?"

Remi felt Declan's gaze switch to her. She shook her head.

"I want to tell her in person."

"She'd like that." Jonah let out a loud, long sigh. "What she *wouldn't* like is you running yourself into the ground while pregnant with her only claim to a grandkid." He fixed her with a mock stern expression. "Get out of here and get some rest."

Remi opened her mouth to complain, but he cut her off.

"I called Rick, Dad's friend, and he said he wants to come up here and stay the night with Dad while I stay with Josh. There's no reason you need to stay here, too." He looked to Declan. "I'm assuming Remi has a place to stay with you, though?"

"She does."

"But what if—" Remi tried.

Jonah still wasn't having it.

"But what if nothing. I'll let you know if *anything* happens. Plus, it's not like the ranch is that far from here anyways." He put his hands on her shoulders to focus her attention so that it stayed solely on him and his next words. "You shot a man to get us off the ranch and then went right back to it to get Dad. Let me do this very simple task of watching over everyone here." His expression softened. "Give me this, Remi. I need it."

So, she did.

Then, before she knew it, Remi was standing in Declan's bathroom back on the Nash Family Ranch and staring at a mirror that was starting to steam over from the shower heating up behind her. She'd already stripped naked but couldn't get her feet to move from the tile floor.

All because of the stain on her skin.

Blood from her father or her brother that had seeped through her shirt.

Remi knew they were okay now, but that crimson smear held too much power still.

Way too much.

It wasn't until two beautiful green eyes met her gaze head-on that Remi realized she was sobbing.

And it wasn't until Declan's arms wrapped around her naked body that she realized how much she needed the man.

Chapter Sixteen

Sometime in the dark of late night or early morning, Remi woke up in bed alone. It wasn't her bed, and she sussed that out pretty quickly through the haze of sleep thanks to the way the pillow smelled beneath her still-wet hair.

It smelled like spice and the woods and Declan Nash.

Remi rolled over and felt the empty space next to her.

After her breakdown in the bathroom, Declan had gone above and beyond the call of supportive. Not only had he taken her into the shower with his jeans still on, he'd scrubbed the blood off her skin and held her while she cried some more. Only after she'd regained her composure, or enough of it to stop crying, did the man dry her off, put a too-big shirt over her head and deposit her like a child in bed.

Remi had been so exhausted from her outburst to the adrenaline-filled day she'd had that sleep had overtaken her within the space of two blinks.

Now she guessed that the man who had saved her from herself hadn't gotten beneath those same sheets next to her.

Remi rolled back over and found her phone on the nightstand. No new calls or texts from Jonah. She took that as good news and slowly got out of bed. She flushed when she realized she was wearing a pair of boxers. She didn't remember putting those on.

Declan surely was a caring and sly man.

If he hadn't already seen her as naked as naked could be, she might have been so embarrassed that she'd try to escape. Instead, she opened the door between the bedroom and living room with all the hope in the world of seeing the sheriff.

She wasn't disappointed.

Declan looked up from his laptop on the coffee table with alarm. That alarm softened after a moment. He smiled.

"Hey, Huds."

It was such a simple greeting, yet it shifted something inside of her that had already been moving.

"Hey, Sheriff."

Remi settled in the chair kitty-corner to the couch so she could face him the best she could.

"Thank you for earlier, by the way. I kind of *lost it*, lost it."

Declan waved off the apology.

"I only did what I could do to help." He sighed and glanced at the computer. "I just wish I could do more."

"I take that to mean no one has found Lydia and the men?"

He ran a hand over the stubble along his jaw. Whatever had softened his expression was now gone. Stress and frustration took its place.

"No. We've checked all the hospitals in the county, and even reached out past it, to see if we can't locate the guy you got. We have so many APBs out on them *and* the three who pulled what they pulled on Main Street that the gossip mill is about to shatter. Mom said that Cooper Mann's grandmother let her know in no uncertain terms that Overlook is losing faith in the department. In me. And, honestly, I can't blame them." He dragged his gaze to hers. "We have so many weird little pieces to this chaotic puzzle, and I just can't seem to find a way to force them to fit. For a moment I'll think I have something and then it gets lost in the chaos. It's driving me crazy."

Remi didn't say anything right away. She knew the man well enough that telling him everything was going to be okay, telling him that he *would* get all of the bad guys in the end, wasn't actually going to help him.

So, instead, she told him a story.

"One time when I was younger Dad and I went to a ranch out in Texas to visit a friend of his named Barry. The boys were too young and Mom had to stay to watch them and, to be honest, I wasn't that excited to be the one who had to go. Dad knew it and tried to talk the place up before we even got there. He told me it was three times bigger than Heartland and had all kinds of animals everywhere you looked. I didn't believe him— to me Heartland was massive—but then we drove the road to the main house and it felt like it took a lifetime to get there. All along the way I watched herds of cows grazing, people horseback riding, and even saw some goats running around. I was mesmerized." Remi couldn't help the smile that she knew passed over her face. The little-kid awe she'd felt then was hard to forget even as an adult. "So when Barry invited us to move the herd of cows to a field at the opposite end of his property, I was actually excited. We got our own horses, our own tents, and some stuff to make s'mores, and rode all day until we got them to where they needed to be. That night I passed out with chocolate on my mouth and a sore butt from riding. It was magic."

Declan smiled in turn at that.

"Later that night, though, I woke up to the sound of two hundred scared cattle. I'd barely gotten on my horse before they took off in all different directions," she continued. "I couldn't figure out what was going on, and neither could Dad or the ranch hands who had come with us. There was too much noise, too much movement, and not enough light. And do you know what Barry did?"

Declan raised his eyebrow in question. Remi leaned forward in her seat.

"He took a breath, tuned the world out and reminded himself that he'd been a rancher for years and was damn good at it. *That's* when he spotted the wolf."

Remi moved from her seat to the spot next to Declan and put her hand on his knee. She wanted to encourage him and comfort him all at the same time. She hoped that she'd at least hit one of her targets.

Declan angled his body so he could meet her gaze more easily.

Once again Remi marveled at how different this scene would have been if they were younger. *He* would have been the one talking while *she* listened in silence.

"With what I know from growing up in Overlook and from what I've heard since I've been gone, chaos seems to be more frequent than not. You've lived in it and still live in it. You're *good* at navigating it. Now you just need to take a breath, tune the world out, and trust that you're—"

Calling him *fast* was an injustice to the move he actually pulled off. In one fluid movement Declan went from a statue beneath her hand to heat against her lips.

He cupped the side of her face and Remi leaned in to the surprise.

She kissed the man back.

Hard.

Their lips parted and the taste of him was all she wanted in the world.

When he broke the kiss, Remi was left blinking and confused.

"You," he rasped out.

"Me?"

"You," he repeated. "That's what I want."

He was back to her lips within the space of a breath. The wild boy from her childhood and teen years. The reunited friend. The good—and not mention to last— fling. The accidental father of her child. The sheriff savior.

Declan Nash had a list of ever-evolving meanings to her.

But what was he now? Between a night of passion that wasn't supposed to last through the next day to always being connected through their unborn child.

What would happen next?

Coparenting across state lines due to her promotion?

Getting married in no-man's-land while her belly grew?

Or some form of in-between?

Remi had no idea about their future.

But she did know something about the present.

She looped her arms around Declan's neck and pulled him against her until they were lying across the couch. He followed her down while never breaking their kiss. In fact, he deepened it with his tongue, trapping a moan of pleasure between them.

Declan's hand tangled in her hair while the other gripped her hip. She moved up and against him as he tried to maneuver himself so his body weight wasn't solely on her. In the process Remi felt how much Declan Nash truly wanted her.

It put fire straight through her. She dropped her hands down and went for the hem of his shirt. Remi had never wanted something gone as badly as she wanted that shirt off.

Declan felt her frustration. He broke their kiss and nearly ripped it in two. The shirt went flying and then he was focused on hers. Which was *also* his. A fact that must have encouraged him. He grabbed its hem and then tore it right up the middle.

Cold air hit Remi's bare chest as the two sides of the fabric fell away, but there were only flames in her blood. When he dropped his mouth down to the skin of her neck and then followed a tantalizing path to her nipple, Remi almost cussed him.

When his hardness pushed against the boxers she was somehow still wearing and through the shorts *he* was somehow still wearing, Remi nearly lost it.

The second he came up for air, she decided to end the torture.

She pulled him back down on top of her and moaned.

It seemed to do the trick.

Remi moved against him as, one-handed, he took off his shorts. Then he focused on her. She moaned again as his hand, strong and warm, skimmed down the boxers on loan and then came back up her leg. Trailing heat and lust right to the spot where she wanted his attention next.

There was no trapping her moans now.

She yelled out in absolute bliss as he pushed inside of her and filled her with hard passion. She moved against him with uncontainable desire.

A man and a woman desperate to be closer.

Lips to lips.

Skin to skin.

Galloping heartbeats.

Remi didn't know what their future held but she did know one thing.

She wanted Declan, too.

THE PHONE CALL didn't wake Declan, Remi did.

Tangled together between the sheets of his bed, she couldn't help thrashing around to escape to the bathroom.

Declan immediately went on high alert, fighting through the haze of the good sleep he'd fallen into with the naked woman wrapped in his arms. He followed her up and out of the bed, fists balled and eyes wild. It didn't matter that he was as naked as the day he was born, he was going to fight tooth and nail to combat whatever had woken Remi so violently.

Then he heard her in the bathroom heaving.

There wasn't anything he could punch or shoot to cure morning sickness.

So after Remi shooed him away, Declan went to the kitchen and poured her a glass of water and took stock of what he had to eat. Nina, Caleb's wife, had claimed that sour candy had been a lifesaver when she'd first been pregnant with their son. Madi hadn't really felt sick with Addison but with her second pregnancy she'd always had crackers, some kind of Popsicle, and a lot of snacks. Declan hadn't been grocery shopping in a hot minute. All he had that met the criteria was a bag of pretzels Desmond had left the week before.

They would have to do.

He plated some, set the water next to it, and brought his phone back out to him.

That was when he saw the missed call. It was from Cussler and time-stamped at just after three in the morning. It was now almost five.

There were no texts or emails as a follow-up. No voice mail, either.

Declan wondered if it had been an accident. His chief deputy was a married man and a father to four. Declan only liked to call him when it was absolutely necessary. He decided to send a text, instead. He put the phone down and the ringer up, surprised he'd missed the call in the first place. Normally he was a light sleeper. Then again, normally, he didn't have a naked Remi Hudson in his bed.

No sooner had he set the phone down than the woman of the hour made her entrance. She was wearing another one of his old T-shirts. It was too big for her and somehow still she made it an attractive piece. The urge to rip it off her like he'd done earlier was nearly overpowering. She frowned at him, picking up on his thoughts.

"Don't go getting any ideas, buddy. I feel like death incarnate. I know it's cliché to blame you for how I feel right now, but—" she took a seat at the dining table next to him "—this is all your fault."

Declan chuckled.

"The words every man wants to hear after a night of rolling around naked in bed with a beautiful woman."

That pulled a smile from her. It was small but there. She motioned to the plate of pretzels. He nodded.

"I didn't know if you would want to eat but read that if you eat a little every few hours that it might help with morning sickness, especially when you first wake up."

Remi's eyebrow arched high.

He unlocked his phone and found the app he was looking for. He tapped it and slid the phone over.

The surprise was clear on her face.

"You downloaded a pregnancy app?"

Declan shrugged.

"I figure I'm already behind on the game, might as well try to catch up best I can."

Remi gave him a look he couldn't quite place and grabbed a handful of pretzels.

"If I didn't feel like I was about to be sick, starve, and cry all at the same time right now I'd kiss you."

Declan smirked.

"And if you kissed me right now I might just destroy another one of my shirts."

Remi's cheeks flushed pink and she laughed.

"Smooth one, Sheriff."

"I try."

The phone between them buzzed.

Remi tensed.

"I missed a call from my chief deputy. I texted him I was up," he explained, spinning the phone around to face him. "If something was wrong he would have called more than once or probably just come here to wake me up himself."

He trailed off when the phone started to ring. He

stopped whatever he was going to say and took the call right there. Cussler was quick and precise. He'd called Declan, then decided to let the sheriff get some sleep when he hadn't answered. It was no secret Declan hadn't gotten enough of it lately. Cussler recounted what had happened and had handled the situation.

Declan thanked him and ordered him to seek the same sleep he'd let Declan get.

As they ended their call, Declan was already slipping deep into his thoughts.

Finally Remi said, "What's wrong? What happened?"

He didn't answer right away. If it had been yesterday afternoon the new information would have been another piece in the bizarre puzzle. Another stroke of chaos. Another reminder that he had no idea what *exactly* was going on.

But Declan had since had some sleep, some comfort, and a woman who'd told a story about a rancher and a wolf.

Now he finally saw some sense in the chaos.

Declan met Remi's gaze. She had a pretzel at her lips and was undoubtedly the most stunning woman he'd ever seen.

"I think it's time I called a family meeting."

Chapter Seventeen

The last time Remi had been in the same room as all of the Nash siblings, they had been in the loft of their stable and hoping they wouldn't get caught by the adults they'd snuck away from. There had been others there, friends and crushes and hangers-on, because being a Nash in Overlook earned a certain amount of fame. Unwanted by them, given by most.

When the triplets were together, even more so.

Remi had never liked the attention thrust upon them. They clearly didn't want it. However, talking to each as they showed up at Declan's house, she was glad to see it hadn't beaten them down.

Like their older brother, the triplets were and were not the same as she remembered.

Outside of the sheriff's department, Caleb was smiles and humor. He had a coffee cup in one hand and a baby teething ring in the other. He declared to everyone that he'd found it in his truck and wasn't going to let it out of his sight until he could pass it to his wife, Nina, since it was one of their son's favorite things to play with. Love had drenched every word.

Madi, who been closed off to everyone who wasn't her family when they were younger, embraced Remi with a warm hug. The scar along her cheek was just as noticeable as it had always been, but it did nothing to dampen her lighthearted spirit. She plopped down on the couch next to Caleb and started to tell him about her two children's current favorite toys. One was the remote control to their TV. The other was a gardening bucket with a painted smiley face on it. Both laughed at that.

Desmond came in last. The limp he walked with hadn't changed from when they were younger but there was definitely something different about it and him. A lightness? A carefree air around him? Remi couldn't place her finger on it but accepted a hug from him with pleasure. He was a businessman who had spent his career helping others. He hadn't had to come with Caleb to Heartland the day before, but he had, no hesitation. Remi thanked him for it and he accepted the kind words with a charming Nash smile before moving into the living room to sit.

Then there they were.

The Nash triplets.

Once they had been three eight-year-olds forced to live through trauma no kid should have to experience.

Taken from a park during a game of hide-and-seek. Hurt, scared and terrified.

Now three adults, happy and healthy—and no idea they were about to revisit a past they'd all seemed to move on from.

Remi knew this same thought was moving through Declan's mind the moment he came in from the bedroom and saw them. He shared a look with her.

She tried on an encouraging smile.

It wasn't missed.

Madi stopped whatever Caleb was saying to Desmond by putting her hands on both of their arms. They followed her gaze to Declan. The three of them looked up at their big brother as he pulled a chair from next to the dining table opposite them. He waited until Remi was sitting in the armchair before he started.

"I'm going to dive in because I've already held off telling any of you this for too long as it is." Still, Declan took a breath before continuing. The triplets lost their earlier humor. Three sets of baby blues were focused solely on him. "The morning before Cooper Mann allegedly attacked Lydia Cartwright he asked to meet me because he thought he had information on a cold case. *Your* cold case." The shift was subtle but there. The triplets tensed in unison. "He said a man in a fancy suit at the Waypoint Bar kept rattling on about a note in the wall at Well Water Cabin that law enforcement had missed. I thought it was a bunch of nonsense but, well, I had to check. Remi was in town and nice enough to indulge me with a fresh pair of eyes. Which made the difference because she found it."

"A note *in* the wall?" Caleb repeated.

Declan nodded.

"It looked like a painted-over wallpaper seam," Remi explained. "Basically it was glued against the wall in the paint. I almost didn't see it."

"What did it say?" Madi scooted to the edge of the couch cushion. Her darkened expression reminded Remi of how she'd often looked as a teen.

Declan pulled out his phone, selected one of the pictures he'd taken of the note and passed it to her. They took turns looking at it even though Declan answered.

"Justin Redman was the only thing written on it."

"Why does that name sound familiar?" Desmond asked.

Caleb was quick to answer.

"Dad was on a case trying to find his attacker just before the abduction, right?"

Declan nodded.

"I took another look at the file last night to see if anything stuck out to me, but it was pretty cut-and-dried. Dad was about to go after his attacker hard and then had to let someone else handle the case after the abduction. Justin was killed in a car accident before another detective could take the case so it was ultimately dropped."

Madi scrolled through Declan's phone.

"I guess he got really lucky, then," she muttered. Then she amended, "The attacker. Not Justin, obviously. You know how good Dad was at cases like that."

They all nodded in agreement. Declan continued.

"Before I could really get a grasp of what we'd found, Cooper was arrested. I assumed he was pulling my leg with the note, painted it in there a while back and used it to distract me. Or it was a twisted way to drum up *more* publicity for himself after he tried to kidnap Lydia. You know how some of these bad guys love the spotlight."

Desmond snorted.

"It would have been a doozy of a news bulletin, too. 'A new lead following Overlook's most infamous kidnapping case found at the same time local idiot kidnaps, or tries to, an innocent woman.' If he did it for attention he'd surely get it."

"But you didn't go public with the note." Caleb's voice held an edge. He was angry he hadn't been told. Not only was he Declan's brother, he was one of his detectives.

"We had to handle the situation as delicately and quickly as we could, given the town's history," Declan defended. "I had to put the *maybe* of the abduction case on the back burner while I dealt with the very real and present attempted abduction. And all before the press tore into us to make that job harder."

Madi continued looking at Declan's phone. Desmond nodded. Caleb was satisfied enough not to argue.

"Cooper denied he attacked Lydia and said *she* attacked him, mutilated her face with his keys, and then jumped into his car. A witness saw him and assumed he was pushing her inside. He said he was trying to get her out while Lydia swore up and down that he attacked and was trying to take her when we interviewed her. I was going to dig deeper into Justin Redman, still, but the next day I got distracted again."

"Claire's Café?" Madi guessed.

What had happened across Main Street had already circulated twice over throughout the county.

"Yeah," Declan answered gruffly. "A man jumps out of a car outside, attacks a woman, and I give chase. Once he's standing still he tells me, in so many words, that he wanted me to chase him away from Claire's. I run back to find out a man and woman, both wearing suits, had come inside and shot a man in the arm before escaping back to their car. They then go and pick up the man I'd been chasing."

None of the triplets commented. Again, they knew this part.

Well, most of it.

They didn't know why Remi hadn't been shot and, somehow, the news hadn't made its way to them.

"And then we have yesterday," he continued. "I

talked to Cooper on a hunch and became convinced he's not lying."

"Then Jazz and I figure out that Lydia Cartwright didn't exist, at least not online, until five years ago," Caleb supplied. "And you go to her house and find out it's empty, meaning she lied."

Remi hadn't known that part. She gave Declan a questioning look. He returned it with an apologetic one.

"I was heading to Heartland to talk to Jonah again. See if he knew anything about the house and why she'd lied. But changed course here when Cooper's grandma showed up to plead his case. I saw you in the field before I ever made it off Winding Road." He redirected his attention to his siblings to, she guessed, tell them about what had happened on Heartland before they'd met in the field. However, the words stuck in his mouth.

Declan became angry. A muscle in his jaw twitched. His hands fisted.

Remi spoke for him.

"My brothers, Dad and I were making some food when Lydia showed up. She said she had come for me, not Jonah, and immediately attacked. I was able to get her out of the house, but she opened fire." Remi felt her own bad memories tensing her body. She took a breath and skipped the heart-wrenching parts. "It wasn't until I made it out to the barn behind our house to where Jonah and Josh were that I found out there were four men with her, all armed. I shot one in the stomach before Josh was shot. After that we managed to ride off. My brothers said no one spoke to them or around them when they were trying to hide. If—if my dad heard anything, it might be a while before we can find out what that was."

Each Nash gave her a sympathetic look. She was

thankful they didn't say anything. There wasn't much reassurance they could give her at the moment. Sometimes a look of understanding or a pat on the back helped more than words. A sentiment the family was, no doubt, well versed in by now.

"Which brings us to early this morning," Declan continued. "Cussler called this morning to tell me that a man named Joe Langley was taken to the ER early. He was attacked during a jog through his neighborhood after he couldn't sleep. He said a man in a suit came out of nowhere, did the deed, and left him with his phone to call for help."

"It seems like the Fixers are our common link between everything that's happened," Caleb jumped in. "We might not be able to see their scorpion tattoos but their suits *and* frustrating-as-hell ability to stay a few steps ahead of law enforcement? It can't be a coincidence."

Declan shared another look with Remi. After his call with Cussler they'd spent the next few hours talking out his theory and going over what they knew.

Once again, Madi didn't let the exchange lie.

"There's more," she stated.

Declan nodded.

"For the last few years the Fixers organization has been popping up in our lives. From talk about men in suits to men in suits actually showing up as hired guns, they've been around. I have no doubt that the man at Waypoint Bar was a Fixer, the two men and woman on Main Street were Fixers, and even Lydia and the men at Heartland were Fixers. But, what is the *only* thing we know about them?"

"They do what they're paid to do," Desmond offered.

"Which means that *someone* out there is pulling the strings."

"But why?" Madi asked. "And to what end?"

Declan sat up straighter and then domed his hands over his lap.

Remi knew what he was about to say and yet goose bumps erupted across her skin when he said it.

"The woman outside of Claire's Café wasn't just attacked. She was pistol-whipped in the face. The man inside the café, Sam, was shot in the arm. The *side* of the arm. And Joe Langley had his leg broken. Badly." Silence filled the room so quickly Remi felt suffocated by it. Declan caused that silence with his deafening theory.

She looked at Madi and the scar that had been created by being pistol-whipped.

She looked at Caleb, remembering the scar across his arm from a bullet grazing it.

She looked at Desmond, the man who had grown up with a limp after having his leg broken from the sheer force of a man twice his size.

No one moved.

Declan had to bring the conversation home.

"I think everything that has happened in the last week is because someone is sending us, the Nash family, a very personal message."

MADI TOUCHED HER SCAR. Caleb rolled his shoulder back. Desmond put his hand on his knee. Then the three did something that only they seemed to be able to do on occasion.

They said the same thing at the same time.

"Why?"

Remi's brown eyes found his. Sometimes he believed

they were a dark amber, beautiful and dangerous depending. Her brow was pinched, expression thoughtful. This was a question they'd already tried to tackle in the early hours of the morning. In fact, the case had become the only thing they'd talked about since Cussler had called.

Yet, here they were with no clear answers.

"One theory is someone is trying to rattle us. Maybe someone from an old case is ticked off at Caleb or me. Maybe someone is angry with Des because of the work he's been doing with the foundation. Maybe it's a blast from the past who's angry with Madi."

"But we know who it is," Caleb said. "It's the Fixers. We find them, we find answers."

Even though he said it, they both knew that was a tall order. As much as it pained Declan to admit, finding the Fixers was a damn near impossible feat. Over the years they'd managed to catch a few, but once behind bars, the Fixers died by their own hands or another Fixer.

That was how their reputation had grown so much and so quickly.

They rarely got caught and, even if they did, they took their job, client and any other nefarious details with them to the grave.

Des had had a run-in with who they believed to be the leader of the Fixers in the last dealings with the group before now. He adopted a look of deep concentration and equal skepticism.

"The only time I was offered an answer from them, the cost would have been Riley and her sister's lives." He shook his head. "And that option was given to me by the man with the scar on his hand."

Declan sighed. The man they thought was the Fixer's head honcho had a scar in the shape of an X on his hand. It was identical to the scar the triplets' captor had had on his own hand when he'd taken them. This discovery was one of the main reasons Declan had been unable to completely walk away from trying to solve the case again.

"Which gives weight to the theory that someone has been playing with us for a while now." He ran a hand through his hair and then curved it down to run the top of his knuckles against the stubble beneath his chin. Frustration coursed through him. How he wished to be back in bed with Remi at his side.

"It could be him." Madi's voice was soft as she said it, and Declan heard the pain. "It could be the man who took us."

That had been another theory. The triplets' abductor was toying with them. Declan didn't put too much stock in that possibility, and Caleb voiced the reason for that.

"Getting away with taking and scarring three little kids, who also happen to have a father in law enforcement, once, was a miracle on its own. For him to come back to mess with us would be an idiotic thing to do. He might as well throw self-preservation out the window."

Declan agreed. What would be the reasoning behind doing that? Especially all these years later?

"But no one knows why you were taken in the first place."

Everyone turned to Remi. Her cheeks tinted at the sudden attention, but she remained focused.

"When you were kids. No one ever figured out *why* you were taken." She straightened in her seat. "Because you're right. It was a miracle the guy never got caught. Everyone in town was looking for you, including your dad, the county's best detective at the time. *Everyone* was looking for you." She turned to Declan. "Which meant no one was looking for Justin Redman's attacker, someone who also was never found. How sure are you that Justin's death was an accident?"

Declan opened his mouth to answer. Nothing came out. Caleb also seemed to be at a loss. In the shadow of the abduction they'd never focused on the case that their father had abandoned.

"You think we were taken as a distraction," Madi spelled out. "So Dad wouldn't look into Justin's attack?"

Remi shrugged.

"If Cooper Mann didn't try to take Lydia, then he probably didn't put that note in the wall at the cabin, either. He was telling the truth and probably heard about it from a Fixer at the bar, knowing it would eventually get back to one of you. Whether they are toying with you all or not, Justin Redman has to have *some* kind of significance to all of this. Right? Why else go through the trouble of painting a note in a wall?"

Declan's heart rate sped up. The wheels in his head began to turn. For a moment no one spoke.

Had Remi just found one of their missing pieces?

Chapter Eighteen

"This is a bad plan."

"You've already said that. Three times now."

"Because it *is* a bad plan."

"For the record, I never said it was a good plan."

Declan snorted.

"Well, that doesn't help me feel better."

Remi ran her fingers through her hair and then tried to flatten the parts of it she'd pinned back. They'd had an eventful day. Some of it had included going back to Heartland. Remi had stayed stone silent as she'd led him to her childhood room. She'd kept that silence while finding the clothes she needed and changed. Declan had gone behind her, packing her bag with things he thought she might need for the foreseeable future. When she eyed him with a question seconds from her lips, he'd told her the simple truth.

"Sorry, Huds, you're stuck with me until this whole thing gets sorted out."

Remi hadn't fought him then, but he was back to fighting her hours later.

They were sitting in the parking lot of Waypoint Bar in Kilwin. He was in his best pair of dark jeans, a black button-up at her request and had on his vacation-only dark blue Stetson. His sheriff's badge was in his back pocket. The blazer in the back seat would hide his shoulder holster.

Remi wasn't armed, which didn't mean she couldn't do some damage. She was decked out in a sheer white blouse that dipped low and tucked into a pair of navy pants—which he noted matched his hat—with legs so wide Declan had thought it was a long skirt at first. She'd chosen black flats that wrapped around her ankles and lipstick that reminded him of a bull's-eye. One he very much wanted to hit.

"I wore this to a party one of my clients threw for Towne & Associates after I cleaned up the absolute mess that was their finances," she'd said after debuting the look. "I packed it on the off chance I could convince Molly to go out while I was in town."

Now, looking at her in the glow from Waypoint's lone light at the back of the parking lot, Declan found the outfit to be too much. Just like the plan.

Remi sighed and slapped him lightly on the shoulder.

"Stop it. Stop that broodiness right now. We need to do this and do it right." She motioned to her outfit and his. Her brows drew in together. She rolled her shoulders back. Then she reminded him why he'd agreed to the bad plan in the first place. "Justin Redman said he was supposed to meet Dean Lawson the day he was attacked. No one ever got around to asking Mr. Lawson what for. Now we can, thanks to your brothers pulling some hefty favors to find this Lawson guy and get us a meeting *twenty-five years* after the fact." She motioned to their outfits again. At the movement his attention redirected to the curve of her breast. Remi was nice enough not to call him out for it. "If Lawson can't

give us any information we can use about Justin Redman, then we can leave him be and mingle with the rest
of the crowd and see if we can't at least find something
about the man who told Cooper about the note in the
wall. If you go in with a sheriff's badge on your chest,
guns blazing, I don't think we'll get the response we
want. Right now we just look like two people on a date.
It's not like everyone in the city knows you're the Wildman county sheriff."

Declan saw the logic in it, but he didn't have to like it.

Remi let out a frustrated huff.

"You told Julian to keep watch on Madi. You have
Desmond with your mom. Caleb is with his wife and
son. Jazz is working with your chief deputy to find
Lydia and the people who have been attacking strangers and my family home." She reached out and took his
chin in her hand. It was soft and warm. "You told me
earlier that you're not leaving me. I'm telling you right
now that *I'm* not leaving *you*."

She kept his gaze for a moment before letting go.

Then she was smiling.

"So, now that that's out of the way, can we please go
in already? I have to pee. Again."

Despite every reservation he had, which numbered
many, Declan chuckled.

"Yes, ma'am."

Declan had already been told that Waypoint had lost
its law enforcement hangout roots, but it was still odd
to see in person. What had once been walls covered in
framed pictures of fallen heroes, graduating classes,
candid stills from on the job and an assortment of police
memorabilia had now been swapped for a moodier aes-
thetic. Posters from old movies, handmade wall art and

pictures of people relaxing after, he assumed, a long day on the job surrounded a clientele who were in varying stages of after-work comfort. Declan led Remi past two dartboards mounted against the interior faded brick, a dimly lit pool table, a wall lined with flat screens, clusters of tables, and up to the massive bar that lined the back wall. No one paid them any mind as they walked through. Not even a wayward glace as Remi stopped just shy of the counter and turned to him.

"That's him," she whispered, trying and failing to be covert about her head nod. The man in question was sitting hunched over in the middle of the bar, a few feet from them. Declan would have questioned her ability to pick him out so easily from the angle if it hadn't been for his hair. Stark white and falling past his shoulders. Just as it had been in the picture from his online profile and the several magazine pieces written about him.

Dean Lawson was a businessman, like Desmond. However, unlike Declan's brother, Lawson was in real estate and was more known for throwing extravagant parties for wealthy clients and driving sports cars with bikini models than charitable giving. His idea of helping the community, as far as Declan could tell from a general Google search, was putting attractive people in expensive houses. The latest article about him had been his announcement that he was passing his business on to his son. They'd been lucky he was visiting Kilwin before heading back to his current home of Miami.

Declan was hoping they'd be even luckier before the night ended.

"How do we play this?" Remi asked. "Good cop, bad cop?"

Declan raised his eyebrow at that.

"We're just going to see if he knows anything about Justin that can help us. We don't really need a good cop or a bad cop."

Remi snorted.

"That's what they always say."

"They?" he asked with a laugh. She nodded. Her eyes darted back to Lawson. She was excited. Declan couldn't much blame her. Just the *chance* of a lead could get his adrenaline going.

"Okay, there, hotshot, why don't we sit next to him and just talk first?"

"All right, but if you want me to turn up the heat or to help you, just say 'coconut.' That can be our safe word."

"Coconut? How am I supposed to work that into a conversation?"

Remi shrugged.

"If anything goes wrong, then you'll find a way."

She threw him a teasing grin and nodded toward Lawson.

The seats on either side of him were unoccupied. Declan touched the small of Remi's back before passing her and sliding onto the bar stool to the man's left while she took the right.

Declan noticed two things about Mr. Lawson from the get-go. One, he was working on at least his third drink. Two empty shot glasses hadn't been cleared yet from in front of him. The current glass his hand was wrapped around looked to contain whiskey. Two, the man matched the mood of three drinks. His shoulders were drooped over, his elbow propped up on the countertop, and his gaze was on the liquid of his drink. The word *dejected* popped into Declan's head at the sight of him.

When he dragged his eyes up to meet Declan's, his expression was blank.

"Mr. Lawson," he greeted, offering his hand to shake. "I'm Declan Nash and this is Remi. Thank you for meeting us."

Dean Lawson's handshake was a half-hearted affair. One he didn't extend to Remi, who gave Declan a disapproving look over the man's shoulder.

"You know, I hadn't been back to Kilwin in ten years and then I'm in town for less than a week and everyone wants a piece." He took a sip of his drink. "What a wild ride."

Again Remi gave Declan a look.

"Well, thank you for coming out to meet us, then," he said, using his cordial voice reserved for press conferences. "We won't keep you long."

Lawson waved his hand dismissively.

"Don't worry, son, tonight is the last time I worry about managing my time. But whatever you're going to ask, better go ahead and ask it."

Declan didn't like Dean Lawson, he decided. Then again, he didn't need to like him to ask a question.

"Do you remember a man named Justin Redman?" he started, easing into it.

Lawson nodded.

"I do."

He didn't make any attempt to elaborate. Declan kept on.

"Twenty-five years ago he was attacked at a gas station by an unidentified man. Justin was killed in a car accident before the case could be investigated. The only information we had about the incident was the day it happened Justin said in a statement he was on the way to meet you. Do you remember why?"

Lawson ran his index finger up and down the side of his glass. He didn't look to Declan as he answered.

"Funnily enough, I don't remember why exactly he wanted to meet then. I remember the man, though." His face became pinched. "A child in men's clothes. That's what he reminded me of. A man who, for whatever reason, thought he was more than he was. An annoying little twerp." He laughed. It was unkind.

Remi's look of concern rivaled Declan's own confusion. Dean Lawson was showing signs of disgust and hostility for a man who had died over two decades ago.

Lawson took the last long drink of his whiskey and shook the glass at the passing bartender. He was an older man who paid no attention to Declan or Remi. Not that either had planned on drinking, but the oversight added to the list of reasons Declan liked the old Waypoint Bar over the new version of it.

The bartender refilled his glass.

Lawson smiled down at the new drink.

"Did you know that I grew up in Kilwin?" he asked. "Not too far from this bar, actually. My dad was in sales and my mom inherited all of her father's money in lieu of an actual job. I grew up watching my dad, a proud and honest man, continue to work himself to the bone to provide for a family already provided for while my mother couldn't understand why he resented her. *Then* he died and Mom finally understood that all he'd been trying to do was show her the best things in life are earned, not bought." Lawson gave Declan a look of such loathing he nearly felt it as a physical thing. "So, in a drastic one-eighty to honor my father she decided

I wouldn't see an ounce of her or his money ever. Not a dime, not a penny." Declan didn't miss his grip tighten around his glass. "Now, that might seem like an okay and even normal thing for most families but, you have to understand, I'd already spent my life relying on that money. My father was always away on business trips and my mother had already made the choice to make my life as easy as possible. When she decided that was a mistake and one she wouldn't continue to make? I was *days* away from striking out on my own."

He took a drink.

Declan's body was tensing on reflex, readying for something. He just wasn't sure what yet. Remi's body language had changed, too. She sat taller, more rigid. Neither had any idea what was going on.

Lawson finished his most recent drink and shook his head.

"Boy, was I stubborn about still sticking to the plan I'd made when I'd had the money and, boy, was I bad at it. It wasn't long at all before I was going to bed hungry in a crappy little apartment, filled with worry over what I'd do next. Then one night everything changed. One night I decided something that has been the guiding motivation of everything I've ever done since." Lawson shook his glass with one decisive shake. "There is no honor in starving, so why be honorable if that's what you'll get?"

Declan couldn't stay quiet any longer.

"Why are you telling us this?"

Lawson went back to staring at his drink. When he spoke next he sounded almost wistful.

"Because I wanted someone to know that, while I don't regret the things I've done over the last few decades to build the life I've lived, I did want someone to understand why I did them."

"And what are the things you've done?" Remi asked.

He didn't look up from his drink as he answered her.

"I made money and I protected that money. No matter the cost."

"Justin Redman didn't die in an accident, did he?" Declan formed it as a question, but his gut was already telling him it was true. "You killed him."

Lawson didn't deny it.

"The man was an idiot. He gets into a fight with one of my suppliers and then has the nerve to give a statement saying he was supposed to be meeting up with me after?" Lawson's anger was as potent as his loathing had been earlier. Declan readied for anything, including body slamming the man against the ground behind them if he even so much as blinked at Remi now or dropped his hands off the countertop. "Our standing arrangement was supposed to be confidential and only one of the many other confidential things he knew. Once your father was tasked with finding his attacker, I knew it was only a matter of time before Justin slipped up and damned me and everything I'd been working for. Deciding to kill him was easy. It was the other parts that were hard."

He laughed. It held no humor and sounded weaker than the one before.

"I thought I'd made it out. I really did. I went twenty-five years without ever hearing Justin's name and, yet, one week back in town and he's one of several names I've heard that I never wanted to again. I shouldn't have come back home." He sighed, pushed his drink away from him and grimaced. Then he was looking squarely at Declan. "You know, I saw you and your siblings, out on Main Street when I was in town once. The triplets were tiny, loud little things. Inseparable and a spectacle all in one. Everyone paid attention to them because of how rare triplets are, especially in Overlook. I admit, I was one of them. To this day I've not met another triplet set. But you? The eldest brother and singleton? No one paid you any mind. You weren't special. Not like they were."

Declan's hands had balled into fists. He couldn't look away from the man who would have been his father's age, staring at him without an ounce of fear of the consequences to what he was saying.

Dean Lawson didn't waver one bit.

Even when what he said next changed absolutely everything.

"That's why I paid him to kidnap you, instead. But he didn't listen to me, did he?"

Chapter Nineteen

Surprised wasn't the right word.

Angry wasn't, either.

Remi watched as Declan's face hardened into an emotion that made her feelings fall somewhere between the two. Fear didn't even register. Why would it?

Dean Lawson was just a sad man in a bar with a drink never that far from his fingertips.

A sad man who'd just said he had paid to have Declan kidnapped which, as history showed, hadn't worked out.

"Come again?" Declan's voice was ice.

Lawson sighed. The hunch he'd already been sitting with became more pronounced.

"Michael Nash was one of those hard-nosed detectives you see on old cop shows. The ones who never lose. If he'd gotten ahold of Justin, he would have gotten ahold of me. There was only one thing in the world that could have distracted him. Taking his kid." He pointed at Declan and shook his head. "But…" He glanced at the bartender. The older man was staring as he wiped a glass dry. Remi wondered if he had heard the patron's admission. "Things escalated. And now we're here."

Declan moved his blazer. She knew beneath it was his gun. They'd come here to get more insight into Justin Redman, and here they were sitting with the man who had paid to make the abduction possible.

"Who did you pay?" Declan's voice was unrecognizable.

Lawson shared a look with Remi. Or at least she thought it was with her. Instead, his eyes skirted to the person on the bar stool to the right of her. He had been in a conversation with a woman on the other side of him when they'd first sat down. Now the couple had gone silent and still. The bartender had also changed states. He placed a still-wet glass on the bar top and kept his dishrag in hand.

The hair on the back of Remi's neck started to stand.

Declan was understandably focused on Lawson, just as she had been, but now other details were blaring. The music that had been somewhat loud when they walked in had now softened. The movement of the bar's patrons eating, drinking and talking had lessened. The bar was quiet enough for her to hear the TV at the other side of the room.

Now that her focus wasn't homed in on Lawson's every word, Remi could tell something was off. *Very* off.

And Lawson was a part of it.

He wasn't answering Declan's question, even though he'd just incriminated himself by supplying information he hadn't really needed to give.

Surely he knew that Declan and the sheriff's department would go at him full force now?

Why did he suddenly seem so hesitant?

"I asked a question," Declan thrummed.

Again, Lawson kept quiet.

Something hit the floor between Lawson and Remi. She glanced down, body already taut with nerves.

Nerves that escalated so quickly it was a struggle not to openly gasp.

Blood.

That was what had hit the ground.

And it was coming from beneath Lawson's blazer.

"Coconut." The word came out before Remi could stop it. Then she chanted it. "Coconut. Coconut. Coconut."

Declan tore his eyes away from Lawson. Remi shook her head. The man between them chuckled. He finally took a long look at her.

That was when Remi *really* saw it. The pale skin, the pain.

The acceptance.

Now she knew why he'd freely admitted to what he'd done.

He was already dead.

"You can't escape them," he said. "He blamed me for complicating his life. He blames the Nashes for ruining it."

"We need to leave," Remi whispered across him, urgency making her heartbeat take off in a gallop.

"For over two decades he planned a way to find his justice." Lawson shook his head. "You'll only leave this place if it's a part of that plan. And, boy, is he big on plans."

Declan was off his bar stool in a flash. The movement seemed to be tied to every person inside the bar. Chairs scraped against wood and glasses clinked against tables as the entirety of Waypoint stood. They all had their guns out before Declan could pull his.

And they all were aimed at Remi.

Lawson was the only one who remained seated.

He turned back to his drink.

Remi, wide-eyed, looked at Declan.

He was furious.

"This was a trap. One we set up ourselves," he said through gritted teeth. "I should have never brought you."

Remi had opened her mouth to say she was sorry for pushing them to come since it had obviously been a bad plan after all when she was interrupted by a man breaking away from a group in the middle of the room. He was dressed in an expensive suit and smiling.

"We didn't give you much choice, now did we?" the man said. "After we realized the value of Miss Hudson, we knew that an attack against her would only make you stick that much closer to her side. Even taking her to a bar for a seemingly insignificant meeting." He stopped a few feet from them. Then he held out his hands and lowered them. Every patron around them put away their guns and sat back down.

Then it was just the three of them standing.

"If you hadn't brought her, then we would have. And killed every innocent person we had to to do it," he continued. "*This* was the best option you could have hoped for."

"I've been looking for you for a while now," Declan said. "The man with the scar on his hand who seems to pop up when us Nashes are involved."

Remi looked down at the man's hand. Sure enough she could see the scar in the shape of an X on it.

He was the leader of the Fixers.

And they were apparently in their den.

The man kept smiling.

"Maybe it's you all who keep popping up in my business. Did you ever think of that?"

Declan's hands were fisted. Remi wanted to hold them, but didn't want to move and start a fight.

"You're too young to have carried out the abduction," he said. "What's your part in all of this now? What do you want with us?"

The man's smile twisted into a nasty smirk.

"*I'm* here to give you some choices. Some hard choices. Then we'll be leaving and you'll never see me again."

Declan wasn't pleased with that answer.

"Let her go and I'll make all the choices you want."

The man shook his head. Then he looked at Remi.

"She's the one who has to make the first choice."

Declan started to move toward her to, she guessed, shield her from the man, his words and the consequences they'd bring. The man in the suit didn't have to lift a hand to stop him. Half of the bar raised their guns again. Declan held up his hands and stopped.

He actually growled.

"It's okay," she said. Then to the man in the suit, she said, "You clearly like the sound of your own voice so why don't you go ahead and give me your bad-guy spiel so you can hear it some more." The man's eyebrow rose. "Sorry, do you want me to sound more like a damsel? Do you want me to cry?"

"Huds," Declan warned.

I'm sassing because of pregnancy hormones and straight up fear, she wanted to explain. Instead, she tried to simmer down.

The man actually sniggered at her.

"I guess it shouldn't surprise me that you have some bite. You *did* manage to escape my men yesterday."

"After I shot one," she added, failing at keeping her sass in check.

The man nodded, conceding.

"You did, and it was such a bold decision given the odds. Which makes this next part interesting for me." He cleared his throat and clasped his hands behind his back. "This entire organization was made with the sole purpose of destroying the Nash family. From root to stem, every job taken, every connection made, has been a means to an end…for some of us. Myself? I'd like to think we're worth more than a revenge plot. But, for now, here I am to get us all to the next stage." His smile dropped and suddenly he was the image of a consummate professional. "You, Remi Hudson, can do one of two things. You can either come with me willingly to be bait for Declan and the triplets to come save you later, or you can refuse and I'll kill Declan and you'll still be bait for the triplets later. The choice is yours."

Remi went ramrod straight. Declan cussed and started telling her no.

She didn't listen.

"So I can either die now or die later? Not much of a choice."

The man shrugged.

"Think of it like this, if you leave voluntarily *he* won't die now and might even save *you* later. It's probably your best option."

"She's not going anywhere with you," Declan yelled. The man paid him no mind again.

"If I go with you, what's to stop your happy helpers from killing him the moment we leave?"

"Nothing, but we'd like his help for this next part. He's the best candidate to convince his siblings to meet us all at Well Water Cabin. Alone."

A shiver went down Remi's spine.

"Why do you want to go there?" Declan had to ask.

"Because it's poetic, I suppose. Because we can. Now, Miss Hudson, make your choice."

Remi looked at Declan.

Beautiful, soulful green eyes. Smart and cunning and, most of all, kind.

Declan Nash was a good man. He would be an even greater father. But to be that, to have that chance, Remi had to keep herself alive. Just as she had to keep him alive, too. Since she wasn't in law enforcement, didn't have a weapon and was standing in a room filled with at least fifteen people who weren't afraid to use theirs, making her choice was laughably simple.

"I'll go."

EVERY MAN AND woman had their weapons back up.

Some were itching to use them.

Declan knew the feeling, but reality was biting him in the backside. He made a rough estimate that there was no way he could get Remi out before one of the fifteen or so guns went off and bullets rained down on them both. Even if he became a human shield, the odds weren't in their favor that he could get her out without being hurt. He also figured there was no way he could get her safely out the back door behind the bar which, he assumed, led to a kitchen or office and eventually to an exit.

In fact, any way he sliced it, there was no good option to save Remi.

Rage boiled beneath his skin. Helplessness only made it hotter.

He should have never sought out information on Justin Redman. Going to Well Water to look for the note in the first place had been a mistake. Just as going back with Remi to find it had been.

He should have locked Remi and him up in his room. Stayed together beneath the sheets.

Definitely not brought her along to Waypoint Bar.

"There's no way in hell you're going," he told her, chancing a slight movement that angled him between her and the man in the suit. She smiled. It made every part of him wish he could protect every part of her.

"I am. And you're going to let me." She lowered her voice to an almost-whisper. "Who knows Well Water better than you do?"

It was a question that hung in the air as the distance between them grew. Declan watched helplessly as his future family walked away from him.

Remi stopped at the man's shoulder. When she spoke, there was fire in her words and she let the entire room hear them.

"I may not have a badge or a gun but if I find out anyone so much as touched him after we left, you will never see me coming. I'll rip you and your cute little suit to shreds."

The man in the suit chuckled and nodded. He motioned to a woman at the table nearest him. She made her way over and then led Remi out.

Remi didn't look back at him.

Which was good.

Declan was doing all he could to keep from running after her and taking out as many guns as he could along the way. And maybe the Fixers around them knew that. Some pulled their guns higher.

When Remi and the woman were out of the bar the man in the suit moved closer. The smile he'd given Remi's sass was gone. His tone reminded Declan of a tired teacher.

"You will bring Madi, Caleb and Desmond to Well Water Cabin at midnight. You will tell no one else where you are going or why. You will lie if anyone asks where Remi is and you will do it convincingly."

"And if it's just me who shows up?"

The man in the suit shook his head.

"That's not part of the plan."

"And that's not a good answer."

He shrugged.

"I'm not here to give you what you want, Declan. I'm here to tell you the only chance you have at saving one family is to sacrifice the other. Like Remi, you have a choice here. Show up at Well Water with your siblings or don't."

"You're just going to kill us all when we get there," Declan said, trying to tamp down his anger. He motioned to Lawson behind them. He'd seen the blood after Remi had started yelling "coconut." Then he'd pieced it all together. They'd done something to Lawson, hurt him. Now he was dying. "Did you give him the same ultimatum? Show up and die, or don't show up and have someone you love die?"

"No," the man answered, voice clipped. "He never had a choice."

Declan flexed his hands, uncurling and curling them into fists.

"If you're really going to let me go, then let me take him with me."

Dean Lawson was a walking and talking answer. He'd paid for the abduction, which meant he knew the man with the scar who'd done it. Because Declan didn't for one second think that the man across from him now would tell him. And, honestly, if he did Declan would have a hard time believing him.

Lawson was the only silver lining of everything that was happening. A small, barely there sliver.

The man in the suit's lips curled up into a grin.

"Like I said, Dean never had a choice," he said. "He was always meant to die here surrounded by us, an empire made from nothing."

Lawson must have known that.

That was why he'd told Declan and Remi what he'd done.

And that was why he hadn't told them who he'd paid. He couldn't. Not with a room filled with Fixers.

He might have been dying, but he hadn't wanted to die yet.

Neither did Declan.

"I'll go," he said, repeating Remi's words.

The man in the suit nodded. He didn't flinch as Declan moved toward him and instead walked him out of the bar. Remi's car was still parked in the same spot they'd left it in, but she and the woman who had gone after her were nowhere to be seen. In fact, there was no one around at all.

It was just him and the man in the suit.

Declan could take him right then and there. Could pull his gun out, could tackle him, could dish out a punch that splayed him out on the concrete, but Declan found that he believed in the man's sincerity about what would happen if he didn't show up at Well Water Cabin.

He'd lose Remi.

He'd lose his baby.

Nothing was worth that.

Instead, Declan decided to throw himself into the next part of the plan he was being forced into. He started to walk away, but the man in the suit had some last words for him.

"You've seen us over the years. You've seen what we do and you know how good we are at doing it. There's also a lot you haven't seen. There's a lot you don't know. Don't underestimate us, Sheriff." It wasn't bragging. It was a warning. One he recapped. "If you or your siblings tell anyone about what's going on, we'll know, and it won't end well. For any of you or your families."

Declan almost decked the man then.

"I've met a lot of criminals in my life," he said with barely contained rage. "Do you know that most of them have a code? Have *some* honor?"

The man in the suit sighed. He actually sighed. Then he met Declan's eyes with a pensive stare.

"You've seen us over the years, and I've seen you Nashes over the years, too. I've seen you drown. I've seen you shot. I've seen you run into the darkness, run into flames, and run into places where the odds were never in your favor. You may think of yourselves as a normal family dealing in bad luck, but me? I see you as survivors, even if it's by the skin of your teeth. I wouldn't bet against you Nashes. You shouldn't, either."

Declan felt his eyebrow rise. The man in the suit gave a brief smile.

"I may not have *honor*, Mr. Nash," he continued.

"But I am smart. Putting all four of you in one place while threatening your partners and children? Well, anyone would be a fool to believe with certainty that you'd lose in the end. I'm just trying to remain realistic."

Pride stirred in Declan's chest at that, but he made sure not to show it as he asked one last question.

One that he already knew the answer to.

"Your client, the one who hired you to orchestrate all of this—he's the one who took the triplets, isn't he? He's come back for them."

The man in the suit was solemn as he answered.

"He's come back for all of you."

Chapter Twenty

Declan went to Caleb's house first.

It was on the Nash Family Ranch and had been re-
built with the help of the siblings. There was a wraparound porch with a swing on it that Declan himself
had hung. That was where he found his brother sitting
with his wife, Nina, and their son, Parker.

It was just after supper and they looked content.

When they saw Declan they all smiled, even Parker.

It tore at his heart as he lied.

"Hey, Caleb, I need your help on something," he
said after they greeted each other. "Do you mind coming with me?"

Nina was readjusting Parker who had started to
squirm, so she didn't see her husband's look of concern. Declan didn't have that triplet telepathy but he
knew Caleb could feel something was majorly off. He
ran his hand over his wife's back and dipped in for a
kiss against her temple.

"Sure thing," he said to Declan. Then to her, Caleb
said, "Nina, why don't you two go over to Mom's while
we're gone. It would be the perfect time to put together
that plastic play set she's been needing help with for
the kids."

"Oh, you mean the one you boys were supposed to put together but always seem to have something better to do?" she responded, teasing clear in her voice. She sighed, all dramatic. "I suppose I always knew us ladies were the more capable ones. Plus, Parker took too long of a nap today and I don't see him going to bed anytime soon. Maybe this will tire him out."

Caleb and Declan helped her get Parker and his things into the car. While he gave Nina a quick kiss, Declan ruffed up Parker's hair and then gave him a tight hug. Caleb, seeing this, spent more time with the goodbye.

It wasn't until they were in the car and heading to pick up Desmond that Caleb turned to him.

"When you went to that bar you told us all to watch our families because they weren't safe. What's going on? And where's Remi? Why are we in her car but she's not here?"

"I can't tell you yet," Declan said with the stiffness of holding on to a world of worries for far too long. "We need to get Desmond and Madi first."

Caleb didn't argue. He didn't question. He listened to his big brother and Declan loved him for it.

Desmond's house had been built behind the main home they'd grown up in and their mother currently lived in but, from Declan's earlier instructions, he and his wife were at the main house. Nina got to the house a few seconds before they did and Caleb jumped out of the car to help her and Parker into the house. Desmond came back outside with him as Declan hung back.

He loved his mother dearly, but if Caleb was picking up on his tension, then their mother would, too.

Desmond's limp only made Declan feel worse. It

must have shown. Both brothers shared a look between them after seeing Declan.

All three got into the car in silence.

Then they were on Winding Road and heading toward Hidden Hills Inn.

"Julian will know something's wrong," Desmond said without prompting. "He won't let her leave without an explanation. Not unless he knows she won't be in any danger."

Declan gritted his teeth.

"Then she'll have to lie."

"It's that bad?" Caleb asked.

"It'll be worse if anyone thinks something's wrong."

That was enough to keep the boys quiet until they made it to the bed-and-breakfast Madi and Julian lived at and ran. There were no guests currently at the inn, but as soon as they cut the engine Julian appeared in the doorway of the house.

"Let me go get her," Caleb said, grabbing Declan's shoulder to keep him from getting up. "I'm closer with Julian than you two."

Declan didn't argue that. Julian had saved Caleb's life and, since then, the two had become close. In fact, Parker's middle name was Julian. Something that had made the older Julian tear up when he'd found out.

Their friendship was put to the test that night. Declan and Desmond couldn't hear what they said, but it was clear that Julian knew something was wrong, too, and wasn't about to let Madi be a part of it. Then Madi appeared. She joined the conversation and must have strengthened whatever argument Caleb had been making.

Then all three went inside.

Only Madi and Caleb came back out a minute later.

Caleb slid into the back seat and Madi buckled into the front.

They left Hidden Hills Inn and were quiet until they got to where Declan hadn't been in years.

He parked next to the river he had drowned in once. It was on land that no one currently lived on. He got out and the triplets followed.

The night was peaceful and cold.

Declan looked at his watch and began.

"I'm about to give you a lot of information really fast. Information that will be a lot to understand, but we're running low on time so I need you all to take it with a nod and let me keep going. Okay?"

They nodded in unison. No one was smiling. They wouldn't be after he was done, either.

"Justin Redman was supposed to meet Dean Lawson. That meeting was supposed to be secret. Lawson has been, as far as I can guess, dealing with drugs to make his fortune. Or, at least, he was back then. Justin got into a fight with one of his suppliers and then said Lawson's name in an official report. Lawson said he knew if Dad looked into the attack at all that Justin would eventually lead him to what Lawson had been doing and everything he worked for would be taken away. So, he decided to pay someone to abduct me to distract Dad. Lawson said that the man he paid didn't listen and, well, we know what happened instead."

Guilt surged through Declan. Guilt so strong he nearly stopped talking. He should have been the one taken. Not them.

"It's not your fault," Madi said, picking up on his thoughts. "Keep going."

Declan sighed.

"Lawson only told me this because he was dying and he was only still alive to get me and Remi to the bar. It was filled with Fixers." At this part he hesitated. Three pairs of true-blue eyes searched his face.

They were adults now. They had children and spouses. Careers, mortgages, and dental insurance.

Declan had walked Madi down the aisle at her wedding in the backyard of the inn she'd made into a home and business.

He'd been at Caleb's graduation and then sworn him in when he'd become a detective.

He'd stood, arm around Desmond, and looked up at a building that had been erected for the foundation he'd created that helped thousands of people daily.

Declan knew they were adults.

Knew that they could handle themselves. Knew they'd grown into thriving individuals.

Yet, standing there looking at them so close to where their father used to take them all fishing as a family, Declan saw only the little kids who had snuck out to a park to play a game of hide-and-seek and had reappeared three days later all grown-up.

How he wished with all his heart and soul he could have changed their fates.

He took another breath and then ripped off the bandage.

"The man who abducted you is back and he wants us to go to Well Water Cabin tonight to die."

There was a moment where no one said a word.

Then that was the last silence for a while.

"Who is he?" Caleb asked.

"I don't know. Lawson wouldn't say."

"He hired the Fixers, though?" Desmond asked.

Declan nodded.

"Apparently they've been in his back pocket for years. All the bad stuff that's gone down with us all? Them, at his order. I don't know why he's coming after us all now, but he is. The man in the suit, the leader we keep running into, said they'll kill everyone we love if we tell a soul about the meeting."

Madi took a small step forward. She put her hand over her heart.

"You want us to go," she said, voice soft, "because they have Remi, don't they?"

He nodded.

"They know something I should have told you yesterday." He gave them a small smile. Happy for the news, angry at how he had to give it. "She's pregnant... with my kid."

Madi was the first to move. She threw her arms around Declan. Caleb and Desmond weren't far behind.

"Oh, Declan, I'm so happy for you," Madi said into his chest.

"Same here, big guy," Desmond said.

"You'll make an awesome dad," Caleb finished.

"Thanks, guys."

The warmth of familial love spread through him at the words. At the group hug. At the way the future seemed brighter with the thought of a baby in it.

Then that warmth cooled until it was ice.

The Nash children stepped back and all joy was gone.

"I'm not like the Fixers. I'm not going to force you to come to Well Water with me. My best guess is this man wants to talk and then he'll kill us all. But there's no guarantee he won't kill us all the moment we drive up." Declan felt the resolution in his heart before the words to back it up left his lips. "But I'm going. Even if it's only to give Remi a better chance at escaping. I just—I wanted you all to know. You've deserved answers for most of your lives. I wanted you to at least get some of them."

The triplets didn't even look at each other.

Madi spoke first.

"You're wrong," she said with bite. "Saving your family, getting our answers, and finally giving that son of a bitch what's coming to him. We deserve it all."

"She's right," Desmond said with vigor. "We're going and we're going to save Remi and we're going to finally put this mystery to rest."

Caleb nodded. Declan was surprised to see him smirk. In fact, he was surprised to see all of them so calm. The man who had scarred them, locked them up and changed all of their lives because of this was waiting for them.

Waiting to kill them.

Yet, there they were.

Suddenly those three children looked exactly as they should have to him.

Two men and a woman ready for justice.

Caleb captured the sentiment well.

"Whoever this man is, whatever his reason is for wanting us, he's overlooked one devastating fact. We're grown-up now and we won't be as easy to push around."

Madi and Desmond agreed.

Declan smiled at this brothers and sister.

"Then it's settled," he said. "Now, we have less than three hours to come up with a plan to find justice for our father, bring peace to our mother, get answers for us, and save the woman I love and our kid. Any objections?"

Not a one of them made a peep.

THE BASEMENT WASN'T as bad as Remi had pictured. In fact, in any other circumstance, she would have thought it was cozy.

A few steps from the stairs was a door that led into a spacious room with a kitchenette in the corner and an open door that showed a bathroom on the other side. The light fixtures were nice and did a good job of lighting up the place, and even the kitchenette was pleasing to look at.

What changed the feel of the room in such a sudden and violent way was the three small cots against the wall and the four locks on the door, reminding her just what the triplets had gone through all those years ago.

When the woman in the pantsuit locked all four locks, Remi quaked in fear. She was alone in the room and leaned into the privacy. She cried. She hoped she hadn't left Declan to die and she hoped she hadn't just led herself and their child to do the same.

She felt exhausted.

She felt helpless.

And then she felt sick.

Remi ran to the bathroom with tears blurring her vision and threw up in the sink.

Because of course morning sickness didn't take a break. Not even when she was being held captive. She tried to compose herself after the deed and instead was hit with another wave of nausea.

This time she threw up in the toilet.

After that she leaned against the wall and cried some more.

It wasn't until a man cleared his throat that Remi realized someone was in the doorway.

The man in the suit from Waypoint was holding a bottle of water and a packet of gum.

"There might be power now, but there's no running water in the house, I'm afraid," he said. "And if you die tonight I'd bet it would feel nicer to die with somewhat fresh-feeling breath."

He stepped back to let her out of the bathroom and shook the bottle when she didn't take it.

"Both are in sealed containers. Not taking them is only going to make *you* more uncomfortable. Not me."

Remi was thirsty and her mouth tasted awful. Denying either point didn't make them go away. She relented and took both, but not without a severe look she hoped hurt the man.

"Being kind to a pregnant woman you're about to kill doesn't make you a good person, you know," she said hotly.

The man shrugged.

"Who says I want to be a good person?"

That sent a shiver of fear down Remi's spine. Whether she wanted to feel it or not.

"But, if it makes you feel better, I won't be the one killing you. That's not part of the plan."

Remi opened the bottle, breaking its seal, and went back to the bathroom to wash her mouth out. When she came back she took a long drink of water and popped two pieces of gum.

Both made her feel light-years better.

So did her barb at the man.

"For someone who thinks they're so clever, it's interesting to find out you're nothing more than someone else's bitch."

The man snorted, trying to seem like he'd blown off the insult, but Remi saw it.

She saw the nostrils flare, saw the anger pass over him.

She'd hit a nerve.

Because she'd spoken the truth.

But the man was more disciplined than she had hoped. He was back to smiling.

"For being the bait that's going to lead almost an entire family to slaughter, you sure are cocky."

Remi wanted to say something clever, something that hurt him, but she didn't have his discipline. She kept quiet and went to one of the cots, and he eventually left without another word.

Then there she sat for hours.

In that time she thought about her father, her brothers, her mother and stepfather, her job, and the Nashes. She thought about Declan and their unborn child the most.

By the time the door to the basement opened, Remi had come to a decision. The only catch was that they all had to survive the night.

Remi didn't recognize the man who walked in but she recognize did the scar on his hand.

The man who had taken the triplets.

The man who wanted them all to die.

And he'd come to see her first.

Chapter Twenty-One

There were at least twenty men and women wearing suits surrounding the cabin. It was such an odd sight to Declan. For the last decade Well Water had been forgotten by most of the world, a desolate structure that was visited by him only for the occasional maintenance. Before that it had been his father visiting. Before that it had been a circus.

Now the abandoned cabin in the woods had too many people in and around it. People dressed for the boardroom with guns in hand like they were going to war.

"If it all goes sideways I'm doing everything in my power to get Remi out," Declan said after he found a place to park among a cluster of inconspicuous cars and trucks. "That includes dying. And you're going to let me if that means you can get out, too."

No one rebuffed him, but Desmond tried to be reassuring.

"This will work. I know it will."

No one backed him up but no one disagreed.

They'd had three hours to come up with a plan to save Remi and themselves without weapons, without help, and without knowing how many people would be at the cabin.

Their plan was at best risky; at worst it was downright idiotic.

And it was all they had.

A man came to the door as Declan got out. He was sneering. It was the one man he'd chased across Main Street. He ran a hand through his red hair, exposing the holster and the gun in it against his side.

"Howdy, Sheriff. If you'd be so kind to allow my associates to check you all for any knives, guns, bombs, *et cetera*, that would be mighty kind of you." He was mocking them but Declan allowed the search. Just as his siblings did. The redhead seemed surprised that none of them had any weapons of any kind on them. No cell phones, either.

Those were back at the river, GPS on, and each holding video recordings for their families and law enforcement. They were hoping their plan would work but prepared if it didn't. Watching his siblings make their videos for their kids and spouses tore Declan apart. They'd noticed and told him again this was their choice to make and they'd made it.

Tonight, for better or worse, one nightmare would end.

Redhead led them inside and cut right to the living room. Declan felt the tension coming off the triplets. This was the first time Madi and Desmond had been back to Well Water since they'd escaped. For Caleb it had been a few years, but that didn't matter.

This place was their personal hell.

One that was filled to the brim with strangers waiting for them.

Among the crowd was the man in the suit. Still the

fanciest in the group. He smiled when they stopped in front of him.

"You didn't bring any weapons and you didn't ask for any help. I don't know if you aren't that smart or if you all are just a bit too confident."

"You gave us terms and we followed them," Declan said. "I'd say that makes us, at least, respectful."

The man in the suit nodded. He was pleased.

"It does make everything go smoothly when you follow the rules."

Declan looked around the room. He knew where she probably was but still had to ask.

"Where's Remi?"

The man's smile faded. He became the ideal image of a businessman.

"She's downstairs with the man of the hour." He held up his hand to stop Declan from saying how much he didn't like that. "She's fine. We can go see her now."

He nodded to the people around them. Most stayed but Redhead, a woman with a sneer and three others followed. They walked behind their group as Declan followed the man in the suit to the only place that was ever an option for this horrible meeting.

Declan turned to his siblings as they got to the top of the stairs to the basement. He lowered his voice.

"You're not little kids anymore."

Caleb nodded. Desmond and Madi grabbed hands and stood straighter.

Then the Nash children followed the man in the suit down into the room they wanted to go in least. Right up to the smiling face of a man Declan had never seen.

Yet the triplets had.

Madi made a guttural, primal growl.

Caleb balled his fists.

Desmond lowered his head but kept eye contact, jaw clenched.

Declan looked past the man at Remi.

Then he yelled.

Guns came out and up from the man in the suit, Redhead and the woman. Declan stopped in his tracks.

Remi was lying across one of the cots, blood visible across the side of her face.

"She's not dead, not yet," the man said. "She got a little too mouthy so I showed her what that gets you in my house. I hit her a little too hard, I suppose. She fell right over like a twig in the wind."

Declan was absolutely seething. His chest was rising and falling in rage-fueled pants. He turned to the man in the suit.

"You said she was fine," he roared.

The man in the suit shared a look with the other. He didn't seem too happy, but he offered Declan no explanation or apology.

Then Declan was staring back at the man he was going to kill.

The triplets had tried their best to describe what their abductor looked like after they were rescued. Madi had talked about his eyes so dark they looked black and made you feel cold when they were on you. Brown hair like dry mud and messy like mud, too. Caleb had focused on his stature. He wasn't too tall but was wide. Strong but slow. Not overweight but not rail thin. Average. Desmond, on the other hand, had gotten more emotional with his descriptions.

One had always stuck with Declan.

"He was quiet but looked like he wanted to break

us just because he could," eight-year-old Desmond had said. It was a statement that had held more weight than the others, considering that same man had badly broken his leg during the initial attack and then made him suffer with it for days.

Now, standing close enough to strangle him, Declan saw what young Desmond had seen.

The man wanted to break them. All of them.

And Declan was over it.

"What do you want?"

The man kept smiling.

"My name is William Gallagher," he started. "And I tell you that to remind you that you won't be leaving this cabin, so having my name does nothing for you. As for you, well, I'll never forget you." He looked past Declan's shoulder and listed the triplets off as he looked at them. "Desmond, Madeline and Caleb. It's been a while, hasn't it? I've been keeping tabs on you three. Late congratulations on your marriages and children. Your careers are also touching. Not what I would have picked had I had a choice, but it doesn't really matter in the end, does it?"

Declan had to breathe in slowly through his nose and let out a breath through his mouth. It was the only way to keep from running at William.

He seemed to sense Declan's struggle with his rage.

"Dean wanted me to take you. Did you know that?" William said. "But if Dean wanted a distraction by taking one of Michael Nash's kids, boy howdy at the distraction taking three would be." His smile twisted upside down. Anger flashed across his expression. "I had everything planned out. But what I hadn't foreseen was how much heat taking you three would be.

And after you escaped?" He shook his head, anger apparent on his face. "Dean decides not to pay me. Skips town. So what do I have to do? Go underground. Give up *my* life to hide as the entire country looks for my face. My scarred hand. *Me*. And all because I *gave a damn about you dying*."

At this he looked at Desmond.

What was more famous than the abduction itself was how the triplets had escaped. After having his leg broken and untreated, by day three Desmond was in immense pain and in a bad way. Madi and Caleb knew that if they didn't get him help soon he could die. So, in a last-ditch effort, they'd decided to have him play dead.

Up until this point William had only ever brought them food. But when they started screaming and crying, saying that Desmond had stopped breathing, he'd run in to check. The moment he was trying to find a pulse was the moment everything changed.

It didn't matter who you asked, neither Madi, Caleb nor Desmond could remember exactly what happened next. The best they could describe it was that they'd simply synced up. Become a hive mind. They'd attacked William as one unit and gotten to the other side of the door to lock it. Together they'd run into the woods, bloody, broken and scarred.

When Caleb had brought the cops back to the cabin after they'd been found, William was gone.

"We couldn't have done it had you not broken my leg in the first place," Desmond shot back.

William let out a low, tense laugh.

"You don't understand the danger you're in, son. For years I missed out on the life I wanted, living in the shadows, waiting. So I decided to spend those years building something that could do what I'd been forced to do. All for the purpose of destroying everyone who forced me to abandon what I'd loved."

"You started the Fixers," Caleb said.

William nodded.

"And I used them to torment you all the last few years. Help those who despised you, who wanted to harm those you loved." He shared a look with the man in the suit. It wasn't a kind one. He didn't explain it, either. "You might have prevailed each time but you also were waiting. Waiting for the other shoe to drop." William extended his hands out wide. "Now it has."

"Why now?" Madi asked, voice sharp.

"I wanted you to build your lives. Make careers. Fall in love. Create families. I was getting restless waiting for our dear sheriff to find someone. But then his truck broke down and, well, the mouthy one behind me came into the picture. That was enough for me to start."

"So, Lydia, she's a Fixer." Declan said it because he already believed it to be true. "She used Jonah to get to Remi."

William snorted.

"You want to know a fun thing about small towns? You get a happy coincidence once in a while. See, Lydia was brought in only to do whatever plan I saw fit. She was supposed to blend in first and build up some grace with the locals until I had that plan. And what better family to attach to than those who ran the Heartland Ranch? Childhood friends to the Nashes? It was a shock to us all when we realized that, not only were you and Miss Hudson no longer just friends, that she was pregnant with your child." His grin was sickening. "Having Lydia and the others try to take the mother of a future Nash child, even though it didn't work out the way I wanted? Well that was almost as fun as planting a note in a wall, knowing that just the mention of it would drive you mad. Watching you Nashes obsess has become a fun pastime of mine throughout the years. I think, when this is over, that's what I'll miss most."

William took a small step forward. Not close enough that Declan could lunge at him but close enough that Declan's muscles started tensing up, ready for anything. His mirth was gone. He had gotten to what he really wanted to say. "I want you all to know that your violent deaths will become a horror story every man, woman and child will know. A nighttime terror that will haunt your families, your loved ones, your friends, your co-workers. Strangers. I had to live in the shadows and you'll never leave the spotlight. Not even in death."

He turned to the man in the suit. He nodded, but neither man made a move. William looked at Declan as he added one last thing.

"Any last words before *all* of you meet horrible ends?"

Declan took a quick breath.

Then he turned to the man in the suit and made sure his words were absolutely sincere.

This was it.

"I want to hire you."

The man in the suit raised his eyebrow. Redhead and the woman laughed. So did William. The man didn't.

"Come again?"

Declan turned to face him completely, angling away from William. So did Madi, Caleb and Desmond.

"My father was a good man," he started. "But when he couldn't find who was behind the abduction, he became obsessed. Every day, every night. Weekends. He worked the case until it was all he did. Holidays, birthdays. He started to hate every special day that families are supposed to enjoy together. They were reminders that the years were going by and he was no closer to figuring it out. He pushed my mother away first, and then, when we all started to move on, he dug in so deep that he sacrificed himself to it. The obsession. Then he died, and even though I knew not to become him because I'd seen what it did, I still followed his example." Declan motioned to the room around him. "I own this place. This hell pit. Because *he* did and he willed it to me. No explanation. No note. Just a deed and an unspoken direction." That was something no one in his family knew. He could feel six baby blue eyes look in his direction. He kept on. "And I went into law enforcement and I started to obsess. I started walking that line between doing what I wanted and doing what he wanted."

Declan glanced at William. He still looked smug.

"When William took the kids, he ended whatever chance we had at a normal life. That includes you." This part was a gamble, but it was a theory they had kicked around before coming to Well Water.

Declan motioned to his hand. To the scar that matched William's.

"You were right earlier. I don't know much about you, but I *do* know you follow contracts. You never betray them. *That's* your code. And since William is your father, I'm going to assume he doesn't have a contract, does he?"

A pin could have dropped and they would have heard it.

The man in the suit didn't dispute a word he'd said.

Which meant they had been right. The man in the suit wasn't the boss, he was their abductor's son.

"You want to hire me to kill my father?" he asked after a moment.

Declan shook his head.

"I want to hire you and the Fixers to get Remi, take her to the hospital and tell them she's pregnant, and then do what you all do best. Disappear." Declan looked around the room to the suits ready to mock such an outrageous idea. He pointed to William, who was looking less smug. "At his prime he was bested by three eight-year-olds. Then he spent most of his life plotting against them when he could have easily killed us time and time again. You've been around here. You know who we are. We're fathers and mothers and husbands and wives. We're law enforcement. We're charitable and charming and kind. This town loves us. If you kill us? All because an old man's pissed he messed up a job by not following orders in the first place? You'll be hunted to the ground by our loved ones. And if they don't find you, they'll have kids that will grow up and hunt your kids down. The cycle will never end."

Declan went back to the man in the suit.

"Let's show our fathers we're stronger than they ever were."

William made a noise. A snort that clearly said he thought Declan was crazy.

But he wasn't paying attention to the suits. Their expressions had turned thoughtful and their gazes had turned to the man in the suit.

He considered Declan. He considered his father. Then he looked at the scar on his hand.

That was when Declan knew.

"There's money in the trunk of the car, where the spare tire is. I don't know your going rate, but it should be enough."

The man turned back to him. He nodded.

"Your contract has been accepted."

"What!" William was livid. His son paid him no mind.

"We'll take Miss Hudson to the hospital and let them know she's pregnant. Then you won't ever see us again." He nodded to Redhead and the woman. They went to Remi and scooped her up. Declan wished it could be him, but the Nash siblings had already guessed that while the man in the suit might accept their contract, he wouldn't go so far as to interfere with his dad.

The other suits seemed to agree and, just like that, the man in the suit became the real boss of the Fixers. He saw to Remi being taken to the stairs and only stopped at the door. He turned around and looked his father up and down. His last words before he left the room, however, were for them all.

"There's a gun in the middle kitchen drawer. Good luck."

The door shut and the sound of it locking became the background noise to a whirl of motion.

William was faster than Declan would ever give him credit for. He couldn't grab him in time. None of them could though they tried.

Madi got to him just as he flung the drawer open. She grabbed at his face, lashing out with her nails. It tore at his skin, making him yell so loud it hurt Declan's ears. Still he pulled the gun out and turned. Desmond gave his own battle cry as he hit the man in the gut with a devastating tackle. He, Madi and William slammed backward into the wall. The gun hit the ground and skidded away but William kept struggling.

Caleb joined the fray next with a punch that hit William's face so hard it echoed.

Declan scooped up the gun. He aimed it at William but there was no reason to use it. William had gone slack from the hit even though Madi held one arm, Desmond held the other, and Caleb had his hands against his chest so he wouldn't move an inch from where he was.

Despite everything, Declan smiled.

The Nash triplets had, once again, bested their abductor.

He wasn't dead but, this time, there wasn't a chance in hell that he was getting away.

Chapter Twenty-Two

Remi was shocked.

By many, many things.

First, she was shocked to wake up in her car being driven by the man in the suit. They were alone, which made her feel such an intense wave of anger and anguish that she nearly got sick again. The throbbing headache from being knocked out by his boss in the basement wasn't helping.

"Declan hired me to take you to the hospital," he'd said when she moved. "From there you can call for help to go out to the cabin. It'll only be the Nash family and one other man."

Remi hadn't known what to say or believe but, sure enough, he'd dropped her off right outside the hospital doors. Then he'd gotten out of her car, which apparently Declan had driven to the cabin, and stepped into one that had been following them.

And then he'd left.

The second shock was, after sending almost every member in law enforcement to Well Water Cabin, she got a call from Declan. Remi blamed the pregnancy hormones on how hard she cried at hearing his voice.

The shocks only got better after that.

Remi was seen by a doctor alongside her mother, who had finally made it to the hospital. Together they learned something that made them both freak out and squeal at the same time. After that Remi found out her father was awake and asking for her.

She hugged him fiercely, told him what she'd just found out and then the decisions she'd come to while being trapped in the basement. She'd cried again as he'd teared up. Josh and Jonah were next on the list for some familial love and the good news.

Then Declan arrived as she settled into a seat in the lobby to wait for him.

He ran in, saw her and was upon her before she could stand. He only broke their kiss to ask a volley of questions.

"Are you okay? Why are you out here? How's the baby?"

Remi laughed.

"I have a headache but am okay. I came out here to wait for you." Remi took a deep breath, then let it out. "And the babies are fine."

Declan's eyes tripled in size.

He smiled like a wild man.

"Babies?"

Remi held up her fingers.

"It's still too early to really tell anyone but, there are two sacs, Declan. *Two.*"

She laughed, unable to stop the giddiness.

Declan shook his head, then was laughing.

"I'm guessing that means you're okay with the idea of having twins?"

"Are kidding me? I'd love it!" He laughed again, throwing his head back. Then he wrapped his arms around her. "Man, my family is going to flip. The singleton Nash might have twins?"

He pulled away from her and dipped low for another kiss.

Then those green eyes she loved were on her. Suddenly his expression changed to a serious one.

"Huds, we said we were going to have a talk about the future and here's what I'm thinking. I want to move to Colorado with you," he said. "I want to raise our kids together, in the same place. I want to wake up next to you and go to sleep with you in my arms."

That was the second biggest shock of the night.

"You'd give up being sheriff? You'd leave your family?"

Declan put his hand on her stomach. Remi could have melted.

"You're my family, too. And I'd cross oceans for you if that's what you wanted."

Butterflies dislodged and had a frenzy in her stomach.

"Well, look at that. My wild cowboy ready to hang up his hat for me." She ran a hand across his cheek. Every part of her softened. "I suppose this is a good time to tell you my new life plan. I have a feeling you're going to really like it."

ONE CHRISTMAS PASSED.

And then another.

By the third Christmas, so much had changed.

And so much hadn't.

Declan sat on his horse wearing his cowboy hat. Desmond and Caleb wore theirs while Madi was sitting on the fence next to the stable wearing her boots. She was pregnant again and her bump was the reason she'd decided to sit on the fence rather than a horse. Still, she wanted to hang around her siblings until Julian showed up so they could go home.

"You know, Ma is bringing a date to Christmas Eve dinner, right?" she asked, no hard feelings in the words. Between Desmond and Riley becoming parents, Caleb and Nina expanding the retreat, and Madi and Julian preparing for their fourth child, spending time together had lessened. They still had Sunday dinners together, but that was at their mother's, which meant gossiping about her hadn't been ideal.

"It's about time," Desmond said with a smile. Caleb mirrored it.

"Y'all do know she's been seeing Christian in secret for over a year, right?"

Declan laughed.

"Yeah, it's not like you can keep a secret in this town. I'm glad she's making it public, though. Now we don't have to pretend like we have no idea why he keeps showing up around the ranch even though he lives in Kilwin."

Madi laughed and bounced her foot in the air. She rubbed her belly.

"I think Dad would approve, despite him and Christian's differences from back in the day."

They all agreed. During what felt like a lifetime ago, their father had believed Christian was connected to the triplets' abduction. It had put a wall of resentment and discord between the men and the Nash family. That was until Christian had proven he was a great man after helping Madi survive the family's first brush with the Fixers. Since then he'd become friends with the family. More so with their mother. Dorothy Nash had been nothing but happy the last year or so and they knew it wasn't all because they'd put William Gallagher behind bars for good. Though, having him locked up had definitely helped.

For a man who had spent years cultivating a group who would rather die than spill their secrets, William became a very talkative man once in handcuffs. He said he did so to take Dean Lawson down with him, detailing their arrangement and what had really happened all those years ago. Lawson, who had passed away at the bar that night, lost the reputation he'd built for years, as well. And that had been William's goal.

He was big on trying to hurt people, even after death.

As for his son, the man in the suit, he mostly stayed true to his word. A month after everything had settled down, he visited Declan outside of the grocery store of all places.

"I don't think you understand what 'I won't see you ever again' means," Declan had greeted. The man in the suit had smirked.

"Don't worry, this is a quick social visit."

Declan knew the man wasn't good, but he couldn't bring himself to be wary of him, either. Especially since the Fixers had been rumored to have disappeared from, not only Overlook, but all of Wildman County.

"For what it's worth, I'm sorry about your dad," Declan had found himself saying. He'd later blame the kindness on the fact that the man had taken Remi to the hospital and, honestly, had saved all of their lives by taking the contract in the first place.

"For what it's worth, I'm sorry about yours, too."

They'd shared a small companionable silence. One

of understanding. Then they were back to their normal roles.

"You know, this is the only time I'll let you go free," Declan had said. "So after you leave my sight, you better stay out of it."

The man in the suit had laughed.

"Remember how we agreed that you don't know me?" he'd asked. "Well, let me enlighten you on something. While my dad was amassing money to help with your destruction, I was stealing and saving it. The second I'm out of your sight I'll be heading to a private airfield and on my way to a beautiful, remote beach somewhere very tropical. And *then* I'll disappear."

"Still, very brazen of you to show back up here again."

The man in the suit started to walk toward a car near them.

"I can afford to be brazen, Sheriff. I bet you still haven't found *any* record of my existence, have you?" He'd said it with a smile and he'd been right. No one had been able to find any hint that he existed, not even his name. "Don't feel bad. While my father spent decades waiting to reveal himself when the right time came, I spent the same time waiting to disappear."

The man in the suit had pointed to Declan's truck.

"Consider that an early baby shower gift," he'd said. "For what it's worth, I don't hate that you Nashes might now have a shot at a happy ending. And consider this the only time I'll ever break a contract."

He'd already been gone by the time Declan saw what he'd left in Fiona's front seat.

It was the bag of money he and his siblings had collected to pay for their contract with the Fixers back at

Well Water. On top of the bag were two ribbons. One pink, one blue.

Declan and Remi had received another gift after they'd married that he believed to be from the man. It was a postcard of an island with well wishes and an exorbitant amount of money that they'd decided to give to charity. The card had been signed "the Whisperer."

Other than that, Declan hadn't seen or heard of the man in the suit or the Fixers since.

"I think Dad would have liked this, too," Caleb said, bringing Declan back to the present. He motioned to the four of them. "Us, I mean, but, especially you."

Declan was surprised to see those three sets of baby blues turn to him. Caleb continued.

"We realized this morning when we were helping set up the Christmas lights that we somehow have been idiots and haven't told you this outright and in clear words. So, get ready for the mushiness."

They all shared a look.

Desmond spoke next.

"Thank you, Declan."

He didn't understand.

"For what?"

Madi's smile was small but true.

"For giving us peace."

It was such a simple statement but it did something Declan hadn't thought possible. A weight had been lifted. The guilt, the heartache… It all blew away in the nice December breeze.

Movement caught his eye at the edge of the field.

"You guys are going to make me cry in front of my wife," he said with a genuine smile.

Madi laughed.

"Like you didn't blubber when Michael and Lysa were born," she teased.

"And don't forget that tearing up you did at the wedding," Caleb added with a grin.

Declan laughed and didn't deny either accusation. Other than his kids being born, his wedding to Remi had been one of the best days of his life.

It had been a small, perfect ceremony held in the no-man's-land between the Nash Family Ranch and Hudson Heartland. To show they approved of Declan, Gale Hudson had officiated while Josh and Jonah had walked Remi down the aisle of flowers and grass. Her mother and stepfather had held the twins while his mother and Christian had distracted the rest of the grandchildren. Every Nash sibling and spouse were either groomsmen or bridesmaids.

"Don't act like you didn't drop a tear or two," Desmond said to Caleb.

Caleb in turn swatted at him, which riled Desmond up. Soon they were racing around the barn and up toward Caleb's house. A car started up the drive and Madi waved Declan off.

"That's Julian," she said. "You can go on to your wife now, Sheriff."

"If I could, I'd swoop down and kiss you on the cheek, little sister," he said, half-mocking. She laughed.

"And if I wasn't the size of a beach ball I'd stand up and accept it."

Declan laughed and soon he was off riding. He slowed as Remi did, meeting him in the middle.

She was as beautiful as a sunset and he told her as much.

"You keep sweet-talking me like that, Mr. Nash, and

we might be catching up to Madi and Julian's kid count tonight."

Declan chuckled.

"We did say we'd start sometime after the kids were walking," he pointed out. "Though now I can't see where the sense in that is."

"We're attracted to adventure, I suppose. Why else would we be building a house with a set of twins and two stressful jobs?"

Declan ticked the reasons off on his fingers as he listed them.

"Because my house was too small. We're sentimental fools who thought it would be nice to live on the same stretch of land we got married on. We didn't plan to get pregnant with twins, though I'm over the moon it happened. *And* because we actually love our jobs."

Remi, who was now chief financial officer at Desmond's foundation, nodded at each point.

"Don't you come at me with answers that make sense."

"Oh, I'll come at you with something all right, cowgirl."

He winked at her, which made Remi throw her head back as she laughed again.

Then she was all smiles.

"Only if you can catch me, cowboy."

Remi was off on her horse, pointed toward their home, faster than Declan could whistle.

Before he followed after her, Declan turned around and looked at his family and the ranch he'd been born on and would probably spend the rest of his days around.

Caleb, Desmond and Madi were still hanging around, laughing, talking and riding. His mother was up at the house, not five minutes away, singing Christmas carols and baking gingerbread cookies, he had no doubt.

Declan had spent years worrying about his family. Worrying that they'd never be whole again. That they'd never *truly* find happiness. That life wasn't as kind as it was mean.

Yet, sitting astride his horse in a field he used to ride with his father, Declan Nash *really* did feel it, too.

Peace.

* * * * *

Prologue

Billy Reed looked down at the body and wished he could punch something. Hard.

"This is ridiculous," Suzy said at his side. "She's not even eighteen."

His partner was right. Courtney Brooks had turned sixteen two weeks ago. The car she had been found in was a birthday present from her father. Billy knew this because he'd known of the girl since she was in middle school. She was a part of one of the many families in the small town of Carpenter, Alabama, who had lived there through at least two generations.

And now she was dead in the back seat of a beat-up Honda.

"Anyone tell her folks yet?" Billy asked. He'd arrived on the scene five minutes after his partner, Suzanne Simmons, had. By the time he'd cut through lunchtime traffic and bumped down the dirt road in his Crown Vic to the spot where poor Courtney had met her end, a set of paramedics, the deputy who had first responded to the call and the boy who had found her were all gathered around, waiting for what was next.

"No, Rockwell wanted to make the call," Suzy answered. Billy raised his eyebrow, questioning why the sheriff would do that when he hadn't even come to the crime scene yet, and she continued. "He's fishing buddies with her dad. He heard Marty call in the name."

Billy could imagine their leader, a man north of sixty with a world of worries to match, breaking the bad news from behind his desk. He'd let his stare get lost in the grain of the oak while he broke a family's heart with news no parents should ever receive.

"There's no signs of foul play, as far as I can tell," Suzy commented. One of the EMTs broke off from the car and headed toward them.

"We both know what this is, Suzy," Billy said. The anger he was nearly getting used to began to flood his system. The deputy could save the EMT time by telling the man he already knew what had killed her. An overdose of a drug called Moxy. The current scourge of Riker County. However, Billy's mother had taught him the importance of being polite. So he listened to the man say that he thought Courtney had been gone a few hours before they'd gotten there, and if the paramedic was a betting man, he'd put his money on an overdose.

"I've already taken pictures, but I'd like to look around again, just in case," Suzy said. Billy was about to follow when a call over the radio drew him to his car instead. He asked dispatch to repeat.

"The sheriff wants you here, Billy," she said. "Now."

That gave him pause but he confirmed he understood. Suzy must have heard, too. She waved him away, saying she could handle it from here. Billy's eye caught the teen who had found Courtney. He was standing with Marty, one of the other deputies from the department, and they were deep in discussion. Every few words he'd glance back at the girl. And each time he looked closer to losing it. He'd likely never seen a dead body before, and judging by his expression, he'd never forget it, either. It made Billy grind his teeth.

No one in Riker County should have that problem. At least, not if Billy had a say about it.

It had been six months since an influx of Moxy hit the county. In that time, Billy had seen four overdoses and an escalation of violence, two of those incidents ending in murder. For all intents and purposes, Moxy brought out the worst tendencies in people and then energized them. While Riker County, its sheriff's department and police departments had had their problems with narcotics in the past, the new drug and its ever-elusive supplier had caught them woefully off guard. It was a fact that kept Billy up at night and one that stayed with him as he drove through the town and then cut his engine in the department's parking lot.

Movement caught his eye, distracting his thoughts, and he realized he was staring at the very man who had called him in. Billy exited the cruiser and leaned against it when the man made no move to go inside the building, arms folded over his chest. Sheriff Rockwell put his cigarette out and stopped in front of him. He looked more world-weary than he had the day before.

"I'm going to cut to the chase, Reed," the sheriff said, leaving no room for greetings. "We need to find the Moxy supplier and we need to find him now. You understand?"

"Yessir," Billy said, nodding.

"Until that happens, I want you to work exclusively on trying to catch the bastard."

"What about Detective Lancaster?" Billy asked. Jamie Lancaster's main focus had been on finding something on the supplier since the second overdose had been reported.

"Lancaster is crap, and we both know it," the sheriff said. "His drive left the second we all had to take a pay cut. No, what we need now is someone whose dedication isn't made by his salary." The sheriff clapped Billy on the shoulder. "In all of my years, I've learned that there's not much that can stand against a person protecting their own. You love not only this town, but the entire county like it's family, Billy."

"I do," Billy confirmed, already feeling his pride swelling.

The sheriff smiled, briefly, and then went stone cold.

"Then go save your family."

Two months later, Billy was sitting in a bar in Carpenter known as the Eagle. In the time since he'd talked to the sheriff in the parking lot, he'd chased every lead known to the department. He'd worked long, hard hours until, finally, he'd found a name.

Bryan Copeland.

A businessman in his upper fifties with thinning gray hair and an affinity for wearing suits despite the Alabama heat, he was running the entire operation from Kipsy. It was the only city within the Riker County Sheriff's Department purview, Carpenter being one of three towns. But where he kept the drugs—whether it was through the city or towns— and when he moved them were mysteries. Which was the reason Billy hadn't had the pleasure of arresting him yet. They couldn't prove anything, not even after two drug dealers admitted who their boss was. Because, according to the judge and Bryan's fancy lawyer, there was no hard evidence. So that was why, late on a Thursday night, Billy Reed was seated at the Eagle finishing off his second beer when a woman sat down next to him and cleared her throat.

"Are you Deputy Reed? Billy Reed?" she asked, voice dropping to a whisper. Billy raised his eyebrow. He didn't recognize the woman. And he would have remembered if he had met her before.

She had long black hair that framed a clear and determined face. Dark eyes that openly searched his expression, trying to figure him out for whatever reason, high cheekbones, pink, pink lips, and an expression that was split between contemplation and caution. All details that created a truly beautiful woman. One who had the deputy's full attention.

"Yes, that's me," he answered. "But I don't think I've had the pleasure."

The woman, who he had placed just under his own age of thirty-two, pasted on a smile and cut her eyes around them before answering.

"I believe you're trying to build a case against my father." Billy immediately went on red alert, ready to field whatever anger or resentment the woman had with him. However, what she said next changed everything. Her dark eyes hardened, resolute. With a voice free of any doubt, she gave Billy exactly what he needed. "And I can help you do just that."

Chapter One

Three years later, Billy Reed was kicking off his shoes, digging into his DVR and turning on a game he'd been meaning to watch for a month. During the season he hadn't had time to keep up with teams or scores but he liked the white noise it produced. And, maybe if it was a close enough game, his focus might leave his work long enough to enjoy it.

He popped off the cap of his beer and smiled at the thought.

He'd been the Riker County sheriff for under two years, although he'd lived his entire life within its lines, just as his father had before him. It was one of the reasons Sheriff Rockwell had personally endorsed Billy to take his place when he'd decided it was time to retire.

"You always want what's best for Riker and I can't think of a better outlook for a sheriff," Rockwell had said. "After what you've helped do for this place already, I can't imagine a better fit."

Billy's eyes traveled to a framed picture of the former sheriff shaking his hand. The picture had been taken during a press conference that had come at one of the most rewarding moments of Billy's career as deputy, when drug supplier Bryan Copeland had been locked behind bars for good.

He didn't know it at the time, but that case would help him become the man he was today—the sheriff who was trying desperately to pretend there was such a thing as a night off. He took a pull on his beer. But as soon as he tried to move his focus to the game on the TV, his phone came to life.

So much for trying.

The caller ID said Suzy. Not a name he'd wanted to see until the next morning. He sighed and answered.

"I just got home, Suzy," he said.

Suzanne Simmons didn't attempt to verbally walk carefully around him. Never mind the fact that he was the boss now. He didn't expect her to, either. She'd been his friend for years.

"That ain't my problem, Sheriff," she snapped. "What *is* my problem is Bernie Lutz's girlfriend drunk and yelling at my desk."

Billy put his beer down on the coffee table, already resigned to the fact that he wouldn't be able to enjoy the rest of it.

"Say again?"

He'd known Suzy since they were in middle school and knew that the short pause she took before answering was her way of trying to rearrange her thoughts without adding in the emotion. As chief deputy she couldn't be seen flying off the handle when her anger flared. The sheriff's right-hand man, or woman in this case, needed to appear more professional than that. Though that hadn't stopped her from expressing herself within the privacy of his office from time to time.

"Bernie Lutz, you remember him?" she asked. "Short guy with that tattoo of his ex-wife on his right arm?"

Billy nodded to himself, mind already going through old files.

"Yeah, drug dealer until he went the straight and narrow about a year ago." Billy remembered something else. "He said he found Jesus and started doing community service when he got out of lockup."

"Well, it looks like he just found a whole lot more than Jesus," Suzy said. "Jessica, his girlfriend, just ran into the station yelling about finding him dead in a ditch when she went out to their house. She's asking for our protection now. And, by asking, I mean yelling for it."

Billy ran his hand down his face, trying to get the facts straight.

"So, did you check out if what she said was true?" he asked.

"Working on it. I tried to get her to come with me to show me exactly where she found him but, Billy, she freaked out big-time. Said they could still be watching her."

Billy stood, already looking for the shoes he'd kicked off when he'd thought his night off might stick. His cowboy hat was always easier to find. He scooped it up off the back of the couch and put it on. The act alone helped focus him even more.

"They?" he asked.

"She claims that two men came to the house last week and asked Bernie for drugs, and when he said he didn't deal anymore, they told him they'd come back and get them both." Suzy lowered her voice a little. "To be honest, I think Jessica is under the influence of *something* right now—why didn't she call us from the scene?—but I sent Dante out there to check it out. I just wanted to give you a heads-up if this thing ends up escalating and poor Bernie really is in a ditch somewhere."

Billy spotted his shoes and went to put them on.

"Go ahead and get descriptions of the men she claims paid them a visit," he said. "They could very well be suspects in a murder. And, if not, at the very least, they could be trying to buy or spread narcotics in the community." His thoughts flew back to Bryan Copeland.

"And we don't want any more of that," she finished.

"No," Billy said. "Definitely not."

"Okay, I'll give you a call when this all pans out."

"Don't worry about it," he said, tying the laces to his shoes. "I'm coming in."

"But—"

"The people of Riker County didn't elect me to sit back when potential murderers could be roaming the streets," he reminded her. "Plus, if there *is* a body and a crime scene, we need to act fast so that the rain doesn't destroy any evidence. Call Matt and tell him to go ahead and head out there. Even if it's a false alarm I'd rather be safe than sorry. Don't let Jessica leave the station until I get there."

Suzy agreed and said goodbye. She might have been his closest friend, but she still knew when to not argue with an order. Even if she had been trying to look out for him.

Billy turned the game off, not bothering to look at the score, and mentally checked out. He tried recalling where Bernie had lived when he'd arrested him and the road that Jessica would travel going there. Billy had grown up in Carpenter, which was one of the three small towns located in Riker County, and Billy had driven all of its roads at least twice. It was the epicenter of a community fused together by humidity, gossip and roots so deep that generations of families never left. Billy Reed was a part of one of those families. He lived in the home he and his father had both grown up in, and a part of him hoped that one day his kids would walk the same hallways. Not that he had any kids. However, it was still a thought that drove him to try and keep the only home he'd ever known a safe, enjoyable one. If Bernie and his past drug habits were back at it, then Billy wanted to nip that in the bud.

Billy tried to rein in thoughts from the past as he searched for his keys, the one item he always seemed to lose, when a knock sounded on the front door. Like a dog trying to figure out a foreign noise, he tilted his head to the side and paused.

It was well past dark and had been raining for the last hour. The list of visitors he'd typically receive was relatively short, considering most wouldn't drop by unannounced. Still, as he walked through the living room to the entryway, he considered the possibility of a friend coming by for a drink or two. Just because he'd become sheriff didn't mean his social life had completely stopped. Then again, for all he knew it could be his mother coming into town early. If so, then he was about to be berated for his lack of Christmas lights and tree despite its being a week away from the holiday. While Billy knew he had to maintain a good image within the community, even when he was off, he hadn't found the time or will to get into a festive mood. Though, if he was being honest with himself, the holidays had lost some charm for him in the last few years. Still, he opened the door with a smile that felt inviting, even genuine.

And immediately was lost for words.

It was like looking in a mirror and recognizing your reflection, yet at the same time still being surprised by it. That's what Billy was going through as he looked at Mara Copeland, dark hair wet from the rain that slid down her poncho, standing on his welcome mat.

"Hey, Billy."

Even her voice pushed Billy deeper into his own personal twilight zone. It kept whatever greeting he had reserved for a normal visitor far behind his tongue.

"I know it's late and I have no business being here but, Billy, I think I need your help."

BILLY DIDN'T MAKE her spell out her situation standing there on his doorstep. He'd regained his composure by the tail end of Mara's plea. Though she could tell it was a struggle.

"Come in," he said, standing back and gesturing wide with his long arms. Mara had almost forgotten how tall he was. Even in the mostly dark space outside his door, she could still make out the appearance of a man who looked the same as he had almost two years before—tall, with broad shoulders and a lean body rather than overly muscled. Lithe, like a soccer player, and no doubt strong, an attractive mix that carried up and through to a hard chin and a prominent nose. His eyes, a wild, ever-moving green, just sweetened the entire pot that was Billy Reed. Mara had realized a long time ago that there wasn't a part of the dark-haired man she didn't find appealing.

Which didn't help what had happened back then.

She hesitated at his invitation to come inside, knowing how meticulous he was with keeping the hardwood in his house clean. Which she clearly was not. The poncho might have kept the clothes underneath dry, but it still was shedding water like a dog would its fur in the summer. Not to mention she hadn't had a hood to keep her long tangles of hair dry.

"Don't worry about it," he said, guessing her thoughts. "It's only water."

His smile, which she'd been afraid she'd broken by her arrival, came back. But only a fraction of it. The lack of its former affection stung. Then again, what had she expected?

"Sorry to intrude," she said, once they were both shut inside the house. Its warmth eased some of the nerves that had been dancing since she'd gotten into the car that morning, although not nearly enough to keep her stomach from fluttering. Although she'd known her destination since she'd buckled her seat belt, seeing the sheriff in person had stunned her, in a way. Like finding a memory she'd tried to forget suddenly within reach. She started to wonder if he had tried to forget her. "I would have called but I couldn't find your number," she lied.

Billy stood back, giving her space. The small part of his smile that had surfaced was disintegrating. Mara's stomach began to knot. She had a feeling that Billy's politeness was sheer Southern reflex.

And now he was starting to remember exactly who she was.

She didn't blame him or the mistrust that distorted his handsome face next.

Though, that stung a bit, too.

"You could have called the department," he deadpanned. "You might not remember, what with you up and leaving so quickly, but I'm the sheriff. I'm sure if you asked for me they'd patch you right on through."

Mara kept the urge to flinch at bay. In her road trip across Alabama, back to the last place she'd ever thought she'd return—especially with Christmas only days away—a small part of her had hoped Billy would have somehow forgotten or forgiven what she'd done. That when and if they ever met again, he would smile that dimpled smile that used to make her go weak in the knees and they'd—what?—be friends? Her thoughts had always derailed at that question. They always seemed to when she thought of Billy.

The little girl asleep and hidden beneath the poncho, held up by Mara's arm, didn't help matters.

"I *do* remember that you're the sheriff," she said. "And, you're right, I should have called there, but—" Mara had rehearsed a speech in the car explaining the exact reason she had driven back to Carpenter, back to his house, instead of just calling. Now, however, the words just wouldn't come. All she could find were his eyes, ever searching for an answer. "Well," she started again, trying to find a stronger voice. "It seemed too important to not talk about face-to-face."

Whatever reply Billy had been brewing behind those perfect lips seemed to stall out. His brows pulled together, his nostrils flared and then, just as quickly, his expression began to relax. He took a deep breath.

"Fine," he finally said. "But make it quick. I just got called out."

That was as warm as she'd bet the man was going to be, so she nodded. The simple movement shook water free from the bright yellow poncho covering her. She tried to give him an apologetic look.

"I didn't have an umbrella," she explained.

"You never did," he said, also, she believed, on reflex. Like the nod, it was such a simple statement that Mara wondered if he'd even registered he'd said it at all. "Here, let me help with that." Billy reached out and took the bag from her shoulder. Any mother might recognize it as a diaper bag, though it was designed to look like an oversized purse, but she could tell Billy Reed hadn't caught on to it yet.

Or the bulge beneath the poncho.

She must have really thrown him for a loop.

"Thanks. Do you have a bag or something I could put this poncho in?" She motioned to the very thing keeping their conversation from diving headlong into the foreign topic of kids.

"Yeah, give me a sec." He set her bag on the entryway bench and headed toward the kitchen. It gave Mara a moment to take two deep breaths before letting each out with a good shake.

It had been two years since she'd seen Billy Reed. More than that since she'd met him in a bar, ready to do her best to help him take down the only family she'd had left. Now here she was, standing in his house, dripping on the hardwood.

"This is all I have to put it in," he said, coming back. His smile was still gone but at least he wasn't stone-faced.

"Oh, thanks," Mara said to the Walmart bag he extended. She didn't take it. "Actually, I'm going to need your help with this one. I don't want to drop her."

And, just like that, Billy Reed must have finally

looked at her—*really* looked at her—taking in the large bulge beneath the poncho. Wordlessly, he helped her pull it off. He stood there, eyes wide, as the dark-haired little girl came into view. She wiggled at the sudden light but, thankfully, stayed asleep. One little blessing that Mara would more than take.

"This is Alexa," Mara introduced her. She watched as his eyes widened. They swept over the little girl with attention she knew he was proud of. For a moment she forgot why she'd come. So many times over the last two years she'd thought about this meeting. Would it happen? What would he say? What would *she* say? However, Mara reminded herself that she hadn't come back to Carpenter because she'd decided to. No, a man and his threats had made that decision for her. Mara cleared her throat. It was now or never. "Billy, meet your daughter."

Chapter Two

Billy, bless him, didn't say a thing for a good minute. Though his eyes ran the gamut of emotions.

Mara took a tentative step toward him, arm still holding their daughter up, and opened her mouth to speak, but Billy's phone went off in his pocket, ringing too loudly to ignore.

He shook off the spell he'd fallen into, though when he spoke, his voice wasn't as strong as it had been before.

"Please, hold that thought. I have to take this," he said, pulling his phone out. He didn't look at the caller ID as he answered. "Reed."

Mara's mouth closed as a woman's voice filled the space between them. She didn't stop for breath as she relayed whatever she needed to the man. Slowly his attention split and refocused on the new information. His brow furrowed and his eyes took on a look Mara knew all too well.

This was Work Billy and she'd come at a bad time. That much was clear.

"Okay, thanks," he said when the woman had finished. "I'll be there in twenty."

Mara's stomach fell as Billy ended the call. She

didn't know what she had expected of the man she'd left with no more than a note on his pillow and no hint whatsoever that she was pregnant with his child. But his taking a work call hadn't been on the list of possibilities. She straightened her back. Alexa squeezed her little arms around Mara's neck in her sleep. The slight movement wasn't missed by Billy. He looked at his daughter before his eyes cut back to her.

"You have a world of explaining to do," he started, voice low. He had finally landed on an emotion. Anger. "First you just up and leave, then you don't talk to me for two years, and now you're saying that—" He stopped his voice from going any louder. Without breaking eye contact he reached for the raincoat on the wall next to them. "A body has just been found and I need to try and get to the crime scene before this rain messes everything up. If it hasn't already." He slid into the coat. "I'm sorry." He ran his finger across the brim of his hat. "It's been a long day and I didn't expect to see you." His eyes trailed down to Alexa before meeting Mara's again. His expression softened, if only a little. "I would ask you along, but I don't think a crime scene in the rain is a good place to have this talk."

"I'll agree to that," Mara said. Before she could add anything the sheriff's expression changed again. It became alert, ready.

"Wait, you said you needed my help?" he asked. The angles of his face seemed to go tight. While Mara had no doubt he was ready to listen to her with all of his attention, he was also still thinking about the crime scene. The sound of pounding rain probably wasn't helping.

"I can wait until you're done," she said. The urgency that had driven her from their home that morning had ebbed considerably, especially now that she was there, standing in Billy's house. Maybe she had been foolish to leave so suddenly and come running back to Carpenter.

And its sheriff.

"Are you sure?" She could see his resolve splitting. She nodded.

"I can go check in to the hotel off Miller Street, if you think it will be a bit."

"Why don't you just wait here? It's not like you don't know your way around." Heat rushed up to Mara's cheeks at the comment. She doubted he'd meant to stir up old memories. He was just stating a fact. She *did* know her way around, having spent countless hours there trying to plan a way to stop her father. A pursuit that had had unexpected outcomes.

"Oh, I wouldn't want to intr—"

"Mara." Billy's voice took on a low edge. "Stay."

An easy command for any smart woman to follow from Billy Reed.

Alexa stirred in her arms.

"Okay," she relented. It would be nice not to have to run Alexa back out into the bad weather. Plus, she doubted after the information she'd just hit him with, Billy would leave his house until he had the whole story. She couldn't blame him. "I'll wait until you get back."

An expression she didn't quite understand flashed across Billy's face, but when he spoke his voice was normal, considering everything.

"Help yourself to any food in the fridge," he said. "I'll be back as soon as I can."

Mara thanked him and moved out of his way as he went out into the storm. The Billy she'd known years before hadn't changed. Justice and protecting those within his jurisdiction still prevailed.

"Well, Alexa," Mara said once she'd heard his Tahoe leave. "This is the Reed family home."

A little uncertainly, Mara slipped off her shoes and padded through the entryway and into the living room. Surprisingly, or maybe not, nothing seemed to have changed since the last time she'd been in the house. The old dark hardwood grounded a room that had been the heart of the Reed family for two generations. Sure, some of the furniture had changed—the black leather couch certainly hadn't been Billy's mother's choice, and neither had the plasma flat-screen—but the cozy feel of a house well loved and well lived-in hadn't diminished one bit.

Mara kept on her tour with a growing smile. From the living room she went to the kitchen, the dining room and the open office. She was looking for clues that might tell her what had happened to Billy since she'd left Carpenter. The family pictures of the Reeds still dotted the walls, including some new additions and marriages, while other pictures specific only to Billy also popped up occasionally. Mara stopped and smiled at one in particular that caught her eye.

Standing in front of a crowd of Riker County residents was the dark-haired man, moments after he'd been officially elected sheriff.

The old affection began to break through an emotional dam she'd spent years building. Then, just as quickly, she was back to that morning, when she'd stood on her front porch across from the stranger who had threatened her life and the life of her child. If anyone could deal with the mystery man it was the Riker County sheriff.

Alexa moved in her arms. This time she woke up.

The cold that had started to spread in the pit of Mara's stomach turned to warmth.

"Well, hello there," she whispered.

Alexa looked up at her mom. Just shy of fifteen months, the toddler might not have known much about the world, but that had never stopped her beautiful green eyes from being curious.

Just like her father's.

It TOOK FIFTEEN minutes to get to the ditch that held Bernie Lutz's body. Billy could have taken three hours—hell, three days—and still not have been able to completely process what had just happened. A herd of elephants could have stampeded alongside his Tahoe as he navigated the muddy back road and it wouldn't have distracted him. Mara's sudden reappearance alone would have stunned him. But this? Alexa? Mara Copeland on his doorstep with a baby?

His baby.

"Get a hold of yourself, Billy," he said out loud. "You've got a job to do first."

Had Mara been wearing a wedding ring? Billy shook his head. He needed to focus on one thing at a time. He needed to put everything that wasn't Bernie Lutz out of his mind. At least for the moment.

He sighed.

Yet, there Mara had been. Staring up at him through her long dark lashes, asking for help.

And he'd just left.

His phone went off, dancing on the dash before he

answered. This time it was Matt Walker, currently Riker County's only detective, thanks to the retirement of his former partner. Like Suzy, Matt was direct when he spoke about work.

"Henry got a tarp up, Billy," he yelled over the weather. "But the road runoff is washing everything away. I went ahead and called in the county coroner."

Billy swore.

"It hasn't rained in weeks, and the one time we need it dry is the one time all hell breaks loose."

"It could be worse," Matt said. "We could be the body in the ditch."

Billy nodded.

"You're right," he said, sobering. "I'm a few minutes out. If the coroner gets there before me, go ahead and load him up. Maybe if we act fast enough we can salvage some evidence."

"Ten-four." Billy started to hang up but Matt cut back in. "And Billy? Just from looking at him, I'm going to say that his girlfriend might have been telling some kind of truth. He's beaten pretty badly. His death wasn't fast, by any means. See you when you get here."

He ended the call.

Thoughts of the past half hour were replaced by the need to solve a murder.

It was just before midnight when Billy unlocked his front door. The storm raged on. Every part of him was soaking wet, and his boots and jeans were more mud than anything. He didn't even try to keep the floor clean. Instead, he sloshed inside and stripped in the entryway.

It wasn't until he was starting to pull off his shirt

that he spotted the bright yellow poncho sticking out of a Walmart bag. He froze as his brain detached from work life and zipped right back to his personal one.

Mara.

With more attention to the noise he was making, he left his shirt on and, instead, got out of his boots. Only one light was on. He followed it into the living room. For one moment he thought it was empty—that Mara had left again, this time with his daughter in tow—but then he spotted a mass of dark hair cascading over the arm of the couch. Coming around to face it, he was met with a sight that used to be familiar.

Mara was asleep, body pulled up so that her knees were close to her stomach, making her look impossibly small. It wasn't the first time he'd come home after work to find her in that exact spot, lights still on, waiting for him. Even when he'd tell her not to wait up, Billy would come in after a long day to find her there. She'd never once complained. Seeing her lying there, face soft and unguarded, Billy took a small moment for himself to remember what it felt like to come home to her. But it didn't last.

There had been too many nights between then and now. Ones where he'd come home to an empty house, wondering why she'd gone.

I'm sorry, but it's over.

Billy shook his head at the one sentence that had changed everything between them and looked at the one idea he'd never entertained after Mara had gone.

Alexa was tucked within her mother's arms, simultaneously fitting and not fitting in the space between. Her hair was dark, but still lighter than his, and it fell just past her shoulders and, from the looks of it, was as thick as her mother's. Before he could police his thoughts, a smile pulled up the corners of his lips.

He might not have known her the day before, but that didn't stop the affection for the little girl.

And, just like before, the feeling of warmth, however brief, was gone.

Why had she been kept a secret?

Billy took a step back. While he had questions, he didn't want to wake either one, but the creak in the floor that had been there since his father was a child sounded under his weight. Mara's eyes fluttered opened and immediately found him.

"I tried to be quiet," he whispered.

Mara shook her head and slowly sat up while trying to disengage herself from the toddler.

"No, I'm sorry," she whispered back once she managed to get free. "I didn't mean to fall asleep."

She followed him through the entryway and into the dining room, far enough away that they could talk in normal tones.

And, boy, did they have a lot to talk about.

"What time is it?" she asked, taking a seat at the table. She stifled a yawn.

"Close to midnight. I was gone a lot longer than I thought I would be," he admitted. Billy took a seat opposite her. "This storm couldn't have come at a worse time."

Mara nodded, but the movement was sluggish. He was tired, too. It was time to stop delaying and finally ask the current question on his mind.

"Mara, why are you here?"

Chapter Three

"A man came to my house this morning and asked about my father," Mara said, knowing full well that once the words were out there Billy wouldn't forget them. Finding a way to take down her father—to catch him in the act—had been an emotional and physical drain on them both. The collective hope that Billy would save Riker County had pressed down heavily on him, while betraying the only family she'd had had never left Mara's mind.

As if an invisible hand had found the strings to his puppet, Billy's entire body snapped to attention.

"They wanted Bryan?"

But he's in prison, Mara silently finished.

"The man didn't want *him*," she said out loud instead. "The guy wanted something important of my father's and I needed to tell him where it was. I had no idea what he was talking about."

Billy's dark brow rose in question. "Something important," he deadpanned.

"He didn't say what, past that," she admitted, recalling how the man had been careful when choosing his words. "But what really spooked me was when he said he wanted to take over what my father had built, my family's business. And I don't think he was talking about my dad's old accounting job."

Billy's forehead creased in thought. She could almost see the red flags popping up behind his eyes.

"Moxy," he supplied.

She nodded. "I told him I had no part in that slice of my father's life, but he didn't seem to care," she continued. She twisted her hands together, and when she recounted what happened next her stomach was a knot of coldness. "Then he saw Alexa playing in the house behind me. He told me that I might change my mind if I had the right incentive."

Billy's body managed to take on an even greater tension.

"What did he want you to change your mind about?" he asked. "Telling him the location of *something important* or wanting nothing to do with your father's past business?"

Mara sighed.

"I don't know. After he looked Alexa's way, I told him he needed to leave." Mara let her gaze drop. "He didn't argue, but he did say he'd be seeing me again soon."

Billy's chair scraped the hardwood as he pushed back. Mara could feel her eyes widen in surprise as she readjusted her attention to his expression.

Anger. And it definitely wasn't meant for her this time.

"I'm assuming he didn't give you a name," Billy said, walking out of the dining room and disappearing. He was back a second later with a small notepad and a pen in his hands.

"Just a first name. Beck."

"And did you call the cops?"

A burst of heat spread up her neck and pooled in her cheeks. Mara had *thought* about filing a police report, but the mention of her father had thrown her completely off-kilter. What she would *normally* have done went out the window. Instead, her thoughts had flown south to Riker County. And the only man who had ever made her feel safe. Suddenly, that feeling that had burned so strongly hours before when she'd packed the car and taken Alexa on a trip across Alabama seemed rash.

"No," she admitted. "I should have but—well, I thought if someone was trying to start up my father's business again that they would start it here. I thought that I should—I don't know—warn you or something." Again, her words sounded lame compared to what she wanted to say. But at least they were true. In his prime, Bryan Copeland had grown a drug network that nearly swallowed the whole of Riker County. His dealings had cost the lives of several residents, including teenagers. Not to mention a cascade of repercussions that were harder to measure. The fact that all of her father's former connections hadn't been found was one that had always made the man in front of her nervous. Part of her father's business hadn't been accounted for…which meant that if this Beck person *was* trying to start up again, it would only stand to reason he might have found the people law enforcement hadn't. Or maybe that's what Beck was looking for.

For the first time since he'd stepped back through the door, Billy's expression softened a fraction. The lines of tension in his shoulders, however, did not.

"Could you describe to me what this Beck guy looks

like?" He flipped open the notebook and clicked his pen. "And did you see his car?"

"Yes and yes."

Mara spent the next few minutes painting a picture of the stranger named Beck until Billy was satisfied it was enough to try and look him up through the department's database.

Mara thought it curious that Billy never asked where she was currently living. It made her wonder if he'd looked her up at all in the last two years. She hadn't gone far, but far enough that Riker County had been firmly in her rearview.

"I want you to come to the station with me tomorrow," Billy said, closing the notepad. "I'm going to see if the sketch artist from the state agency can come in and work with you. Maybe the new guy can draw us a good picture to work with if this Beck person isn't on our list of people with warrants out on them."

"So, you think Beck was serious?"

Mara sat straighter. The possibility of someone revitalizing Moxy, or any drug, within the community using the foundation her father had laid was finally sinking in. Just another reason for the residents of Riker County to despise her and her family. "You think he's really going to try and start up where Dad left off?"

Billy let out a long breath. He ran his hands through his hair. How attractive she still found him was not lost on Mara. Looking at him now, a well-built, fine-tuned man with miles and miles of goodwill and good intentions, she could feel the stirring of feelings she needed to stay still. Not to mention the heat of attraction that always lit within her when Billy was anywhere near. But now wasn't the time or place. If there was a chance he could forgive her for leaving, she doubted he'd forgive her for keeping their daughter a secret—a topic of conversation she was sure would take place once the cop side of him was done flexing his professional muscles.

The sheriff cleared his throat. His eyes hardened. He had something to say and she doubted she'd like it.

"We found Bernie Lutz in a ditch tonight," he started. Mara felt recognition flare but couldn't keep it burning long enough to connect. Billy helped her out. "He was one of the drug dealers your dad used who escaped the serious charges after Bryan went to court." There it was.

"The one with the ex-wife tattoo," she said. He nodded.

"This was never confirmed, but the story his girlfriend spun was that two men came to their house looking for something the other day. Whatever it was, Bernie didn't know or didn't tell. This could all be a coincidence, but you know me, I don't believe in those." Billy put his finger on the paper he'd just written on. He jabbed it once. "Not only do I think this mystery man is going to try to start up your dad's old business, but I think he might have already started."

BILLY WAITED FOR Mara to process everything and then excused himself to go to his room. He slipped into his attached bathroom and splashed cold water on his face. The night had thrown him several curveballs and he hadn't hit one of them.

Even if he filtered out Mara's sudden reappearance and the absolute bombshell that was their daughter, Billy still had Bryan Copeland's legacy to worry about. Whoever this Beck person was, Billy would be damned if he was going to let him repeat what had caused Riker

County so much pain years ago. Especially not during the holiday. That was no present any family should have to get.

Billy splashed another wave of water on his face. He stayed hunched over, resting his elbows on the edge of the sink, and kept his eyes closed. There. He could feel the weight of Riker County's newest burden settling against him. It pressed down on his shoulders and kept going until it hit his chest. No, he wasn't going to stand by while the residents of his county endured another Bryan Copeland incident.

Billy opened his eyes.

Not while he was sheriff.

He dried his face, and without changing out of his wet clothes, he walked out to find Mara, his mind already made up.

She was standing in the living room, Alexa asleep in her arms. Her bag was thrown over her shoulder and her expression was already telling him goodbye.

"You're leaving."

Mara's cheeks reddened but her answer came out clear, concrete.

"Yes, but not town. To be honest, I don't like Beck knowing where I live so I don't want to go back there just yet," she answered. "Plus, to be even more honest, I'm really tired. The faster we get to the hotel, the happier I'll be."

Billy wasn't a complicated man. At least, he didn't think he was. Yet, standing there a few feet from a woman who had left him in the dust, he knew he shouldn't have felt any joy at her admission that she was staying. Or an ounce of desire from looking at her hardened nipples through her light pink T-shirt—the result, he guessed, from the AC he had turned up despite the cool they were getting from the storm—or how her jeans hugged her legs just right. But he did.

"Stay here instead," Billy said before he realized he'd even thought it. Mara's eyes widened a fraction. Her cheeks darkened slightly. "The guest bedroom is free, the sheets are clean and you don't have to drive in the rain to get there. Plus, Miller's parking lot looked pretty full. Probably lousy with in-laws and extended family members that no one wants in their house."

He grinned, trying to drive his point home. It didn't work.

"I don't think it's a good idea," Mara said, eyes straying from his. He wondered if she knew he was thinking about her naked and against him. It was a fleeting thought, but by God it was there. "I've already upset your life enough by coming here."

Billy cleared his throat and tried to clear the feelings of attraction he was currently wading through. He needed some space from her, but he wasn't about to let her leave without a fight, either. Something he wished he could have done two years before.

"Then stay in the guesthouse," he offered.

Mara met his gaze.

"I finished it last summer," he explained, remembering she hadn't known he'd thrown all of his spare time into finishing the apartment that used to be the detached garage. It had been less for his mother when she came for long visits and more of a distraction. "Come on, Mara," he continued when she still seemed to be weighing her options. He moved closer but stopped when the floorboard squeaked. It earned a small movement from Alexa. Billy let himself look at the little girl before fixing her mama with a look he hoped didn't show how hard it was to just talk to her. "Please, Mara. Just stay."

Mara shifted Alexa so she was more firmly on her hip. A wisp of a smile pulled up her lips but it blew away before she answered.

"Okay, we'll stay in the guesthouse if it really doesn't bother you."

Billy nodded and moved to grab her bag. His eyes lingered on Alexa but he didn't ask to hold her. He couldn't be a father right now. Not when things in Riker County were starting to heat up. Not when Mara had attracted the attention of a mysterious man who had no problem threatening children. Not when he'd been in contact with Mara for less than an hour and was already having trouble focusing on anything else. He shouldered the bag and led the two down the hall and to the back door, grabbing an umbrella in the process.

It wasn't raining as hard as it had been, but it was enough to warrant pulling Mara close to him to stay dry beneath the umbrella. She didn't move away or argue as she folded into his left arm and against his side. The inner war he was fighting was downright impossible to ignore as they walked in silence along the stone path that led to the guesthouse door. Billy pulled the keys out of his pocket and unlocked it.

"Here you go," he said, voice low, even to his ears.

He watched as she stepped inside and wordlessly looked around the living space. A kitchenette, three-piece bathroom and a small bedroom made up the rest of the apartment. He'd built on to expand it but everything was still small. At least it was private.

And far enough away from him that he'd never know if she left.

"Oh, it's beautiful, Billy," Mara said after a moment. "You did a wonderful job."

Billy would have taken the compliment with pride if anyone else had given it at any other time. But Mara's words flipped a switch within him. He felt his body stiffen, his expression harden. The pain of finding her note on his pillow came back to him in full.

"I'll come get you at seven," he said. He stepped back out into the rain but didn't look away from those dark eyes that made him crazy. "And, Mara, try not to leave this time. Once we get this guy you're going to tell me exactly why you kept my daughter a secret."

Chapter Four

Mara and Alexa were up and ready when Billy knocked on the guesthouse door the next morning.

"You're late," Mara greeted him, a hand on her hip. She nodded to the clock on the wall behind her. It was ten past seven.

"I thought I'd give you some wiggle room," he admitted. He looked down at Alexa, who was, for the first time, wide-awake since they'd shown up on his doorstep. Her attention stayed on the stuffed dog in her hands as she played on the floor.

"There's no such thing as wiggle room when you have a toddler," she said with a smirk. It was meant as a quick comment, but Billy couldn't help but wonder about the foundation it was born from. When had Mara learned that lesson? Whenever it was, all he knew was it was without him.

Mara's smirk sank into a frown. She cleared her throat, humor gone.

"Listen, about Alexa," she started, but Billy was already a step ahead of her. He held his hand up for her to stop.

"Again, I want to have this talk. I really would like to know why you kept my daughter from me," he said, serious. "But not right now." Mara opened and closed her mouth, like a fish out of water, trying to find what words, Billy didn't know, but he didn't have time to find out. "Right now we need to find Beck and figure out what it is he's done and is trying to do so we can stop him," he continued. "My first priority is to keep you two safe. You can tell me all about your reasoning for not letting me know I was a father later." While he spoke with what he was trying to pass off as authority, he couldn't help but hear the anger at the end of it.

He'd spent most of the night lying awake in bed, coming up with a plan of action for the day. In the plan was a large section related to how he wanted to handle Mara and Alexa. After hours of no sleep, he'd decided the best way to do his job—to keep everyone safe— was to detach himself emotionally from the dark-haired beauties in front of him.

However, maybe that was going to be harder than he'd thought.

"Okay," Mara finally said. "I'll follow you to the station."

She grabbed her bag and scooped up Alexa. The little girl clung to her stuffed animal with laser-like focus. Billy wondered what other toys she liked.

"There's a coffeehouse that opened up across the street that has pretty good breakfast," Billy said as he locked up the guesthouse behind them.

"I actually packed enough cereal to last for weeks for this one," Mara said, motioning to Alexa. "She's a nut about Cheerios as soon as she wakes up in the morning." Alexa swung her head up to face Mara and let out a trill of laughter. It surprised Billy how he instantly loved the sound. "Yeah, you've already scarfed

down two helpings, haven't you, you little chowhound?"
Mara cooed at the girl. Together they laughed, bonded
in their own little world.

One that Billy didn't know.

He cleared his throat and Mara straightened.

"But," she continued, expression turning to the same
focus her daughter had worn before. "If they have good
coffee, I won't turn that down." She smiled but it didn't
last long. "And, Billy, I know it's not my place, but I
noticed you didn't have a tree or any Christmas decorations or lights…"

Billy sighed.

No matter what was happening in their lives, leave
it to the women of the South to still care about Christmas decorations.

THE RIKER COUNTY SHERIFF'S DEPARTMENT was located
in the very heart of Carpenter but was by no means in
an extravagant headquarters. That never stopped Billy
from feeling a boost of pride when it swung into view.
Placed between the county courthouse and the local
television station, the sheriff's department was two stories tall and full of men and women tasked with protecting their Southern home.

Wrapped in faded orange brick and concrete, its entrance opened up to a street almost every Carpenter
resident had to drive along to get somewhere, while its
parking lot around back butted up against a business
park that housed a bistro, a coffeehouse and a clothing
boutique called Pepper's. Billy and Mara angled their
cars into the assigned and guest parking, respectively,
and headed straight to the coffeehouse. Billy had tried
to convince Mara to ride with him but she'd pointed out

his day could get hectic and she liked having the option of her own transportation. Not to mention the car seat was already in her car. Billy decided not to push the topic since she was a flight risk. Instead, he decided to act like everything was normal when they went into the coffeehouse. There they earned a double take from one half of the owner pair known as the Chambers. Becky, a bigger woman with short hair and an even shorter temper, was surprisingly tactful as she addressed them.

"Well, Sheriff, can't say I was expecting to see you on your day off," she started, then she switched her attention to Mara and Alexa. "And certainly not with two lovely ladies in tow."

Billy ignored the affectionate part of the statement, along with what felt suspiciously like pride, and showed just how happy he was about being in on his off day with a frown.

"A sheriff's job is never done," he said solemnly.

"Not with that attitude." Becky winked at Mara, but the dark-haired beauty's gaze had been drawn to the corner booth.

"I'll take my usual," Billy said. "She'll take one of your mocha iced coffee concoctions I always complain about."

Becky raised her eyebrow.

"Does the lady not get a say?" she asked, voice beginning to thread with disapproval. Her changing tone must have snagged Mara's attention. She turned back to them with a small smile.

"She definitely does, but this one here apparently hasn't forgotten my guilty mocha pleasures," she said. "With whipped cream, too, if you have it, please."

Becky seemed appeased that Billy wasn't rolling

over Mara and went about making their drinks while they hung off to the side of the counter. Billy expected Mara to comment about his remembering her favorite caffeinated drink but the woman seemed focused on the corner booth again. So much so that she hardly noticed when he moved close enough to drop his voice so no one else heard him.

"What's going on?"

Alexa looked up from her place on Mara's hip and stared at Billy with an expression caught somewhere between inquisitive and concerned. He couldn't help but stare right back into those green eyes. Like looking into a mirror when it came to the same green.

"That's Donna Ramsey," Mara answered, in an equally low voice. Billy broke his staring contest with Alexa and angled his body to glance at the other side of the room. True to her words, Donna Ramsey was sitting in the corner booth, head bent over the magazine and coffee on the table in front of her. He nodded.

"It is."

Billy watched as Mara's face grew tight. She furrowed her brow.

"Do you know Donna personally?" he asked, his own concern pushing to the forefront. Mara shook her head.

"I've only spoken to her once."

"About?"

He knew Mara well enough to know that her thoughts had turned dark. From anger or sadness or something else, though, he couldn't tell.

"About my father," she answered, voice nearly lost amidst the clatter of the espresso machine. Mara lost her dark look and replaced it with something akin to nonchalance.

"Don't worry," she said. "It was before I left and nothing I didn't already know."

Becky bustled into view before he could question Mara further. She handed them their drinks and looked at Billy.

"Remember, Sheriff, complaining always makes problems ten times worse," she said sagely. "So stop complaining and start drinking some of the best coffee this town has to offer."

Billy couldn't help but smirk.

"You got it, Becky."

Mara waved goodbye while Alexa giggled, and soon the three of them were walking to the back of the station.

"I like her," Mara commented.

"Next time you order from her, tell her that," Billy said. "Suzy did and now she gets a discount."

Mara laughed and Alexa started to babble. Billy craned his neck to look down at her face. Whatever she was saying must have been normal because Mara didn't skip a beat.

"Suzy," she started. "I—I haven't seen her since you were sworn in."

They had made it to the back door used by employees only. Billy pulled out his key and went ahead and addressed the elephant in their shared room.

"She's still one of the few in the department who knows about us working together to bring down your dad. I never told anyone else about the other us. Or what we used to be," he amended. With his key hanging in the lock he looked over his shoulder to the woman he'd been ready to spend forever with and then to their child. "I'll leave it up to you what personal details you want to disclose to my staff. And I'll follow your lead. But whatever you choose to do today, don't think I won't undermine it tomorrow if I need to."

Then Billy opened the door and headed inside, mind already going into work mode. He had a murder to solve and a man named Beck to find.

IT WAS COMFORTING, in a way, to walk into the department alongside Billy. Because, unlike their lives in the last two years, the building hadn't changed. At least, not any way that Mara could tell.

They took the back hallway that ran behind dispatch and the break room and turned the corner to where Mara knew offices lined one of the hallways that led back toward the lobby. Billy's office was smack dab in the middle of the others. His nameplate shone with importance. Mara couldn't help but feel some pride creep in at the sight of it.

"Walden, the sketch artist, said he'd be here by eight thirty," Billy said, walking them past his office. "Until then I'd like you to officially make a statement about this Beck fellow. I'm going to double-check that no one fitting Beck's description is a part of an open case with us or local PD." He stopped two doors over and motioned her inside. It was the conference room and it definitely wasn't empty.

Mara felt her cheeks immediately heat at the sight of mostly familiar faces. Alexa tucked her head into the side of her neck, suddenly shy. Mara didn't blame her. Billy motioned to an open chair, one of many, around the long table in the middle of the room. Mara sat down with tired grace. Alexa's sudden shyness didn't help either one of them adjust from standing to sitting down.

"Most of you already know Mara, and Mara you know them." Billy continued to stand. He motioned to Suzy, Matt Walker and Dane Jones. The last time she'd seen them Suzy had been a deputy along with Billy, Matt had been a deputy, too and Dane had been on his way to being sheriff. Now, sitting across from them, Mara doubted their titles were the same. She wondered what title Dane had now but she wasn't about to ask for clarification.

On the same side of the table was the one face she didn't recognize, a pretty young woman with curly blond hair and a smile that looked genuine. Before Mara could stop the thought, she wondered if Billy found the woman pretty, too.

"Mara, this is Cassie Gates," Billy said, making the introduction. "She's training to be a dispatcher." Mara couldn't stop the confusion that must have crossed her expression as to why a dispatcher, a *trainee* dispatcher, was in the room with them when the woman answered the question herself.

"I'm the youngest of six siblings, most of whom have a kid or two under their belt, so I'm very experienced in the art of keeping little ones entertained when their mamas need to do something important," she said, voice as sweet as her appearance. She flashed a quick smile at Alexa and addressed the toddler directly. "And what's your name? I bet it's something pretty."

The entire room seemed to wait as Alexa peeked out at Cassie. There was nothing like waiting for a toddler's judgment. Seemingly based on some unknown factor, there was no telling how a child would react to something new. That included people. However, instead of hiding away again, Alexa seemed intrigued. She looked back at Mara for a moment, as if asking for permission.

"This is Alexa," Mara introduced them with a smile, showing Alexa her approval of the woman next to them. She might have been a stranger to her but she wasn't to Billy. Mara trusted his judgment. And Alexa trusted Mara's.

"Well, what do you know. That *is* a pretty name," Cassie said, animation in her words. It reeled in Alexa's attention. The blonde reached for a bag next to her. From her seat Mara could see it was filled with books and toys. Billy had prepared for the morning, despite short notice. "If it's okay with your mama, how about we go next door and play in the sheriff's office? You could even help me read this." Cassie held up the children's book *Pat the Pet* and Alexa nearly lost it.

"Dog! Dog," she exclaimed, already trying to get off Mara's lap.

It earned a surprised laugh from Cassie. Mara reached into her own bag and produced the same book.

"Welcome to her favorite book," she said to the trainee. "She likes petting the dog the most."

Mara gave Cassie permission to go next door and play, since Alexa seemed to have lost any doubt about the woman as soon as the book had come into view. Mara didn't miss the way Billy's eyes stuck to the cover of the copy Mara had brought along. With more than a twinge of guilt, she realized that, like the stranger who was Cassie, he hadn't had a clue in the world what his daughter did and didn't like.

But Mara couldn't change what she'd already done and turned to face what was left of the group. The men each gave her a friendly smile. Suzy, on the other hand, gave her a stiff nod. While the other two had known about their working relationship, Suzy alone had known about Mara and Billy's romantic one and her sudden departure. As one of Billy's closest friends, Suzy probably knew better than even her how he'd handled it, too.

"Now, Mara," Billy started, setting a tape recorder in the middle of the table. "If you could start at the beginning, when the man named Beck visited you."

Mara repeated the story she'd told Billy the night before, making sure to give them as clear a picture as she could of Beck. Before she could finish describing his clothes and car, however, a man knocked at the door. Despite his dark complexion, Mara mentally likened his expression to "looks like he's seen a ghost."

"Excuse me, Sheriff, we have a problem," he interrupted. Like fans passing on a wave in a football stadium's stands, Billy and his staff became visibly tense.

"What is it?" The man hesitated and looked at Mara. "It's fine. Tell me," Billy added, showing that Mara's presence didn't bother them with whatever news he had.

Which wasn't good news at all.

"We just got a call about two teens who are being taken to the hospital," he started. "They were both overdoses."

Mara's eyes widened. She asked him what everyone else was thinking.

"Of what?"

Bless him, he didn't hesitate in responding to her, though Mara would have been happier if it had been with a different answer.

"Moxy. They overdosed on Moxy."

Chapter Five

Billy tried to not feel like he was suddenly several years in the past, staring at the deceased Courtney Brooks in her car. But there he was, sitting in a conference room and feeling exactly as he had then.

Sad.

Guilty.

Angry.

If he had been alone, he would probably have thrown something. Instead, the best he could do was toss a few expletives in the direction of Deputy Dante Mills, who, thankfully, didn't seem to take open frustration personally.

"They were at the abandoned drive-in theater out past the town limits," Deputy Mills continued. "The owner of the gas station across the street saw their cars hadn't moved in a while and decided to investigate with her husband. Neither had ID on them. As far as their status, it was unclear how bad the damage was, other than they needed medical attention ASAP."

Billy had heard enough. He turned to Suzy, who rose at the same time.

"We're going to the hospital," he told her. Then to Matt, "And I want you to go to the theater grounds and look around. Talk to the gas station owner, too." Billy turned to Dane Jones and a look of understanding passed between them. For his own personal reasons, Dane had taken himself out of the running for sheriff and, instead, applied for Captain of Investigative Bureau within the department after Rockwell had retired. He preferred fighting the good fight from behind a desk instead of out on the streets. Billy couldn't blame him after what had happened to the man years before. Some cases just went south and there wasn't anything anyone could do about it. That was a lesson Dane hadn't let himself learn yet.

"I'll finish up here and see what we can do to find this Beck person. See if we can't connect some dots to Bernie Lutz, too," Dane said. "I'll even give Chief Hawser a call and see if he's had anything come across his desk."

Billy nodded. It was a good idea to go ahead and touch base with Carpenter's police department. Although Billy was sheriff of Riker County, the town of Carpenter and the city of Kipsy had their own police departments and anything that happened within those municipalities was their jurisdiction. Bernie's body and the overdoses had been found just outside the town limits, which meant Billy was running the show. But he didn't have an ego too big to not have an open dialogue with the local PD. He happened to be a fan of Chief Hawser, too.

Billy finally looked at Mara. Her expression was pinched and worn at the same time. He assumed the news had put her on the line between the present and the past, just as it had him, anger and guilt both squarely on her shoulders. He wanted to go to her, even took a small step forward, but caught himself.

"The sketch artist should be here soon," Billy said. "You can wait in my office if he takes too long."

Mara's jaw tightened.

"As long as you figure out who's doing this," she said.

"Believe me. I will."

Suzy wordlessly followed him to the parking lot and into his Tahoe as the rest of the department went on with their tasks. She kept quiet as he pulled away from the department and got on the main road that would lead them to Carpenter's hospital. However, no sooner had they passed the first intersection when Suzy asked the one question Billy knew she would.

"Is Alexa yours?"

Billy had already resigned himself to following whatever lead Mara wanted to take about telling the department who the father was. But she hadn't expressed herself one way or the other.

"Yes," he answered, surprising himself. "I just found out last night."

He cast a look over at his friend. Suzy, a mother herself, didn't seem to pass any judgment either way on the information. Instead, she kept her gaze focused out the windshield.

"She's a cute kid," she said, as if they were talking about the weather. "I'm glad she didn't get your nose."

Billy laughed. He somehow felt better.

THE SKETCH ARTIST'S name was Walden and he very much looked like what Mara suspected a Walden would look like. Slightly rounded in the gut, thick glasses, a crown of blond hair around a shiny spot of baldness and a patient, even temperament, the man took his time in sketching out Beck.

"Is this close?" he asked when he was finished. He slid his notebook over to her. Alexa, who had taken a snack break next to her mother, peeked over at the drawing.

"That's perfect," Mara said, quickly moving the notebook out of Alexa's line of sight. As if the man could do her harm from it. "You're very good at your job, Walden," she added, thoroughly impressed. He'd even managed to add in the sneer that had pulled up the corner of Beck's lips as he said goodbye.

"I'd always wanted to be an artist, though even I'm surprised that I wound up here." Walden motioned around the conference room but she knew he meant the department as a whole.

"I can understand that," she admitted. "I used to dream of running my own interior design business. Now I work at a flooring company trying to convince people redoing their floors is the first step to a happy home." Mara gave him a wry smile. Walden shrugged.

"Hey, the floors are the foundation of a home. Not a bad place to start at all," he pointed out. Mara laughed.

"You seem to be a very optimistic man. I suppose your glass is always half full?" Walden pushed his glasses back up the bridge of his nose and stood with his notebook.

"It's better to have a half-full glass than an entirely empty bottle." He gave her a nod. "I'm going to take this to the captain now. It was nice to meet you, Mara."

It took her a moment to return the sentiment, as she was slightly stunned by the weight of his previous statement. She wasn't the only one with pain in her life, and compared to most, hers wasn't the worst. Her thoughts went to the teens in the hospital. She looked at Alexa, transfixed by her bag of cereal. At a time when families and loved ones were supposed to be coming together for holidays, Mara couldn't imagine what she'd feel like if she were to get a call like the one the families of the teens were no doubt receiving.

"Knock, knock." Mara shook herself out of such dark thoughts and focused on Cassie standing in the doorway. "Now that you're finished, I've been told to tell you that you don't have to hang around here any longer," she said, all smiles. Her gaze went to Alexa. "I'm sure there are much more exciting places to be than a sheriff's department."

Although Cassie was no doubt being polite, Mara couldn't help but wonder who'd told the woman that Mara should leave when finished. Had it been a polite suggestion to start off with or had the young woman changed the tone to stay nice? Mara mentally let out a long, loud sigh. Feelings of uncertainty, self-consciousness and guilt began to crop up within her again.

And she hadn't even been in Riker County for a full twenty-four hours yet.

Instead of telling the truth—that she'd like to stay until Billy came back—Mara stood with an equally warm, if not entirely true, smile.

"There are a few places I'd like to visit," she tried, attempting to wrangle her child's toys and food back into their appropriate places within her bag. "Plus, it does seem to be a nice day outside."

Cassie nodded, following Mara's glance out of the conference room windows. Every Southerner had a

love-hate relationship with winter. South Alabama
had an annoying habit of being humid and hot when it
should be chilly or cold. Christmastime was no excep-
tion. Mara had left her jacket in the car. She doubted
she'd need it while in Carpenter, though she wouldn't
have minded being proven wrong. At least in North
Alabama, where she lived with Alexa, the promise of
being cold in time for the holidays was sometimes kept.

"Could you ask the sheriff to call me when he gets a
chance?" Mara asked when Alexa and her things were
finally ready to go. Cassie nodded and promised she
would. Together they walked past the hall that led to
the back door and, instead, moved past the offices to
the lobby.

It was hard to not smile at the department's attempt
at decorating. Colored lights and garlands covered every
available inch. On the lobby desk there was even a small
Charlie Brown Christmas tree—twigs and a few colorful glass ornaments. An unexpected wave of guilt
pushed against Mara at the sight. Not only had she dis-
rupted the life of the sheriff by showing up, but she'd
also left behind her own planned Christmas with Alexa
back home. Decorations and toys, even holiday treats
she'd already baked and packaged. But now that Billy
knew about her, what would the holiday look like?

The deputy who had given the news of the overdoses
earlier gave them a quick smile while still talking to the
secretary, another person Mara didn't recognize. The
only other people in the lobby were two women waiting in the chairs.

As she had with Donna Ramsey in the coffee shop,
Mara recognized one of them, a woman named Leigh
Cullen. Unlike Donna, Leigh recognized Mara right

back. She stood abruptly, pausing in whatever she had been saying.

"Thank you again for everything," Mara said in a rush, cutting off eye contact and disengaging from her spot next to Cassie. "See you later."

"You," Leigh exclaimed, loud enough to catch the entire lobby's attention. Mara had the wild thought that if she could run out of the building fast enough, Leigh would somehow forget about seeing her. That she could literally outrun her past. But then Leigh began to hurry over toward them, her face reddening as she yelled, "How dare you show your face here again!"

Mara angled Alexa behind her and braced for a confrontation. One she hoped wouldn't be physical. It was one she deserved but not one she was ready to let Alexa witness. However, Cassie surprised them all.

In all of her compassionate glory, she stepped between Leigh and Mara, and held up her hand like she was a traffic guard telling the driver of a vehicle that they'd better halt their horses. It stunned both women into silence.

"No ma'am," Cassie said, voice high but firm. "You do not act that way in a sheriff's department and certainly not in front of a child."

For the first time, Leigh seemed to notice Alexa on Mara's hip. Still, her eyes remained fiery.

"Don't you know who this woman is?" Leigh continued, though her voice had gone from an explosion to a low burn. Probably because the deputy's attention was fully on them now. "Do you know what she let happen?"

Mara's face heated. Her heartbeat sped up. How had she thought coming back to Riker County wouldn't end in disaster? That someone wouldn't recognize her?

"I know exactly who she is and you don't see me hollering at her like this," Cassie said. Though she'd been polite before, Mara could see her sharp edges poking out in defense now.

"Maybe you should take a breather, Leigh," the deputy added with absolute authority. He looked confused by the situation but determined to stop it.

"You shouldn't be here," Leigh said. She turned away, grumbling a few more not-so-becoming words beneath her breath, and stomped back to her companion, who'd remained seated.

"I'm so sorry, Mara." Cassie didn't take her eyes off Leigh's retreating back. "I don't know what came over her."

That clinched it. Cassie didn't know who Mara was.

"Thank you," Mara said, honest. "But it's alright. I don't blame her one bit." Without explaining herself, Mara took Alexa and left the department.

It wasn't until they were locked inside the car, "Jingle Bells" playing over the radio, that Mara broke down and cried.

Leigh's husband had been gunned down while trying to stop an armed robbery almost three years ago. His killer had been one of Bryan Copeland's drug dealers. If Mara had tried to turn her father in the moment she found out who he was and what he had done, then Leigh's husband wouldn't have bled out in the convenience store on Cherry Street. Mara knew that.

And so did Leigh.

A HALF HOUR LATER, Mara was letting the laughter of her child soothe her wounds as best it could.

They had gone from the department straight to Anthony's Park. Not as green as it was in the summer, the three-mile stretch of trees, walking paths and recreational spots was located near the town's limits, closest to the city of Kipsy. Because of that fact, Mara had often visited the park when she'd first started to meet up with Billy. They'd sit in the parking lot, huddled in Billy's late father's old Bronco, and try to figure out the best way to stop *her* father and his drugs.

Are you sure you want to do this? I can take over from here. You can go home and I won't ever fault you for it, Billy had said one night. Mara still remembered how he'd looked at her then. Concern pulling his brows together, eyes soft, lips set in a thoughtful frown. Compassionate to a fault, Billy had offered her an out.

And would you go home if you were in my place, Billy?

Despite his lower rank back then, in hindsight Mara realized Billy Reed had always been a sheriff at heart. The resolution that had rolled off him in nearly staggering waves as he'd answered had helped Mara come to terms with her own choice to stay.

No. I would see this through to the end.

Mara smiled as Alexa began to giggle uncontrollably at the sand hill she'd just made. Who knew that *seeing it through* then would have resulted in a daughter.

"You're brave."

Mara jumped at the new voice behind her. Afraid it belonged to Beck, she didn't feel much better when she saw it belonged to another man she didn't know. That didn't stop her from assuming he was into some kind of drug, either. Thin, with red, almost-hollow eyes and stringy brown hair, there was a restlessness about him that kept his body constantly moving. He rubbed the thumb of his right hand across his index finger over and over again but, thankfully, the rest of him stayed still on the other side of the bench.

"Excuse me?" Mara said, body tensing so fast that she nearly stood.

"You're brave to let her play in the sand box," he said, motioning to Alexa. The little girl looked up from her spot a few feet away but lost interest immediately after.

"How so?"

Mara slowly moved her hand to the top of her bag. The playground they were at was out in the open, which made it very easy to see how alone the three of them were now. The man could have looked like George Clooney and Mara still would have been trying to get her phone out without being noticed.

"The sand. It's going to get everywhere," he offered. "I'm sure it won't be fun to clean up."

"I've dealt with worse," she replied, politely. "Plus, she loves it."

The man shrugged.

"I guess you're a better parent than most." He never stopped rubbing his finger, like a nervous tick. It made Mara's skin start to crawl. She opened her bag slowly and reached her hand inside. "So, Mara, was Bryan a good parent?"

Her blood ran cold and froze her to the spot. The man's smile was back.

"Who are you?" she managed. "What do you want?"

He answered with a laugh.

"Let's just say I'm a friend of a friend." Mara's fingers brushed against the screen of her phone. All she had to do was unlock it and tap twice and it would connect straight to 911. But apparently the man had different plans. "If you don't take your hand out right now, I'm going to teach you a lesson in manners in front of your daughter," he said, his smile dissolving into a look that promised he'd carry through on his threat.

Mara pulled her hand out to comply, but she wasn't about to submit to him completely. She stood, slowly, never taking her eyes off him.

"What do you want?" she repeated.

All the fake politeness left him. When he answered his tone was harsh and low. It made the hair rise on the back of her neck.

"Bryan Copeland's drugs and blood money. What else?"

Chapter Six

Her father might have been a lot of things, but Mara had learned a few good lessons from him. Once he'd told her a story about when he was a young man working in a big city. He'd decided to walk home instead of taking a cab, wanting to enjoy the night air, and a man tried to mug him at knifepoint.

Bryan refused to let anyone take advantage of him and used the only weapon he had on him. He took his house keys, already in his hand, and slid the keys between his fingers so when he made a fist, his keys were sticking out, ready to teach his attacker a lesson.

Mara had never heard the rest of the story, only that her father had left that alley with all of his belongings still with him. He would use that story throughout her youth to try and teach her to, at the very least, always keep her keys in her pocket instead of her purse. Because no attacker feared a weapon their victim couldn't get to in time. And usually they didn't care about keys, either.

So as soon as her new friend asked about drugs and blood money, Mara's hand went straight into her pocket.

"I don't know what you're talking about," she said,

pulling her keys out. "I think it's time for us to leave now."

The man shook his head, which Mara expected. Leaving, she gathered, wouldn't be easy, but at least now she had *something* that would hurt him if he got physical. Which she prayed wouldn't be the case. Alexa could still be heard playing behind her.

"You don't leave until I say you leave," the man bit out.

Mara angled her body slightly to hide the hand with her keys. She threaded one between her index and middle fingers and then another between her middle and ring fingers. If he noticed her making the fist, he didn't comment on it.

"My father doesn't have any blood money or drugs left to find," she answered. "And if he does, I'm the last person who would know where they are."

The man seemed to consider her words for the briefest of moments before a sneer lit his face.

"He said you'd deny it."

That made Mara pause.

"Who?" she asked. "My father?" Billy hadn't been the only man in her life she'd not spoken to since she'd left Riker County. She hadn't communicated with her father in any form or fashion since he'd been sentenced. And even then that had been brief.

In the time in between then and the present, had he been talking about her?

"Your friend Beck."

Mara's stomach iced over. She tightened her grip on her keys until they bit into her skin. Apparently Beck worked fast, whoever he was.

"I haven't talked to my father in years," Mara said,

trying to keep her voice even. The man behind the bench looked like he would prey on anyone showing fear. Like a shark waiting for blood. "If he has anything hidden, I'm not the one to ask to find it."

"You know, you keep talkin' but I still don't believe you."

He cut his eyes to the space behind her that Mara knew contained Alexa. On reflex, Mara stepped to the side to block his view. The ice in her stomach might have been created in fear but that didn't mean she wouldn't use that to fight tooth and nail to keep the creep away from her daughter.

Maybe the man sensed that. He lazily slid his gaze back to hers and put up his hands in defense.

"Now, I don't have any weapons on me, little miss," he started. "But if you don't come with me I can still make some trouble. For all of us." He dropped his gaze to show he was trying to look at Alexa again. The mistake cost Mara her patience.

"I'm leaving," she said. "If you try to stop me I'll call the cops."

"There won't be any need for that," he replied, his sneer dropping again. In its place was an expression filled with intent. Evil or not, Mara wasn't going to stick around and find out. Mara tried to recall everything Billy had ever taught her about protecting herself in the few seconds it took for the man to round the bench. But all she could think about was a football game she'd watched with her father a few weeks before they'd caught him.

Sometimes the best defense is a good offense.

So, with Billy's voice ringing in her ears, Mara lunged out at the man with her fist of protruding keys.

However, Mara's lunge turned more into a stumble. No matter how much she wanted to keep the creep away from her and her daughter, her lack of experience in attacking strange men and the surge of adrenaline through her wasn't helping her. Her fist missed his face but snagged his ear before she lost her footing.

The man let out a strangled cry as one of the keys cut into the side of his ear. Mara tried to steady herself enough to throw another punch that would do more damage, but the man was faster. He grabbed her wrist and squeezed hard.

"You little—" he snarled, but Mara refused to give in. She brought her knee up hard into the man's groin. The hit connected and whatever thoughts he was going to convey died on his yell of pain. He let her go and immediately sank to the ground.

It was the opening she needed.

Mara turned tail and went to Alexa. She grabbed her so quickly that the little girl instantly started to fuss. When Mara started to run toward her car, the little girl went from annoyed to scared.

Maybe she sensed her mother's fear.

Or maybe she heard the man get up and start chasing them.

BILLY WASN'T HAVING a good day.

Though he knew he had no room to complain. Not after he'd seen Jeff Briggs's mother in Santa earrings weeping for her son who was lying in the hospital in a coma. Stanley Morgan wasn't much better than his friend. The doctor had told Billy and Suzy they were certain that Stanley would wake up, they just couldn't say when.

Billy had personally given each set of parents the news once a nurse identified the teens from her neighborhood. None of them had any idea that either boy had been using drugs.

Billy let out a long, loud breath.

"I'm going to call the office to see if we have a good sketch of Beck to work with," Suzy said when they were back to driving.

Billy nodded and turned the morning talk show down as Suzy spoke with Dane. He watched as downtown Carpenter flashed by their windows. It was a warm day, but not as humid as it could have been. Still, Billy wouldn't have minded changing out of his blazer to one of his running tees. His sheriff's star shone on his belt, reminding him that just because it was warm didn't mean he could start slacking in his appearance.

"She did what?" Suzy asked, voice laced with surprise and simultaneously coated with disapproval. Billy turned the radio off. He raised his eyebrow in question but Suzy held up her index finger to tell him to hold on. "Yeah. Okay, I'll tell him," she continued into the phone. "Shouldn't be a problem. Thanks, Dane."

"What was that about?" Billy asked once Suzy ended the call. For a brief moment he wondered if Mara had left town again. This time taking a daughter he knew about.

"Leigh Cullen tried to start something with Mara after she was done with the sketch artist. Apparently Leigh's been saving up some anger for her." The knot Billy hadn't realized had formed in his chest loosened. Mara hadn't decided to run off into the night, or day, again.

"What do you mean, she tried to start something?"

"While Mara was leaving the station, Leigh started hollering and came at her." Billy tensed with a flash of anger. Suzy didn't miss it. "Don't worry, she didn't get far. Deputy Mills and Cassie handled it while Mara went off to take Alexa to the park. At least, that's where Jones said he thinks they were going. He wasn't sure. You know how he is when Cassie's trying to talk to him. His attention breaks a hundred which ways."

Billy couldn't help but let out a chuckle. He had, in fact, noticed how Dane couldn't help but lose some of his concentration when the trainee dispatcher was around.

"You give him such a hard time about her, you know?" he pointed out. Instead of continuing straight, taking them in the direction of the office, Billy was already putting on his blinker to turn. Anthony's Park wasn't that far away.

"And he gave me a hard time when I went out with Rodney a few years back, so I'm still getting even." She gave an indifferent shrug. Billy couldn't argue with that. "So, we're heading to the park?"

"I don't know how serious this Beck person is, but I don't want to take any chances until we catch him, or at least know more. And after seeing those kids laid up in hospital beds, and knowing that Beck showed up at Mara's house and threatened Alexa—" Billy's grip momentarily tightened around the steering wheel. "Well, I'd feel a lot more comfortable if Mara and Alexa stayed a little more hidden while in town." Billy didn't slow down as he took another turn, his sense of urgency growing. "Plus, I have a feeling I'm going to need to have a talk with Mara."

"You want to visit her father," Suzy guessed.

Billy nodded.

"If things start escalating, then I want to talk to the source himself before this thing gets out—"

"Billy!"

Suzy pointed out her window into Anthony's Park to their left. Billy had already been focused on driving to the running trail entrance, what used to be Mara's favorite path to walk, and hadn't noticed the playground or the green expanse between it and the parking lot.

But one look at Mara running with Alexa in her arms and a man chasing them, and a meteor could have crashed down next to them and he wouldn't have noticed.

"Hold on!"

The side road that ran to the parking lot was too far away for his comfort, not when the man was so close to Mara and Alexa, so he cut the wheel hard. The Tahoe went up and over the curb with ease.

"Can you see a gun on him?" Billy yelled, blood pumping as he sped up.

"Not that I can tell," Suzy hollered back.

The man heard the approaching vehicle and turned. Billy was close enough to read the shock on his face. Apparently seeing a Tahoe barreling toward him was enough of a threat to make him rethink his current plan of action.

"He's changing direction," Suzy yelled. "Heading for the walking trail!"

Billy floored it toward the concrete trail that ran through the woods, knowing that once the man broke through the first line of trees the Tahoe wouldn't have enough room to follow. The man, however, was fast.

Billy slammed on the brakes as the fugitive slipped between the trees.

But that wasn't going to stop Billy.

He flung his door open and only hesitated a moment to look behind them at Mara.

"Are you okay?" he called, adrenaline bombarding his system. The second he saw her nod, Billy turned and was running. "Stay with them," he yelled to Suzy.

And then Billy was in the trees.

Chapter Seven

The man opted to avoid the only paved walkway that Anthony's Park had to offer. Under normal circumstances that would have been just fine. While there wasn't enough space for a vehicle to drive between the trees, there was more than enough for someone to explore or deviate if you were truly bored with the even, smooth path.

However, chasing someone?

That was a different story.

Billy weaved through the trees, attempting to copy the perp's zigzag route while adjusting his pace to the uneven terrain. At least if the man had a gun, Billy would be able to fall back to cover without much issue.

"Riker County Sheriff, stop *now*," Billy yelled out as he swung around another tree and barely avoided the next. The man didn't even hesitate. "Stop now or I'll shoot!"

That did the trick in breaking the man's concentration.

His foot caught on a tree root and down he went. Billy was on him in seconds, gun drawn and ready for a fight if needed.

"Don't move," he commanded. "Put your hands on your back!"

The man obliged, but not without complaint. He wheezed and groaned into the dirt before catching his breath enough to mumble out some heated language. It didn't bother Billy. He'd heard worse.

"I didn't do anything." The man finally had the brass to yell as Billy pulled his cuffs out and slapped them on his captive's wrists. The run seemed to have burned him out. The heat wasn't helping matters.

"It looked to me like you were chasing a woman and her kid," Billy said, tugging on the cuffs to make sure they were secure. "And I don't know about you, but to me, that looked like something."

"You don't know what you're talkin' about," the man hurled back.

"Well, good thing I'm going to explain it to you back at the station." Billy secured his gun and helped the man get to his feet. "You run again, or try anything funny, I'll show you just how much more in shape I am than you," Billy warned. The man, covered in sweat, spat off to the side in anger. "And you spit on me or mine, and that's felony assault against an officer of the law. Got it?"

The man grumbled but didn't kick up too much of a fuss as Billy led him out of the woods. Suzy, ever alert, was standing in front of Mara and Alexa, sandwiching them between the Tahoe and herself. Her hand was hovering over the gun at her hip, ready to defend the civilians at her back. When she saw them, there was nothing but focus in her expression.

"I called for backup," she said, not leaving her spot. "Deputy Mills was in the area. Should be here soon."

On cue, the sound of a distant cruiser's siren began to sing.

"You're making a mistake," the man tried again. "I'm the victim here! Did you see what that bitch did to my ear?" Billy kicked out at the back of the man's leg. "Hey," he cried out, stumbling forward. Billy pulled back on his cuffs to keep the man from falling.

"Watch your step there, buddy," Billy said. "Wouldn't want you to hurt yourself."

Deputy Mills came into view soon after. He drove around to the parking lot that looked out at the playground and stopped. Billy used his free hand to fish out the keys to the Tahoe he'd shoved into his pocket before.

"Will you take the Tahoe back to the office?" he asked Suzy. "Our friend here can ride with Mills." Billy glanced at Mara. She was rubbing Alexa's back while the little girl cried into her neck. "I'll catch a ride back with you."

It wasn't a question, but still Mara nodded. Her face was pinched, concerned.

"Sounds good, boss." Suzy caught Billy's keys. "I'll go ahead and call Chief Hawser and tell him what's happening. I'm sure he won't mind, though. As long as we get men who like to terrorize women and children off the streets." She cut a piercing look at the man.

"Agreed. Call ahead and tell them to make the interrogation room *comfortable* too," he added, in a tone that let his perp know that his humor was sarcasm only.

"Will do," Suzy said. She was already dialing the department's number. Billy passed her but made sure to angle his body between the man and Mara and Alexa as they passed.

Mara didn't comment as they all walked over to

Deputy Mills's cruiser, a few spots down from Mara's car, but Billy didn't miss her soft reassurances to their daughter that everything was going to be okay. It sent another flash of anger through him. When Deputy Mills helped get the man into the cruiser Billy might have been a little rougher than usual with him.

"Read him his rights, deputy," Billy said when he was shut in the back of the car. "And don't let him give you any trouble."

Deputy Mills nodded.

"Yessir."

Billy watched as the cruiser pulled out and away before he went to Mara. She was leaning against the side of her car, still rubbing Alexa's back. The little girl wasn't crying anymore but a few sniffs could be heard. Those little sounds carried a much stronger punch than Billy thought was possible.

"Is she okay?"

"Oh, yeah, she's fine," she assured. "I just scared her a little when I had to grab her and run."

"Tell me what happened, Mara."

"Can we get out of here first?" she asked. Her gaze swiveled past him to the playground in the distance.

"Yeah, we can." Billy tried to search her face for an indication of how she felt. The Mara he knew had been easier to read than the mother standing in front of him. She was guarded. Once again he wondered what her life had been like in the last two years.

"How long have you been here?" he asked. Mara shifted Alexa so they both slid into the back of the car.

"Not long," she said, starting the dance of buckling the toddler into her car seat. Alexa's eyes were red. Tear tracks stained her cheeks. Billy didn't like the sight.

Not at all. "Oh, Billy, can you open my bag and grab a wipe or two?" She motioned to the bag she'd put down next to the car. Billy complied, thinking the wipes were for Alexa, but Mara held out her keys to him instead.

"You want me to drive?" he asked, confused.

Mara gave him a small smile.

"There's blood on my keys," she explained. "But if you want to drive, I don't mind that, either."

"YOU USED YOUR keys like Wolverine uses his claws," Billy deadpanned after she'd told him the story of what happened in the park. "I can say that I've never seen that self-defense tactic used in Riker County. Though I guess it was effective."

Mara looked into the rearview mirror and gave him a sly smile.

"Believe me, if I'd had something more useful I would have used it instead."

Billy held up one of his hands to stop her thought. "Hey, it did the trick, didn't it?"

Mara's attention shifted to Alexa strapped into the car seat next to her. She had calmed down in the few minutes they'd been driving, but Mara couldn't help but see the little girl who had cried out as Mara had grabbed her and run. More for her sake than Alexa's, Mara held on to her daughter's little hands.

"It helped us get away, but who knows what would have happened had he caught me." Mara paused. "Actually, I know what would have happened," she said, sure of her thought. Billy kept his eyes on the road but she knew he was listening with all of his attention. "He would have taken me and tried to make me tell him where this fictional stash of my father's is. And when I didn't tell him, he would have used our daughter against me."

Mara had gotten so swept up in her own anger that the words had flown from her mouth without realizing she'd used the word *our*. One little word that had never meant much to her had made Billy react in a very small yet profound way. No sooner had she spoken than his hands tightened around the steering wheel.

"Billy, I—" she started, feeling the immediate need to apologize. Though the car ride wasn't long enough to explain herself or her actions, and certainly not long enough to apologize for them.

"So you think the stash isn't real?" Billy interrupted. There was a tightness to his voice. It caught Mara off guard but she didn't ignore the question.

"I think that guy and this Beck person believe there is," she admitted. "But, really, I can't see how. The investigation into my father's business was exhaustive. Don't you think we—or you and the department— would have come across this cache of money or narcotics? At least have heard a rumor about it?"

In the rearview mirror Mara could see Billy agree with that.

"Still, like you said yesterday, we never were able to fully flush out your father's network," he pointed out. "Maybe that includes this stash."

Mara felt her cheeks heat. She was frustrated and she had a feeling it was only going to get worse. Putting her father in prison should have been the end of this particular brand of headache. And, with some loathing on her part, she realized, heartache. Memories of her childhood filled with a loving father, always watching out for her and taking care of her, tried to break through the mental block she kept up at all times. It was too difficult to remember the good times when she had so thoroughly helped bring in the bad.

"Either way, I don't think it really matters whether or not it's real," she said, hearing the bitterness in her tone just as clearly as she assumed Billy did. "As long as they think *I* know where it is, then Alexa is in danger."

The car slowed as they took the turn into the parking lot of the station. Billy pulled into a staff spot, quiet. Mara wondered what was going on behind those forest green eyes of his. He cut the engine and she didn't have to wait long for him to tell her.

"Well, then, we're going to have to convince them that you don't."

The man's name was Caleb Richards and he'd made a nice little petty criminal career for himself in the past decade. With breaking and entering, convenience store theft, a multitude of speeding tickets and an aggravated assault charge, Caleb's history painted a picture of a man who didn't mind stepping over the line of what was right or wrong. Law be damned.

"That's quite the track record," Billy said to the man after reading his record out loud. They were on opposite sides of a small metal table in the department's lone interrogation room. Behind a two-way mirror sat Suzy and Captain Jones, watching. He'd asked Mara to stay in his office. She might not have admitted it, but her run-in with Caleb had shaken her up more than she was letting on. "And now running from the cops after attempted—what?—kidnapping? That's a bit of an escalation for you, don't you think?"

Caleb's face contorted into an ugly expression of anger.

"Kidnapping? That woman attacked *me*," he yelled. "I was just minding my own business. She should be the one wearing these, not me!" He yanked his hands up as much as his restraints would let him.

"She said you came up to her asking about money and drugs," Billy went on, playing it cool. "In your words, *blood* money. Again, from where I'm sitting that doesn't sound like you were the innocent one in all of this." Caleb shook his head but didn't respond. Which was probably the smartest thing he'd done that morning. Billy pressed on. "Listen, Caleb, Mara doesn't know where the stash is. Despite what Beck tells you, I assure you, she doesn't. I would know," he said honestly. "And I think it's time I tell him that face-to-face. Caleb, where is Beck?"

The man's anger seemingly transformed. Fear registered clearly when he uttered the four words Billy hated in interrogations.

"I want a lawyer."

"This would all be a lot easier if you'd just cooperate with us," Billy tried. "Make a deal and tell us everything you know about your boss and we might take running from a cop off the table."

Billy already knew Caleb wouldn't bite. He was that special kind of stupid criminal, motivated purely by fear. And right now he wasn't afraid of Billy or being charged. Which was more telling than if he'd just stayed quiet.

"I'm not talking until I have a lawyer," Caleb responded. "Got that?"

Billy rapped his fist against the tabletop and smiled.

"Got it."

He shut the interrogation door behind him just as Captain Jones and Suzy stepped out of the observation room.

"What now?" Suzy asked, following him as he started to go to his office. He paused long enough to catch Dane's eye.

"I have an idea," he said. "But I think it's time the captain takes a coffee break."

Dane respected, and what's more, trusted Billy, so he decided to play along.

"I've been needing a refill anyways," he said. "And anything that happens while I'm getting that refill, I'll have no knowledge or part of, is that understood?"

"I wouldn't steer you wrong," Billy assured him. Dane nodded and left them outside Billy's office.

"Okay," Suzy said, unable to hide her trepidation. "What's this bad plan of yours?"

Chapter Eight

No sooner had Mara slipped into the interrogation room than Caleb tried to tell her to leave. He was more than surprised when she shushed him.

"Be quiet, you idiot," she said in a harsh whisper. She shut the door quietly behind her but paused to listen for anyone who might have heard. At least Caleb was good at following some instructions. He didn't make a peep.

"I suggest you don't raise your voice," she said, taking a seat in the chair opposite the man. He watched her through a shade of confusion and an even darker shade of mistrust, both apparent in his widened eyes and pursed lips. He hadn't expected to see her, she suspected. Certainly not alone. That was just fine by Mara. She didn't need his trust. She just needed to avoid his suspicion. "The sheriff just stepped out on a call and the rest of them are otherwise distracted, but I wouldn't push our luck by wasting any time."

Mara leaned back in the chair, crossed her arms over her chest and lifted her chin enough to show that she was above the business she was about to discuss. And, by proxy, above Caleb. His round eyes took on more of a slit as he, in turn, tried to size her up. Criminal background or not, Mara knew she was smarter than he was.

"I told you all that I'm not talking until I get a lawyer." He said it slowly, testing her.

"Well, good thing I don't care about all of that," Mara said dismissively. "What I *do* care about is this." She dropped her arms from her chest and jabbed one finger on the tabletop. Not dropping her fixed stare into his beady little eyes, Mara kept her voice clear, yet low. "How did Beck find out about my father's stash when we spent so much time trying to keep it a secret?"

Caleb's reaction was almost laughable. His eyebrows floated up so high they nearly disappeared into his hairline.

"You're saying you do know about the stash, then," he said with notable excitement.

Mara shushed him again for his volume.

"Yes. What do you think I am? An idiot like you? Of course I know about the stash. I'm Bryan Copeland's only child. Do you really think he'd build his own drug empire and *not* tell me? We always knew he might get caught, so he came up with a backup plan. Me."

Caleb's look of surprise morphed into a smugness. He leaned toward her.

"I wasn't buying you not knowing anything," he said, matter-of-factly.

"Glad to know you've got some brains in that head of yours," Mara replied with a little too much salt.

"Hey, you better watch that mouth of yours," Caleb warned.

Mara snorted.

"Or what? You going to magically uncuff yourself and beat me while in the middle of the sheriff's department? Honey, you can't honestly think *that's* a good idea."

Whatever smart retort, or at least his version of one, was about to tumble from between Caleb's crooked teeth stalled on his tongue. Like she'd suspected, Caleb was a small fish in a big pond. If he had been prepared to kidnap a woman and her child for Beck then he was either a very loyal lackey or just one who responded to the confidence of the man in charge.

Or, in her case, the woman.

"Now, here's the deal," Mara continued, lowering her voice but not enough to lose its strength. "I want to know how Beck found out about the stash and, for that matter, who this Beck person is. Because I've heard of a lot of people—a lot of big players—and I promise you I haven't heard his name even once."

There it was.

Clear behind his damp straw-colored eyes. An internal struggle while he weighed his options. To help her image Mara tapped her fingers on the tabletop.

"Don't let my mom jeans fool you," she added. "I'm not this soft, compassionate creature you think I am. And more than the same goes for my father. So answer me. *Now.*"

"Or what?" Caleb shot back with more bite than Mara had anticipated. If she couldn't sway him to see her, or her father, as more threatening than Beck, then he wouldn't give her any of the information they needed.

"Or what?" she repeated, stalling. "I'll tell you what."

And then it was Mara's turn to have a terrible idea.

BILLY WATCHED THROUGH the two-way mirror in absolute awe as the woman he thought he knew completely and intimately grabbed the front of Caleb Richards's shirt and, in one quick, smooth motion, pulled him down hard. The man was so caught off guard that he didn't even try to shield his face. It connected with the top of the table, making a *whack* so loud it was nearly comical.

"If you don't tell me, my father will figure it out soon anyways and then he'll tell everyone it was you who snitched on Beck," Mara said, sitting back in her seat like she wasn't the cause of Caleb's current pain. He put his elbows on the table so he could cradle his nose. There was no blood that Billy could see, but that didn't mean the man wasn't hurting. "Then you'll have not only Bryan Copeland and his associates gunning for your head, you'll also have this Beck fellow and whoever it is he deals with waiting for you to show up. Jail or not, you'll become a target. And I don't have to spell out what will happen when your boss finally catches up to you." Even from Billy's angle he could see the corner of her lips pull up. "Or do I?"

Caleb let out a volley of muttered curse words but he didn't outright try to fight Mara.

"Damn, she's good," Suzy whispered from Billy's side.

He had to agree.

Caleb took a beat to calm his anger.

"I'm screwed either way, then," he finally said.

Mara held up her finger and waved it.

"You tell me what you know and us Copelands will take that as a sign of good faith," she said, diplomatically. "We'll forget your indiscretion of working for a competitor and may even reward you for being helpful. That is, if you *can* be helpful."

A smarter man would have pointed out that Bryan Copeland was no longer competing for anything. That even though some hardened criminals still had a network outside of their prison cells, Bryan's operation had been thoroughly dismantled. Largely thanks to the woman sitting opposite him, promising him a fictional safe haven. However, Caleb Richards didn't appear to be the brightest of men. Mara had found a spot to put pressure on, and after one more long look at her, he cracked.

"I've only heard him go by the name Beck," Caleb started, not looking at all pleased at what he was doing, but doing it all the same. "He found me in a bar, knew my name and asked if I liked money." Caleb shrugged. "I said *hell, yeah, I do*, and he said I could make a lot of it if I came and worked for him."

"Doing what, specifically?" Mara interjected. "Grabbing me?"

Caleb nodded and scrunched up his face in pain. He rubbed the bridge of his nose.

"He said he'd already done the hard part of getting you to town. All I had to do was get you to tell me where the stash was and grab you if you didn't. Then let him get the rest out of you."

"Wait, Beck said *he* got me to come to town?" Mara asked, picking up on Billy's own question.

"Yeah, he said he knew if he let you know he was trying to find the money that you'd probably freak out and want to check on it." A grin split his lips. "He tried to follow you last night but got a flat tire. By the time he changed it he couldn't find where you'd gone so *bam* he tells me to keep checking all of your favorite spots in town to wait you out."

Billy felt his anger start to ooze up through his pores and turn into a second skin. His hands fisted at his sides.

"And how would he know my favorite spots? Is he from Carpenter or Kipsy, or is he just blowing smoke and guessing?" Mara's relaxed facade was starting to harden. She was uncomfortable.

"No, I don't think he's from here. He was complaining about the GPS on his phone the other day."

"Then he just got lucky today with guessing I'd go to the park," Mara offered. Caleb shook his head.

"He told me you used to go running there a lot and probably wanted to show your kid the playground since the sun was shining and all. Though, I guess that was a leap of faith on his part."

"But how did he know that?" Billy asked aloud.

"If he's not from here then how did he know I used to go to the park?" Mara asked a split second later.

"He said his friend knows you. And before you ask, no, I don't know his friend or anyone else he works with, really. I only ever met him at the hotel he's staying at."

"And what hotel is that?"

By God, if Caleb didn't tell her.

A KNOCK ON the door stopped Mara from asking any more questions. Expecting to see Billy or Suzy, she was surprised to find a squat man, sweating in his suit.

The lawyer.

"May I ask what you're doing in here with my client?" the man asked, already bolstering himself up. Mara stood too fast, but recovered with a smile that started with a look at Caleb and ended with the new man.

"Oh, I'm just a friend trying to keep him company until you arrived" was all she said. The lawyer opened his mouth, to protest, most likely, but she was already moving past him into the hallway. It was one thing to pull the wool over Caleb's eyes. It was another to try it with a lawyer.

Mara didn't look back as she walked straight toward Billy's office. The closer she came the more she realized that, while she was happy with the outcome of what she'd just done, something felt off. A lot of Riker County's residents hadn't believed that Mara had been oblivious to her father's dealings. Since it had never been made public that Mara was integral in providing evidence against him, a good number of the general public had assumed she was just clever in how she'd gotten away with avoiding any charge by association. Even though *Mara* knew the truth, she realized now that maybe a part of her didn't.

Maybe there was some side of her that had always known the kind of man her father was. Maybe the person she'd just pretended to be in the interrogation room was the woman she really was, deep down.

Maybe the sweet, compassionate person she portrayed to everyone *was* the cover.

Just like her father.

Mara walked into Billy's office and stopped in the middle. Her heart was galloping and her breathing had gone slightly erratic. She pushed her hands together and twisted them around, trying to physically remove herself from whatever hole she was falling into.

"You did great," Billy exclaimed from behind her. Mara jumped but didn't turn around until she heard the soft click of the door shutting. "I mean, he just opened up and—Mara?"

The warmth and weight of Billy's hand pressed down on her shoulder. Even though she couldn't see his face, she felt his concern through that touch.

When she turned to him, she could feel tears sliding down her cheeks.

"Oh, Billy," she cried.

Billy's expression skirted around deeper concern and hardened. His hands moved to the sides of her shoulders, steadying her. Still, she could feel the warmth of his skin through her shirt. She hadn't realized how much she'd missed it.

"What's wrong?" he asked, lowering his head to meet her gaze straight on. His eyes, a wild green that constantly changed their hue and mesmerized whoever was in their sights, pulled the reluctant truth straight from Mara's heart.

"What if I *am* like my father?"

Mara didn't know if she was looking for an answer from the sheriff or, really, if she even deserved one from him, of all people. But, bless Billy's heart, he gave her one.

Though not the one she expected.

He took a step closer until her breasts were pressed against his chest. The closeness brought on a new reminder. One of her body naked against his. Sharing his warmth until it became their heat.

"You are *not* like your father," he said. His voice had dropped an octave. Its rich new volume surrounded Mara, trailing across every inch of her body like a silk ribbon. She resisted the urge to let her eyelids flutter closed. It had been too long since she'd heard Billy talk to her like that, and it wasn't helping the images already starting to pop up in her mind. The fear of being like her father started to chip away. But not from his words. It was because the man himself was less than a breath away. If she moved her head up enough she'd be able to meet his lips with hers. Would it be the worst idea she'd had?

No. It wouldn't.

"Mara," Billy whispered, though to her ears, it sounded more like a plea. Mara couldn't find the words to respond, if that's what it really was.

A warm flush started to spread through her body as Billy loosened his hold. Instead of backing away, his fingers trailed down her arms and then made the jump to her hips. The air between them went from fear and concern to something else entirely, charged enough that Mara was left speechless.

That was how it went with the two of them. They only needed an instant for their fire to ignite.

"Mara," Billy repeated. He dropped his head but not his gaze. He angled his lips toward hers and Mara, God help her, finally closed her eyes, ready to feel Billy's lips on hers after two years without him.

But Beck wasn't done with them yet.

The sound of glass shattering ripped away whatever moment they were about to have. But it was the sound of Alexa's high-pitched cry that had them running out the door.

Chapter Nine

The possibility that the sound was something as simple as a cup falling off a table and breaking was quickly dismissed when another crash of glass sounded. This time it was followed by Billy throwing his body into Mara's and pulling her down to the floor. He made a cage around her, his hand flying to the gun at his hip in the process.

"Shooter outside," he yelled. On the end of his words were other shouts from the rest of the department. The empty hallway filled as everyone tried to find the source.

"Shots through the conference room," Billy yelled as a *thunk* split the air.

"Alexa," Mara cried. She nearly broke Billy's hold to go the couple of feet to the conference room door. The room where Alexa had been playing with Cassie. The half wall of glass that made up the interior wall of the room crashed to the hallway floor. Billy's hold was concrete around her. Alexa's continued crying was physically pulling Mara but the sheriff was having none of it.

"Stay here, Mara."

"Alexa—" she tried, but Billy wasn't budging.

"I'll get her."

Mara willed her body to stay still long enough to convince the man she wasn't going to run into the line of fire. The hallway around them was filled with noise as Billy and Suzy barked out orders and relayed information back and forth.

Then Billy was calling out to Cassie, the only person watching Alexa.

She didn't answer.

Billy pulled his gun up high and moved in a crouch until he was in the conference room.

"We need a medic," he yelled as soon as he disappeared from view.

In that moment Mara knew that nothing on earth or in heaven could have kept her from going into that conference room. She mimicked Billy's crouch and was about to rush in when someone grabbed her shoulder.

"Let me go first," Suzy said, brandishing her own firearm.

Mara had enough sense to pause, but no sooner had the chief deputy cleared the door than Mara was in the room.

"Oh, my God!"

The window that looked out onto the street was broken, glass sprinkled on the floor in front of it and on the conference table. However, it was what she saw on the other side of that table that had Mara's stomach dropping to the ground.

Among the scattered LEGOs and books was a blood trail that led to the opposite side of the room, just out of view of the window. There, tucked in the corner, was Cassie, sitting up and bracing herself against the wall with Alexa pushed into the corner behind her.

Even though Billy was at Cassie's side, the injured woman found Mara's gaze and spoke to her.

"She-she-she's o-okay," she gasped.

"Don't talk, Cassie. Save your strength," Billy ordered, tone sharp. He put his hand to the side of Cassie's neck. Blood ran between his fingers.

Mara kept her crouch low as she hurried to their side.

"Get Alexa," Billy ordered. His voice was cold. No doubt helped by the blood he was trying to keep staunched by holding the trainee's neck. Cassie started to move but he stopped her. "Mara can grab her. Don't move."

"Thank you, Cassie," Mara said. She touched the woman's shoulder and focused on her daughter. It was clear Cassie had been shot, yet she still had been trying to protect Alexa. Mara reached over her and grabbed for her daughter. Once the little girl realized who she was, her crying only became more pronounced and large tears slid down her cheeks.

"You're okay," Mara whispered, trying to soothe them both. "You're okay."

"Suzy, take them out of here," Billy ordered as soon as Alexa was pressed against Mara's chest. "Somewhere with no windows. Don't come back until you have a medic with you."

Billy didn't meet Mara's eyes. Instead, he started to talk to Cassie in low, reassuring tones. The whole scene squeezed at her heart.

There was so much blood.

Suzy led them to the dispatcher's small break room, separate from the one law enforcement used, and set down Mara's bag by the door. She hadn't realized Suzy had grabbed it in the first place.

"Stay here until we know everything's alright," Suzy said.

Mara nodded.

Alexa continued to sob into her shirt.

It was Suzy who came to get Mara and Alexa when everything calmed down. The department was filling with people and Suzy had to take them out the back to her car to avoid most of them. She wouldn't explain what was happening until they were driving out of the lot. All Mara knew was that Billy was on the search to find the gunman, along with Chief Hawser and some of his officers. It wasn't every day that someone was brazen enough to attack a law enforcement department. Even more rare was the reality that the shooter had managed to kill, which was the first bit of news Suzy relayed.

"Caleb Richards is dead. The second shot hit him in the head."

"But how?" Mara was shocked. "He was in the interrogation room. There's definitely no windows in there."

"The poor SOB had to use the bathroom. He got his lawyer to let him go as soon as he walked in. He was shot in the hallway, right in front of the door."

A chill ran up Mara's spine and then invaded every inch of her. The one place she'd thought was completely safe hadn't been able to prevent a death.

"We think the first shot was meant for Caleb," Suzy continued, not stopping for Mara's thoughts. She looked out the windshield, directing her car through traffic. They'd decided that leaving Mara's car in the department parking lot was a good idea. They'd only paused to put Alexa's car seat in Suzy's. "He meant to shoot through the conference room windows once at Caleb,

I'm assuming, but—" Suzy paused and seemed to re-think what she'd been about to say.

"But Cassie had the bad luck to walk by the window when he shot," Mara guessed. She looked in the rear-view mirror to the back seat, where Alexa was nodding off. She'd been able to calm the toddler down during the half hour or so they'd been in the break room. Pure white rage streamed through Mara at the thought that someone could have...

Mara stopped her thoughts before they went to the darkest *what if* she could imagine. Alexa had had a ter-rifying day, but at the end of it she was safe.

"How is Cassie?" Mara had heard when the first re-sponders had carted the woman out but hadn't stepped out from the break room to see firsthand. She hadn't wanted Alexa to see any more blood than she already had.

"She went into surgery as soon as she got to the hospital. Her sister met her there. Beyond that, I don't know."

Mara felt tears prick behind her eyes. She fisted her hand against her thigh.

"Any idea who the shooter is?"

Suzy's knuckles turned white as she gripped the steering wheel.

"No," she admitted. "But believe you me, the sheriff is sure going to find out."

"Good."

They didn't talk the rest of the way to Billy's and Mara couldn't imagine it another way. When she'd started to work with Billy to help bring down her father they'd kept Mara's involvement a well-guarded secret. Suzy had been the only person in the department who had known from the start. At first, Mara had wondered if Billy's insistence on including the woman was born from a relationship that was more than professional. Now Mara knew Suzy was his best friend.

Suzy is good people, Billy had told her, simply. *I trust her more than anyone. And you should, too. She'll never steer you wrong and will always have your back.*

And that's how Mara knew Suzy knew about Alexa.

"You haven't asked why I left," Mara said when the car rolled to a stop in Billy's driveway. Suzy cut the engine. She'd be staying with the two of them until Billy was back, just in case.

"I assume you had your reasons." Suzy turned to face her for the first time, keys in the palm of her hand. "And to leave a man that in love with you, they better have been really good reasons."

"I used to think they were," Mara admitted, more honestly than she'd meant. Her cheeks flushed in response.

"And now?" Suzy asked. Her expression softened.

Mara didn't know how to answer that. Luckily, she didn't have to.

"Mama," Alexa fussed. "Mama!"

Suzy smiled. The tension in the air dissipated. Now Mara could see the mother in the woman next to her coming to the helm.

"Now *that's* a sound I have to admit I miss," she said. "There might be some uncertainty you're feeling in your life right now but I can promise you this. Enjoy this time of her life because babies surely don't keep."

For the first time since coming to town, Mara forgot about her troubles. The three of them went into the sheriff's house, talking about the joys of motherhood, and the Alabama heat and humidity, and the rising price of gasoline.

Anything other than the current dangers of Riker County.

SOMETIME LATER THAT NIGHT, Suzy left. Mara woke up from her spot on Billy's bed with a start, heart racing and breath coming out in gasps. She threw her legs over the side of the bed and tried to get her bearings. The sound of glass breaking faded away as full consciousness replaced the nightmare she'd been having. That's when she saw the note on the nightstand.

> I have to run. Two deputies are outside and I'm locking you in. I set the alarm so don't try to leave because I don't know the code to disarm it if you trip it.
> Suzy

Mara put the note back down and looked over at her daughter. The sleeping child with her dark hair framing her face looked like a princess. Tranquil during sleep, unaware of the world around her.

And those in that world who would use her mother's love against her.

Mara leaned over and gave the girl a kiss on the cheek before getting out of bed carefully. Her bare feet touched the same hardwood Billy walked across daily. It made her wonder if any other women had been in his room—his bed—since she'd gone. Surely they had. Billy was a great catch by anyone's standards. Why shouldn't he have taken a lover since? With a sinking feeling in the pit of her stomach, Mara realized Billy could indeed *still* be in a relationship with someone. It wasn't like either one of them had asked about the other's love life. Maybe showing up with his daughter had shocked him enough that he'd forgotten to mention his relationship status.

Mara exhaled until her body sagged. She followed the once-familiar trail that she'd walked during the five months they'd been together from the bed to the bathroom and turned on the hot water in the sink.

Suzy had grabbed her things from the guesthouse, both of them deciding that it would be easier for everyone to be under one roof. No matter the fact that close proximity and Billy Reed were an almost irresistible combination. Suzy had eaten in the kitchen with them before Mara had been able to go through the task of giving Alexa a bath. After that she'd played with her child until both had fallen asleep. That had been welcome yet unintentional. And Mara knew the sleep that had been easy before would now elude her until she heard from Billy.

The water felt great against her skin, warm and soothing. If she wasn't going to go close her eyes again, she might as well use Alexa's being asleep to freshen up. Mara turned off the faucet and went to the shower. Standing under the water she'd still be able to see Alexa, asleep on the bed in the other room. So, more than ready to wash the day off, Mara opened the door as wide as it would go and quickly undressed.

When she stepped into the water stream, she sighed. Then, just to make sure, she moved the shower curtain to the side enough to peek at Alexa. The little girl hadn't moved from her spot. Not even an inch.

Satisfied, Mara stepped directly under the water. It

drenched her hair and skimmed down her back while the warmth wrapped around the rest of her. She tried to clear her mind, but all it wanted was to go back to earlier that day.

And to Billy.

Thoughts alone conjured up feelings of pleasure and desire she'd thought would never come again. They weren't complicated feelings, but when they had to do with their past, how could those feelings be anything *but* complicated?

Then, as if just thinking about the man gave her the power to conjure him up, Mara heard the sheriff call out her name. Guilt flooded through her as she tried to erase where her mind had just taken her. She stepped back and quickly wiped at her eyes.

"In here," she answered, reflexively taking a step back so she couldn't be seen through the gap between the shower curtain and the tub. Billy's heavy shoes sounded outside the door.

"Can I come in?" he asked. Something in his voice snagged on a branch of her concern but she answered all the same.

"Yeah. Just please leave the door open for Alexa." Mara reached out, ready to move the curtain to look at the man, but hesitated. "Is she still asleep?"

There was a pause as he checked.

"Yeah, she's snoring a little."

"Good," she said, glad Billy's entrance hadn't woken the little girl.

They both grew silent, only the sound of water hitting Mara's chest filling the small room.

"I'm sorry for being in your space. I would have asked but you were busy and, well, the guesthouse didn't feel as safe," Mara finally said, unable to keep the quiet going any longer. Every part of her body was on alert. Even more so when Billy didn't answer. "You there?" she ventured.

"Can we talk?" He asked it overlapping her question. Something definitely was wrong. Billy's voice was low and ragged.

Raw.

"Of course."

The sound of plastic running along metal made Mara turn to face the other end of the shower. Billy pushed the shower curtain open enough for him to step over the lip and into the tub.

Mara froze, watching as the sheriff, completely clothed, stood in front of a very naked her.

Billy had seen her naked on several different occasions while they had been together. What was beneath her clothes wasn't a mystery to the man. However, she expected him to at least give her a once-over. Even if she was utterly confused as to why he was standing in front of her in the first place.

Yet Billy's gaze never left her own.

He closed the space between them so fast that she didn't have time to question it. He grabbed her face in his hands and crashed his lips into hers. Heat and pressure and an almost dream-like softness all pulsed between their lips. Mara, too stunned to react, let alone speak, stood stock-still as he pulled back, breaking the kiss. He pressed his forehead against hers and spoke with such a strong sound of relief, Mara felt her heart skip a beat.

"I'm just glad you're okay."

Chapter Ten

The first time Billy ever kissed Mara they'd been in the dining room of his house. It had been a long night of trying to track down a dealer who would decide to flip on Bryan, and Billy could tell the world was weighing heavy on Mara. As he had been bringing in their reheated coffee, he'd caught the woman in a moment she'd been trying to hide.

Elbows on the table, head in her hands, shoulders hunched, and with what must have been a myriad of emotions running up her spine and filling her shoulders, Mara had looked beyond the definition of exhausted. And not just physically.

Billy hadn't known he had romantic feelings for the woman until that moment, though he supposed he'd suspected they were there all along. Seeing her so obviously hurting, he had wanted nothing more than to comfort her. To soothe her wounds. To assure her that, even though things were grim, it didn't mean they always would be. And so Billy had pulled her up to him, kissed her full on the mouth and then, while resting his forehead against hers, told Mara that everything would be okay.

How funny that over two years later, and two rooms

over, he'd be doing almost the same thing. Yet this time he was the one who needed strength. Though, admittedly, he hadn't planned on seeking it out fully clothed in the shower.

He'd come into the house without any thoughts in his head of kissing Mara Copeland. But then she'd spoken to him through the shower curtain, just like old times, and everything in him had shifted. What if Caleb had taken her in the park? What if she'd been the one shot trying to protect Alexa? Then he'd looked at Alexa on the bed, snoring soundly, wrapped in a pink blanket with some Disney character or another on it.

When Mara had asked if he was there, Billy hadn't cared about the question. Just the voice asking it. In that moment, he'd only been certain of one thing.

He needed to touch Mara, to feel her. To know that without a doubt she was real and alive and simply *there*.

Now, though, Billy wasn't so certain of himself.

True, moments before he'd all but forgotten the world around them. But now?

He raised his forehead off hers and let his arms fall down to his sides.

"I'm sorry," he said, more aware than ever that he was standing fully clothed in front of a naked Mara. "I shouldn't have just—"

Mara threw her arms around his neck, pushing her mouth back over his. Any hesitation on his part went down the drain with the hot water. Billy pulled her body against him while deepening the kiss and letting his tongue roam a familiar path. Their lips burned against each other, suddenly alive with a mutual attention that always flamed red hot.

The rest of him began to wake as his hands pushed

against her soft, wet skin. Unable to stay still, he turned and pushed her against the wall. Water cascaded down his sides as he deepened the kiss, pulling a moan from her. He suddenly wished he had taken his clothes off *before* entering the tub.

And maybe Mara had the same thought.

She broke the kiss long enough to grab the bottom of his shirt and pull up. It stuck halfway off. Billy moved away from her to do the deed himself. He yanked it off and shucked it somewhere over his shoulder. Mara openly looked over his chest before moving her lips right back to his. She let her hands linger at the buckle of his belt. Soon it, along with everything else Billy had been wearing, was kicked out of the tub until there was nothing but skin between them. Billy hoisted Mara up and against the wall. She wrapped her legs around his waist.

They might have lived separate lives in the last two years, but in that moment, it felt like nothing had changed.

THE HOUSE HAD sounded the same for two years.

Occasionally, it creaked, thanks to the wind, despite having long since settled. Sometimes the branches of the tree outside the guest bedroom scraped against the outside wall. An owl that lived somewhere in the trees away from the house would hoot every so often, while the frogs and insects had a constant rhythm that carried from dark until light. The refrigerator's ice maker and the air conditioner both fussed a little when they came on, too. These were the noises Billy was used to, the ones he heard but never really thought too much about.

However, lying awake in his bed, two new sounds began to mingle with the house.

He turned his head to the right and looked at Mara.

Dimly illuminated from the bathroom light that filtered under the door, Billy could see the woman's face, relaxed in sleep. Her hair was splayed across her pillow like something wild and her lips were downturned. His gaze stayed on those lips for a moment.

He hadn't meant for anything to happen between them. But once Mara had kissed him, he'd known that he couldn't resist her. They might have a complicated past but there was no denying the two of them were connected by something stronger than simple attraction. They'd started a relationship during an intense investigation because being together without *being together* had been too much for either one of them to resist. They needed skin against skin, mind to mind. They needed each other, even when it wasn't what they needed separately. And it was that need that had given him something unexpected.

His attention moved to the little girl between them. Mara had curved her body toward Alexa, protecting her even when sleeping, while Billy had taken up guard on the other side.

After he and Mara had gotten dressed, Billy had been ready to sleep in the guest room or even on the couch. They both knew that their time together hadn't fixed their time apart. Especially when it came down to the fact that Mara had kept Alexa a secret. However, Mara had been quick to ask him to stay.

If only to make sure Alexa doesn't roll off the bed, she had said with a little laugh. Billy didn't know if she was joking or not, but he took the job seriously.

It *was* the first one he'd been given, after all.

For the umpteenth time since their shower together, Billy couldn't stop the blanket of questions that was being woven around him. Holding in every question he had for the mother of his child. The child she'd kept a secret. Why?

And why hadn't he asked her. Why hadn't he gotten an answer before they'd kissed or before they'd gone further?

Billy knew why.

His body hadn't cared that he didn't have answers to why she kept Alexa a secret or why she'd left at all. All it had needed was to know that Mara was safe and then all it had needed was her.

Still, lying there now, Billy knew he should have asked. Because, even if he didn't like the answer—how could he?—he needed one. Just as badly as he needed to stop Beck.

To protect Mara and his daughter.

Billy's cell phone started to vibrate just as thoughts of being a father picked back up in his mind. Both dark-haired ladies stirred. As quickly and quietly as he could, Billy got out of bed and took his phone into the hallway.

"Reed," he answered.

"We found Bernie Lutz's girlfriend," Detective Walker said, not wasting time. "After we let her go the other night she apparently jackrabbited to the next county over and got stopped going forty over the speed limit. One of the officers knew we were looking for her so they called up and we got them the sketch of Beck and Caleb. She confirmed Beck was one of the two men who threatened Bernie before he died, but had never seen Caleb."

"At least that's one mystery put to bed," Billy admitted.

"They are going to hold her for reckless driving until they can get the sketch artist back in tomorrow so we can try to figure out who this mystery friend of Beck's is. She didn't recognize any of the men she saw from the database. They warned me it probably wouldn't be until the afternoon that they could get it going, though. Apparently Walden's visit to help us was his last stop before his vacation kicked in."

"Figures," Billy muttered.

He told Matt he'd done a good job and they talked a bit more about everything that needed doing the next day before Billy ordered the man to go get some sleep. He ended the call and figured he should take the advice himself. Being exhausted wouldn't help anyone, especially when he needed to focus.

"Everything alright?" Mara whispered, surprising him when he'd lowered himself back into bed. He stayed on his back but turned to face her. Her eyes were closed and he suspected she wasn't even fully awake. Still, he answered.

"Just found another connection to Beck," he whispered.

"That's nice," she responded, the corners of her lips turning up.

Billy mimicked the smile. It had been a long time since he'd had a conversation with half-asleep Mara.

"We also caught the mayor hooking up with Will Dunlap," he whispered. "It was a pretty big scandal but I got to tase them both, so that was fun."

Will Dunlap was Mara's ex-boyfriend and he'd lived in Kipsy most of his life. They'd stopped dating a year before she'd approached Billy in the bar. Mara had said that she'd broken up with Will because her father didn't like him. In hindsight, Billy wondered if that had meant Will was a really good guy or a really, really bad one. Either way, Will left for Georgia after the breakup and Billy had checked into him in secret over the last two years. Trying to see if he had been working with Bryan, he told himself. But, if he was being honest, Billy had thought maybe Mara had gone to be with him.

Because, again, he still didn't know why she'd left. Pregnant at that.

"Good," Mara answered automatically. "I'm glad."

Billy smirked, satisfied the woman wasn't really coherent, and decided to try and get some sleep instead of continuing to mess with her. The last thing he needed to do was accidentally wake up Alexa, too.

"I missed you, Billy."

Billy froze, waiting for Mara to continue.

But she didn't.

Instead, she reached out her hand and found his, her arm going across Alexa's chest. Neither one of them woke up from the movement. Billy stayed still, eyes wide, looking into the darkness, Mara's hand in his.

Her skin was warm and soft.

Only when Mara's breathing turned even again did he finally answer.

"Once you two aren't in danger anymore you're going to tell me everything, Mara," he whispered. However, he couldn't deny one poignant fact any longer. He dropped his voice even lower. "I missed you, too."

SUNLIGHT CUT THROUGH the curtains with annoying persistence. Mara could only guess that the pervading light was what had woken her. She tried to ignore it and fall back to sleep—because if Alexa was still asleep it couldn't have been past seven—but no sooner had she shut her eyes than she realized it wouldn't happen, for two reasons.

First, the moment she had woken and stared up at the wooden beams that ran across the ceiling, she'd remembered exactly where she was. And what had happened the night before. Even as she shifted slightly in bed, Mara felt the familiar soreness of a night well spent with Billy. Just thinking about him taking her in the shower, both of them riding a wave of raw emotion, made heat crawl from below her waist and straight up her neck.

Second, when Mara turned to look at him, a different kind of pleasure started to spread within her. The sheriff was lying on his back, eyes closed and face relaxed, a sight Mara had seen many times during the time they'd been together. However, what she'd never seen before was Alexa tucked into Billy's side, also sound asleep. His arm was looped around her back, protectively, while Alexa had her face against his shoulder, her wild hair splayed around them both.

Together, the three of them made a family.

Or would have, had Mara not left.

You had a good reason, she thought to herself angrily. *You wanted to keep him safe, happy.* Mara balled her fists in the sheets. Tears pricked at the corners of her eyes. *You made a choice.*

Alexa stretched her arm out across Billy's chest and then gave him a knee to the side, as she usually did when she slept with Mara, but the sheriff took it without issue. In sleep he readjusted the arm around the little girl until both settled back to comfortable positions.

You made a choice, Mara thought again. *But now it's not just you anymore.*

Mara felt her chest swell as the idea of the three of them together flashed through her mind. Was that even possible after everything? Did Billy even want that? Sure, they'd had quite the experience in the shower the night before, but that could be chalked up to the heat of the moment. But one night didn't erase her abandonment.

Two *thuds* from somewhere in the house shattered Mara's thought process.

"Billy," she immediately whispered. She grabbed his arm but didn't wait for him to stir. Trying to be quiet, she threw her legs over the side of the bed and ran to the bedroom door. It was already shut, but she threw the lock. When she turned, Billy was not only awake, but untangling himself from Alexa, trying to get out of bed.

"I think someone is in the house," she whispered, coming to his side. Alexa rolled over to the middle of the bed and blinked up at the two of them as Billy stood. "Wait, is someone *supposed* to be in the house?" Mara asked, realizing with a drop of her stomach that maybe the night before *had* been just their heightened emotions and that Billy could have a lady friend who frequented his place.

"*No one* is supposed to be here but the two of you." It was a relief that didn't last long. Another noise sounded from the front of the house. "Take Alexa and get in the bathroom. Call Suzy." He grabbed his cell phone from the nightstand and handed it to her. Then he opened the drawer and took out his gun. Mara grabbed Alexa, trying not to seem too alarmed. Thankfully, when the little girl first woke up in the morning, she was the calmest she ever was. She yawned and let herself be picked up.

"Mama," she cooed.

Billy was about to say something else when a floorboard creaked in the hallway near the bedroom door. The handle started to turn. Mara remembered the lock was busted. Billy pushed Mara with Alexa behind him and raised his gun.

Mara's heart hammered in her chest. Was Beck brazen enough to break into the sheriff's house or send someone else to do it? Was the intruder there to take Mara? Or maybe find out what Caleb had told them at the station? What if the shooter was just there to clean house?

"I have a gun trained on the door and I won't hesitate to use it," Billy barked out.

Another creak sounded.

"Billy Marlow Reed, if you shoot me and ruin my favorite blouse, so help me I will come back and haunt you!"

Billy instantly lowered his gun but Mara didn't loosen her stance. She didn't recognize the voice. Another creak sounded and soon a woman was opening the door, a hand firmly on her hip.

"Sorry," Billy said, sounding like it. "But next time, Mom, you've got to call before you show up."

Chapter Eleven

What a sight they must have been for Claire Ann Reed.

Billy had a pair of flannel sleep pants on and a white T-shirt, and he had a crazy case of bed hair not to mention a gun in his hands. Alexa was in Mara's arms and sporting equally wild hair and a Little Mermaid nightgown that went to her shins. And Mara? Well, she wished she could have met Billy's mom wearing more than one of his old sports shirts, two sizes too big, and a pair of his boxers. Why she hadn't declined the clothes he'd handed her after their shower and simply grabbed her own out of her bags, no more than two steps from the bathroom, she didn't know.

"To be fair, I *did* call," Claire said with a pointed glare at her only son. "Twice. And when you didn't answer I decided to let myself in. And, to be fair *again*, I'm your mother, it's Christmastime and you should have known I'd come in early!" For the first time she looked at Mara and Alexa. Her demeanor changed from scolding to polite. She smiled. "Now, I have fresh coffee in the kitchen, if you'd like some."

"Fresh coffee? How long have you been here?" Billy asked.

Claire laughed.

"Long enough to slice up some apples and oranges for a healthier breakfast than I'm sure you usually eat." Claire looked at Mara. "Maybe the girl might like some?"

"Alexa," Mara offered. "Her name is Alexa. And she does love oranges."

Claire's smile grew until she looked back at her son.

"Now get dressed and come explain to me why you almost shot me." Her eyes turned to slits. "And why there's no big green tree with ornaments and lights all over it in the living room."

And then she was gone.

Mara and Billy stood still for a moment. Mara's cheeks started to cool. She hadn't realized she'd been blushing. While she knew the woman's name and had heard stories, she'd never met Claire in person. Now the chance at a normal first impression was gone.

"Well, this was unexpected," Billy finally said, moving to shut the bedroom door. He managed to look sheepish. "That was my mom."

"I gathered that," Mara said, putting Alexa down on the bed. Mara dragged her hands down her face and let out a long sigh. "Of all of the times I wanted to meet your mother, it wasn't while I'm wearing her son's boxers."

That got the sheriff to crack a smile.

"At least we had Alexa with us," he pointed out. "We could have been in a much more…compromising situation."

He was trying to lighten the mood but the comment reminded Mara to ask an uncomfortable question.

"Does she know about us? Or did she?"

The humor drained from Billy's face. He shook his head.

"She knew we were spending a lot of time together but I said you were a friend. I wanted to keep things under wraps during the investigation and trial. She doesn't know you're Bryan's daughter, though."

"Mama," Alexa said again, drawing the word out. She knew what was next but kept her eyes on Billy. They had less than five minutes before Alexa started yelling for num-nums, her favorite phrase for food.

"And how do we explain us?" Mara asked.

Billy put a hand to his chin, thoughtful.

"We don't," he finally said. "Not yet. Not until we figure out what *us* is. And not until we get this Beck situation straightened out."

It was a sobering statement but one Mara took with her chin up.

"Okay," she agreed. "Then I guess I should change."

Billy went to the closet next to the bathroom. Without looking back he said, "You look pretty good to me."

Mara put Alexa in her favorite blue shorts, a flowery shirt with the words The Boss across the front and tried to manage the girl's thick hair into a braid. It was sloppy, at best, but the toddler was hungry and let her mama know quickly she wasn't going to sit still any longer.

"I can take her out there while you get ready, if you want," Billy said after surveying the process in silence. Though he had laughed when he saw what Alexa's shirt said. Mara didn't want the man and his mother to feel burdened by attempting to negotiate with an early-morning Alexa but she also wanted to look decent before she had to sit down across from Claire Reed.

"Good luck, then," Mara said to the man. He smirked. The image sent a jolt through her. Billy Reed looked good no matter the time of day or situation. He was just one hell of an attractive man.

"Alexa, want to come eat with a crazy lady who likes to barge into houses unannounced?" he asked the girl with a slightly high-pitched voice.

"Yeah," Alexa shot back with her own high octaves.

"Then let's get out there, partner!"

Alexa was so excited by having someone seemingly on the same wavelength that she reached for Billy's hand. He grabbed hers without skipping a beat. But Mara saw him stiffen, if only for a moment. She realized that it was the first time he'd held his daughter's hand. As they disappeared from view, Mara couldn't help but feel the weight of guilt crushing her heart.

The sheriff was too good for her.

BILLY WAS HELPING Alexa with her orange slices and Cheerios when Mara came into the kitchen frowning. She'd put her hair into a ponytail and was wearing a white blouse and a pair of jeans that hugged her legs.

Those same legs had been wrapped around his waist last night while hot water ran across nothing but naked skin. Maybe when he'd gone into the bathroom to talk to her he hadn't expected or planned for them to end up having sex.

But that didn't mean he hadn't enjoyed it.

He cleared his throat. Sitting in between his daughter and mother was not the place to be thinking such thoughts. Instead, he focused on Mara's downturned lips.

"What's wrong?"

"I hope you don't mind, but Suzy called and I answered," she said, holding out his cell phone. His mom showing up was enough of a surprise to make him forget he'd left it with Mara. He wiped orange juice off his hand and took the phone.

"Suzy?"

"Billy, we've got another problem," the chief deputy said without missing a beat. "I suggest you go into a room Alexa and your mother are not in so I can use profane language."

Billy stood and held his index finger up to Mara.

"How did you know my mom was here?" he asked. He walked to the bedroom and pushed the door almost closed behind him.

"When you didn't answer, she called me. I told her you should be at home."

"Thanks for that," he said, sarcastic.

"No problem, boss." There was no hint of humor in her tone. Whatever news she had, Billy was sure he wouldn't like it.

"Okay, I'm alone now. Go ahead and get your frustration out and then tell me what's going on."

Suzy took a moment to spew some very colorful words before circling back to the reason she'd called.

"Bernie Lutz's girlfriend is dead."

Billy paused in his pacing.

"Wait, what? How? Wasn't the local PD holding her on reckless driving until the sketch artist could get there? Did they let her go?"

"No."

"But then, how was she killed?" Billy put his hand to his face and closed his eyes. "Tell me she wasn't shot while she was *in* the police station."

"She wasn't."

Billy opened his eyes again and looked at the wall of his bedroom as if it would make sense of everything. It couldn't, but Suzy could.

"Okay, tell me everything and I'll hold my questions until the end."

"I HAVE TO go visit our neighbors in law enforcement," Billy said when he came back into the dining room. He was already wearing his gun in his hip holster, badge on his belt and a button-up shirt beneath his dark blazer. His cowboy hat was even in its position of honor atop his head.

"What happened?"

"Bernie Lutz's girlfriend was supposed to talk to a sketch artist today about the man who was with Beck when he threatened Bernie." Billy went into the kitchen and came back with one of his to-go coffee mugs. "She was in the county over, being held at their police station last night, when a fire behind their building made them evacuate. By the time everything calmed down they realized she was gone."

"She escaped?" Mara asked, surprised.

"That's what they thought. Until a jogger found her a few miles away in a ditch."

"What?" A coldness started to seep into Mara's skin. "So, as far as we know, two of only three people who have had direct contact with Beck have been killed."

Billy shared a look with Mara that she couldn't define. He nodded.

"It looks that way," he said. "I'm going to head out there with Detective Walker to see if we can find anything to help us nail down Beck or his friend."

"Is Beck the man who shot poor Cassie?" Claire asked. She had set down her food to listen when Billy had come in.

"How the heck did you know about Cassie?" Billy asked. "We've been stonewalling the media until we figure out who's doing what."

If Claire was offended by her son's bluntness, she didn't voice it.

"Betty Mills, you know, that nosy old coot who lives in the house behind the Red Hot Nail Salon off Cherry, called me after she talked to her daughter who has a son who works with you—"

"Dante," Billy guessed.

"I suppose so. Anyways, *he* had the decency to call his mama to let her know he was okay because word got around that two people had been shot, including Cassie, at the department. I figured I'd have better luck communicating with you if I came to town a day earlier instead of waiting by the phone." Claire didn't give her son any room to apologize for not calling her. She turned to Mara. "I was here when Cassie first got accepted as a trainee. She was so nice and bubbly."

Guilt dropped in Mara's stomach. She realized she hadn't asked about the woman's condition when Billy had come home the night before.

"How *is* Cassie doing?" she asked, hoping the answer would ease some of her worry.

"The surgery was a success yesterday, but she hadn't woken up yet by the time I got in last night." Billy's shoulders stiffened. No doubt thinking about one of his own being shot in his domain. "Her sister said she'd keep us updated, though."

"I guess you don't have time to tell me what all is

going on?" Claire jumped in. "And why this Beck person seems to be killing everyone he meets?"

This time it was Mara who stiffened. Billy didn't miss it. His frown deepened.

"I don't want you to leave this house," he ordered. "Two deputies are already on the way, including Dante Mills. They'll be watching the front and back of the house and will check up on you every half hour." He looked to his mother. "Mom, I can't make you do anything, but I would really appreciate it if you stayed here. If Mara wouldn't mind, she can go over what's happening with you, as long as you don't tell anyone else. Not even Betty Mills, okay?"

Claire sat up straighter, if that was possible, but she nodded, her short bob of hair bouncing at the movement.

Billy walked over and kissed the top of Alexa's head. He hesitated before leaving the room. Mara knew then that Billy Reed was already 100 percent in love with his daughter. Leaving now would be impossible. Even if Billy didn't want Mara to stay.

She sighed. There were bigger issues to contend with.

For instance, Claire was staring daggers at her.

"He's scared someone will hurt you two," Claire guessed. "Why?"

Mara looked at Alexa and felt fear clamp around her heart.

"Because now I'm the only person we know of to have direct contact with Beck, who is still alive."

CLAIRE WAS A LOT like her son. Or perhaps it was the other way around. The older woman listened patiently as Mara told her everything that had happened, starting with Beck visiting her house. One detail Mara didn't include, however, was her past relationship with Billy. And that Alexa was his daughter.

"So, this Beck man wants you alive because he needs you," Claire said when Mara finished. "At least that's a silver lining, considering he seems to have a friend keen on killing."

Mara couldn't help but agree.

"As sad as it is to admit, yes, there's that."

Claire drained the rest of her coffee from the cup and looked at the toddler across the table from her. Alexa crunched on her Cheerios and became transfixed by a cartoon about pigs Mara had playing on her smartphone. While watching television wasn't exactly a tradition at their house, sometimes it was the only way for Mara to distract the girl.

"So, you came back to town to tell Billy, since he was in charge of the case against your father and is now the sheriff," Claire spelled out. Mara nodded. "And I'm guessing you also told him that Alexa is his daughter."

Mara froze, coffee cup hanging in midair.

"Excuse me?" she said, trying to recover.

Claire actually smirked.

"Any mother worth her salt is going to figure out when she's looking at her grandchild, especially when the little girl has the exact same eyes as her son," she started. "Not to mention, you don't strike me as the type of woman to let your daughter—and you for that matter—sleep in a bed with a stranger. Am I right?"

Mara didn't know what to say, so she answered in a roundabout way.

"I was the one who helped Billy build the case against my father when he first took it over. During that time we…became close," Mara admitted. She paused, trying to figure out what she wanted to say next but found the words weren't coming.

Claire's smirk softened into a small smile. She held up a hand in a stopping motion.

"Listen, my husband was a very private man and I know Billy has picked up that trait," she began. "I've learned a thing or two about respecting his decisions. Because, in the end, he usually has a good reason for everything he does. I'm going to extend that courtesy to you, too, because my son doesn't pick his company lightly. So, I'm going to assume you are a good woman. And a strong one at that, considering what you must have gone through with your father," Claire continued. "But, you coming back here lets me know that at one point you left. And while my son can keep a secret, I know he wouldn't keep one about having a daughter from me for too long." Claire reached over and took one of Mara's hands in hers. "I won't ask you why you didn't tell him about her until now, but I don't want you to sit here and deny that Alexa's my granddaughter, okay?"

Mara, despite the decision she and Billy had made to wait to tell Claire, gave a small nod, unable to look away from the woman. As if she was caught in a trance. Claire squeezed her hand before dropping it. She leaned back in her chair. She still wore a pleasant, warm smile.

"Now, if I wasn't sure you loved my son, I wouldn't be this nice," Claire tacked on. It was a startling statement that instantly got a reaction.

"Love your son? But I—" Mara started, heat rushing up her neck. This time she was interrupted by Claire's laughter.

"Don't you try to deny it," she said, wagging her finger good-naturedly. "The girl's name is proof enough you loved my son—once, anyway. And, if I had to guess, proof that you always intended to tell him about her." She shrugged. "At least, that's my feelings on it."

Mara felt the heat in her cheeks intensify. But this time she too smiled.

"Her name?" Mara asked, though she knew it was pointless. Claire Reed seemed to pick up on things quickly. Much more so than her son. She would have been a phenomenal sheriff.

"Alexa, after Alexander. Which is my late husband's name and one of Billy's favorite people in the entire world." Claire's smile widened. "You named her after her grandfather, didn't you?"

Mara couldn't help it. She laughed out loud.

"Do you know that Billy hasn't even mentioned that yet?" Mara knew it was no use denying the connection between them all. "I thought it would be one of the first things he asked me about but, no, he hasn't said a word!"

"Well, my Billy might be a lot of good things," Claire said. "But, bless him, that boy can sometimes be just plain oblivious to what's right in front of him, too."

Chapter Twelve

"How in the world did she slip away without anyone noticing?"

Billy looked over at Detective Matt Walker in the driver's seat. They'd spent the morning talking to officers and witnesses to the fire, trying to figure out what had really happened. So far, no one knew anything other than that Jessica had been there one moment and then, the next, she was gone.

"Incompetence on the officers' behalf?" the detective asked. "The fire wasn't bad enough to require all of their attention, especially since the fire department was a few doors down, and yet they still managed to lose someone in their custody."

Billy wanted to say no, because everyone he had met that morning had seemed, well, competent.

"A suspect was killed, not only in custody at our department but *inside* of it," Billy pointed out. "Whoever is behind this, whether it's Beck or his friend, they seem to have a skill for avoiding detection."

"The hotel being a good example of that," Matt said.

Billy nodded. He hadn't gotten the chance to tell Mara yet, but the hotel room where Caleb had said he'd met Beck had been searched.

Thoroughly.

They'd found nothing. Just a cash payment for six days, starting the week before, under John Smith, of all names. The hotel manager and staff had been told to call if there were any more check-ins or sightings of Beck. Discreetly.

"I should have brought more coffee," Billy finally said, massaging the bridge of his nose. "This case is giving me one of those headaches that feels like it will never go away. I've lived in Riker County my entire life and you've been here for years. How is it that two people who've never been here are navigating our home turf so well?"

"Beck's friend could be a local."

It was a thought that Billy had already discussed with Suzy. And one he hated to entertain. Though just because his love for his town and the area surrounding it was great, that didn't mean everyone else saw Riker County with the same fondness.

"If Bryan's so-called stash is in fact real then knowing where it is would help clear everything up, or at least give us a better chance at stopping this guy," Matt continued. "We could use it to bait Beck and end this mess."

Billy sat up straighter. But then he thought about Mara and her body against his, and how much he would hate it if something happened to her or to Alexa.

They'd have to use Mara for any baiting plan to work. That's why Billy hadn't put much stock in that plan yet. He didn't want her to be in any more danger. They'd just have to figure out a way to pull it off with Mara and Alexa out of harm's way.

Finally, Billy balled his fist.

"I need to talk to Bryan Copeland," he admitted.

"*That's* what I need to do. Get him to tell me where the hell this stash is if it's real."

"You think he'd tell you anything, though?" Matt asked. "Considering you're one of the reasons he's in prison?"

Billy shrugged.

"I'll just have to be persuasive."

"You think he'd tell Mara?" Matt ventured with notable caution in his tone. While Billy hadn't told the man about his relationship with Mara, he knew Matt was a good detective. Billy hoped no one else suspected a personal connection between him and Mara. Because, if they did, that meant Beck could possibly know, too. If it hadn't been for the storm the night Mara had shown up, he could have followed her straight to his house.

Just the thought made Billy even more anxious. His phone ringing with the caller ID for Mara didn't help.

"Reed," he answered.

"Billy, it's Mara."

"Everything okay?"

"Yeah, we're fine," she said quickly. Then her voice dropped to a whisper. "Billy, do you think you could come pick me up?"

Her tone made him hesitate. He cast a quick look at Matt, wondering if he should also be quiet.

"Why? What's going on?"

There was movement on the other side of phone. A door shut.

"I think I know where Dad's stash is."

"A MAN NAMED Calvin Jackson was a very unhappy man in the state of Washington who, almost a decade ago, decided to use a local high school's basement as his own personal meth lab," Mara said from her spot at the table. Billy stood at its head while Matt and Suzy were across from her. All eyes were focused as she spoke. "No one would have probably caught him had the lab not exploded—taking Calvin with it—because no one expects a meth lab to be underneath Honors English.

"That's what my father said after we saw it on the news," she continued. "He said if you ever want to hide, you do it not in the last place someone would look, but the last place someone would even associate whatever you are doing with. He said Calvin Jackson had the right idea, just not the right approach." Mara let out a quick breath. "I should have realized then and there that something was off about him, but you know. I just didn't."

Billy fought the urge to put his hand over hers. They might have shared a lot in the last twenty-four hours, but since Mara had called they had fallen into a more professional rhythm. Plus, Mara had left right when Billy had thought things between them were going great two years ago. Maybe chalking up their night together as a one-time nod to their past—and their lack of control when the other was around—would give them a chance at sharing a civil future. One where they could be friends.

One where she wouldn't leave and take their daughter with her.

The thought of never seeing Mara or Alexa again made Billy almost physically uncomfortable.

"So when Mom got out my high school yearbook from the attic, it reminded you of that," Billy guessed. He didn't miss the smile in her voice or the fact that she didn't deny his mother had done just that.

"Yes, it did."

Hiding a stash of money and drugs in a high school had seemed a far-fetched notion until Billy had remembered the school had been completely renovated almost three years ago after a series of storms that had taken their toll.

And that Bryan Copeland had been at the ribbon cutting when the addition had been unveiled.

Mara had remembered that detail because she said she'd been tickled to see her dad on the news, even if he had been in the background. It was the best lead they'd had so far. Even if that didn't automatically mean the stash was hidden somewhere on the grounds.

"But where could he have hidden it without anyone noticing?" Matt asked after Mara was done.

"Well, as far as I know, there's no basement," Billy said, trying to recall the layout. "Then again, I've been told it doesn't look like it did during my high school days. I haven't been there in years. If Bryan *was* going to try to sincerely hide it where no one but him could reach it, he could have used the construction as a way to do just that. And it meets the timeline of when the investigation started to get going. He could have used the storm as an opportunity to make his own personal fallback plan."

Suzy nodded in agreement and then cringed.

"So I guess this means we're going back to high school?"

Billy cracked a quick grin.

"I guess it does."

After several calls made by all three members of his team, Billy went back to standing at the head of the table. This time with a plan.

"Here's the deal," Billy said to the group. "Matt, I

want you to keep your attention on finding Beck and his helper or helpers. Because at the end of the day, even if we do find the stash, that doesn't mean our problems with them are over. Work the local angle. If someone we know is feeding this Beck information, we need to plug that hole quick. Talk to the local PD again. See if they have anything to help us."

"Got it," Matt said. "I think I might already have a good spot to start looking."

"Good." Billy looked at Suzy. "Suzy, I want you to come with us, because three sets of eyes are better than two."

Suzy crossed her hands over her chest.

"And?" she asked.

Billy let out a long breath.

"And I hate dealing with Robert by myself," he admitted.

"Robert?" Mara asked.

Suzy was quick to answer.

"The principal. He's something of a chatterbox."

"Which wouldn't be bad if he wasn't always talking about nonsense," Matt added.

"But we need him unless we want to wait for a warrant, which might leak to the public what exactly it is we're looking for," Billy pointed out. "Plus, if we're going to search the high school for a cache of drugs and blood money it only feels right that the principal is at least on the premises."

CARPENTER HIGH DIDN'T look like the school Billy remembered.

Its once-stained, shabby and seen-better-days structure was cleaner, brighter and nearly pristine.

One of the last places anyone would look for a stash of drugs and blood money.

Billy followed Suzy into the staff parking lot, where a man was standing next to an old Mazda.

"Is that Robert?" Mara asked from the passenger's seat.

Billy nodded.

"And we're going to let Suzy distract him while we conduct our own search," he said. "Because I can stand a lot of things, but there are some people on this earth I believe were put here just to test our patience."

Mara laughed and soon they were standing across from Robert. He was a short man with a crown of dark hair that had a shiny bald spot in the middle. His gut used to extend past the belt and dress khakis that he habitually wore, but he was much slimmer than he had been the last time Billy saw him.

"New diet," he said, looking straight at Billy. He patted his stomach. "Mama said I wasn't getting any younger and told me it was now or never to take control of my life. Health included." He sent a wayward wink to Mara at Billy's side. "She really just wants me to settle down and give her some grandbabies. I said one thing at a time, Ma!"

Mara gave a polite little laugh.

Suzy cleared her throat. "We're kind of in a hurry, Robert," she said, taking a step forward so that his attention stuck to her. "You understand what we're here to do? And why only you can help us, right?"

Robert, feeling the weight of importance on his shoulders, puffed out his chest and straightened his back. His playful smile turned into a determined crease.

"Yes, ma'am." He made a grand gesture and swept

his arm toward the front entrance. "I'm ready when you are."

Billy could tell Suzy was holding back an eye roll, just as he could tell Mara was trying not to laugh, but soon the four of them were heading up the walkway.

"Did you really tell him what we were looking for?" Mara whispered when Robert got out his keys. Since it was a Saturday, he'd promised no one else would be inside during the day.

"That we had reason to believe that harmful substances could have been hidden on the premises and we'd like to take a cursory look on the down low before causing a panic."

"And he just agreed to that?"

Billy shrugged. "He'd rather be sure before he subjects his school to good ole small-town scrutiny."

"I can't blame him there," Mara conceded.

Robert opened the door and they all stepped into the lobby. Like the outside, the inside looked much nicer than the school Billy had attended. Still, he inhaled and couldn't help but feel a twinge of nostalgia. The urge to tell the story about a fifteen-year-old Suzy giving Kasey Donaldson a black eye for saying she shouldn't be allowed to play capture the flag because she was a girl was almost too great to resist. Especially when Billy realized the principal's office was still straight ahead, next to the stairs that led to the second floor. He'd watched Suzy do several marches into that office with her chin held high.

Hell, he'd done a few himself.

"Okay, why don't we split up to make this faster," Billy said, shaking himself out of his reverie. "Suzy, you and Robert take the gym and detached buildings, and we'll search the first and second floors of the main building."

Suzy didn't even bat an eye at being paired up with Robert. By the hard set of her jaw, Billy saw that she was in work mode. They had a problem that needed to be solved.

Finding Bryan Copeland's stash would solve it.

Robert followed Suzy, already babbling about something, while Mara turned her attention to him.

"You know, in movies, it's usually a bad idea to split up," she mused.

"Stick with me and you'll be alright, kiddo."

Mara was quick to respond with a wicked grin. It made Billy feel a lot of things he shouldn't be feeling. Maybe they should be splitting up, after all.

It wasn't until they made it to a second-floor classroom that the idea of *them* pairing up showed itself to be a bad one.

Mara noticed a panel of ceiling tiles that were painted a different color than the many others they'd already seen. Since their motto was to leave no stone unturned, she pulled a table over and stood on top of it. She wasn't short, but she wasn't the tallest woman, either. She pushed one tile up but she couldn't see inside the ceiling. She needed just a little more height.

"Billy, get up here and look."

"I don't think so," he said seriously. "I'd snap that table in two."

"Then—"

"It's probably not the best idea for me to get on those chairs, either. Donnie Mathers tried to jump from one to the other in tenth grade and one broke from under him. Broke his arm, bone sticking out and everything." Billy shook his head. "But what I can do without breaking anything is hoist you up."

"Then how about we nix the table and chairs. You're certainly tall enough to be better than a table."

Mara didn't wait to be invited to him. She jumped down and stood in front of him expectantly.

"Just like the time I helped you get that branch that was hanging off of your roof," she said. When he hesitated, Mara feigned offense. "Unless you think I'm too heavy to pick up."

"Don't even pull that," he said, but it got the job done. He wrapped his hands around her and hoisted her up until she was able to move a tile.

"A little more," she said, trying to keep her mind on the task at hand and not *Billy's* hands. He was quiet but adjusted to give her a little more height. It always amazed her how strong Billy Reed was. Mara brought her phone up and shone the light around inside the ceiling.

"Nothing," she reported, not surprised. "At least we looked."

Mara braced for Billy to let her down fast but, instead, he lowered her slowly. Like molasses crawling down a tree, her body slid against his until her shirt caught on him. It had dragged the fabric up to expose her bra by the time her feet were back on the floor. She moved to pull it down, but Billy caught her hand.

She felt her eyes widen and her breath catch. The heat of his hand burned into her skin, but it was his stare that almost set her ablaze. It pierced through the few inches of space between them, and frightened and excited her more than she wanted to admit. Mara couldn't read what the man was thinking.

She sure found out.

He dipped his head down until his mouth found her own. But it was his hand that surprised Mara. While his tongue parted her lips, his hand let go of hers and traveled down to the cup of her bra. She let out a gasp as he thumbed her nipple until it hardened. It wasn't the only thing. She could feel Billy's arousal as he used his free hand to pull her flush against him.

It was fuel to their already burning fire.

Mara grabbed his belt and pulled the man closer, trying to show him she wanted him just as much as he wanted her. Right then. Right there. However, Billy surprised her by breaking their kiss. His hand dropped away, leaving her exposed skin cold.

Billy met her gaze.

Those green eyes spelled out one word to her.

Regret.

"I-I'll check the rooms at the other end of the hallway," she said, tugging her shirt down quickly. Before Billy could stop her, Mara rushed from the room.

But, with a heavy heart, she realized he didn't even try.

Chapter Thirteen

Mara opened her eyes and tried to make sense of what she was seeing.

Her head pounded and her side lit up in pain. She sucked in a breath and regretted how much it hurt. She tried to move, if only to distance herself from the physical discomfort on reflex, but realized with panic that she couldn't. Her eyes swiveled down to the object pinning her to the ground.

It was a set of metal lockers.

But why were they on top of her? And where—

Then it came back to her.

Mara moved her head from side to side to try and see the rest of the storage room behind her. Except for more lockers and cleaning supplies, she was alone.

She turned her attention back to the weight keeping her against the floor. Tentatively, she pushed her shoulder up to try and free one of her arms. Pain shot fast and hard through her side again but she managed to get her left arm free.

Mara hesitated as footsteps pounded the tile outside the closed door. Someone was coming toward it.

Fast.

Mara put her left hand under the top part of the

locker across her chest. She started to push up just as the door swung open.

"Billy," she exclaimed in profound relief.

The sheriff's eyes widened in surprise and then almost immediately narrowed. He came around to her head.

"What happened? I heard you scream," he said, already putting his hands under the top of the locker.

"I'll tell you if you get this off me," she promised, readying herself for the weight to be lifted. A part of her was afraid to see the extent of the damage done to her. She just hoped nothing was broken.

"Alright, get ready."

Billy pulled up and soon the locker was hovering over her. Mara didn't waste any time. She rolled over onto her stomach and dragged herself across the tile between Billy's legs. The pain she'd felt before nearly bowled her over at the movement.

"I'm out!"

Mara turned back to watch the lockers crash to the ground. The noise rang loudly through the room and into the hallway outside. She'd been gone from Billy's side for less than ten minutes. It had been more than enough time for trouble to find her.

"Get your gun out, Billy," she said, a bit breathless. Bless the man, he didn't hesitate. He unholstered his gun, kept his back to the wall and crouched down next to her.

"Someone pushed those over on you?" He motioned to the lockers.

Mara nodded.

"I was looking in them and heard someone walk up.

I thought it was you but the next thing I knew I was waking up on the floor under them."

Billy said a slew of curses that would make his mama angrier than a bull seeing red and pulled his cell phone from his pocket. He must have dialed Suzy, because she answered with an update already going, loud enough for Mara to hear. They hadn't found anything yet in their search.

"Suzy, someone's here with us. Tell Robert to lock himself in a room and you come up to the main building pronto. We're on the second floor."

"Want me to call in some—"

The unmistakable sound of gunshots rang through the air. Mara heard it through and outside of the phone. Billy stood so fast she couldn't hear whatever it was that Suzy yelled.

But she knew it wasn't good.

"Suzy?" he called. "What's happening?"

She didn't answer but another gunshot sounded.

Billy cursed again and pulled the radio from his belt. He called for backup using a tone that absolutely rang with authority. It inspired Mara to get to her feet, though it was a struggle.

Acute pain that made her inhale lit up her side—or, more accurately, her ribs. If she hadn't broken any, she'd at least bruised them something mighty. No other part of her seemed worse for wear. Not even the knot on the back of her head where she'd hit the floor.

The moment Billy had finished his call, he turned to Mara. Surprise was clear on his face.

"I'm fine, let's go," she yelled, waving him toward the door.

He didn't wait to argue with her. Instead, he tossed

her his cell phone and then whirled back around, gun drawn.

"Stay behind me," he barked.

Mara had no intention of doing anything else.

They left the supply closet and, when Billy was convinced the coast was clear, moved down the hall, heading for the set of stairs at the end.

The second floor of the school was two wide hallways in an L-shape with classrooms lining both sides. The stairs were where the hallways converged and Mara had marched by them when she was fleeing from Billy minutes before. She'd been so embarrassed, and filled with shame and loathing and a hundred other emotions, that she'd gone to the farthest room she could find. She should have been more careful, or at least cautious, but no one should have known about their search other than Matt, Suzy, Robert and a few deputies who'd been ordered on standby.

They should have been alone in the school.

Another shot rang through the air. This time, Mara didn't hear the echo come through the phone. This time, the call ended. A cold knot of worry tightened in Mara's stomach for the chief deputy and the principal.

Billy quickened his steps, moving with his gun high and ready. Mara sucked in a breath and started to follow when the sheriff stopped so quickly she nearly ran into his back.

"What—" she started, but Billy cut her off.

"Listen," he whispered.

Mara froze.

The unmistakable sound of footsteps echoed up the stairs from the first floor. Someone was coming. And by the set of Billy's shoulders, Mara knew it probably wasn't a friendly. Without turning his back to the stairs the sheriff began to backtrack. Mara gasped as the quick reversal made the constant thrum of pain in her side triple.

The footsteps stopped but Billy didn't.

He kept moving until they were off the stairs.

"Go hide," he ordered, voice low. He nodded in the direction of the part of the second floor she hadn't explored. But she wasn't about to question him.

"Be careful," Mara whispered. She tried to be quiet as she moved as quickly as she could toward the classrooms at the end of the hallway. She chose the middle of three and turned in the doorway so she could still see Billy.

He was looking at her. With a quick jerk of his head he motioned for her to get inside the room. So she went, leaving the sheriff alone.

The bullet grazed Billy's arm, but it was the man lunging at him that made him lose his gun. It hit the tile and skidded away while his back connected with a wall. Billy took a punch to his face as the infamous Beck snarled, "Where is it?"

Billy pulled his head back up and slung the man off him. If Beck hadn't shot half a magazine at him as soon as he'd seen Billy on the stairs, forcing the man to take cover long enough so Beck could run up, he wouldn't have had the chance to question Billy. Let alone lunge at him.

Blond hair cropped short against his scalp, blue eyes that held nothing but hatred for Billy, and the thin, drawn face of a man who looked to be in his late thirties, all wrapped in a pair of khaki slacks and a collared shirt, Beck didn't look nearly as threatening as Billy had imagined. Certainly not a man trying to create another boom in the drug industry of Riker County.

But neither had Bryan Copeland.

Billy knew that bad men didn't have just one look. Bad men were just men who did bad things. Whether one wore a suit or a wifebeater, it didn't matter.

While Beck tried to regain his balance, Billy threw his own myriad punches. One connected with Beck's jaw, another with his ribcage. The latter blow pushed his breath out in a wheeze but he didn't go down. Instead, he used Billy's attack against him. Bending low, Beck rammed his shoulder into Billy's stomach, throwing him back against the wall.

"Where is it?" he roared again. Beck's anger was getting the better of him. The man took the time to rear his fist back, like he was winding up for the big pitch.

It gave Billy time to bring up his own fist. Hard. It connected with Beck's chin with considerable force. The man made a strangled noise and staggered backward. He held his jaw with both hands. Billy didn't waste time watching what he did next. He turned to look around for his gun.

It lay beneath a water fountain a few feet away.

Billy was running for it, already mentally picking it up and swinging it around on Beck, when he registered a new noise. Footsteps, coming fast.

Could Mara have tried running up to help?

But it wasn't Mara.

He turned in time for something to slam against his head.

Then everything went dark.

"WHERE'S BILLY?"

Matt Walker stood in the doorway, a frown pulling down his lips. Sirens sounded in the distance.

"He's okay, but—"

"But what?" Mara walked past him, pain be damned.

"Mara, I need you to stay, just in case," Matt tried, but she was already looking for the sheriff.

"Billy!"

Billy was on the ground. Sitting up, but still, on the ground. He had a hand to the back of his head. His face was pinched. He was obviously in pain.

"I'm okay. Got caught by surprise. Apparently Beck's friend is here." His gaze shot to her side. Mara realized she'd been clutching it. The pain kept intensifying the more she moved.

"Bruising, that's all," Mara said. "What happened out here?"

"I turned my back on the stairs and I shouldn't have." Billy looked to Matt. "One minute I was fighting him and then the next I got slammed with something. Then I could hear the sirens. Beck and his buddy must have run."

"Did you pass out?" Mara asked, worry clotting in her chest. She put her hand to the spot Billy was holding to inspect it closer. There was blood.

"For a second," he said dismissively. The detective must have cleared the other rooms down the hallway she'd been hiding off and jogged back to them. "Matt, Suzy should be outside at one of the buildings. She had Robert with her. Someone was shooting at them."

Matt nodded and grabbed his radio. He told everyone who was listening to keep their eyes out for two suspects and to find Suzy. Apparently he had no intention of leaving Mara and Billy. She was glad for the detective's company. Billy wasn't looking too hot.

"Don't move," Mara chided when he tried to stand.

Billy, of course, tried anyway.

Mara rose with him, hands out to steady the sheriff if needed.

"I'm fine, I promise," he said, swatting at her. As soon as his hand cut through the air, though, he started to sway.

"Billy," Mara exclaimed. She grabbed his arm and gasped at the pain from her ribs.

"You *both* need seeing about," Matt said.

"I'm *fine*," Billy tried again. He steadied himself. The hand he'd had against the back of his head was red with blood. Mara pointed to it.

"That isn't fine, Billy."

He shook his head a little, trying to be dismissive again.

"I just need to take a seat—" he started. But then the man tipped backward.

"Matt," Mara squealed, trying to keep Billy from hitting the tile floor. Matt was fast. Between the two of them they managed to stop the sheriff's fall. They eased him back down to the tile as gently as they could.

"He's unconscious," Matt said, reaching for his radio again. However, before he could call anything in, a voice was already yelling into the airwaves.

"We need a paramedic!"

Chapter Fourteen

The ER nurse was brisk when she told Billy he had a concussion and needed to take it easy. At the very least, for the rest of the day.

"I have a job to do," he objected, already slipping his badge back on. His cowboy hat soon followed.

"So do I," she retorted, her brows drawing together. The effect made her look severely disapproving. "And it's to tell you that you need to rest. Sheriff or not, you're just as human as the rest of us."

Billy was getting ready to harp on the fact that he was a human *who happened to be* a sheriff when Matt walked around the privacy curtain. He gave a polite nod to the nurse who, in turn, smiled.

"I'll go check on my other, less stubborn patients now," she said before throwing Billy a parting look of annoyance. Then she turned to Matt. "I'm going to tell you what I told him. He needs rest."

"Yes, ma'am," Matt responded, dutiful. Billy rolled his eyes.

She pulled the curtain back again so they were out of sight of the rest of the nooks that lined the emergency room. Thankfully, it wasn't crowded.

"I thought everyone was supposed to love the sheriff," Matt said with a smirk the moment she was gone.

Billy shrugged.

"Apparently not everyone got that memo." The nurse had been more kind to Mara when he'd insisted she get checked out first. Then, when the tables had turned, Mara wouldn't stop fussing. It wasn't until she went upstairs that Billy realized the nurse wasn't going to cut him any slack. "So, what's going on?"

"Like I told you on the way over here, it's been confirmed that Bryan's stash isn't at the school," Matt started, taking a seat on the doctor's stool. He pulled out his pad to look at the notes he'd written. "After hearing what happened, Chief Hawser offered up a few of his off-duty officers to comb the school again, just in case. He said if that's stepping on your toes to let him know, but he didn't sound like he cared either way."

"I reckon he probably doesn't mind about stepping on anyone's toes," Billy said. "But that's not a bad idea."

"He also said his communications head suggests you hold a press conference to try and let the public know to look out for Beck, his associate and any suspicious activity." Matt cut him a grin. "I told him you already contacted the news station, right after you yelled at the EMTs to turn off the damn sirens because you couldn't hear yourself think."

Billy knew there was humor in what he'd done, but when he'd woken in the ambulance on a stretcher, Mara peering down at him through her long, dark lashes, he'd been feeling anything but humorous. Part of him knew he needed to take it easy but the other part, the sheriff side of him, knew that time was wasting. Beck and his friend weren't going to take a break just because he needed one.

"Was Hawser the only chief in the county that called in so far?" Matt nodded. Billy bet Chief Calloway, from the city of Kipsy, would be on him soon. They were usually a bit busier than the rest of Riker, but Alexandria Calloway was not the kind of chief to sit back and twiddle her thumbs about any case.

Billy figured he might as well beat her to the punch. "I'll get Dane to talk to Chief Calloway and see if she can make sure all of her officers stay in the loop." His head thrummed with a dull ache. Like putting a shell up to his ear and hearing the ocean but, in Billy's case, he couldn't seem to put the shell down. The doctor had given him something for the pain and nausea but he'd refused to get the really good stuff. He had a job to do. He needed to stay sharp.

"While all of this posturing is going on, I need you to keep on trying to figure out who this Beck person is and who's helping him," Billy said. "Use Caleb as a start since he's the only person we actually know the identity of. Once I get out of here I'm going to call in a few reserve deputies to see if we can't narrow down a possibility as to where our friends are at least staying since we burned their hotel bridge."

Matt nodded. He wrote something down and closed the pad. He looked a bit alarmed when Billy swung his legs over the bed and stood. Billy pointed at him.

"If you tell me to rest, I'll fire you on the spot," he threatened.

Matt's grin was back.

"Wouldn't dream of it."

"Good, now get to work. I'm going to go upstairs and then head back to the office."

It hadn't been until a little after he'd come to in the ambulance that Billy had learned Suzy had been shot. Luckily she'd been wearing her bulletproof vest beneath her uniform. The impact, however, had caused her to fall, shattering her radio and pushing her away from her cell phone. Robert, in terror, had started to run, and she'd had her hands full wrangling him back inside the gym. He had been so frenzied that he'd hyperventilated and passed out. Which no one blamed him for. He'd expected to simply show them around the school, maybe find something interesting in the process. Not almost get killed by an unknown shooter.

Suzy was standing in the hallway on the second floor in the east wing. She had a scowl on her face and her vest in her hand. Instead of her Riker County Sheriff's Department shirt, she was wearing a plain white T-shirt. When she saw Billy, her scowl deepened.

"He ruined my shirt," she greeted. "The bullet tore right through it."

"I'm sure we could order you a new one."

"Good."

Billy was next to her now and could tell she was holding back. But that's who Suzy was. She held her emotions close to her chest. Sometimes she didn't even let Billy in, and he was her closest friend.

"Besides the shirt, how's everything else?" he asked. Suzy brought her eyes up quick, her mouth stretching into a thin line. Defensive. Billy amended his question. "I mean with the vest. How's the vest doing?"

Suzy started to say something but paused. She let out a breath and played along.

"Okay," she admitted, face softening for a moment. "Glad it wasn't shot more than once, though. It's going to bruise something wicked."

Billy smiled.

"Won't we all."

Suzy nodded, gave her own little smirk and motioned to the room behind her. The door was shut but Billy knew who was behind it.

"How's Cassie doing?" He nodded to the room.

Suzy glanced over her shoulder.

"To be honest, I don't know. All I got is that she hasn't woken up since the surgery, but she's on some pretty intense meds so that's normal."

Billy tensed. For several reasons. One was that he hadn't seen Mara since she'd left him to go with Suzy to check on the trainee. Surely Suzy wouldn't just let her wander off.

"So, Mara's not in there?" he had to ask. It made Suzy's lip quirk up for a second. She pointed down to the other end of the hall.

"Don't worry, Sheriff. Your gal's right there."

Billy ignored the comment but was glad to see the dark-haired woman a few yards away. She stood talking to an older couple he recognized as Mr. and Mrs. Gates, Cassie's parents. He hadn't realized they had already flown in, probably relieving her sister who had a few kids at home. He'd meant to meet with them, but that intention had fallen through the cracks as their case had gone nowhere but south since Cassie had been hurt. Billy scrubbed his hand down his face and sighed. It sat heavy on his chest.

"Buck up, partner," Suzy whispered. "They're coming over."

"Mr. and Mrs. Gates, it's good to see you," Billy greeted them when they stopped. He had no doubt in that moment that neither would leave the hospital until their daughter did. "I'm just sorry it had to be under these circumstances."

Mrs. Gates, a woman who probably exercised her laugh lines during happier times, gave him a weak smile. She looked exhausted and withdrawn. A shadow of the woman Billy had met at Cassie's informal birthday gathering a handful of months before. Mr. Gates, who held the strain of his daughter's near-death experience clearly on his shoulders, was faster with a verbal greeting and a handshake.

"I'd have to agree with you there," he said, pumping Billy's hand once and letting it drop. His eyes dropped with it and focused on Suzy's vest. The chief deputy had tried to angle it behind her as they'd walked up, but Mr. Gates had a sharp eye. Or maybe he was just suspicious of anything and everything. Billy didn't blame him, considering. "The man who did that to Cassie shot you?" he asked Suzy.

"We can't say for certain," she responded. "But it's a possibility."

"Either way, both incidents are being investigated thoroughly by our entire department and other departments in the county," Billy assured him. "And we're about to go back out there and join them." The words didn't seem to offer Mrs. Gates any relief the way they did her husband. Mara must have sensed it. She lightly touched the woman's arm.

"These are good, smart people," she said. "Everyone responsible will be caught and dealt with. Don't you worry about that."

Mrs. Gates turned to look at Mara. She patted her hand and nodded.

"How's she doing, by the way?" Suzy asked. "We couldn't find the doctor, and the nurse just said she was sleeping."

This was a question Mrs. Gates was quicker to answer. There was a noticeable tremble in her voice as she did.

"She's good. The surgery was quick and they say everything will heal." She touched her neck. Her voice broke as she added, "She'll, uh—she'll have a scar, though."

"But a scar we'll take," Mr. Gates jumped in. He put his hands on his wife's arms and squeezed. The pressure seemed to jog her out of the worry she'd been falling back into.

She turned to him and smiled.

"You're right." She took one of his hands and they seemed to get lost in their own silent conversation. They loved each other. That much was apparent. It made Billy want to look at Mara.

He shouldn't have done what he'd done earlier. But being that close to Mara—touching her—he'd just wanted more. His body had taken hold over his mind and reached out for her again.

And she'd reached back.

"Well, you let us know if there's anything we can do for you, but it's time for us to get back out there," Billy said, eyes firm on the couple. He didn't need to look at Mara.

What had happened between them couldn't happen again. Not now.

"THEY GAVE ME something for the pain and wrapped me up," Mara said when she was riding shotgun in Billy's car. "Like I said, it's only a little bruising. No broken ribs. So I'm fine."

"I believe you."

His eyes flickered over to her but didn't settle. It made the guilt of everything that had happened rise again within her.

"Billy, I'm sorry," she said. "I thought the money and drugs would be at the school. I was wrong and you got hurt and Suzy got shot. I just—I'm so sorry."

"It's not your fault," he said with force. "It was a good lead. One we had to chase down, one way or the other." He slapped his hand on the steering wheel. It made Mara jump. "A lead *I* should have chased down. Not you. I shouldn't have dropped my guard." There appeared to be something else he wanted to say, but his original thought must have won out. "You got hurt, too."

Mara wanted to wave off his concern, but she realized he was right. In part. Her presence might have been the reason Beck and his lackey had shown up in the first place, thinking she knew where the stash was and following her to the school. If she'd stayed at Billy's, then the sheriff and his chief deputy wouldn't have had their lives put in danger. At least, no more than usual.

That line of thinking was a straight shot to Alexa. She was still at the Reed family home with Claire, unaware that she'd come close to losing her father.

"I'm sorry, Billy," Mara whispered before she even realized what she was saying. The haze of medication wasn't as thick as she wished it was. The kind of pain that couldn't be seen was coming to the forefront. The present danger they were in was just salt in her past choices' wounds. She wasn't talking about what had happened at the school anymore. "I know you must hate me."

Billy was silent a moment, probably piecing together a polite way to agree with her, when something she hadn't expected interrupted them.

A truck slammed into the side of their car, right behind Billy. It happened so fast that Mara didn't even have time to scream. The impact rocketed them off the road, past the shoulder and right into the ditch.

Wham-bam-bam!

It wasn't until they settled that Mara realized with relief that they hadn't flipped. She turned to look at Billy, ready to voice the thought, when she saw the sheriff's eyes were closed.

"Billy?" she heard herself screech.

When he opened his eyes, she would have jumped for joy if it wasn't for the seat belt that held her tight. He shook his head a little, dazed, and then seemed to snap out of it.

"You okay?" he asked, already moving.

"Yeah, I think so. What about who hit us?"

Billy whipped his head around and looked back out at the road. The Tahoe was turned at an angle that blocked whoever had hit them from Mara's view. So when Billy started cussing, she didn't understand. But then he said one name that put everything into terrifying perspective.

"Beck."

Chapter Fifteen

Mara's heartbeat was in her ears, thumping with unforgiving relentlessness. The spike in adrenaline wasn't helping. Nor Billy's warning for her to stay down.

And it sure didn't help matters that he'd pulled his gun out.

"Call Suzy" was all Billy said before he opened his door and took aim past the back end of the vehicle.

Mara undid her seat belt and tried to get as low as possible while fumbling for Billy's phone. She found it in a cup holder and dialed Suzy, trying to get her panic under control.

"Beck just hit us off the road," Mara rushed to explain as soon as the call connected. She followed with their location before Billy yelled.

"Come out with your hands up or I'll shoot," he warned. Mara couldn't hear if Beck answered.

"I'm a minute away," Suzy said. "Keep me on the line." Mara nodded to no one in particular and put the phone on speaker. She relayed the information to Billy.

"Having a shoot-out with the sheriff isn't a good idea," Billy hollered.

Mara wished she could see what was going on. Billy

had half his body hanging out the open door and gun held high, but Mara couldn't believe it was good cover.

Would Beck really try to shoot him?

She didn't have to wonder for long.

A shot rang out. Mara gasped as the vehicle rocked.

"What happened?" Suzy yelled, but Billy had his own answer ready. He fired his gun once. It wasn't long before Beck returned fire, causing Billy to retaliate. Soon all Mara could hear was gunfire slamming into metal and glass. She couldn't tell who was hitting what. She kept her head covered and her body as low against the floorboards as she could, praying that Billy wasn't getting hit. When she saw the driver's side window spiderweb from a bullet, mere inches from Billy, Mara nearly cried.

However, when the back windshield shattered, covering the interior in a hail of glass, Mara couldn't help but scream. She closed her eyes tight and covered her head. Around the pounding of her own heart, she expected to hear the shots even more clearly without the back window, but then everything went silent.

"What's going on?" she whispered to Billy.

The sheriff's posture was rigid—a stance that said there was no way in hell he was moving until this was over—but he answered her after a moment.

"Beck got back into the car," he said. "The windows are tinted. I can't see either one of them now."

So Beck had his friend with him.

Maybe because that left him more vulnerable than he liked, Billy got back into the driver's seat and shut his door. His head stayed turned, keeping an eye on the truck. It was still on the road, level with them, but at an angle that gave neither Billy nor Beck a good, clean shot.

"They're leaving," Billy yelled, angry.

"Let's go after them!" Mara might not have liked the danger but, with a surge of anger herself, she knew then that the men weren't going to stop.

So *they* needed to be stopped.

"They shot out a tire. I tried to do the same but my angle was off," he growled. "Suzy, they're moving down Meadows, southbound. Driving the same truck Mara described when she came to town. They're missing some windows."

Suzy confirmed she heard while Billy got his radio. He gave an order for the deputies in the area to help Suzy. He also told dispatch to send a tow truck. She asked if they needed medical attention. It seemed to snap Billy out of sheriff mode. His eyes softened with concern. So much of it that Mara felt the sudden urge to wrap herself around him. To comfort him. To feel comfort from him. To feel him.

"I'm okay," she assured him instead. "Are you?"

Billy nodded, but Mara still traced every inch of him she could with her eyes. He told dispatch to hold off on the medic. When he was done with his orders, Billy scrubbed a hand down his face. A sigh as heavy as a boulder seemed to crush him.

"I agree with that sigh," Mara said, moving slowly, gingerly, back to a sitting position. She couldn't help but wince, pain meds or not. Billy's hand covered hers.

Expecting his eyes to be as soft as they had been moments before, Mara was surprised again by the man. He looked like he was ready to kill.

"We have to end this," he said, voice hard as stone.

Mara was about to agree, but then the sheriff said something that stopped her cold. "Mara, we have to talk to your father."

THE DRIVE OUT to Walter Correctional Facility took them an hour out of Riker County. In that hour, Mara had barely spoken a word. As he sat across from her father now, Billy didn't blame her one bit for needing the silence to collect her thoughts. She might have to face a man not even Billy wanted to deal with. But the fact of the matter was that Beck was escalating. Ambushing them at the school and then less than a few hours later attacking them again, this time on a well-traveled public road?

It all reeked of desperation.

Billy believed that if Mara hadn't screamed, probably making Beck and his associate remember they needed her alive, that the outcome would have been different. But she had and they'd sped off, disappearing before Suzy or any deputies could catch up to them.

Now here Billy was. In an interview room within the prison looking at a man he'd wished to never see again.

Bryan Copeland had been balding for years but he had never let a thing like losing his hair conflict with his image. He was a confident man. Always had been. He'd always worn suits and expensive cologne, and had a quick wit about him that made people laugh. He was a people person, a schmoozer, a go-get-them type filled with determination and steeped in self-esteem.

Bryan Copeland had been kind and cunning in his dealings with the general public and one hell of a dancer at parties. To his underlings, however, he had been cutthroat. Like night and day, when Bryan needed to get down to business he stripped off his disguise and showed his true face. His wit became a weapon, his charm a tool. Whatever compassion he exuded in his home life and within the community was replaced with menace and greed.

That was the man Billy sat in front of now.

Dressed in prison orange, Bryan Copeland looked across the table at him with the eyes of a snake ready to strike.

"Well merry Christmas to me," he greeted Billy. "Couldn't stay away from the man who made your career possible, *Sheriff*?"

Billy had nothing to prove to the man. Nothing to defend, either. At the time, Billy hadn't known stopping Bryan would help him become sheriff. He'd just wanted to stop the man and his business before both destroyed his home.

A choice he didn't regret and never would.

"I have some questions for you."

Bryan scoffed.

"If you can't do your job, *Sheriff*, then I'm certainly not going to do it for you."

Billy ignored his comment and put the sketch of Beck on the table between them. He kept it turned over. Bryan's eyes never strayed to it.

"Where's your secret stash?"

Bryan didn't flinch.

"First of all, that's a ridiculous question that makes you sound like you're some preteen on a treasure hunt," Bryan said. "Secondly, I don't have a secret stash."

"And third?" Billy asked with a low sigh. Bryan's nostrils flared. He didn't like it when the person he was talking to showed disinterest or contempt. It rubbed against his ego, something he'd been fluffing for decades.

"If I did have a secret stash, of whatever it is you think I have, why in hell would I ever tell you about it?" Bryan was nearly seething. His dislike for Billy was pure. The moment he'd found out that Mara had betrayed him and helped Billy was the moment Bryan Copeland began to hate him more than anyone in the world.

That's how Billy knew that just asking would get him nowhere.

So, he was going to gun for the man's precious pride instead.

"Because, if you don't tell me where it is, this man will eventually find it." Billy flipped over the picture and pushed it toward him. "And he'll use it to pick up where you left off. But this time he'll do it better, smarter and with your help whether you want to give it or not. He'll take your legacy and make it his own. In fact, he's already started."

Bryan's lips had thinned but his expression remained blank. His eyes, however, trailed down to the picture. If he recognized Beck, it didn't register in his face or posture. When he answered, he seemed as uptight as he had been when he'd been escorted into the room.

"I don't know what you came here to try and accomplish, but I can tell you now that you should have saved the gas." Bryan fingered the picture. "I don't know this man and I don't know his business. What I *do* know is that if I had a *secret stash* it would have been found during the investigation. Unless you're admitting to me now that you're not that great at your job. Which, again, to be honest, I already knew." Bryan's eyes turned to slits. His nostrils flared. "Why else would you need my daughter's help to catch me?"

Billy knew in that moment that the only way he'd get an answer was to use Mara. Because Bryan Copeland might appear to be a man who wasn't affected by the world, but the truth was he had one weakness.

His daughter.

He'd loved her so much that he hadn't ever entertained the idea that she could turn on him. That she *would* turn on him. That's why he was handcuffed to a table, sitting in an interrogation room with an armed guard behind him.

But Billy wanted to keep her out of the room for as long as he could. So he leveled with her father.

"This man goes by the name Beck," Billy started. "As far as we know, he has one associate who isn't afraid of killing. One or both of them were involved in the murders of three people, two of whom were in police custody when they were killed. They are also responsible for putting three people in the hospital, but that wasn't because of mercy. It's because the people they hurt got lucky." Billy purposely didn't name anyone who had been killed or attacked. He knew Bryan wouldn't care. His response confirmed that belief.

"So? I've had nothing to do with this Beck person or his friend. And if you don't believe me then I'm sure the warden won't mind giving me an alibi." He motioned to the room around them, as if Billy needed the fact that he was in prison emphasized.

"I'm telling you because the only reason we know about Beck is because he showed up at your daughter's house and threatened her." An almost imperceptible shift occurred in the man across from him. Billy didn't know if Bryan did or did not know Beck but the fact that the man had been to see his daughter was news to him. "Since then he's had people try to kidnap her, put her in the hospital and they've even shot at her. All because they think she knows where this stash of yours is located."

Bryan laughed out loud. This time Billy was the one who was surprised.

"They think she might be in cahoots with her old man, huh?" he said around another bite of laughter. It wasn't the kind filled with mirth or humor. It was dark. Menacing. "You and I both know how wrong the assumption that my daughter and I work together is, don't we, *Sheriff*?" He lowered his voice. Despite the decrease in volume, his words thundered. "The one who would rather be in your bed than a part of my life."

Billy was trying not to let Bryan get to him, but that one comment created an almost feral reaction within him. One where he felt the need to protect Mara's name and, to some degree, protect himself.

It bothered Billy the way Mara's only family talked about her with such distaste—such hate—while he also had never liked the fact that Bryan suspected he and Mara had been together. It wasn't that Billy had been ashamed of her—he hadn't ever been—but they'd told only a few people about their relationship. Bryan had not only guessed but been certain that Billy and Mara were together. Which meant Bryan Copeland was either really good at reading his daughter or Billy…or someone had told him.

Regardless of which it was, Billy was still bothered by it. He stood and went to the guard next to the door.

"Bring her in," he said, low enough that Bryan couldn't hear.

The guard nodded and left.

Billy returned to the table but didn't sit down. Instead, he moved to the corner of the room.

"And what tactic is this?" Bryan asked, amused. "Trying to intimidate me by sending the guard away? There are much more intimidating men in this place, Sheriff. With some tricks that end in death. This isn't going to—"

The door started to open.

"This isn't a trick," Billy interrupted. He nodded in the direction of the guard. Mara was behind him. Her back was straight, her shoulders straight, and her eyes sharp and cautious. She rounded the table and took a seat across from her father.

The amusement Bryan had shown Billy disappeared in an instant. If it was possible, he seemed to sit up straighter, as if a board had been attached to his back. With the two of them mirroring each other, Billy realized how much the father and daughter looked alike.

Mara was the first to speak.

"Hey, Dad."

Chapter Sixteen

"You've got more nerve coming here than he does."

Mara wasn't surprised by her father's response, but that didn't mean it didn't still hurt a little. She kept her face as expressionless as she could and tried to remember why they were there. Why she was subjecting herself to the emotional torture she'd tried to avoid for two years.

For Alexa, she thought. *To stop this madness once and for all.*

"I'm tired of being hunted, Dad," she said. "Beck—"

Bryan slammed his fist against the tabletop. Mara jumped.

"You wouldn't be hunted if you hadn't betrayed me," he snarled. "You made your bed when you turned on the only family you had and *both* of you are just going to have to lie in it!"

Billy started to move forward, already trying to defend her, Mara was sure, but she hadn't had her say yet.

"You tried to create a drug empire out of an entire county, Dad. That's three towns and a city worth of people," she responded. "What was I supposed to do when I found out? Sit back and watch?"

"You should have come to me," he seethed. "Not

him. I'm your *father*, your flesh and blood. I raised you, kept food on the table and a roof over your head. I bent over backwards to make sure you never wanted for anything. And now, what do I get in return? A prison cell, Mara! A damn prison cell!"

This time Mara heard Billy begin to speak but she'd had enough.

"Do you remember what you told me when you decided to move to Kipsy? You said you moved because you needed a slower pace. That you wanted to relax. Those were *your* words. And then you asked me to move there, too. Do you remember what I told you?" Mara was yelling now. Whatever dam was holding her emotions back had broken the moment her father spoke. When he didn't answer, it was Mara's turn to slam her hand against the table. It hurt but she ignored the pain.

"I said I didn't want to," she continued. "I had a good life that I didn't want to leave. I had a good job, friends and a home. But no. When I came down to visit, you talked about missing me and being lonely and how Kipsy was a good city filled with good people. You painted this picture of a life you knew I'd always wanted. One where we'd be happy, where I'd meet a good man, raise a family, and you'd sit on your front porch swinging with your grandkids and sipping sweet tea. I could even start a business and have the dream job I'd always wished for. You tried so hard to convince me to love the idea of Kipsy that it worked. I fell in love with it. So, what did you expect would happen when you started to destroy it all?"

"You could have still had all of those things," he responded, more quietly than he had been before. "I always protected you. You were never in any danger.

You could have had everything, but, instead, you sided with *him*."

Her father's eyes cut to Billy with such a look of disgust in them that the dam within her disintegrated further until there was nothing left. Mara fisted her hands and, for the first time in years, yelled at her father so loudly she felt her face heat.

"Don't you *dare* blame Billy or me or *anyone* else for your mistakes. You made them and now you're the one who has to take responsibility for them!" Mara took out the picture she'd tucked into her back pocket. She hadn't planned on using it, but she'd recognized the possibility that she might have to. She slammed the picture down and slid it over to him, next to the picture of Beck.

"You may hate me, Dad. You may not care what Beck and his friends will do to me. You may even want something bad to happen to me. But what about her?" Just seeing the smiling face of Alexa looking up from the picture calmed Mara. Her voice lowered to an even level but she didn't drop any of the hostility. Her father's eyes stayed on the picture as she continued. "This is your granddaughter, Alexa. She didn't investigate you and she certainly didn't have a hand in putting you in here. So, *please*, *Dad*, don't make her pay for our mistakes."

Mara was done. There was nothing left for her to say—to add—to try and sway her father to tell them if he really had a stash and, if so, where it was. She was exhausted. Drained. Yet relieved in a way, too. Not only was she facing her father but she had said exactly what she'd always wanted to.

His eyes stayed on the picture but he didn't say anything right away. Billy took advantage of the silence, perhaps sensing Mara was out of ideas.

"These men believe without a doubt that you have a stash and Mara knows exactly where it is. They've also made it clear that they don't care what happens to Alexa in the process of trying to find it or use Mara. They'll kill her, and then eventually they'll kill your daughter." Even as he said it, she knew he hated the words. Mara knew the feeling. Just the mention of harm to Alexa had a knot forming in her stomach.

"There's no wedding ring on your finger," her father said after a moment. "But she's his, isn't she?" His eyes were slits of rage as he looked at Billy, but she knew what he said next was aimed at her. "Don't you dare lie to me about this."

"We're not together, but yes, she's mine," Billy answered.

The simple admission that Billy was, indeed, Alexa's father should have made Mara happy, and it did—but the first part of the sentence hurt more than she expected. She strained to keep her expression as blank as possible. Maybe the last few days had just been two people caught up in madness, trying to comfort each other for different reasons. Maybe, when everything was said and done, they'd go back to their lives with the only link between them being Alexa. Maybe it had been lust and not love that had tangled them together.

Her father was watching her intently. She didn't need to think about the future when the present was being threatened.

"You two come up here like I owe you something I don't," Bryan Copeland said, standing. "Using a granddaughter I didn't even know existed isn't the way to get me to tell you anything. I can't help you." He turned and looked to the guard. "I'm done talking with them."

"Bryan," Billy tried, but the man wasn't having any of it. Before he was escorted from the room, he looked at Billy. There was nothing but sincerity when he spoke.

"Watch out for daughters, Sheriff. They'll stab you in the back every time."

"Reed, hold up a second."

Billy paused in his walk to the car. Mara, however, didn't. She hadn't said a word since Bryan left. Her eyes, dark and deep, had stayed dead ahead as they went through the process of leaving the prison.

The guard who'd been in the room with the three of them, a man named Ned, jogged up to Billy, mouth already open and ready to talk. Billy wondered if he'd forgotten some procedure for signing out. If so, he hoped it wouldn't take too long. The day had turned into a scorcher.

"I know it was none of my business to listen but sometimes you can't help it when you're in the room." Ned shrugged. "But I didn't know if you caught on to what Mr. Copeland was talking about when he said he wouldn't tell you anything."

Billy felt his eyebrow rise.

"And you do?"

"I guess I can't speak with complete certainty in Mr. Copeland's case, but you see, there's a different kind of world here," he said, thrusting his thumb over his shoulder to the prison. "There are men serving time in there who have done a hell of a lot worse than run drugs. Men who take to killing like it was nothing. Heck, some of them don't even break a sweat trying to do the same thing even when they're living in a cell."

"Yeah, I'd imagine that's true. But what's that have

to do with anything?" Billy was frustrated. Not at the man in front of him, but in general. He didn't want to stand out in the heat and talk about prison politics if he could help it.

"What I'm saying is that a man like Bryan Copeland may look intimidating to the general public with his tidiness and fancy talk, but in there—" again he thrust his thumb back over his shoulder "—in there he doesn't have anything going for him. But he's never had any problems as far as we know."

Billy was about to tell the man to go back inside if he wasn't going to be helpful, but then he heard Bryan's words again.

"He said, *I can't help you* not *I won't*," Billy realized. Ned nodded.

"My guess, if that money or whatever exists, he's using it as insurance to keep him safe in here." Ned shrugged. "I could be way off, but it's happened before."

"So keeping the stash hidden might be the only thing keeping him alive in there."

Ned nodded. "He could use it to buy protection from certain inmates or use it as leverage," Ned confirmed.

"Any idea who he might be targeted by if someone was trying to kill him?"

Ned's expression hardened. The new tension in his shoulders let Billy know he'd not be getting an answer from the guard.

"I don't know," he supplied. "Sorry."

"No problem," Billy said. "At least we have an idea of why he won't tell us." Billy cast a look at Mara. She was leaning against the car, looking out at the road in the distance. Even from where he stood, Billy knew she wasn't there with them. Her thoughts had carried her miles and miles away. "But knowing that might not be a good thing."

"Why's that?" the guard asked.

"Because it still means that Bryan would rather protect himself than protect his daughter and granddaughter."

MARA DIDN'T SAY anything for the majority of their drive back, much like the drive there. But this time, she wasn't sure if it was for the same reasons.

She kept her gaze out the windshield, watching as the road disappeared beneath them. Billy had told her what Ned the guard had said, but that was only the cherry on top of a trip she shouldn't have taken. Any relief she'd felt at finally confronting her dad, telling him about his granddaughter and admitting Billy was the father was no longer warming the cold that had been sitting like a rock in her stomach.

Not only was her father not going to help them, he'd made it very clear that she was no longer wanted in his life. Which, to be honest, she had expected—yet there she was, feeling the sting of it still.

Mara leaned her head back against the headrest and closed her eyes.

The emotional strain of seeing her father—and the past that she'd never be able to change, even if she wanted to—had wiped Mara out physically.

However, no sooner had her eyes closed than Mara was back in that room with Billy saying they weren't together. It shouldn't have bothered her, considering it was a fact she already knew, but still… The finality of the words, said in the strong, clear voice she'd come to enjoy more than she should have, had broken something within her. In a way that she hadn't expected.

Mara let out what she thought was a quiet sigh. One that let the outside world know she was having an internal battle.

"We need to talk about everything that happened."

She opened one eye and looked over at the sheriff. He was frowning something fierce. Mara closed her eye again.

"I don't want to," she admitted. "Not right now, at least."

"But, Mara—"

"Billy, please, don't," she interrupted. "There's only so much a person can deal with all at once. I just want to get back and see my daughter. Okay?"

The Bronco lurched to the side. Mara's eyes flashed open to see Billy cutting the wheel. They'd made it into Riker County according to a sign they'd passed a few miles back, but that didn't mean Mara recognized the Presbyterian church or the parking lot they now were turning into.

"What are you doing?" Mara asked, anger coming to the forefront of her question. It was misplaced, she knew, but that didn't stop it from turning her cheeks hot or spiking her adrenaline enough to make her sit up straight.

"We're going to talk," Billy said, parking in a row of cars already in the lot. A few people were meandering near the entrance to the church but didn't seem interested in them.

"What do you mean we're going to talk? Isn't that what we've been doing?"

Billy put the car in Park, took off his seat belt and

turned his body enough that he was facing her straight on. His mouth was set in a frown and yet, somehow, it still begged to be touched.

To be kissed.

Mara shook her head, trying to clear the thought, as Billy confronted her.

"You're shutting down," he said, serious. His eyes had changed their shade of green from forest to that of tall ferns bowing in a breeze.

"I don't even know what that means," she said, keeping her eyes firmly on his gaze.

Billy's expression didn't soften. He wasn't interested in playing nice anymore. Before he said a word, Mara knew where the conversation would eventually lead.

"What you just went through can't have been easy and now you don't want to talk about it? Even with me?"

"Even with you?" The last shred of emotional sanity Mara had started to fray. "You know everything I do about this case. You heard everything my father said in there. Beyond that, there's nothing you have to do to help me. It isn't your job to make sure I talk about my feelings. We aren't together, Billy. Not anymore."

For whatever reason, using Billy's words from earlier against him made Mara break further. She unbuckled her seat belt and fumbled for the door handle. Tears began to blur her vision.

"I-I need a moment," she said before Billy could get a word in edgewise. Mara opened the door and walked out into the heat.

And swiftly away from the Riker County sheriff.

Chapter Seventeen

Mara had to think. She had to walk. She had to move so the pain of everything wouldn't settle. Her father's words, Billy's words, Beck's words all rattled around in her mind. Taunting her, comforting her, threatening her. Why couldn't life have stayed simple? Why had her father turned out the way he had? Why had she fallen in love with the one man Riker County had needed to protect it?

Mara made it out of the parking lot and to a small park beside the church before she heard footsteps behind her. She'd spent the short walk trying desperately not to cry. The strain already was pushing in a headache.

Sure, it made sense to be upset about everything. Her father *had* just chosen himself over her and her child. But what bothered her the most was that, at the moment, all she could do was think about Billy.

"Mara, stop."

A hand closed around her arm and gently held her still. Mara blinked several times to try and dissuade any tears from falling. Instead of turning her around, Billy stepped into view.

Mara felt the sudden urge to take his hat off and put her hand through his hair.

It all hurt even more, knowing with absolute certainty that she'd never stop wanting Billy Reed.

"Talk to me," he prodded. He lowered his head to look into her eyes more easily.

"Why haven't you asked me?" Mara blurted before she could police her thoughts. "Why haven't you asked one single question about why I left or why I didn't tell you about Alexa?" Billy dropped his hand from her arm. A piece of her heart fell with it. "Just ask me, Billy. At least one question. Please."

Tears threatened to spill again, but Mara stilled herself, waiting for an answer. This time, they weren't interrupted and Billy asked a question Mara hadn't expected.

"Would you have ever told me about her?"

Mara realized then that there would never have been a good time to talk about the choices she'd made. That, at the end of the day, she'd kept one heck of a secret. One that would hurt someone, no matter what. Billy's expression was open and clear as a bell, but she knew his tone well enough to realize it was a man waiting for bad news.

She had already hurt him with her silence. It was time to tell him the truth.

All of it.

"You may not believe me now, and I don't blame you for that, but I never meant to keep her a secret in the first place," Mara started. A breeze swept through the park. She wrapped her arms around herself, even though she wasn't cold. "I found out I was pregnant with her two days before you became sheriff. You remember how quiet I was then? You kept asking me if I was okay."

She watched as Billy slipped back into his own memories.

"I thought it was because of your dad," he admitted. "He'd just gotten sentenced." Mara gave him a sympathetic smile. His eyes widened. "Why didn't you tell me then?"

"I planned to, at dinner that night," she said. "I wanted everything to be nice… But I forgot to get eggs for the cake."

Billy's eyebrow rose in question. Why did that matter? he was most likely wondering.

"Do you remember Donna Ramsey? The woman we saw at the coffee shop?" Billy nodded. "Well, I went back out to buy eggs and ran into her. She wasn't happy at seeing me." Mara remembered the look of absolute hatred burning in the woman's eyes. It wasn't a look she'd ever forget. "Do you know that her husband died overseas? And that her daughter was all the family she had left in the world?" Mara didn't wait for Billy to answer. "Kennedy Ramsey killed herself when her girlfriend overdosed on Moxy. Donna was the one who found her." Mara felt her face harden. Her vision started to blur with the tears she couldn't stop. Caught between anger and sadness, she couldn't tell which emotion had its claws in her heart at the moment.

"I didn't know that," Billy admitted. "But around then it was hard to see all of the repercussions."

"Well, Donna's hatred for me is one that I saw up close."

"It wasn't your fault what happened," Billy asserted.

"If I had come to you earlier about my father—" she started.

"It could have taken us just as long to figure out how

to trap him," he jumped in. "Despite our intentions, your father was a very clever man. Two weeks might not have made any difference at all."

Mara shrugged.

"Either way, Donna let me know I was just as much to blame as my father was," Mara continued. "She told me that she would never accept me in Carpenter or Kipsy and neither would anyone else. To prove her point, the cashier who had overheard the exchange refused to check me out." Mara tried a small smile. "That's why there was no cake at dinner."

"But—"

"I didn't want to tell you that night because all I could think about was Donna, all alone, cursing my family's name," Mara explained, cutting him off. "And so I decided I'd tell you the next day, but then you spent it with Sheriff Rockwell and were so excited that, once again, I decided to wait. I wanted you to celebrate to your heart's content. You'd waited so long for the opportunity to be sheriff."

Mara was getting to the part that she'd once thought she'd never tell Billy. But, standing together now, Mara finally felt like she could tell him everything. She didn't want anything left unsaid. She wanted a clean slate again.

She *needed* it.

"I was going to tell you after the ceremony because I couldn't keep it in anymore. I was scared but excited," she continued. The dull throb in her side started to gnaw at her, as if opening up emotional wounds was somehow affecting her physical ones. "I was at the ceremony, standing in the crowd, off to the side, where I hoped no one would notice me. But then someone did.

He asked me if I was proud of you—and I was, Billy. I was so proud of you. And he used that against me. He told me that as long as we were together, everything you had worked for would fall apart when people found out about us. The daughter of a man who nearly destroyed the county with the new sheriff sworn to protect it. Billy, I looked up at you and you were so happy, and I couldn't get Donna out of my head and—" Mara couldn't help it. A sob tore from her lips and she began to cry. Overcome with emotions long since buried, she finally got to the heart of the matter. "And, Billy, I believed him. If I stayed, I was sure people would hate you because of me, and I just couldn't take that. I'd rather live with the guilt of being Bryan Copeland's daughter than knowing I was the reason you lost your home."

Billy remained quiet for a moment. His expression was unreadable. Even to her. Every part of Mara felt exposed, raw. Leaving Billy Reed had been the hardest thing she'd ever done.

She waited, trying to rein in her tears. Then, like a switch had been flipped, Billy smiled.

"But Mara, you're forgetting something," he said, closing the space between them. He put his hands on either side of her face, holding every ounce of her attention within his gaze. Every hope she had of the future, every regret she had from the past. All at the mercy of the dark-haired sheriff.

"What?" she whispered, tears sliding down her cheeks. Billy brushed one away with his thumb, his skin leaving a trail of warmth across her cheek.

"*You* are my home."

Then Billy kissed her full on the lips.

Finally, Mara Copeland felt peace.

Unlike their shared moment earlier in the day, this kiss was slower. Deeper. It seemed to extend past her lips and dip into her very core. If he hadn't been holding her, Mara was sure she would have fallen. The kiss was affecting every part of her body, not excluding her knees. They trembled with relief and pleasure and promise as the kiss kept going.

If they had been anywhere other than a public park, it might have gone even further, but reality broke through the fantasy quickly. Billy pulled away, lips red, eyes hooded and with a question already poised.

"Wait, who talked to you at the ceremony?" Billy asked. "I respected your wishes for us to be a secret until things settled down. I only told the people who needed to know and I trusted all of them. They wouldn't have told," he added, sure in his words.

Mara let out a small sigh. She didn't want to create any bad blood between the sheriff and one of his deputies. Marsden had only told her his opinion. She had been the one who had listened to it.

"Deputy Marsden," she confessed. Billy's body instantly tensed. Mara rushed to defuse his anger. "He seemed really concerned. I think he was just looking out for you. You can't get mad at someone for loyalty."

Billy didn't appear to be listening to her. His eyes were locked with hers, but he wasn't seeing her.

"What is it?" Mara grabbed his hand. She squeezed it. "Billy?" The contact shook him out of his head. He didn't look like he'd be smiling any time soon.

"Marsden held no loyalty or fondness for me," he growled. "The last order of business Sheriff Rockwell attended to before I stepped in was letting Marsden go. That was one of the reasons Rockwell wanted to talk before the ceremony. If he found out about us, it was by accident. I never would have told him. Gene Marsden is not a good man, and the last I talked to him, he cursed my name."

"What?" Mara asked, surprised. She didn't remember hearing about Marsden being fired. Then again, it wasn't like she had stuck around to get the news, either.

"I'd completely forgotten about him. He was with us when we arrested Bryan. He must have heard your father when *he* was cursing my name about being with you. He—"

They both heard the noise too late, both wrapped up in their conversation.

"Sorry to interrupt."

All Mara had time to do was watch Billy tense.

Beck had the element of surprise and he used it swiftly. He pointed the shotgun right at Billy's chest.

"We'll just call this take three for the day."

BILLY WAS LOOKING at the wrong end of the barrel of a shotgun. Holding it was Beck, smiling ear to ear. Billy noticed a cut across the man's cheek, and he took some small satisfaction that he'd probably caused it not more than four hours ago.

"Hey there, Sheriff," Beck said, voice calm. "How you doing this fine day?"

When Billy had turned, he'd put Mara behind him. Even though she was out of the line of fire, that didn't mean he felt good about their situation. Especially since Beck was holding a shotgun. It would be hard to shield Mara from a shell blast from only a few feet away.

"Hadn't figured I'd see you again any time soon. I thought after shooting up your truck you'd be long gone," Billy admitted. "Where is your friend? I'd like to repay him for the knock on the head he gave me." He glanced over Beck's shoulder to see if anyone at the church had noticed that there was a man holding a gun on them. But no one seemed to be any the wiser.

"Oh, look at you, always the dutiful sheriff. In a bad situation and still trying to fish for information." Even though there was humor in his tone, Beck's hold on the gun was serious. Billy's own gun was burning in its holster. They never should have left the car. He never should have pulled over. Not when none of the deputies had found even a trace of the truck. But, when Mara was involved, Billy's actions didn't always make sense. He cursed himself. He'd let his guard down again. There was no excuse for that. "Well, I'm sorry to disappoint you. I'm not here to answer your questions or theories or even suspicions. I have work to do."

"You're not as clever as you think," Mara said at Billy's shoulder. He was proud that her voice was even. *That's my girl.*

Beck's smile turned to a smirk, a transformation that gave away the pleasure he must be feeling holding a gun on them. So far he'd shown he didn't believe in an even playing field. Why should now be any different? He was just going to have to find out the hard way that Billy was the kind of man who would go down fighting, especially when there was someone to fight for.

"You don't think I'm clever enough?" Beck asked. "Because I've been so bad at following you, hurting you and pulling guns on you? Or am I not that clever because I haven't killed you two yet?"

Billy's muscles tingled in anticipation.

If he could close the gap between him and the end

of the shotgun, he might be able to grab it and move it enough that Mara could run for the car. If he was faster than the shot, that was. If he could disarm Beck or manage to get his own gun out, he could end this. Once and for all.

"Sheriff, calm down," Beck chided. "I'm not going to kill you or Miss Copeland right now. Maybe down the line, if it becomes an issue, but not right now."

"Then put down the gun," Billy ground out. It made Beck laugh.

"Don't mistake mercy for being an idiot. I still have a job to do right now. I didn't just follow you to have a little chat, now, did I?"

"What do you want, then?" Mara asked.

"Funny you should ask, Miss Copeland. Considering it's you."

"I don't think so," Billy cut in. "You're not taking her."

"Oh, but Sheriff, I am. And, what's more, you're going to let me."

Chapter Eighteen

Billy didn't like the confidence the man in front of him was exuding. There was no shaking of his hands as he held the gun, no quiver or tremble or even a fluctuation in his voice. Standing outside, in a public place, holding a gun on a sheriff and a civilian, Beck should have been showing some signs of anxiety or nervousness.

When, in reality, he was showing none.

Which meant one of two things. He was either stupid or he had one hell of an ace up his sleeve.

"And how do you figure that?" Billy asked. "Because I'm here to tell you, that's a tall order you're placing."

"It's because I know your secret," Beck said, simply. "And I intend to use that to make you two do exactly as I please."

Billy didn't need to see Mara to know she reacted in some way to Beck's threat. He himself had tensed, despite trying to appear impassive.

"Secret?" He didn't want to play into Beck's game but, at the same time, he didn't really have a choice.

"If I hadn't already known you two were an item, I would have guessed by that kiss just now," Beck pointed out. "You two really are terrible at hiding this *thing*." He nodded to them when he said *thing*.

"So?" Mara said. "We kissed. How are you going to make me leave willingly with that?"

"I can't." Beck shrugged. "But luckily that's not the only secret you two share. In fact, right now my associate is looking at that other secret of yours. She's pretty cute, you know."

Beck shifted his gaze to Billy with a level of nonchalance he didn't like. Pure rage and fear exploded within Billy's chest. It must have extended to Mara. He felt her hand on his back. A light touch, but with a heaviness only a worrying parent could carry. Beck tilted his head a little, as if waiting for them to fall over themselves responding. His impatience got the better of him. He exhaled, all dramatic.

"Do I need to spell it out for you, Sheriff?" he added.

Billy wasn't ready to believe the man had any kind of connection to his daughter. He could be bluffing for all Billy knew.

"Yes, you do," Billy answered. "We don't want to play any more games with you."

Beck's smile twitched, his nostrils flared and then he was all smirk again. His eyes went over Billy's shoulder to the park behind them. It remained focused on something—or someone—but Billy wasn't going to turn his back to the man.

"I guess you're right," Beck agreed. "Who has time for stupid little games. Here's the deal—the bottom line. I'm short staffed, thanks to the two of you, I'm impatient and I'm over being out in this damn heat. Mara's going to tell me where that stash is and then I'm going to keep her until I've moved it. Then I'll let her go. You may be asking why should you trust me on that? Well." Beck's sneer fell into the most serious expression

Billy had ever seen on the man. "Considering you two seem to be an item, how smart would I be if I killed the lover of the beloved sheriff? You'd never stop hunting me until it consumed you or you caught me. Those are odds I don't like playing. Am I wrong?"

Billy shook his head. "No. You aren't."

Mara moved her thumb on his back, a few strokes to show affection or appreciation. Either way, it eased a part of Billy. If only a little.

"Only a fool, or someone out of options, would make that mistake. I don't fall into either category," Beck assured them. "Also only a fool would directly kill the sheriff if it could be avoided, because then that's just painting a target on my head." Beck shook the shotgun a little, not taking it off them but reminding them he still had it. And that they were still in its sights. "But don't misunderstand that as me saying I won't shoot you. I will. But how could you help Alexa and Mara then, Billy?"

The hand on Billy's back dropped. Mara stepped from behind him and stopped at his side. Her expression was blank, but he knew she was filled with a cocktail of emotions, ready to spill out if she was pushed too hard.

"The bottom line," Billy said, words dripping with absolute disgust.

"Mara is going to come with me now and you're going to let her, or you'll never see your daughter again."

"You son of a—" Billy started, but Mara cut him off.

"What have you done?" she asked. Her voice was so calm, so even, it made Billy pause in his rant. It was the steady ice of a mother calculating a situation.

"Nothing. Yet. And it'll stay that way if you come with me." This time Beck's attention was on Mara.

"Alexa is safe," Billy cut in. "You're bluffing."

"And what if she isn't? What if I'm not bluffing?" Beck asked. "Are you going to take that chance, Sheriff?" He returned his attention to Mara. "And are you going to let him take that chance?"

"Mara—" Billy started.

"I want proof," she interrupted. "Or I won't go."

Beck let out a small exhale, frustrated. But he at least was accommodating. Even if it wasn't at all what Billy wanted to hear.

"Billy's mother, Claire, put up more of a fight than Deputy Mills did," Beck started. Every part of Billy contracted. A cold fire spread through him. Anger and fear warred with each other inside him. If that shotgun hadn't been between them, Billy could have ripped the man apart with his bare hands. "In his defense, he never saw my guy coming. But Claire was looking out the kitchen window, so by the time my associate went inside she'd already grabbed a gun and tried to hide the girl. Luckily for both of us, Claire's a bad shot and my guy has a code about killing the elderly, something to do with being raised by his grandmother, I suppose." Mara's hand went to her mouth. Billy fisted his hand so hard he'd bet he was drawing blood. Beck went on as though he was recapping a soap opera episode and not sharing one of the most terrifying situations a parent could hear. "Alexa was in the corner of a closet, a blanket thrown over her head. She was crying so hard that my associate grabbed her bag of toys. I haven't heard yet if they've worked on calming her down."

"You bastard," Billy snarled. His heartbeat was racing now, adrenaline mixing up everything he was already feeling.

"She's just a baby," Mara added. Her voice shook.

"And I'm just a businessman," Beck added. "An impatient one. If you don't come with me now, so help me, I will throw out what little morals I have left and make you two regret ever trying to get in my way."

Billy's stomach bottomed out. He glanced at Mara. She was looking at him. Her dark eyes were glassed over and wide, searching for some way to save Alexa. To save him. Because he knew she'd do anything to keep everyone safe. Just like Billy knew right then that Beck had won. Mara would go with him. And Billy would let her.

Beck's attention swiveled over his shoulder again. This time it was followed by a woman gasping.

"Hey, come here slowly or I'll shoot you," Beck yelled. Billy turned to see an older woman standing a few feet behind them. She must not have noticed there had been a shotgun in their discussion until she was closer. Her terrified eyes took the three of them in. "Come here now," Beck demanded. It was a few shades darker than any tone he'd used with Billy and Mara. It was made to intimidate quickly.

And it worked.

The woman walked over to them. Billy hoped she didn't have a heart attack.

"Now, what's your name?"

"Sa-Sally."

"Hey, Sally. My friend here needs his gun taken away," Beck said with a nod to Billy. "And I need you to do it for me."

Sally looked at Billy, probably trying to understand what was going on. He nodded to her.

"It's okay," he said, afraid she might try to disobey

and incur the wrath of Beck. While Billy thought Beck would keep his promise not to kill the lover or child of the sheriff, they all knew Sally had no connection to them whatsoever. "Do as he says," Billy said gently.

Sally, who looked to be in her late sixties, finally moved toward them. She stopped at Billy's other side and looked at Beck.

"Billy, take your gun out and give the clip to Mara," Beck ordered. For the first time, he moved the shotgun. Now it was pointing squarely at Mara. "If you so much as try to take aim at me, I will end this now and you'll lose everyone you love in one fell swoop. So do it now."

Billy did as he was told. He unholstered his gun and ejected the clip. He handed it to Mara. She took it with a slightly shaking hand. He wished he could hold her. Let her know everything was going to be okay.

"Empty the chamber and then give it to our new friend, Sally."

Billy ejected the bullet in the chamber and then handed his service weapon to Sally. She, too, was shaking.

"Now, Sally, I want you to run."

"R-run?" Her face paled considerably.

Beck nodded in the direction from which she'd come.

"I want you to run as fast as you can in that direction and don't stop or come back, or I'll kill these good people. You wouldn't want that on your conscience, now, would you, Sally?"

The woman shook her head. Her eyes began to water.

"Then go!"

Sally began to walk away before picking up the pace, gun in her hand. Billy hoped she didn't hurt herself. He also hoped she had the sense to get help.

"Okay, say *see you soon*, *Billy*, and let's go," Beck said to Mara.

"I—" Billy started, but Mara interrupted him again.

"I'm going," she said.

Billy took her face back into his hands and brushed his lips across hers. He hoped the kiss told her everything he couldn't say.

He would save Alexa.

He would save Mara.

He would destroy Beck.

In that order.

"Now, Billy, you know the drill. You move, I end this today. Both of their deaths will be because you tried to be a hero. And ended up protecting no one but yourself. Understood?"

Billy gave a curt nod. Anger flowed through his veins like blood. He'd never wanted another man to come to as much harm as he did the man in front of him.

"I'll get you in the end," Billy promised.

Beck grinned. "I expect you'll try."

Beck walked Mara, shotgun to the back of her neck, away from him. He kept looking back to make sure Billy was still there. Billy made sure not to move an inch. He didn't want to push the already crazed man.

A few people outside the church had finally spotted the procession and, Billy hoped, had called 911. No one moved to help Mara. It angered and also relieved Billy. Instead, they all watched in muted terror, some fleeing back into the church, as Beck angled Mara into a car he'd never seen before, parked right next to Billy's Bronco.

He ground his teeth hard, watching, helpless, as the mother of his child was taken away.

BILLY ROCKETED THROUGH the streets of Carpenter toward his house. He had absolutely no way to contact the world outside of his car. When he'd run back to the Bronco, the driver's side door had been open. His cellphone and radio were gone. Thank God he'd had enough sense to at least keep the car keys in his pocket when he'd followed Mara.

He'd tried, in vain, to keep his eyes on Beck's new car as they left the parking lot, but by the time he'd run to the Bronco, they were gone. It had left Billy with too many options. Too many routes to follow.

Though, if he was being honest with himself, there was really only one place he needed to go.

Chapter Nineteen

Deputy Mills's cruiser was still parked on the street outside the Reed family home. Just like it had been when Billy and Mara had left that morning. However, where Billy had expected chaos on his lawn, shattered house windows and a front door broken off its hinges, all Billy could see was what they'd left behind that morning. Everything looked orderly, calm.

Normal.

But that didn't ease Billy's mind.

He hit his brakes at the end of the driveway and jumped out, already running to the front door.

"Sheriff," someone yelled from behind him. He turned so fast he nearly fell. It was Deputy Mills, standing in the now-open door of his cruiser. Again, Billy expected him to look one way—angry, wounded from the attack—but he looked another—confused, alert. "What's going on?"

"What happened?" Billy asked. He could tell it put the man further on edge.

"What are you talking about?"

Billy heard the squeal from inside the house. He didn't wait on the porch to question the deputy. He flung open the front door and ran inside, attention sticking to a sound he hadn't thought he'd hear in the house.

"Don't move," came a growl of a voice. Billy turned in the entry to see a startled Suzy, gun raised.

"Billy? What are you doing?" she asked, surprised. She lowered her gun but didn't put it away.

"Is Alexa here?" he asked, knowing he must have looked crazy. He didn't care.

"Of course she's here." Suzy pointed into the living room. Billy hurried past her, hearing another squeal of laughter.

Sitting on the floor was his mother, alarmed but seemingly unhurt. Plastic containers of Christmas decorations littered the space in front of her. At her side, amid an explosion of toys that nearly rivaled the decorations, was the most beautiful sight Billy had ever seen.

"Alexa!"

The little girl looked up at him, green eyes wide and curious. She had a stuffed dog in her hand. She held it out to him, unaware of the sheer amount of love flooding through Billy from just seeing her.

"Dog," she yelled. It was enough to get him moving.

In two long strides Billy scooped Alexa up and hugged her tight. He might not have been in her life up until this point, but Billy had never been more certain of any one thing in all his life.

He loved his daughter.

He held on to the moment, closing his eyes and burying his face in her hair. Alexa giggled.

That sound of perfect innocence split Billy's heart in two.

Yes, Alexa was safe.

But what about Mara?

Billy kissed Alexa's forehead before putting her back down, a plan already forming in his head. He turned to his mother.

"Pack your bag and one for her, too."

He turned to Suzy and the deputy as Dante hustled through the front door. He didn't talk to them until all three were back in the entryway. Where he promptly punched the wall.

"Billy," he heard his mom exclaim, but Suzy was closer. She holstered her gun.

"What happened?" she asked. "Where's Mara?"

"Beck lied. He took Mara." Billy heard his mother gasp, but he didn't have time to deal with the emotions behind what had happened. "And I let him."

BECK HAD BLINDFOLDED and handcuffed Mara so quickly she hadn't been able to see the person who ended up driving them away from the church and its neighboring park. All Mara knew was that it wasn't Beck. He'd stayed in the back with her, rambling on about how proud he was to finally have her in his possession. And not only that, but he'd also managed to take her from the sheriff himself.

It wasn't surprising to Mara to find out the man liked to gloat, but that didn't mean that listening wasn't disconcerting.

She tried to keep her nerves as calm as possible by thinking of Alexa. Even if she had no idea what was going on with her little girl, the love Mara felt strengthened her resolve to survive this.

Mara remained quiet for the length of the drive. There were too many questions and she had no way of answering half of them. She couldn't control what Billy was doing, what her daughter was feeling and the fact that she was handcuffed next to someone who was obviously insane. What she *could* do, however, was try and pay attention to how many times the car turned and how long they drove. She might not know the town of Carpenter as thoroughly as Billy, but it couldn't hurt to try and remember as much of the route as possible.

After almost fifteen minutes the smooth road became bumpy, pocked. A few minutes later, they left asphalt altogether. The change in terrain was rough. A dirt road.

Which meant one of two things.

They were either on some back road in Riker County that she didn't know about, or they had left a road altogether and were out in the country.

Mara didn't know which option was better.

"Pull around to the side," Beck said to the driver, giving rise to another question Mara didn't have the answer to. Was the driver the "associate" who had taken her daughter? Was that the same person who'd killed Caleb and Jessica, and wounded Cassie?

Mara tensed as the car slowed and then stopped. The engine remained on.

"Time to go," Beck said, opening his door. Mara sat up, fighting the urge to try and, well, fight—she didn't want to jeopardize Alexa's safety, wherever she might be—and waited until the door next to her was opened. "Stay smart," Beck cooed beside her ear. Mara flinched as he grabbed the handcuff's chain and pulled her out. Once her feet hit the ground, she knew she was standing on grass.

"Stay in the car," Beck ordered his partner. Whoever that was didn't answer. Beck moved his grip from the handcuffs to Mara's upper arm and directed her forward a few feet before turning. In that time, Mara tried to keep her adrenaline in check so she could pay attention once again to her surroundings.

It was colder now, finally starting to feel like Christmas. Though that didn't help Mara narrow down the possibilities of where she might be. But after straining her ears to try to listen around the running car and their footsteps, there was one thing she didn't hear that made her feel even more uneasy.

She didn't hear any other cars.

Which meant they probably *were* in the country, cut off from any normal traffic. Cut off from any easy help. Just plain cut off.

"We're going to go inside and I'm going to take your blindfold off," Beck said at her ear. "If you try to fight me or do anything stupid, I won't kill you, but I'll hurt you really badly. Okay?"

Mara didn't answer. He must have taken her silence as agreement. The sound of a door scrubbing against the floor preceded her being pushed inside a building. She smelled something that was between a wet dog and freshly mowed grass but couldn't pinpoint it any more accurately than that. She didn't have the time, either, before Beck was giving her yet another order.

"Don't move."

The pressure of his hand on her arm went away and soon she could hear him moving something. It scraped against whatever was beneath it, sounding much heavier than a table or chair.

Terror started to seize her chest. Questions and fears shot off in succession in her mind. What was going on? Where were they? What was going to happen to her? Was Beck really not going to kill her? Where was Alexa? Was she scared? Hurt?

Mara jumped as hands moved to the sides of her head. Quick fingers undid the blindfold. She blinked several times, trying to get her bearings. Wherever they were, it was darker than she'd like. Her eyes weren't adjusting quickly enough to make out the location.

"There's a set of stairs behind you," Beck said, motioning for her to turn. "I want you to go down them." Mara looked over her shoulder. The sound she'd heard of something heavy being moved was a large, rectangular canister. It stood next to a hole in the floor.

Not a hole. A trap door.

There was a faint light radiating out of it, but she couldn't tell where it led. She took a second to let her eyes adjust, but still couldn't make out what exactly was down those stairs.

Seeing the trap door and the hidden stairwell might have made some people feel adventurous, but right now, the image only heightened Mara's acute fear of having to walk down them.

Good thing she still had a few questions to ask before she would.

"Where's Alexa?"

Beck cracked a smile. It sent a shiver down her spine. The shotgun he held against his side didn't help.

"She's safe with her dad," he answered. She searched his face, looking for the lie. She was surprised to realize she believed he was being sincere. Besides, if he *had* done something to Alexa, Mara bet he would have been gloating about it.

And she would have already killed him with her bare hands.

Plus, there wasn't much more to do than believe him and hope Billy was doing everything he could to ensure Alexa stayed safe. She had little doubt he would do anything else.

Just thinking about the two of them, without her in the picture, warmed and broke Mara's heart. Despair at potentially never seeing them again inspired her backbone to stiffen. Suddenly, the danger of the man across from her lessened. Mara had much bigger things to fear than a man who had to threaten a toddler to get what he wanted.

"You do know I have no idea where the drugs and money are, right?" Mara asked, pleased at the steadiness of her voice. She raised her chin a fraction to show the man she was above lying to him. Why waste her time doing it?

For one moment, Mara felt like she had the upper hand. Like she had stumped the man who had been nothing but cocky. But then the moment was shattered.

All it took was one smirk to let Mara know she hadn't won.

"I believe you," he said, seeming amused.

"What?"

Beck gave a little chuckle.

"I know you don't have any idea where the stash is," he continued. "In fact, I've known for a bit."

Mara was dumbfounded.

"Then why come after me?" she asked. "Why go through all of this trouble to get me if I can't even help?"

Beck's smirk stayed sharp when he answered, as if he'd been waiting for those questions for a while and it was finally time for him to deliver.

"Because now I have the only leverage in all the

world that would make your father finally tell me where it is."

Mara couldn't help it. She laughed. It wasn't in the least kind.

"Good luck with that. My father wouldn't help me when I asked for it. What makes you think he'll help you now, just because you have me?"

"Because I'm not bartering for your release. I'm bartering for your life," Beck said simply. "You aren't leaving this place alive unless your father does everything I need him to, what I told the sheriff earlier be damned. He's a handsome fella, though, so don't worry. I'm sure he can find another woman to get into his bed and raise your kid if you're gone."

The shiver that had run down Mara's spine before was back with a vengeance. It crippled any confidence she'd been wielding as a shield against her current situation. And the madman across from her. The strength that had kept her voice steady was gone when she answered.

"My father won't help you," she said.

"You'd be surprised what a father will do for his daughter." He brought the shotgun up and pointed it at her. "Now, get down there, Miss Copeland," he ordered. "I've got things to do."

The last thing Mara wanted to do was go down those steps. To find out where that dim light was and what the destination might mean for her future. But Mara couldn't deny that she felt deflated. She'd done what she could and now she might have to let whatever was going to happen play out.

Without another look at her captor, Mara started the descent down the stairs. She was less than four steps in when the door above her was dragged closed. She waited as the sound of the metal scraping filled the air. Something heavy went on top of the trap door. Mara backtracked until she could put her shoulders and back against it. She tried to push up, but the door didn't budge.

Letting out an exhale of defeat, she started her descent again.

The stairs weren't as long as she'd expected, and soon she was standing in a surprisingly large room lit by two hanging bulbs. They cast enough light to reach the corners.

Which was good and bad for Mara.

It was good because she could tell with certainty that she was standing in a basement, maybe used as a storage room at some point, judging by the lumps of furniture covered by dust cloths and pushed against the walls. And knowing *where* she was felt a lot better than sitting in the dark, wondering.

However, for every silver lining there was something bad that had to be coped with, and tied in a chair against the wall was a woman who looked like she'd seen a heck of a lot better days.

"Leigh?" Mara started, beyond confused.

Leigh Cullen had her mouth taped over and blood on her face. She looked just as surprised to see Mara as Mara was to see her.

That, in itself, would have been enough to make a terrifying situation even more dark, but then Mara noticed the boy in the corner, tied to an old oak rocking chair. His mouth was duct taped, his eyes wide. He didn't look much older than ten.

What the hell was going on?

Chapter Twenty

Mara rocked backward on the floor so that her knees were in the air. Before she'd had Alexa she could have gotten the handcuffs from behind her back to in front of herself without much fuss, but since she'd given birth and become a single parent, her exercise habits had disappeared. That included the yoga routine that had kept her flexible. As it was, it took several tries before she was able to get her hands in front of her. They were still bound, but at least now she could use them.

Her maternal instincts had gone from zero to a hundred the moment she'd seen the boy. She didn't recognize him. Still, she hurried over to him with the most soothing voice she could muster.

"Hey, there, my name's Mara," she started, honey coating every syllable. "I'm going to take the tape off your mouth. Is that okay?" The boy, short brown hair, freckles galore and wide blue eyes already filling up with tears, cut his gaze to Leigh. The woman, in turn, slit her eyes at Mara. "I'm not with them, Leigh. A man named Beck took me and brought me here."

It was the vaguest of answers but seemed enough to satisfy the woman. She nodded to the boy. He looked back at Mara and nodded.

"This might hurt a little, but I'll try to be extra gentle," she warned him.

The boy gave another curt nod. He closed his eyes tight as Mara got a grip on the edge of the tape and did her best to ease it off without causing the boy pain. No sooner had it passed over his lips did he give a cry of relief. It made Mara's heart squeeze.

"You did so good," Mara said, knowing the tears in his eyes were a thin dam away from being an all-out waterfall. "I'm going to try and untie you now, and then you can help me untie her." The boy nodded, sniffling. Mara went to the side of the chair and then to the back trying to find the main knot. Thankfully, it wasn't too complicated, resting at the base of the chair. Then again, the boy was small enough that he probably didn't need much help keeping him tied down. "So, what's your name?"

"Eric," he said, tears behind his words. "Er-Eric Cullen."

"Leigh's your mama," she guessed.

"Yes, ma'am."

She'd known that Leigh had a kid, but what had happened with her husband had always taken priority in Mara's mind. A swell of guilt rose at the realization that she'd never even asked after the boy, but Mara batted it down. She needed to focus. And she needed to try and calm Eric down. Even from her crouched position behind him, she could see he was trembling.

"So, Eric, what grade are you in?" she asked, working on undoing the first part of the knot.

"Fo-fourth."

"Oh, nice! That's a fun grade. So you have any favorite classes you're looking forward to after Christmas break?"

The first part of the knot gave way. There were two more to go.

"I like practicing football," he said flatly. "But Mama says I can't play on the team if I don't bring up my grades."

The second part fell away. Mara found herself smiling at his answer.

"I'd have to agree with her there," she said.

He nodded but didn't say anything else. Mara wanted to know how they'd gotten down here and what had happened to them, but she didn't want to push the little guy to relive whatever they'd gone through. She'd just have to ask his mama instead.

"Okay, there we go."

Mara stood, wincing as the pain in her side reminded her she should have been resting, and helped take the rope from around him.

"You okay?" Mara asked.

He nodded but she helped him stand all the same. Another part of her heart squeezed when she noticed a bruise on the side of his face. Like he'd been hit.

"Now, you think you can help me untie her?"

Leigh's eyes were shining but she didn't cry when Mara took the tape off her mouth.

"Oh, Eric, are you okay?" were the first words out of her mouth. The boy's chin started to tremble but he nodded.

Mara let him stand in front of his mom while she checked him over, uttering assurances that they'd all be alright, while she jumped into untying Leigh. The ropes had more knots, including at her ankles and wrists.

Judging by the blood and marks all over the woman, Mara'd bet she'd put up one heck of a fight before they'd been able to get her tied down.

"This might take a little bit," Mara said, fingers fumbling with the knot at the back of her chair. "So let's not waste any time. What the heck is going on? And where are we?"

"We're at the house," Eric said, matter-of-factly.

"The house?"

"We're in a barn," Leigh clarified. "It's on my family's farm. Our house is a mile in that direction."

She nodded to the right wall.

"And this charming little room?" Mara asked, fingers tugging at another knot.

"My great-grandfather put it in to serve as a storm shelter of sorts. It's always creeped me out, so we never come out here. Until today." Leigh said a string of curses before apologizing to her son for doing just that. A heavy sigh followed. "I wanted an old picture of the main house my daddy took when he was a boy that's in one of these boxes. I was going to reframe it as a present for him. Lucky for us, it just happened to be the same day two thugs decided to camp out in the barn. They surprised us after I opened the trap door."

There it was again.

The swelling of guilt. This time Mara didn't let it sit and stew.

This time she let it out.

"It's my fault they're here," she admitted. "They're trying to use me to get something that's hidden somewhere in Riker County."

Mara didn't need to be looking at the woman to know she wasn't happy.

"Eric, why don't you go look for that picture?" Leigh said quietly. "It should be in one of those boxes."

Eric must have known his mom's tones. He obeyed without hesitation, walking across the room from them and pulling off a dust cloth. Mara undid the back knot and was in front of Leigh when the woman had collected herself enough to respond.

"It's about that no-good father of yours, isn't it?" she whispered, low and angry.

Mara nodded. She tried to get into a better position to work on the ropes holding Leigh's ankles to the legs of the chair. Pain flashed up her side again.

"What's wrong?" Leigh asked. Her eyes trailed to the bruise on Mara's head.

"Let's just say I've had a long day," she hedged.

Leigh kept quiet as Mara finished untying her. Such a seemingly simple task had left her exhausted. Instead of jumping up, as the now-free woman did, she pushed her back up against the wall and sat down. All the adrenaline spikes she'd had that day were long past gone. Now Mara felt pain and weariness.

She watched in silence as Leigh ran to her son and nearly crushed him in a hug.

Mara smiled. Pain aside, she'd give Alexa the same greeting.

If she ever saw her again.

BILLY HUGGED HIS mother and kissed his daughter's cheek.

"Are you sure there's no other way? We could just keep all the doors locked and maybe—"

"Mom."

Billy's mother let her arguments go and nodded to

her son. She had Alexa on her hip, the diaper bag on her arm and pure concern on her face. But she wasn't going to argue anymore. Time was a luxury they had little of.

"You be careful," she said instead. "And bring her back."

"I will."

She touched the side of his face before giving him and Suzy some privacy. Alexa waved at him, although her eyes trailed between all the adults in the house. She'd been surprisingly quiet since he'd arrived. It made Billy wonder if she was looking for Mara among everyone. It was a good thing she'd taken such a shine to his mother, or else the next step in his plan wouldn't go over as well as they wanted.

"I don't like this," Suzy said, coming to stand in front of him. She met and held his eyes.

"I know, but it needs to be done."

"And you're not asking me just because I'm a woman, right?"

Billy returned the serious question with an equal answer.

"You know damn well it's not that," he said. Still, he saw some doubt there. He tried to diminish it as quickly as he could. "Beck played me like a fiddle just by talking about Alexa. I can't afford to let him do that again, so I need to *know* that she'll be okay. Which means I need someone I trust. Not only with my life, but with my mother's and child's lives, too. Like it or not, that's you, Suze. None of this will work if you're not the one to take them out of town and hide them." He gave her a small smile. "I'm asking as the little boy you once called dumb as nails for tanking the spelling bee in fourth grade. Not as your sheriff."

That seemed to soften the woman. She let out a sigh before her shoulders pushed back. She raised her chin. Not out of pride. It was determination.

"Who misspells elephant?" She smirked and then was deadly serious. "Go get your gal, Sheriff."

And then Suzy was gone, her own bag slung across her shoulder. No one knew how long it would take to find Mara and stop Beck, but Suzy wasn't bringing Alexa or his mother back until both happened.

Billy just hoped that was sooner rather than later.

Dane met Billy in the lobby the moment he walked in. He looked impeccable, letting Billy know he'd already done the press conference. Which he confirmed with his greeting.

"The public should be on the lookout for Beck and his associate, and both the car they drove away in and the truck they had earlier, too. Mara's picture is also out there. Dante is briefing the reserve deputies who just came in, while we have some of our deputies manning the tip lines and social media. The rest, including the local PD, are out on the streets and in the country."

"And no bites yet?" Billy asked, already knowing the answer.

Dane shook his head.

"Nothing we didn't already know. But I think Matt's ready to talk to us about what he's found on Beck's friend."

Billy nodded and they headed deeper into the building.

"Let's hope we finally have a lead."

BILLY STOOD AT the front of the squad room and looked out at his deputies. Those who were close by had been asked to come in. Those on patrol were being filled in on the new situation in person by Mills and one of the reserve deputies. Because the radios were now a problem.

A bigger one than they already had.

"Gene Marsden worked at Riker County Sheriff's Department for twelve years before he was fired by the last sheriff," Billy started. "There was a list a mile long of reasons why he should have been let go sooner but Sheriff Rockwell liked giving second—and sometimes third—chances to his deputies because he knew that this job can be a hard one. But then, when we were working the Bryan Copeland case, Rockwell noticed that crime scenes and evidence were being tampered with on Marsden's watch. He never found concrete proof that it was Marsden. but after a late night of drinking at a local bar, Marsden started to brag about having his own personal collection of Moxy. Courtesy of the department. He was fired as Rockwell's last act as sheriff, and when he came to me to rehire him, I flat out said no." Billy crossed his arms over his chest. "To put it bluntly, he lost his damn mind."

Two deputies sitting in the back agreed, using more colorful language. Billy pointed to them. Along with Dane and Matt, they'd been present for the scene. "He had to be escorted out. After that, he moved to Georgia, where his sister lives, and didn't make so much as a peep." Billy gave Matt a nod.

The detective cleared his throat to address the room.

"Until two months ago, when he apparently came back." Matt pinned the picture of Marsden they'd been able to get from the security camera at the local bar, the Eagle. "The owner of the Eagle said Marsden has been paying in cash only. One night he got so drunk they called him a cab, which took him to the same hotel where the recently deceased Caleb Richards had been meeting Beck. Around the same time Beck fled, Marsden disappeared."

"We think he might have a police radio, which is why they've always been right there with us every step of the investigation," Billy added. "Even though it was checked in when he was fired, we can't find it." Just saying the words made Billy angrier than he already was.

"Is that the only evidence we have on him? Coming back to town, staying in the same hotel and hating you?" one of the reserve deputies asked. The question might have seemed like the man was unimpressed but Billy knew he was just a straight shooter. He wanted all the information they had before trying to bring down a former cop.

Which brought Billy to a crossroads.

He could tell his deputies to trust him right then and there without any more information and they would. Maybe.

Or Billy could follow Mara's earlier example in the park.

He could finally tell the truth.

"Mara Copeland and I became involved during the case against her father." He didn't wait for any reactions. "After he was convicted, we were going to go public with the relationship but Mara was approached by Marsden, who had found out about us. He threatened Mara with the idea that I would lose my career because of her. So she left." The words tasted bitter in his mouth but Billy continued. "Only a handful of people knew about Mara and I, and none of them have since told.

When I talked to Beck, he already knew about the relationship, making me believe Marsden had found out by overhearing Bryan Copeland talking to me about it the day we arrested him." Billy readjusted his stance. When he spoke again he could hear the hardness in his voice. The bottom line. "While it might not be professional, I love Mara Copeland a whole hell of a lot. That goes double for our daughter."

A few surprised looks swept over the deputies' faces but no one stopped him. "That might not be reason enough to warrant us going after a former cop considering, you're right, we don't have anything concrete to tie him to Beck, but Marsden is the best lead we have. We track Marsden, there's a good chance we find Beck. We find Beck, we find Mara. And if any of you have any reservations about this, well..." Billy paused a second to work up a smirk. "Too bad for you. Because I'm the sheriff and this is an order."

He'd been waiting for some opposition, so Billy was surprised when none came. The men and women sitting in front of him all seemed to agree with gusto.

In fact, some even cheered.

"Alright, let's get to work!"

Chapter Twenty-One

"Why were you at the sheriff's department the other day?" Mara finally thought to ask Leigh.

She let her gaze linger on the picture of Alexa she'd had in her pocket before putting it back. According to Leigh's watch they'd been in the basement for more than three hours. In that time Mara had told the woman everything that had happened, including her part in taking her father down. Something that might not have softened the woman toward her but did seem to surprise her.

The fact of the matter was that Leigh's husband was still dead because of the Copelands. Something she was reminded of every time she looked at Eric, who had finally fallen asleep in the corner. While Mara had been there for a few hours, Leigh and Eric had been there since that morning. The stress of it had been exhausting for the boy.

Mara couldn't blame him. If the need to escape hadn't been so great, she might have tried to get a few minutes of shut-eye herself.

Leigh stopped looking in the box in front of her and turned, already scowling. She motioned to Eric.

"While I was at the grocery store, some man showed up at the house asking all sorts of weird questions," she said. "When Eric asked what his name was, the man refused to tell him. After he left, Eric called me. I was already near the department so I thought I'd drop in."

Mara was about to dismiss Leigh's story when a cold thought slid into her head.

"What did the man look like?"

Leigh pursed her lips, still not happy being stuck in the basement with Mara, but she answered.

"Eric said he was really tall, had brown hair cut really close, almost like what the army fellows wear, looked around his Uncle Daniel's age—midforties—and, not so much like his uncle, he was skinny. Why?"

Mara let out a sigh of relief. Definitely not Beck. She was about to say as much when another terrible thought pushed in. The knot that had sunk to the bottom of her stomach began to spawn other knots.

"What questions did he ask?"

The man might not have been Beck but that didn't mean she didn't recognize the description.

Leigh must have read the fear in her expression. She dropped the contempt she'd been treating Mara with and answered.

"He asked if we'd had any construction done two or three years ago and, if so, where." The knots in Mara's stomach turned cold. Her heart rate started to pick up. "But, of course, all Eric could think about was his dad being killed two years ago, so he said he didn't know. Then he asked if Eric was home alone and, thank God, he lied. That's when he asked what the man's name was and he left."

Mara nearly missed the end of Leigh's sentence. Her thoughts were racing alongside her heart now.

"Leigh, *did* you have any construction done in the

last three years? Anyone coming in and out of the property with trucks or trailers?"

Leigh's eyebrow rose but she nodded.

"Right after my husband passed. We had a bad storm blow through. It flung a tree over and messed up the roof." She pointed up, meaning the barn's roof. "Had a company come in to replace it. They were really nice, too. Cut me a deal on account of being a recent widow. Even planted a new tree near the barn and left a note saying I could watch it and Eric grow up together. I thought it was really sweet. Okay, Mara, what is it? You look like you've seen a ghost."

Mara felt like it, too.

"My father hid a stash of drugs and money right before he went to court, as a fail-safe. We thought that there was a possibility that he used construction as a way to help him hide it, but we've only looked one place. The high school." Mara was struck with such a strong realization that a laugh escaped between her lips. "I never would have *ever* thought to look here. The guilt of what happened to you—to your family— would have made me, and maybe Billy, too, never even think to come here. And my father knew that. It's the perfect place."

Mara shook her head again, but she felt like she was right.

"Leigh, I think my dad's stash is here."

"But you said Beck was still looking for it," Leigh pointed out.

"That's just it. I don't think Beck even knows. I think he picked this place because it's remote and he knows only you and Eric live here. You probably would have never noticed them had you not wanted that picture."

Leigh's face contorted into an emotion that Mara was sure was laced with more than a few colorful words, when a scraping sound cut through the air. Someone was moving the canister off the trap door. It made Mara remember the original thought she'd had.

"I think that man who talked to Eric was Gene Marsden," Mara hurried while she and Leigh retreated to Eric. Mara paused and then switched directions. She grabbed an old lamp she'd pulled from a box earlier and pointed to the vintage baseball bat Leigh had found. "And if he's found out the stash is here, I think he'll kill us."

WHEN IT RAINED, it poured.

That was Billy's first thought when his office received a call from an unknown number. He didn't know what to expect, but he thought it wouldn't be good. So when the caller turned out to be Bryan Copeland, Billy was more than a little thrown.

"I told Beck where the stash was," he started.

"You what?" Billy rocked out of his chair, already spitting mad.

Bryan didn't seem bothered by his anger. In fact, he seemed to be harboring his own.

"The deal was Mara's life for the location." Bryan went on. "Apparently, I still love my daughter. Now, you got a pen?"

Billy wrote down the address Bryan rattled off and couldn't help but be surprised by it but didn't have the time to say so. He also didn't have the time to ask what number the man was calling from or how Beck had gotten hold of him. Those were issues he'd tackle later.

"Now hurry, Sheriff, and go save the girl. I don't believe for a second this Beck will let her go alive," Bryan said, already cutting the conversation short. Billy almost didn't hear it when he tacked on a last question. "And, Billy, is Alexa safe?"

While he had no reason in the world to answer the man, Billy did.

"Yeah, she's safe."

"Good."

Bryan ended the call. Seconds later, Billy was out the door.

No SOONER HAD Beck walked off the last step than Mara smashed the lamp against his head. He made a wild noise as the glass shattered against him, but the wrath of the women he'd imprisoned wasn't finished. Mara slid to the side as Leigh swung her bat for all she was worth into his crotch.

Beck never had a chance.

He hit the ground hard and didn't move. The shotgun he'd been holding thunked next to him. It was closer to Leigh, so she scurried to grab it while Mara readied for the next bad guy, hoping she could still do damage even though her grip was off thanks to the handcuffs.

But no one came.

The two of them froze and listened.

"I don't hear anything," Mara whispered.

"Maybe Marsden isn't here?"

"Let's not just stand here and wait to find out."

Leigh nodded, but hesitated.

"Have you ever shot a gun?" she asked, motioning to the shotgun in her hands.

"Not one of those."

Leigh gritted her teeth.

"I'll hold on to it, then," she said. "Follow me up. Eric, get behind Mara."

Eric crawled out from his hiding spot in the corner and listened to his mom. He stood behind Mara and kept his eyes off Beck.

"Wait, he's got a phone on him!"

Mara saw the light from his pocket as his cell phone vibrated. Leigh trained the shotgun on him as Mara fished the phone out. The caller ID was *M.*

"Marsden," Leigh guessed.

"Which means he's probably not up there?"

The thought got them moving. Mara held the phone, careful not to answer it, and followed Leigh up the stairs while Eric held on to the back of her shirt. If Marsden wasn't in the barn, then there was a good chance they'd be able to get to the house. She could even use Beck's cell phone to call for help once Marsden stopped calling. If he didn't know they had escaped, Mara definitely wasn't going to let him know by answering the phone.

Leigh moved slowly when she ascended, shotgun swiveling side to side, until she was out of view. Mara held her breath, waiting for the go-ahead. Her heart was hammering in her ears.

"We're alone," Leigh whispered down to them after what felt like hours.

Mara, relieved for the dose of good news, led Eric up the stairs. The air smelled musty and damp. The sun that had barely lit the space earlier in the day was gone. Like the basement, there were sets of hanging bulbs. They hung from the rafters, looking tired and weak. The light they emitted wasn't anything to write home about, but Mara welcomed it all the same. At least she could see. A silver lining to the nightmare the day had turned into.

"The house is a mile that way," Leigh whispered, pointing to the wall on their right. "Call your sheriff and tell him we're headed there. I have a lot more guns in that house than I bet Marsden brought to town." Despite their strained, nearly nonexistent relationship, Mara found herself grateful that out of all the women she could have been held captive with, Beck had been stupid enough to pick Leigh Cullen.

Mara fumbled with the phone and dialed 911 with her cuffed hand, ready to tell the dispatcher as quickly as possible everything that was happening and get Billy sent their way. Because they were out of Carpenter's town limits, the call should go straight to the Riker County Sheriff's Department instead of the local police. Which meant Billy would get to them faster.

Get to *her* faster.

That thought alone put some pep in her step. The idea of seeing Billy after everything that had happened was more than a desire to Mara. Now it was a need. As real and essential as breathing. She needed Billy Reed.

Sitting in the basement for hours had given her more than enough time to think about the sheriff. While she'd known that he would keep Alexa in his life now that he knew about her, Mara didn't know where that left the two of them.

Would they coparent from two different homes? Two different towns?

The mere idea of being away from Billy tore through Mara with surprising ferocity. For two years it had been only her and Alexa. But now that Mara remembered what having Billy around again was like, could she go back to living a life without him by her side?

Going through boxes of Leigh's family's antiques, Mara had realized that, no, she couldn't. She didn't want to go back to a house that didn't have the sheriff between its walls. She didn't want to take Alexa away from her father anymore, not even for the briefest of moments. For the first time in years, Mara had come to a realization so poignant that she'd nearly cried right there in the basement.

Two years ago, she should have fought for Billy—for *them*—instead of running.

She wasn't going to make the same mistake again.

However, Mara never found out how fast her 911 call would have reached the sheriff. Before she could hit the send button, the door in the corner of the barn was flung open.

Mara recognized the former cop, Gene Marsden, as easily as she'd heard his words at the ceremony years ago. He hadn't changed in the time since, matching Eric's description to a T, but the gun he was carrying definitely wasn't police issue. He pointed it at Leigh so quickly that it didn't seem humanly possible.

"I'll kill you first," he warned. His voice was steady, calm. It made his threat all the more believable. So much so that Leigh didn't shoot. Which probably was for the best, since there were several feet between them. If she'd missed…

"Kick the gun over here," he ordered before looking at Mara. "And toss the phone this way, too. You call anyone and I'll shoot the boy in the head."

Eric pulled on her shirt a little and she immediately did as she was told. The same went for Leigh. Even if it meant giving up the only upper hand they had. There were just some chances you didn't take. Especially when you believed the threat if you failed.

One look at Marsden's grin and Mara believed his every word.

"Now, back into the basement," he said, using his gun to make a shooing motion at them. Mara shared a look with Leigh. He didn't miss it. "I'll kill the boy, remember?"

"We're going," Mara said quickly. She put the trembling boy in front of her and followed him back into what was becoming Mara's least favorite place in the entire world.

Beck was still lying on the floor and, for a moment, she wondered if he was dead. It wasn't until they had all stepped over him and were in the middle of the room that he let out a low groan.

"You let two women and some little kid get the better of you," Marsden said, showing nothing but disgust for his partner. "How can you live with yourself?" If Beck tried to answer, Mara couldn't tell. The lamp had cut his face up something awful. Blood ran down it like a fountain. It was almost too much to look at, but Marsden seemed to have no trouble sneering at him. "You know, some men would take their lives rather than lose their dignity," Marsden drawled. "But I already know you'd never have the jewels to do that." Marsden took a step back and pointed his gun down. "So I'll do it for you."

And then he shot Beck in the head.

Chapter Twenty-Two

Eric was crying.

Mara wanted to join him.

Killing someone in cold blood was enough to terrify any witness. Killing your partner in cold blood was downright bone-chilling.

"Don't worry, I was going to do that anyways," Marsden said. "Beck liked to talk a lot, but words aren't street smarts. I don't know how he planned to make this business idea of his work." He looked at Mara expectantly.

"You—you mean bringing Moxy back to Riker County," she guessed when he didn't look away.

Marsden laughed.

"I don't think as small as Beck here does." He paused, then corrected himself. "Or did." Mara kept her eyes on Marsden and not the growing puddle of blood around the man he was so casually dismissing. She wondered if he could hear her heart trying to ram itself clear out of her body.

Marsden took a moment to give each of them an appraising look. It made Leigh move so that Eric was hidden behind her completely. If he was offended, he didn't comment on it.

"Now, here's the deal," he said when no one made

a peep. What were they supposed to say? Mara had no idea what he knew or what he planned to do with them. "Unlike Beck here, I'm not going to bore you with nonstop chatter and I expect the same from you." He pointed to Mara then thrust his thumb back to the stairs. Panic jolted through her, rooting her to the spot. "You're coming with me."

"Why?" she couldn't help but ask. As much as she disliked the basement, going anywhere alone with Marsden was worse.

"We've got treasure to dig up, that's why." He pointed his gun at Leigh's head. Eric's crying intensified. "They're only alive because of you right now. If you fight me, I'll kill them."

"Why are you doing this?" Mara cried out. The question seemed to amuse him. He actually laughed.

"For money, what else?" That one little laugh sounded twisted. Marsden had lost his patience. "Now, move it or I kill the boy first."

Mara didn't hesitate this time. She never wanted to be the cause of pain for the Cullens again. She didn't want to be the reason Leigh lost her son or Eric lost his mother.

Mara straightened her back, held up her chin and started to walk. It wasn't until she was outside and looking at the flat, open area between the barn and the woods that her confidence faded.

Her thoughts flew to her daughter, who she prayed was safe, and then to the man who had given her Alexa.

Mara's heart squeezed.

She should have told Billy she still loved him.

And always would.

BILLY RACED ACROSS Leigh Cullen's property in the Bronco cussing. He led a stream of deputies while the local SWAT team was fifteen minutes behind.

He didn't have time to wait for them. While Billy thought Beck might hold off on killing Mara after Bryan had finally given up the location of the stash, he knew that Marsden wouldn't. He was a greedy man with a power complex. And a former cop. He knew firsthand how witnesses and loose ends could undo even the smartest man's plans.

"Marsden won't go down easily," Matt said from the passenger's seat. He had his gun in his hand, ready. "I can't say the same for Beck. I don't know what kind of man he is."

"He likes to talk," Billy said. "If you need to stall, ask him a question about humanity or the line between right or wrong or if he's an Auburn or Alabama fan. I'm sure that'll get him rattling on for a while." Matt snorted. "But you're right about Marsden. If he doesn't have an escape plan set up, he'll make one. And if he can't escape..." Billy didn't finish the thought out loud but they both knew Marsden would kill Mara and Leigh and her kid. As soon as Bryan had told them the stash was next to the barn, marked by a tree that had been planted when he'd brought the cache in, the department had tried to track the Cullens down. Turned out they were missing. Billy only hoped they still alive, held captive with Mara.

Who also needed to still be alive.

Just the thought of the alternative made Billy cuss some more. It didn't help that in the distance they could just make out a faint light on what must have been the barn. Billy knew Riker County and he'd been out to the Cullens once before, but he didn't know this part of their property. He didn't like the added disadvantage.

"Picked one hell of a night for a showdown," Matt said, leaning forward to look up at the sky. Clouds blanketed the moon and stars. Being out in the country, with no light from above, put them at a further disadvantage. But it at least helped with the next part of Billy's plan.

He slowed and pulled into the grass. Matt radioed the men behind them to do the same. While taking Beck and Marsden by force would be easier, Billy had a feeling it ran the best chance of ending in blood. It was time to rely on stealth.

"Ready?" Matt asked after he checked his gun again. Billy did the same. There was no room to make mistakes.

"Let's finally put an end to this."

There was half a football field's length of flat grass and dirt between them and the barn. An outdoor light hung over one of the doors but it didn't worry Billy. He could make out the outline of a vehicle tucked against the side of the barn they were sneaking toward. Billy'd bet dollars to donuts it was the car Mara had been taken in earlier that day. He knew Beck and Marsden were there. He just didn't know if they were in the barn or on the other side of it.

And he didn't know where Mara was, either.

Billy let his questions shut off as he made it close enough to confirm it was the car he'd seen before. He and Matt stepped quietly while looking in the front and back seats. Then, together, they remained quiet and listened.

The Southern lullaby of cicadas and frogs held steady around them, as normal as the humidity and as loyal to the South as football fans to the game. Billy wouldn't have even noticed the song if he hadn't been trying to hear through it. So when an odd noise went against the natural grain of sound, he tilted his head in confusion.

Matt heard it, too.

"Other side of the barn," he whispered, so quietly Billy barely heard him. But he agreed.

Billy led them along the outer wall, away from the side with the light. He held his breath and kept his body loose as he took a look around the corner. Nothing but more grass, open space and a small amount of clutter lining the back wall of the barn. Even before Leigh had lost her husband, the barn hadn't been used for several years. That fact was merely highlighted when Billy and Matt crept past a door that was heavily chained shut.

They weren't going to be getting anyone in or out that way.

The weird noise Billy couldn't place stopped as soon as they cleared the door. In tandem both men froze at the corner of the barn, guns high and ready.

"I took your cuffs off. You shouldn't be stalling anymore," a man said, loud and clearly frustrated. Billy knew instantly the voice belonged to Gene Marsden. Like nails on a chalkboard, his one sentence was enough to grate on Billy's nerves.

"My ribs are bruised, no thanks to you. If I'm going slow you can thank yourself for that."

Billy could have sung right then and there. Mara was alive.

"You've got a lot of mouth for someone standing in a hole that could be their grave." Billy's joy at hearing Mara's voice plummeted straight down into the fiery depths of pure anger.

No one talked like that to his woman.

"Cover me," he whispered to Matt. He didn't need to see the detective to know he nodded.

Billy crouched, kept his gun straight and swung around the corner of the barn. When bullets didn't fly, he took in several details at once.

There was an old tractor with a flat tire sitting a few feet from the barn's side. Two battery-powered lanterns sat on the ground on the other side of the tractor, casting wide circles of light over two figures. One was Marsden, tall and holding something—a gun, most likely— while Mara was farther away. She was holding a shovel and standing in a hole up to her knees. Next to Marsden was Beck's truck, looking the worse for wear. Neither Marsden nor Mara was directly facing Billy, so he took a beat to look for Beck, Leigh or Eric. When he didn't see anyone else, he started to move toward the back of the tractor.

He could have shot Marsden right then and there— and been happy about it, too—but Mara was too close to the ex-deputy. Billy needed a cleaner shot or a better angle to force the man to disarm himself. Then any chance of that went out the window. Without the lantern's light going past the skeleton of metal, Billy didn't see the beer bottles on the ground until it was too late. His foot connected with one and sent it flying into the other. They sounded off like church bells on a Sunday.

And Marsden didn't waste any time second-guessing the noise. He turned and started shooting.

"Drop your gun, Marsden," Billy yelled after lunging behind the wheel of the tractor. Bullets hit the metal and wood around him, but Marsden didn't answer. He kept Billy pinned down for a few shots until Matt responded to the man in kind. The sounds of gunfire shifted as Marsden must have taken cover behind the truck to take aim at Matt.

"Mara," Billy yelled out, worried she'd be hit in the process. There wasn't any cover she could take easily.

"Billy!"

Like magic Mara appeared around the front of the tractor, seemingly unharmed. There were so many things he wanted to do to her right then and there—appropriate and not so much—but it wasn't the time or place. So he swallowed his desires and got down to business.

"Where's Beck?"

Mara shook her head.

"Dead," she said. "Marsden shot him in the basement." Her eyes widened. "Eric and Leigh are down there still. I need to get them."

The exchange of bullets ceased. Billy bet everyone was reloading.

"You get down there and stay with them," Billy said hurriedly. "Backup is down the road. We'll call them in if you'll stay there."

Mara nodded and turned her body, ready to run, but hesitated. She found his gaze again.

"I never stopped loving you, Billy Reed," she said, voice completely calm. "I promise I'll never leave you again."

Billy, caught more off guard than when the gunfire started up again, didn't have time to respond. Mara didn't wait but kept low, using the tractor as a shield, and soon disappeared around the front of the barn. He heard what must have been the door they'd been using to get in and out of the structure.

The sound shook him from the moment. Billy took a beat to call in their backup and then yelled out to Marsden.

"You're outnumbered," he yelled out. "Put the gun down, Marsden! It's over!"

The shooting stopped again. Billy waited a moment before sticking his head out around the tractor's tire, gun ready. Had Marsden listened to him? Would it be that easy?

"Grenade!"

The two syllables Matt yelled were enough to spike Billy's adrenaline and get him moving, but it wasn't enough time to clear it. He saw the flash-bang arc through the air in the space between him and Matt. Billy dove as far away from it as he could before a deafening blast went off behind him.

The flash blinded him; the sound stunned him.

For several seconds Billy tried to regain some control of his body, his balance, his senses. But before he could, Marsden went for the only option he had left to possibly get out of this mess alive.

Mara.

It took Mara longer than she would have liked to push the metal canister off the trap door, but she eventually managed.

"It's me," Mara yelled, hands going up to cover her face seconds before Leigh could pummel her with the bat she'd beaten Beck with. His body was still at the bottom of the stairs, in a puddle of blood. Mara jumped over it as Leigh backed away to the side again. Eric popped up from his hiding spot against the wall.

"What's going on up there?" Leigh asked, not dropping the bat to her side.

"Billy showed up." Mara couldn't help but smile. "He told us to stay here. Backup is down the road."

Mara saw the relief in Leigh's shoulders. She leaned the bat against the wall.

"I guess our friend isn't surrendering," she said as more *thunks* could be heard from above.

Mara wrung her hands and shook her head.

"He's definitely not su—"

"Grenade!"

Mara flinched backward and put her hand to her mouth. She gasped as a loud *bang* shook the barn above them. Leigh shared a look with her, eyes wide, as silence filled the world above the basement stairs.

"No," Mara said, shaking her head and still backpedaling. Surely it was Billy who had thrown it, right? He'd had enough of Marsden and thrown a grenade to end it?

Even as Mara thought it, she knew that wasn't the case.

"Is it over?" Eric asked, bringing her attention to the fact she was at the back wall. Her hand still over her mouth, she didn't have the will to pretend to look like everything was okay.

She wouldn't do that until Billy came down those stairs.

"Should we—" Leigh started. She was cut off by the sound of footsteps coming down into the basement. Mara dropped her hand, a smile coming to her lips thinking of Billy. It was because of that smile that Leigh dropped her guard.

And that's why she didn't beat Marsden to a pulp as soon as his feet hit the floor.

Instead, when she belatedly tried to do some damage, Marsden hauled off and pistol-whipped her. Eric yelled as the force of the hit made Leigh sink to the floor. All she had time to do was look up as Marsden brought up his gun and pointed it at her son.

"For that, I'll kill him before I kill you," he sneered. He looked at Mara. "And then we're leaving."

Mara didn't have time to tell the man that she had no intention of leaving with him.

So, instead, she showed him.

With nothing but the image of Alexa firmly planted in her mind, Mara jumped in front of Eric just as Marsden fired.

BILLY RAN DOWN into the basement and shot Gene Marsden in the head.

His ears rang something awful, his movements were still sluggish and he was having trouble seeing, but none of that could hide one horrifying fact.

Marsden had created Billy's worst nightmare.

He'd shot Mara and he'd done it seconds before Billy could stop him.

"Mara's been shot," he yelled back to Matt.

She was on the ground with Eric standing behind her, crying.

"Are you okay?" Billy yelled at him even though he knew the boy was. Where Mara was lying on her side, it was obvious she'd taken the bullet for the boy. Eric nodded just as Leigh swooped in and grabbed him. They gave Billy space while he dropped down to his knees.

"Mara," he said, still yelling. As gently as he could, he rolled her onto her back. Immediately he cursed. The shot had been to the chest. "It's okay," he said, surprised when her eyes opened. "You're going to be okay. Matt's called in some help."

Mara smiled up at him, but it was as soft as a whisper. Her eyelids fluttered closed.

Billy couldn't help the fear that tore from his mouth.

"No, stay with me!" Billy pulled her into his lap. Matt appeared at his side and, without words, put pressure on the wound. "Come on, Mara," he said, trying to keep her conscious. Despite Matt's attempt, blood poured out around the detective's hand.

The sight alone tore at Billy worse than any pain he'd ever known.

"You promised you'd never leave me again," he said to her. "You can't leave me again. You promised!"

But Mara kept quiet.

Chapter Twenty-Three

Alexa's hair was a mess. Billy was man enough to admit that that was his fault. He'd finally gotten her used to him brushing out her hair after bath time and right after she woke up, so he'd gotten cocky and tried to do something a bit more adventurous that morning. He'd searched hairstyles for little girls and found a video that showed him how to do a fishtail braid.

Now, looking down at her sleeping against his chest, Billy accepted that the braid looked more like a rat's tail than a fishtail anything. He sighed. Maybe one day he'd get it right. But, for now, no one who'd visited had given him grief about his fathering. That included his mother, surprisingly enough.

He turned to look at the chair next to his. It was empty. She must have stepped out to get coffee or another book while he and Alexa dozed off in his own chair. There was just something about hospital machines and their beeping that created a noise that carried him off to sleep.

Then again, he hadn't gotten much sleep in the last few days.

Billy's eyes traveled to the hospital bed in front of him.

He'd positioned his chair next to Mara's feet so he was facing her. He wanted to know the second she woke up. He wanted to be there for her. If it hadn't been for Alexa, he wouldn't have left her side during the last few days.

Billy closed his eyes again and rested his chin on top of his daughter's head. It was nice to feel her against him after everything that had happened.

Beck's and Marsden's bodies had been collected and buried outside Riker County with their families. Beck turned out to be Kevin Rickman, a college dropout who had tried to desperately follow his father's long criminal career. But, like his father, he'd been killed over power, money and drugs. Beck had only focused on Bryan Copeland's legacy because his father had helped Bryan at the beginning of his drug running, right before he'd been killed. Bryan hadn't ever met Beck, but was able to pick the man's father out of an old picture. Kevin had used an old friend of his father's to get a message to Bryan in prison. Then Bryan had used his connections to relay the stash's location and then call Billy and warn him.

Billy felt the letter folded in his wallet like it was on fire. It was from Bryan to Mara and had been sent to Billy's office. As guilty as he'd felt about reading it, Billy was glad he had. Bryan hadn't given Mara any grief and he hadn't apologized for his past. He'd only said he was glad she was okay and asked if she would send him pictures of both herself and Alexa.

Billy would never like Bryan, but he was glad he'd finally put his daughter's life above his own. So much so that Billy called in a lot of favors, including some of Sheriff Rockwell's, and gotten the news that Bryan

Copeland's stash had been found, or even ever existed, kept secret. Just until Bryan could be moved to a prison out of state. Then Billy would personally let everyone know, including anyone with bad intentions, that there was no reason to ever dig on Leigh Cullen's property again. Otherwise there would always be someone who would look for it. The stash had been right where Bryan had told him. A handful of deputies had spent the night digging out a metal container that held more money than Billy would probably make in a lifetime. Plus enough Moxy and other assorted drugs to help any budding drug runner start out strong.

Billy had just started to think about all the paperwork he'd have to fill out when a sound made his eyes flash open.

"Mara," he said, surprised.

Mara, propped up on a pillow, was looking right at him. There was a smile across her lips.

"Don't—" she started but coughed. Billy was already getting up, trying not to jostle Alexa too much. She squirmed once before he laid her down on the love seat on the other side of the room.

"Here," Billy said, voice low, as he grabbed his cup of water and popped a straw into it. He held it up to Mara and she drank a few sips.

"Thanks," she said. "My mouth was really dry."

Billy put the water down on the table and sat on the edge of the bed to face her. He couldn't help but smile. She was the most beautiful woman he'd ever seen.

"I didn't want you to move," Mara said, giving her own smile. "You two were so cute."

Billy glanced back at Alexa and felt a bit sheepish.

"I tried to braid her hair," he explained. "It looked better yesterday."

Mara's brow furrowed. She looked around the room and then down at herself.

"How bad is it?" she whispered.

Billy felt his smile falter.

"You're expected to fully recover. But…" Billy let his hand hover over her chest. The doctor said there'd be a scar there but she'd been damned lucky. The second woman to get the same diagnosis in a week on his watch. "There were a few close calls to get you there."

Billy felt the pain and fear and anguish he'd experienced when Mara had flatlined twice in the ambulance. He'd nearly lost his mind with worry as he'd paced outside surgery afterward.

"I'm okay now, then," Mara said softly. She reached out and patted the top of his hand. Billy realized that, even though she was the one in the hospital bed, she was trying to comfort him.

It made his smile come back and he finally did something he should have done two years before. Reaching into his pocket, he pulled out a small box. He held it up to Mara. Her eyes widened.

"I always thought I'd do something elaborate and romantic when I proposed to you but dammit, Mara, I can't wait anymore." Billy opened the box. He'd tell her later that he'd bought her the ring two years before, but for now he had to tell her what he wanted in the future. "You don't have to marry me now, tomorrow or even next year, but Mara Copeland, I sure do need you to be my wife." He took the ring out and held it up. "Marry me and let's grow old together?"

Mara's expression softened. Those beautiful lips

turned up into the smallest of smiles. When she answered, Billy couldn't help but laugh.

"Sounds good to me, Sheriff."

THE CHRISTMAS TREE was going to fall over. Its branches hung down with the weight of too many ornaments, half from Billy's childhood and the others they'd bought together for Alexa. At the time, Mara had been more than happy to fill their cart with bits and bobbles, but now she was worried the sheer weight of them all was going to kill their tree. Even if it was fake.

"Personally, I think it looks amazing."

Mara turned and smiled. Billy was grinning ear to ear. "I'm sure everyone at the party is going to be jealous that their trees aren't as great as this one." He opened his arms wide, motioning to the tree. Mara caught sight of the wedding band on his finger. It made her glance at hers before answering him. The sight made her feel a warmth spread through her. Every single time.

"That their trees *weren't* as good," she corrected him. "You know, considering it's the end of February and no one has decorations up anymore. Or are celebrating Christmas."

Billy waved his hand dismissively.

"I wasn't about to let my first Christmas with my girls go by without a proper celebration," he said, defiance in his voice. Billy sidled up beside her and placed his arm around her waist. "Plus, I think we deserve a pass to do that, don't you?"

Mara's smile grew.

It had been almost three months since Mara had woken up in the hospital. In that time, several things had happened. The first was that she'd learned Christmas had come and gone while she'd been unconscious. Claire had still taken the day to shower her in gifts and love, but Billy had told everyone that he'd wait until the three of them could celebrate together. As a family.

The idea of their first Christmas together had made her cry, which had, in turn, alarmed the sheriff, but she'd promised they were tears of happiness. Something she realized she'd always feel after Suzy, of all people, had been ordained and married them on the back porch of Billy's house. It had been a short and sweet ceremony. Claire had cried while holding Alexa, while Detective Walker and Captain Jones had been the official witnesses.

Since then, life had moved quickly. Mara quit her job, broke her lease and together with off-duty sheriff's department employees, Billy and she had moved all of her belongings into the Reed family home.

While she felt the love from the department, a part of Mara had been more than worried that the residents of Carpenter wouldn't ever accept her because of who she was. Especially after the news that she and Billy had a child had traveled through the town like wildfire. However, so far no one had said a rude thing to her. And if they even looked like they were thinking about it, Leigh Cullen would puff up, ready to point out that Mara had died—twice if you counted her heart stopping—to save her son, and if they didn't like her they'd have to deal with Leigh. She'd only used that speech once on a man who hadn't meant any disrespect, but Mara couldn't deny it made her feel good that Leigh didn't seem to hold any more animosity toward her. In fact, while Mara had been in the hospital, Leigh had visited her almost every day.

They'd talked about the serious things first—the sorrys and thank yous for anything and everything that had happened—and then moved on to the personal sides of who they were. It turned out Leigh had been wanting to start her own business—something creative and hands-on—but hadn't found a worthwhile fit. When she found out that Mara had wanted to start up an interior design shop, Leigh had decided that not only could they be friends but they could be business partners, too.

Once Mara was out of the hospital, Leigh proved to have meant every word she'd said. They were already working up the design for an office space downtown. It wasn't large, but it was a start. One Mara was looking forward to. One that her father also praised in a letter. Mara didn't know what their particular future held, especially concerning Alexa, but she couldn't deny she missed her father. They'd agreed to start writing to each other. It, too, was a new start.

Which left one last, life-altering decision that had surprised them. Tough-as-nails, sweet-as-honey Claire Reed. Instead of going back home, she'd pulled a Mara and sold her house, instead.

"I've been bored in retirement anyways," she'd told them one night at supper. "Plus, now that I have a grand-baby, you won't be able to keep me away." She was currently living in the guesthouse but promised she was looking for a place of her own. Though Mara had to admit, it was nice having someone to help with Alexa when she and Billy wanted some alone time.

Which was just as much fun as she'd remembered.

Mara sighed, the warmth of the man next to her seeping into her heart. It made his gaze shift downward.

"Who would have thought that we'd really end up together?" Mara mused.

"I knew we would," he said, matter-of-factly.

"You have to admit, it was quite the journey," she said. "Ups and downs and bad men with guns. Not to mention your mother."

Billy let out a hoot of laughter.

"I hadn't seen *that* one coming," he admitted. "But..."

Mara let out a small yelp of excitement as Billy spun her around. His lips covered hers in a kiss that she'd never forget. When it ended, he stayed close.

"But, as for us, I always knew we'd be here eventually," he whispered, lips pulling up into his famous smirk. It was a sight she was ready to see every day for the rest of her life. "Merry Christmas, Mrs. Reed."

Mara didn't miss a beat.

"Merry Christmas, Sheriff."

* * * * *